MW00878505

WREATHED IN DISGRACE

COVENTRY SAGA
BOOK 8

ROBIN PATCHEN

JDO PUBLISHING

For Tony and René Bancroft.
Thank you for welcoming my son into your family and for
sharing your daughter with mine.

CHAPTER ONE

D enise Masters watched from where she sat on a picnic table, not exactly *afraid* to approach, but not ready either.

When she was a kid, this "festival" had consisted of a Christmas tree-lighting ceremony, a snowball fight—if there was snow—and hot chocolate for the kids whose parents had been smart enough to bring a thermos.

Coventry had changed over the last eight years. Maybe as much as Denise herself had.

Christmas music carried across the park, blasting from speakers set up around the activity.

On an ice-skating rink, lovers twirled. Toddlers wobbled. Teenagers raced. Plenty of them landed on their rumps, usually laughing. Denise itched to show them how it was done. She'd been a good skater in her past life. She'd loved it, gliding across the ice like a bird in flight, the feel of the wind in her hair.

She couldn't remember the last time she'd gone ice skating.

Games had been set up throughout the grassy area—corn hole, horseshoes, giant Jenga. A couple of teens played volleyball on the sand, despite the fact that the weather wasn't exactly fit for the beach. Fortunately, the clouds weren't too thick, and the temperature hovered in the low fifties, warm for November in the New Hampshire mountains.

There was a food truck—a food truck!—with the name of a local coffee shop emblazoned on the side. Denise would never have guessed that tiny Coventry could support a couple of restaurants and a coffee shop, much less a food truck.

Santa Claus had come for the event and was chatting with little ones perched on his knee while a photographer snapped photos.

The year before, Ella had scrambled onto Santa's lap. Would she now, or would she claim that, at eight-and-a-half, she was too mature for Santa?

Denise hated that she had no idea. She hadn't seen her daughter since their month-long visit last summer, though she'd thought of her daily. Hourly.

Scanning the faces in the crowd, she caught sight of the first man she'd ever loved. Maybe, if she were honest, the only man she'd ever loved, even if her love had proved pretty paltry in the end.

Not that she wanted Reid back. He loathed her. Sure, they'd come to a truce of sorts a couple of years before, but it had been a tenuous truce quickly forgotten when she demanded more time with Ella and he argued that she deserved less. He'd agreed to a visitation schedule but then tried repeatedly to wiggle out of it. He considered Ella *his* daughter, and he didn't like to share.

And then Denise would threaten to get lawyers involved. And then they'd fight.

The pattern had repeated more times than Denise wanted to count. She and her ex were cordial to each other now only when Ella was nearby.

Denise hoped to change that.

Reid's pretty redheaded wife prompted not a twinge of jealousy. Jacqui's parka was pulled snug around her middle. Either the slender woman had put on weight, or she was expecting.

The second, no doubt. And nobody had bothered to tell Denise. Maybe they didn't think it was her business, but Ella *was* her business, even if Reid didn't want to admit it. That her stepmother was having a baby seemed like important information. Why hadn't Ella told her? Had Reid asked her not to?

Where was Ella?

Finally, Denise saw her daughter, and her heart flipped. She was proud of the girl her baby had become, with her dark brown hair so similar to Denise's, Reid's brown eyes, a spattering of freckles across her nose. She was proud of Ella's wide smile, her kindness, her contentment.

Not that Denise could take credit for anything beyond the DNA.

She loved Ella, loved her in a way she'd never known one person could love another. Those first few months after Ella's birth had been so hard, with depression suffocating her, coloring everything with a film of gray. Even then, Denise had loved Ella. Now, with the depression and the events that had chased her from New Hampshire so small in the rearview mirror, her love for Ella had only grown and expanded.

And yet...and yet she'd left. What kind of mother leaves her baby?

No wonder Reid hated her. No wonder the rest of Coventry wasn't proud to claim her as their own, at least not the people who'd really known her. Ella, precious, loving girl that she was, forgave Denise for her long absences from her life, but Reid never had and never would. And their old friends... Most were only Reid's friends now.

Love, pride, and shame. That was the cocktail that filled her stomach as she watched her daughter walk between her father and her stepmother, chattering like a squirrel and beaming with joy. Denise's daughter was always beaming with joy.

Reid had raised her well.

The happy family went to the little playground, and Ella climbed up on the swing and pumped. Ella was already halfway through her childhood and, except for a few weeks here and there, Denise had missed it all.

She'd achieved success, but every acting role, every award, every paycheck got lost in a haze of regret. If only she'd done everything differently.

If only she'd told Reid the truth from the start. He believed, everybody believed, that she'd left Coventry—left him and Ella —because she'd wanted to chase her dream. She'd led them all to believe that because that was what she'd ended up doing.

But it wasn't why she'd left.

Now, what she wanted, *all* she wanted, was to be a part of Ella's life.

If that meant she had to tell them all the truth...

One step at a time. Right now, she needed to take literal steps. She hopped off the picnic table and started toward the crowd.

Father, give me the strength and courage...

A loud bang reverberated across the water.

She turned that direction in time to glimpse a boat speeding away. In November? Who would...?

She was tackled.

Hit the grass, facedown. A man on top of her.

Long-buried memories flashed, and she struggled to free herself, desperate to get away. She pushed at his arm propped beside her, but it didn't budge. She shifted, tried to get close enough to his wrist to bite him, but he moved to guard his skin and keep her in place.

"Ma'am, I'm trying to protect you. Please stop." He hovered

over her, not crushing her but allowing enough pressure that she couldn't move.

She got one leg free and whipped it back, catching flesh with her heel.

"Oomph." He lowered himself on top of her. "Stop fighting me."

The words were a demand. His voice, deep and terrifying.

A scream crawled up her throat, tried to claw its way out, but she couldn't seem to make any noise.

"Ms. Masters." The man's voice was calm. "My name is Jon Donley. I'm a bodyguard. I'm trying to keep you alive."

A bodyguard? What was he—?

"There's a shooter. Stay down."

Shooter?

She was still processing that when the man said, "He's gone." He popped off Denise, and she crawled away, desperate to put space between them.

"Whoa, whoa. Stay here, ma'am." He grabbed her wrist. "Come on. Let me help you up."

Confused, she tried to get away, but he didn't let go. His grip was surprisingly gentle.

She didn't have bodyguards, certainly not here. She was trying to remain incognito.

"Ma'am." A blond woman approached from the other side. "You need to go with Donley to the car. We have to get you out of here. My name is Lake. I'm his partner. There's been a credible threat, and somebody just took a shot—"

"Not at me." Denise's voice was high, almost screeching. She lowered the pitch and started over. "That had nothing to do with me." There, that sounded better. "It was probably a hunter."

"In town?" The man crowded her, too close. Was he trying to intimidate? "At a festival?"

She tried to back away, but he gripped her other shoulder. "Maybe you're right," he said. "Just to be safe, we're going to protect you." He kept his voice level, though she heard a hint of frustration. "Please, come with me."

She tore her gaze away from the stranger's to look at the crowd just a hundred yards distant. Was Ella all right? It seemed the music was loud enough that nobody had heard the shot, or if they had, they'd discounted it as inconsequential. Written it off as a car backfiring, or maybe a firecracker some-where. A few people were staring toward the lake, but most had returned to their activities. People still skated on the rink, still stood in line at the food truck.

Ella still swung in the playground. Safe, thank God.

Reid was looking Denise's direction, though. Did he see her?

This was not how she'd wanted the day to go. This was exactly the opposite of what Denise had planned.

As long as Ella was safe. That was all that mattered.

"Ma'am," the bodyguard said. "We need to go."

This was crazy. Was Denise in danger? Had somebody taken a shot at her?

Just a few hundred feet from her *daughter*?

"Come on." He wrapped an arm around her back and started walking.

Denise was too stunned to argue. She let herself be led across the grass. He didn't walk toward her Tesla, though.

"I'm not going anywhere with you," she said.

He didn't falter or slow, just continued in the same direction.

"Where's the woman you were with?" Denise asked.

"Talking to the police."

"Sure she is. Let me go."

The man didn't comply until they'd crossed the street and

reached an ice cream shop. Despite the cold temperature, people stood in line at the counter inside.

When Denise and her assailant, or bodyguard, or whatever he was stood beside the brick building, he situated himself between her and the lake—either to protect her or to hide her from somebody who might rescue her. She figured the odds were fifty-fifty.

He angled to point back toward the park, where the tall blonde was indeed having a conversation with a uniformed police officer. She waved toward the water, and the cop spoke into the little microphone on his jacket, then jogged away.

"See." The man let her go and lifted both arms. "I'm just trying to keep you alive." He shoved a hand in his back pocket and came out with a leather case, which he opened to show her a private investigator license from Massachusetts.

"Take a picture of it and send it to somebody who loves you. Somebody who'll check to make sure you get home safely. Do it now." His voice was deep and commanding. "You have ten seconds, and then you're getting into my SUV."

"Who hired you?"

"Bruce Taggart."

Denise's agent.

She should have guessed.

She pulled her phone from her jacket pocket, snapped a photo of the man and another of his ID. Then, she walked to the rear of his vehicle—he kept in step with her the whole way, blocking her from the park and lake—and snapped a photo of the license plate.

"In the back."

"My car—"

"We'll take care of it."

"Your partner—"

"Get in the vehicle. Please."

It was insane. She didn't know this person, had never seen him before. But it would be just like Bruce to hire security for her against her wishes and without her knowledge.

The man opened the rear door of the Lincoln Navigator, and she slid inside. She selected the three photos on her phone. He'd told her to send them to somebody who loved her.

There were her parents and Ella. Obviously, she wouldn't send the information to an eight-year-old. Denise's parents were in Florida. She'd caused them enough worry.

She could send the pictures to one of her church friends, but they were in LA. They had lives and families. Better things to do than worry about her.

She could send them to Monroe, her house sitter, someone else she'd met at church. But though he was a friend, she wasn't sure she wanted him quite that involved in her business.

She sent the photos to Bruce. Her agent might not love her, but he could be trusted, and he had a vested interest in keeping her safe.

Plus, he was always available. She tapped out a text. *If you didn't hire this guy, then I'm being abducted.*

The bodyguard sat in the front seat, slammed the door, and started the car, but he didn't move.

If he was abducting her, he was sure taking his time about it.

"Are we going somewhere?" she asked.

"Waiting for Lake,"

Lake? What kind of a name...?

Denise's phone vibrated, and she read Bruce's response. *I hired him.*

Why?

Call me when you're safe, and I'll explain.

He'd better. She'd left Hollywood to escape the craziness. The last thing she wanted was for the craziness to follow her home.

"You want Lake to drive your car," the man asked, "or do you want to leave it here?"

"I'll drive it." She reached for the door handle, but he locked the doors. She tried to disengage hers, but it was a child safety lock.

"Sorry, ma'am. After we get you home, we'll discuss what to do next. For now, you're going to have to trust me."

Trust him? She didn't even know him. Before she could say that, the passenger door opened, and the blonde slid in. "Cops are searching for the driver of the boat. So far, nobody knows anything."

He turned to Denise. "Keys?"

It seemed she had no choice. Typical. She had all the money she could ever want, but money didn't buy the things she desired most. Like her daughter's affection. Like the freedom to go to a small-town Christmas lighting ceremony without bringing chaos with her.

Whatever. She pulled the keys from her pocket and handed them over the seat to the blonde.

"See you at the house." She stepped out and jogged away.

The man shifted gears and pulled onto the street that ringed the lake.

Denise stared at the crowd as they passed it. If she'd had any doubt that Reid had seen her before, the way he was watching the SUV now confirmed her worry. He looked furious.

Of course.

All the courage it had taken her to show up here, to walk toward the crowd, to try to fit in with her old friends, and this was how it turned out?

"I'm sorry I frightened you." The bodyguard stopped at the intersection and met her eyes in the rearview mirror. "I hope I didn't hurt you."

She did a quick survey and was surprised to find she didn't

feel a single ache. Cold, sure. The grass had been damp. But he'd somehow managed to tackle her without causing injury. She had the vague memory of the man's arm around her middle when he'd taken her down. He'd supported her and protected her.

Maybe she could trust him.

His eyes narrowed. They were gray and serious beneath dark brown eyebrows. "Are you hurt?"

Was she? She didn't think so. "What is your name?"

"Donley. Jon Donley."

"Okay." She wasn't sure what she was supposed to say now. If somebody really had taken a shot at her, he'd likely saved her life. But she didn't want to believe anybody had been trying to kill her. In which case, this guy had ruined her plans.

"You didn't hurt me, Jon. Scared me, but didn't hurt me."

He nodded and turned onto Main Street.

Leaving Ella, Denise's ex, her old friends—and maybe a killer—behind.

CHAPTER TWO

The sound of the gunshot reverberated in his head.

Jon replayed the moment as he drove through Coventry toward Ms. Master's house. He and Lake had been told she drove a red Tesla—not exactly a dime a dozen in central New Hampshire—so when they'd seen the car driving the opposite direction on Rattlesnake Road as they'd headed toward her house, they'd done a U-turn and followed.

They didn't generally stalk their clients from afar, but the man who hired them had asked that they keep an eye on her without letting her know for the time being. Jon wouldn't have agreed, but Bartlett hadn't consulted him. Apparently, Denise Masters didn't think she needed protection in her hometown.

That gunshot said differently.

He'd heard enough rifle fire to recognize the sound instantly. He and Lake had snapped into action. Jon had sprinted across the grass and tackled the client, trying not to hurt her.

Lake had followed but kept her eyes toward the threat.

The boat had taken off before Lake could make out many

markings, information she'd relayed through the earpiece that connected them. The local police were already investigating.

In the backseat, Denise Masters's eyes were wide, flicking from one window to the next. She was afraid, rightfully so. But she didn't seem to be in shock.

She'd called him Jon.

Nobody but his parents called him Jon. It was Donley, always Donley. But for some reason, he hadn't corrected her. He would when she was safe.

He was making a right on Rattlesnake Road before she spoke. "How do you know where I live?"

"Mr. Taggart."

"How long have you been watching me?"

"We just got to town an hour ago. We were headed this way earlier when we saw you driving down the mountain."

He let his gaze skim the surroundings. Trees towered on the left, where the slope climbed higher. A steep drop-off edged the other side of the road. Between trunks and bare branches, he saw the lake below. Though the skies were gray, the world mostly colorless, he remembered the beauty of the small town from when he'd been here the previous summer, protecting Josie Smith, a senator's daughter.

Josie had almost died because of Jon's incompetence. Although nobody else labeled what happened the same way, Jon should have been prepared. He should have insisted on more bodyguards. There were a lot of things he should have done differently and hadn't because he'd elevated pleasing his client over doing what he thought was best.

He wouldn't make that mistake again.

Ms. Masters remained silent in the backseat, and Jon managed not to look at her again, though there was something magnetic about her thick brown hair, those striking blue eyes. Her skin was darker than his, though naturally or from the sun, he wasn't sure. Of course, he'd already known she was beautiful. Every man with eyes knew that. His sister had two sons, and he'd watched all the latest superhero movies with them. It was his way of connecting with his nephews, and it gave his sister and brother-in-law some time alone. Denise Masters had been in a lot of those movies. Most of the time her character, Ember Flare, was a supporting character, though she'd been the star of one. She was a good actor, but he'd have guessed she wasn't as pretty in person as she was on the screen.

Wrong. She was prettier in person, maybe because her face was clear of makeup. She had freckles across the bridge of her nose he'd never seen on the big screen. Her hair wasn't all fancied up like it was in the movies. It was long and wavy, wind-blown from her time at the lake. Nobody would confuse Denise Masters with the girl next door. She was gorgeous.

And tough. When he'd tackled her, she'd fought like crazy. If he hadn't shifted, she'd have clamped her teeth down on his wrist. And somehow she'd gotten in a good kick to his thigh. Impressive flexibility.

Hopefully, he'd hidden his sudden, shocking flash of attraction. Not that it would be all that shocking to Denise Masters. She was probably accustomed to being drooled over.

He needed to stop thinking of her as *Denise Masters, movie star*. She was a client. Just another client.

They passed a condo development, then nothing for miles until they finally reached her driveway. He did a quick scan. No cameras, no gate, no obvious security of any kind.

He'd fix that immediately.

He parked and heard his client yank the door handle again, to no avail.

"Ma'am, let's wait for Lake. She'll be here any minute and clear the house."

"I don't appreciate being locked in the car."

"Yes, ma'am."

A moment passed, and then the woman sighed. "Will you *please* unlock the doors?" Heavy sarcasm on the "please."

"No, ma'am. We're going to wait for Lake to clear the house."

"Stop calling me ma'am. Makes me feel old."

"Yes, m—" He clamped his lips shut.

"So I'm locked in."

Irritation spiked, and he forced a calm tone. "Somebody shot at you"—he glanced at his watch—"twenty-seven minutes ago. That person could have docked the boat, gotten into a car, and driven up here. He could be waiting for you right now."

"And we're sitting ducks."

He knocked on the window. "Bulletproof glass."

She glared at him in the rearview mirror. Before she could formulate a scathing reply, Lake turned the red Tesla into the driveway and parked.

Through his earpiece, she said, "I have the keys. I'll clear the house."

He pressed the button on the two-way attached to his hip. "Be alert."

"Isn't that your job?" Ms. Masters asked.

He let go of the button. "Talking to my partner. She's going inside your house. We'll follow when we know it's safe."

Lake jogged up the walk and steps to the front door, where she bent to scoop something off the porch before letting herself inside with Denise's keys.

"No alarm," Lake said.

"What if I don't want her inside my house?" Ms. Masters asked.

He shifted to face her. "We've been hired to protect you. If you don't want our protection, then we'll leave. But before you make that decision, you need all the information."

"What information don't I have?"

"When we get inside—"

"What else do we have to do besides talk?"

He faced forward again. The guy who'd hired them, Taggart, was supposed to have sent some documents that would explain his decision to hire bodyguards. Maybe those documents would convince Ms. Masters that she needed protection. If that didn't work—and if getting *shot at* didn't convince her—then he and Lake would head back to Boston. They weren't about to intrude where they weren't wanted.

Rather than explain all of that, he said, "We'll discuss it when we get inside."

Ms. Masters huffed but said nothing else.

Minutes passed before Lake spoke in his ear again. "All clear."

"On our way." He climbed out and opened the rear door, gaze skimming the area all around the house. It was secluded, but that didn't make it safe.

Ms. Masters stepped out, and he stayed right behind her up the walk.

After she climbed the three steps to the door, she looked over her shoulder at him. "Could you back off?"

"When you're inside."

The woman sighed and pushed her way into the house.

He half hoped she'd refuse protection. The only thing worse than guarding prima donnas was guarding prima donnas who didn't think they needed to be guarded. He'd had his share of assignments like that, and he didn't relish another.

But the memory of that gunshot...

Unlike most prima donnas, Ms. Masters seemed to legitimately be in danger. So, as unpleasant as this was proving to be, he'd stick around until the threat was secured or she sent them away, no matter how difficult she was.

CHAPTER THREE

This was supposed to be Denise's refuge from the storm.

After viewing photos online, she'd bought the house the previous summer and planned to visit as soon as she completed the obligations that came with her latest movie. Meanwhile, she'd hired a decorator and had a pool and guesthouse built in the backyard.

It had taken her longer to visit than she'd hoped.

Fine. If she were honest with herself, she'd admit it had taken longer to build up her courage than it had to build the guest house. As much as she craved her daughter's company, she knew what Reid believed about her, and deep down, she feared he was right. He'd told her often enough—both in words and attitude—that she was a terrible mother, that she could only bring her daughter pain and hardship.

Would more time with Ella further highlight Denise's deficiencies? Could she offer her daughter anything but trouble?

It was easier to stay in California and dream of what life could be like back in New Hampshire than to come here and deal with the truth. So maybe she'd manufactured a whole bunch of *obligations* that had been more like *excuses*.

But she was here now, in this house she'd hoped would be a sanctuary.

She crossed the great room toward the kitchen.

The bodyguard followed, not as close as he'd been outside. The man needed to learn the meaning of the term *personal space.*

The one who looked like some kind of blond Amazon warrior walked toward her from her place near the rear French doors. "Ms. Masters, I'm sorry we didn't get a better introduction. My name is Lake." She neared Denise and held out her hand.

Denise gripped it. "Lake what?"

"Just Lake, ma'am."

"Don't call me ma'am." She added, "Please," as an afterthought. "What's your first name?"

The woman's eyes narrowed slightly. "I go by Lake."

Fine. If the woman wanted to be known as a body of water, more power to her.

Denise continued into the kitchen. "I'm freezing." She'd already been chilly, and getting tackled into damp grass hadn't helped. If not for the unexpected company, she'd change into her cozy velveteen loungewear. "I'm having some tea. You two want any?"

Lake shook her head.

Behind Denise, Jon said, "No, thank you."

After she turned on the electric kettle, Denise busied herself finding a mug. They were here somewhere. Her decorator had outfitted the place with everything Denise thought she'd need, including bedding, towels, dishes, and appliances. When she'd finally built up the courage to visit, she'd called the company that managed the house and had them stock her fridge and pantry. Since arriving the night before, she hadn't familiarized herself with where everything was.

While the kettle hissed and bubbled, she yanked open cabinets and found what she needed. All the mugs were gray, like pretty much everything else in the space. The bones of the house were beautiful, but the decor was all sophistication and understated elegance.

In other words, blah.

"There was a package for you on the front stoop." Lake nodded to a manila envelope on the kitchen table. "Mr. Taggart told our boss he would have some information sent to you. I suspect that's it."

Information that explained the bodyguards, Denise assumed.

She'd deal with that when she warmed up. She poured steaming water over the teabag, and the aroma of Earl Grey rose into the room while she added honey and stirred. "You two sure you don't want any?"

Neither responded.

Bad enough these people were in her house. Would it kill them to pretend to be normal?

The hot, fragrant tea soothed her. She'd been in California too long and wasn't accustomed to New England weather. She'd reacclimate, staying through the holidays, maybe longer.

Maybe forever.

Assuming she didn't screw everything up.

Jon and Lake were both watching her as if she were onstage. She was used to that in public, but this was her home, even if it didn't look like it. Or feel like it. She wanted nothing more than to send them both away, but that manila envelope needed to be opened and dealt with.

Bruce wouldn't have hired bodyguards—against her expressed will—without a very good reason.

So, fine.

She was on her way to the offending mail when somebody knocked.

Jon's gaze snapped to hers. "You expecting—?"

"No."

He crossed the living room and spoke through the door. "Who is it?"

"Detective Pollard, Coventry PD."

Jon opened the door and ushered the older man inside.

The detective wasn't short, but Jon dwarfed him. Pollard had dark brown hair and nondescript hazel eyes in a pudgy face. He looked eager as he crossed the room toward Denise, hand outstretched. "Detective Paul Pollard, ma'am."

She smiled, shaking his hand, which was as oversized as his face. And sweaty. The temperature had probably dropped to the thirties, and this guy had sweaty hands. "Nice to meet you, Detective."

"Been assigned to the shooting."

"Oh. Well, maybe somebody fired a weapon, but it wasn't at me."

"'Fraid it was. We dug a bullet out of a tree just a few feet from where you were standing, according to your guards, anyway." His gaze skimmed past Denise for a moment, and he nodded at Lake.

"You're saying somebody really was trying to shoot me?" Denise's words were laced with shock, too high and too loud. She'd been so sure the bodyguards had overreacted.

But the detective's head wagged back and forth. "Maybe. Maybe somebody was trying to scare you."

Beside them, Jon said, "Anything on the bullet?"

"We'll send it for analysis, but it'll take some time." He faced Denise again. "Anybody in town have a grudge against you?"

"I can't think of anybody." Except Reid, but as much as he

hated her, he wouldn't hurt her. And anyway, he'd been at the park. "You think the person fired from the boat?"

"No question."

"Any info on that front?" Jon asked.

"Possibly." He pulled a little notebook from his jacket pocket and flipped it open. "Witnesses say it was a fishing boat with a red stripe down the side. Is that what you saw?"

Jon nodded. "It looked well worn. One occupant, a man. He wore a knit cap and a sweatshirt, dark green. Couldn't see below the waist. Headed to the northeast." He turned to Lake. "Anything to add?"

"He fired once, then took off at a good clip. He was around the bend and out of sight in seconds."

The detective looked at Denise. "What did you see?"

"I have nothing to add. My focus was elsewhere."

"Assuming this was aimed at you specifically and not random," Pollard said, "any ideas who could have done it?"

"None."

"Who knew you'd be at the tree lighting ceremony today?"

Denise shook her head. "I hadn't told anybody my plans. Nobody even knows I'm here."

The man's eyes scrunched, wrinkling the space between his eyebrows. "You're sure? No friends, family"—he indicated the bodyguards—"these two?"

"I've never seen them before today."

Jon explained who hired them and how they'd come to be at the lake.

"Okay," Pollard said. "So you're saying..." He turned to Denise. "Your agent thinks you're in danger?"

"Not exactly," Denise said.

"Yes," Jon said.

The cop looked between them before focusing on Denise again. "You're saying nobody knew you were in town?"

"Bruce. My house sitter in LA. And the company that manages the house when I'm not here, Rossi Properties. They turned on the heat and bought groceries."

Pollard wrote that down. "I'll start with Rossi Properties." He slid his notebook back into his pocket. "Unless the guy firing at you was a terrible shot, which is possible, I'd guess he was just trying to scare you. Maybe it was a kid playing a prank who didn't even realize who he was shooting at. But until we know for sure, I recommend you be careful. We wouldn't want anything to happen to you." His cheeks turned a little pink as he said the last sentence.

"Thank you, Detective."

Jon started for the front door. "You have my number and my partner's. You'll let us know what you learn?"

The detective seemed in no hurry to leave, but he walked beside the bodyguard. "Yeah. And you too." He turned to focus on Denise. "If anything else happens, or if you think of anyone who might want you to leave town—"

"I'll call you."

The detective walked out, and Jon closed and locked the door behind him.

This was crazy. Somebody'd actually *shot* at her?

And her daughter had been fifty, maybe seventy-five yards away, not to mention the hundreds of other people who'd been in the park today.

It was horrifying.

She sipped the tea, trying to warm a chill caused by more than just the temperature.

But as long as she was dealing with bad news... She snatched the oversize envelope and tried to tear open the end. It had practically been laminated in packaging tape.

"Let me." Jon stepped forward, holding one of those red pocket knives with a million tools.

She handed him the envelope, and he sliced open the end and handed it back.

She shook a thick stack of papers into her hand.

The one on top was a printout from the *LA Times*, an article about the latest high-profile killing. Why would Bruce send her this? It wasn't as if she didn't know about the murdered female actors. Heck, that was one of the reasons she'd finally decided to return to New Hampshire.

Not that she feared being a victim, not really. There were thousands of actors in Hollywood. Why would she be a target?

That was the problem, though. Nobody could figure out how the victims were related. Aside from all being female actors, they had nothing in common, nothing that any authorities could determine, anyway. At least according to the media, but maybe the police were holding back information.

The first victim had starred in a sitcom that aired for a few years on some cable channel. Denise had never seen it, nor had she ever met the woman. She'd never met any of the victims.

That page was stapled to a few more—the rest of the article, it looked like. Denise flipped to the next bundle. It was an article about the second murdered actor, a woman who'd played a detective in a long-running TV series.

Moving on to the third stapled bundle, she saw an article about the third victim.

Denise wasn't the brightest bulb in the stage lights, but she was sensing a pattern.

Why had her agent sent her this? She lifted the larger envelope again and looked inside, hoping for an explanation. One slip of paper hadn't come out with the rest.

This package was delivered to my office for you. I called the police, and they took the originals. This is a copy. Call me.
—*Bruce*

Lake had returned to her spot near the rear doors, but Jon leaned in to see. "Articles about the Starlet Slayings?"

Starlet Slayings. Some reporter had coined the moniker, and it had stuck.

"That was sent to you?" the guard asked.

"To my agent." She didn't look at him. "Probably just some-body trying to freak me out."

He made a sound low in his throat. "You'd better call Mr. Taggart."

"I'm sure it's nothing. He's just being paranoid." Except Bruce wouldn't have forwarded this if he didn't think she had reason to worry.

She glanced at the bodyguard, who was giving her a look she guessed was a combination of impatience and annoyance. Similar to a look he'd given her in the car. He had to know who she was. Seemed he wasn't impressed.

She dialed, and Bruce answered immediately. "Did you get the package?"

"I don't understand what the big deal is. So somebody sent me articles about the victims. What difference—?"

"Did you look through it?" Bruce's normally low voice pitched higher when he was upset. Like now. "You need to look through the whole thing."

"Okay." She scanned each printout, trying to figure out what the point was.

Jon hovered over her shoulder to see what she was seeing.

"Hold on, Bruce." She set her cell on the table. "You're on speaker. The bodyguards are here as well."

"Good, good," Bruce said. "Denise, go to the bottom of the pile."

She lifted the stack, leaving the last bundle of papers on the table, and stared at the image. This woman she knew, an A-lister known for her roles in romantic comedies. Shannon Butler wasn't a friend exactly, but Denise had met her and liked her. They'd connected at parties. They had mutual acquaintances. But Shannon wasn't one of the killer's victims, and this wasn't an article about a murder. It was a puff piece about Shannon's work with some charity.

"I'm confused," Denise said. "What does Shannon have to do with anything?"

"You haven't heard?"

She got that acid-drop feeling in her middle.

She hadn't looked at the news that morning. This house of hers was so secluded, so peaceful. The last thing she'd wanted was to let the world intrude.

She didn't want to know. She didn't want to hear what Bruce was about to say.

His voice was lower than usual when he spoke. "What you have is a copy of a packet that was left leaning against the agency's back door at some point between Wednesday evening, when we closed for Thanksgiving, and this morning, when I went in to get some work done. Maybe it came today."

"If you didn't see it until this morning," Jon asked, "how did you get it here so fast?"

"Courier," Denise said.

Jon's eyebrows hiked, but she paid little attention. When Bruce wanted something done, it got done, and obviously this was too important to toss in the mail. She figured there'd been a local attorney in the middle, someone paid well for confidentiality.

Her agent continued. "Maybe the package came last night

or the night before, and if it did, if I'd seen it sooner..." Bruce was a tough guy, an old-school Hollywood agent, the kind who wasn't against raising his voice and dropping threats as liberally as he dropped profanities. When his voice broke, tears pricked Denise's eyes.

Jon pulled out a kitchen chair and motioned her into it.

She sat, dreading what her agent would say next.

"Shannon Butler was murdered last night."

Denise couldn't comprehend what was happening.

Jon spoke into the silence. "The killer sent that package before he pulled off the murder. He wanted you to know who his next victim would be."

Before Denise could speak, Bruce said, "That's the theory."

"Cameras?" Jon asked.

"Not in the back," Bruce said. "Only employees use that entrance."

The bodyguard wore a scowl when he turned to her. "Why you?"

She couldn't speak for the emotion clogging her throat. She shook her head.

"Maybe it's a...like a John Hinckley thing," Bruce said. "You know, the guy who tried to kill Ronald Reagan to impress Jodie Foster?"

Denise knew the story. Surely somebody wouldn't murder... how many women so far? Seven, eight? Surely somebody wouldn't do that to get Denise's attention.

She'd had her share of crazy fans, no question about it. But a murderer?

"What did the police say?" Denise asked.

"They're looking for connections from these women to you. They're going to call you as soon as I give them your number. I wanted to break the news to you myself."

"There are no connections," Denise said. "I knew Shannon,

but it wasn't like we were friends. We never worked together. And the other victims... I don't think I ever met any of them." The pitch of her voice was rising with her panic. "What does any of this have to do with me?"

"I don't know." Bruce cleared his throat. "Just stay safe, okay? Do what your bodyguards tell you. Make sure you have top-notch security at your house. Can you do that?"

"Yeah. Yeah, I guess."

"I gotta call the detective. He'll be reaching out, so answer it, all right? The sooner we get to the bottom of this, the better."

When Bruce ended the call, she stared at her cell phone as if it might have the answers she needed. She didn't understand. What did the Starlet Slayings have to do with her? Why would the killer send her the information?

If somebody had opened that envelope sooner, Shannon might have been warned. She might have been saved.

The murders had nothing to do with Denise. Nothing

It seemed the killer thought differently.

"Are you convinced now that you need us?"

Denise forced her gaze up to the bodyguard beside her. She wanted so badly for the answer to be no. No, she didn't need bodyguards. No, she wasn't in danger.

But she wasn't stupid. She nodded.

"We have some ground rules."

She'd worked with bodyguards before and was accustomed to their rules. They always wanted to go over them. "Okay."

"We're here to protect you. Our whole job is to make sure you're safe. If we tell you to do something, we're telling you for a reason that involves your safety."

"Makes sense."

"So if I tell you to duck, you duck. If I tell you to run, you run. If I tell you to stay, you stay."

"Like a well-trained dog."

If he thought her funny—or annoying—his facial expression didn't give him away. "You need to obey us."

"If you say jump, I ask how high."

"No." The single word was sharp. "If I say jump, you jump. No questions asked. Can you do that?"

"I can try."

"There is no 'try.'"

"Thank you, Yoda."

His lips didn't even quirk. "And I'll be bringing in a larger team to protect you."

"What if I don't want a larger team?"

Only the slight narrowing of his eyes gave away his frustration. "Then you can find another agency."

"Wow. Demanding much?" When he didn't respond, she sighed. "Do what you think is best, and I'll obey your every order."

"Thank you, ma'am."

"As long as you quit calling me ma'am."

"I'll try."

She raised one eyebrow, and he almost smiled.

"Yeah, I know. There is no 'try.'" He motioned to the packet of papers. "Do you mind?"

While Jon read the newspaper articles, Denise stared at the phone, sipping her cooling tea and waiting for the California police to call. In the minutes since she'd spoken to Bruce, everything had changed.

Someone banged on the front door.

She gasped and pressed her hand against her chest, her heart pounding beneath her palm. Was the detective back? He'd knocked like a normal person, though, not like an enraged gorilla.

The bodyguards moved like performers in a choreographed dance. Lake shifted back to the slider and glanced outside. Her hand rested on the firearm at her hip. Outside, the sun had already dipped below the tree line.

Jon crossed to the front door, also seemingly primed to draw his weapon. "Who is it?"

"Reid Cote."

And here she'd thought the day couldn't get any worse.

Jon turned to her, eyebrows lifted.

"My ex-husband."

"Open up or send him away?" the guard asked.

This wasn't how she'd wanted to do this. She'd planned to let Reid in on her plans slowly, carefully, to mitigate his reaction. But nothing had gone according to plan so far, so why was she surprised he'd found her?

She stood. "Let him in."

Jon opened the door, and Reid stormed past it. He was tall and slender and still handsome, despite the scowl on his face. When they'd been together a million years ago, his eyes had often been filled with amusement, always with love when he looked at her. Now, those same eyes conveyed anger as his gaze bounced off Jon and landed on her. But before he said anything, he snapped back to the guard.

"I know you. How do I...?" He studied Jon's face a long moment, then looked past Denise to Lake on the far end of the great room. After a beat, he glared at Denise, taking a few steps toward where she stood beside the kitchen table. "You have bodyguards?"

How did he know?

Before she could ask, Reid said, "Why do you need—?"

"What are you doing here, Reid?" Denise kept her voice level despite his rudeness. "How did you—?"

"What am *I* doing here? I live here. What are *you* doing here?"

"I live here too."

The words had the desired effect. Horror flicked across his face.

Lovely greeting from the man who'd once sworn to love her till death parted them.

Not that she could blame him.

He looked around at the space again. The front part of the great room sported a cathedral ceiling with a stone fireplace that reached to the peak. Soft white sofas were flanked by gray end tables that matched the coffee table. Just inside the front door, stairs led to a second-floor hallway that was visible from the ground floor, beneath which were her kitchen and dining area. The only interesting thing in the room—besides the grand fireplace—was the undecorated Christmas tree the management company had put up for her. Twelve feet tall, it stood against the wall between the living area and the kitchen.

She hoped Ella could help her decorate it.

The house had been built in the sixties, or maybe the seventies, but had been completely remodeled earlier that year. And if it was a little bland—despite the preferences she'd given to the overpriced decorator—she'd add her own personal touches over time.

Reid's face turned a shade of red that rivaled that of an heirloom tomato. Bright red with hints of purple.

If she didn't know better, she'd think he was suffering a heart attack. But no, this was just Reid being Reid. He spent his life perpetually enraged at Denise.

He started toward her again, but Jon grabbed his arm. He must've held tightly because Reid tried to twist out of his grip—and failed.

"Call off your dog," he said through gritted teeth.

"Sir." If Jon was offended, it didn't come out in his voice, which was even, though a little cool. "It's my job to protect Ms. Masters. In your current state, I suggest you keep your distance."

Reid shot her another hateful look. "Fine."

Jon released Reid's arm, and he shook it out.

"How did you know where I was?" Denise asked.

"Saw you get into the SUV. Then I saw the Tesla drive off and figured it was yours. Nobody else in town is that pretentious."

He'd been in her house thirty whole seconds before he'd insulted her. A personal record.

"I lost it on Rattlesnake," Reid said, "but I knew you wouldn't be in one of the condos. When I saw the Tesla in the driveway, I made some calls. You bought this place?"

"Who did you call?" Denise had purchased the house through a corporation set up to protect her. How could Reid have figured it out so quickly?

"The former owner is a friend of mine," he said. "Aspen dug into her paperwork from the closing. She said it was bought by EMC & Son. I cracked the code."

EMC. Ella Marie Cote. And *Son*, as in Masterson, Denise's maiden name.

"Why are you here, Reid?"

He stood taller. "This is my town, Denise."

"It's not like you got Coventry in the divorce. I grew up here too. As far as I know, it's still a free country. I can live wherever I want."

"Not here," he said.

She was about to toss out a retort—how he had no right to tell her where to live. How he was lucky she hadn't sued for custody of their daughter yet. Instead, she tried very hard to see this from his perspective.

He'd raised Ella by himself. He was her custodial parent, her real parent in every sense of the word.

Denise had left them both, and Reid didn't understand why. Nobody did.

That was her fault, not Reid's.

Denise had rights, rights she hadn't pressed for. Her presence had to feel threatening, which was why she'd hoped to ease into this slowly.

Summoning all her acting skills, she let a smile fill her face and chose a nonthreatening tone of voice. "I'm not here to ruin your life, Reid."

"Why are you here then?"

"Because I want more time with my daughter. Not vacations, but real, everyday-life kind of time."

"You aren't capable of that." His words sounded so final, so confident. So true.

"Maybe I'll surprise you."

"Remind me not to hold my breath."

She deserved his contempt. She'd messed up everything. But God had forgiven her. Ella had forgiven her. According to Ella, Reid and Jacqui attended church every Sunday. But he couldn't seem to manage the forgiveness thing where she was concerned. "I hope, if Ella ever disappoints you, you'll show her more mercy than you've shown me."

"You don't deserve mercy."

"I don't think that word means what you think it means." If he recognized the reference from *The Princess Bride*, a movie they'd watched repeatedly in high school, he didn't show it.

He crossed his arms and glanced at the bodyguards again. "What's going on? Do you always travel with bodyguards? Or is there something...?" He stepped forward a few steps.

Jon stayed beside him, crowding Reid like he'd crowded

Denise earlier. He kept his gaze on Denise, maybe waiting for some signal that he should stop him from getting too close.

She didn't want Reid to know what was going on. He'd only use the knowledge against her. Use it to keep her from Ella.

But he was Ella's father. If Denise wanted a real place in her daughter's life, she and Reid would need to find a way to work together.

Reid reached the kitchen table and peered at the papers spread out there. "These are the Starlet Slayer's victims. Why do you have...?" He rounded on Denise. "Are you a target?"

Was that concern in his voice? "I have no reason to believe—"

"You're a target, and you came *to Coventry,* where your *daughter* lives?" He moved toward her, but Jon stepped in the way.

Jon's body was just inches from hers as he stood between them. His back was broad, his shoulders wide and strong.

Reid glared past the man at her. "Seriously?"

"It's okay, Jon."

Near the back door, Lake's eyebrows hiked in surprise. At what? Did she think Denise should be afraid of her ex? Reid wasn't dangerous.

Denise patted the man's back. "Reid won't hurt me. It's okay."

The muscles beneath her hand tensed, but the bodyguard stepped out of the way silently. He stopped just a few feet from her, poised, it seemed, to jump between them again.

Reid tempered his voice. "Will you please tell me what's going on?"

"I told you I wanted to buy a house here to be closer to Ella."

"And then you didn't. I thought it was a passing whim."

"I've been busy with contractual obligations. Filming, interviews, tours—you know."

He didn't look impressed, not that she'd expected him to be.

"My contract is up at the end of the year. The studio's trying to renew it. My agent is working on that. Meanwhile, I had time on my hands. I bought the house this summer, got it ready, and now I'm here."

"For how long?"

"I don't know exactly. Through the holidays, for sure. Maybe longer." Maybe forever, but she didn't tell him that. *One step at a time.*

His eyes narrowed. "Does Ella know?"

Did he suspect their daughter had kept it from him? Would she have, if Denise had asked her to?

"I would never ask her to keep something like that from you."

He blinked, glanced away.

"Unlike you," she said. "When were you going to tell me Jacqui's pregnant?"

"How is that any of your business?"

"That my daughter's about to get a baby sister or brother? Kind of a big thing in a kid's life. Seems she might want to talk to her mother about it."

"She doesn't need you. She has Jacqui."

Denise absorbed the blow the same way she'd absorbed all of Reid's hits for years.

"Nevertheless." Denise kept her voice even. "I am her mother. It's not kind of you to ask her to keep things from me. That puts her in a very awkward position. Don't you think?"

He pressed his lips together, ran his hand over his short hair. "Yeah. You're right."

Whoa. Just like that?

"And about the other thing," he said. "The whole...mercy thing. I'm usually pretty good at it. Forgiveness. But with you..."

She didn't expect him to finish the sentence. He didn't need to.

She snatched her mug from the kitchen table and moved around the island into the kitchen. "Would you like a cup of tea?"

"No, thanks."

"Jon? Lake?"

"No, ma'am," Lake said.

Denise speared her with a look.

"Habit. Sorry."

Denise poured out the cold Earl Grey, grabbed another tea bag—herbal with hints of cinnamon and cloves—and poured the still-hot water over it. "I came here to be near Ella." She added honey to the mug before looking at Reid. "Did the murders have something to do with me making the decision now? Maybe. I mean, I wasn't nervous, not really. But... yeah, it's a little disconcerting to have women in the same line of work as mine be murdered. I honestly didn't think they had anything to do with me."

"You *didn't* think. But now you do?"

She indicated the table with her chin. "Somebody sent me that packet of papers with articles about the murders. The last one is the victim who was killed last night, Shannon—"

"Butler. I saw."

"It's *possible*"—she placed heavy emphasis on that word—"that the packet was left for me with my agent before Shannon was killed. Meaning it's *possible* that the killer left it. But it's just as likely the packet was left this morning."

The color in Reid's face had returned to normal. Now, it paled. "You're saying maybe the killer sent it to you?"

"Maybe. But I didn't know about any of that when I came here. That all happened today."

"How long have you been here?"

"Since last night."

"Why were you stalking us at the festival today?"

She plopped the mug on the counter, spilling a little across the white marble. "I wasn't *stalking* you, Reid. I was trying to get up my courage to...to join you. Join Cassidy and James. Can you understand that? Can you understand that it's not easy for me to be back here? I knew how you'd react. I thought Ella would be happy to see me. But everybody else..."

Maybe the slightest tinge of compassion flitted across his face, but it didn't last. "You thought you'd just show up, no warning."

"A surprise."

He let that settle. "Ella would have liked that." The admission seemed to hurt. "I'm glad she didn't see you. It would break her heart to have you show up and then leave again."

"I'm not going anywhere."

"You might be in danger. You really want to bring that danger to your daughter's doorstep?"

Jon cleared his throat. "There's no reason to believe the girl is—"

"She's not your daughter," Reid snapped. To Denise, he said, "You need to go back to Beverly Hills."

Before Denise could process what he'd said, Jon grabbed his arm and dragged him across the room.

"Hey, take your hands off me."

But Jon ignored him. He yanked open the front door, and the two disappeared outside.

CHAPTER FOUR

Jon managed to keep himself from pitching the man down the steps.

"Take your hands off me!" Ms. Masters's ex-husband had made the demand—while attempting to free himself—more than once as Jon yanked him down the front steps and toward the driveway. This guy was strong, just not strong enough.

Jon ignored him until they were beside the silver sedan. The sun was setting, though it wasn't even four o'clock yet, and the temperatures were already dropping, but Jon's anger kept him plenty warm.

Cote yanked away again, and Jon let him go.

He stumbled back and crashed into his car, barely keeping his feet. He turned and squared up with Jon like he was preparing for a fight.

"Don't make an enemy out of me." Jon kept his voice low and even.

"I need to talk to her. We need to figure this out. And I wasn't going to hurt her."

"My job is to keep Ms. Masters safe. The instant you

suggested she return to the place where she's most likely to be murdered, you threatened her safety."

His mouth opened. Closed. "I didn't..." He ran a hand over his short hair. "I didn't think of it that way. I just meant that she shouldn't be here."

"Every one of those murders happened in California. Your ex-wife just revealed to you that she might be a target. But it didn't occur to you—?"

"I get it. I'm just...I'm trying to keep my daughter safe."

"This guy hasn't harmed any children. From what I've learned of the case, every victim has been an adult actress. A couple of them had children, but none of those children were harmed. Every murder occurred when the children weren't present. There is absolutely zero reason to believe your daughter might be a target. Her mother, on the other hand—"

"Okay. Okay. I see what you're saying. But she docsn't have to stay here."

"This is her house. She has more right to be on this property"—he tapped his foot against the asphalt—"than you do. You might not like that fact, but you can't argue it."

"Fine." He looked past Jon at the doorway. "I'd like to go back inside and speak to her."

"Not tonight."

"Ask her. You don't get to decide—"

"You can call her later and tell her what a brute I am. Right now, we need to manage her protection, and you're getting in the way." Jon reached past him and opened the car door. There was something else he needed to say before the guy left, though. "You recognized me earlier."

"You were Josie Smith's bodyguard."

"I saw you at that Fourth of July dinner," Jon said. "There was one other time, but I doubt you saw me. It was the following Sunday, at church."

Cote's eyebrows hiked.

Jon wasn't about to explain what had motivated the decision, the self-loathing that descended after his client had been kidnapped and almost killed, the desperate need to know that nobody's protection rested solely on his shoulders. That maybe there was a God who was watching, who was helping.

Thomas and Josie had prayed a lot leading up to that terrible weekend. When they'd been taken, Jon had thought what a waste of time all that prayer had been.

But they'd escaped. They'd both survived. It had been...miraculous.

Which had sent him to church.

"You were at church that day," Jon said. "Standing next to your wife, your little girl between you. You had your hands up in the air like you were really into the music. Like you were—"

"Thomas and Josie almost died that weekend. I was thanking God."

Jon considered that. "I've been doing some studying about this faith thing. Here's what I'm trying to figure out. How can a guy who claims to be a Christian worship God like you did that day and still be so filled with hatred? Hatred directed at a woman he used to love, the mother of his child?" He stepped closer, held his eye contact. "Which is the real you? Are you a hypocrite, or a liar?"

The man blinked, and his shoulders drooped. "I'm working on it. It's a process, this 'faith thing,' as you call it."

Jon backed off. "I think you'd better step up that work. Ms. Masters is here. And she's not leaving." Jon was about to head inside when Lake spoke in his earpiece.

"Client wants to provide protection for her daughter," Lake said, "and she's insisting I leave with the ex tonight."

Which would leave only Jon to protect Ms. Masters. He tapped the two-way at his hip. "Bad idea. We need two here."

Cote's eyebrows lifted, so Jon motioned to his earpiece.

"Bartlett says it's your call," Lake said. "He's working on getting more manpower, but nobody can be up here until late."

Just a few months earlier, Jon had almost gotten his client killed, and there'd been two guards on her that day, not to mention a station full of police officers. How could he keep Ms. Masters safe by himself? What if he made another tactical error? "I don't like it."

"Me either. But..." Lake lowered her voice, and he imagined her turning away so the client couldn't hear. "She's stubborn. It's either she sends me with the ex, or she sends us both away."

He stifled a sigh. Prima donnas.

"Fine," Jon said. "Meet you at the door. Keep her inside." He spoke to the ex. "Don't leave yet."

"Told you she'd want to talk to me."

"Wrong again." He started back toward the house, Cote at his side. "Ms. Masters is insisting Lake go with you to protect your daughter."

Rather than look relieved, the man seemed irritated. They were nearly to the steps when the door opened.

The client stepped outside, and Jon hopped up to stand in front of her, turning to face Reid. What part of *keep her inside* had Lake not understood?

The actress clearly had no sense of the danger she was in.

"Is this really necessary?" Ms. Masters asked from behind him. "I'm trying to have a conversation."

"I'm trying to keep you alive." He positioned himself so she'd be able to see Reid but would be hidden from the woods at the side of her house. If he were trying to kill her, that was where he'd hide—with his sniper rifle.

Assuming the would-be killer had half a brain, Ms. Masters should be safe for now.

He still didn't like it.

After a long-suffering sigh, Ms. Masters spoke again. "Lake is going with you, Reid. I guess there'll be a whole team, but the rest won't be here until tomorrow."

"I don't want that," Cote said. "It'll freak Ella out."

"Ella will be fine." Her voice was patient, more than his would have been in a similar situation. "I always have security when she's with me in California."

"If you'd just leave town—"

"This isn't a negotiation," Ms. Masters snapped. Then, she started over in a calmer tone. "I'm going to be at church tomorrow. Don't tell Ella. I want to surprise her. And then I'd like to bring her back here for the afternoon."

Cote's jaw clenched so tight, Jon figured it was giving him a headache. "I'd prefer more notice."

"You have something planned?"

"That's not the point. The point is—"

"She's my daughter too."

Tension stretched between them. Ms. Masters didn't back down as Cote seemed to wrestle with his response.

After a moment, he said, "Fine. Until dinnertime. She has school on Monday."

"Thank you." Ms. Masters's voice was lower when she spoke again. "Thanks for doing this." Though he couldn't see her, he assumed shows speaking to Lake. "There's nothing more important to me than Ella."

Lake jogged down the steps, giving Jon a look as she passed him.

Yeah, he recognized that look.

Lake was no happier about this plan than he was.

Their number of clients had just doubled—more than doubled if he considered the ex and his wife—and Donley and Lake had to split up.

A heap of papers inside the house underscored that Ms. Masters was in danger.

Not to mention the attempt on her life that day.

This was just getting better and better.

CHAPTER FIVE

They'd barely stepped back into the house when Denise's phone rang. The California number wasn't familiar, but she had a guess.

"Hello?"

"Denise Masters?" It was a man, his voice rough like he smoked a lot of cigarettes or drank a lot of whiskey. "Special Agent Martin Frank, California Bureau of Investigation."

"Agent." She eyed Jon beside her.

He said low, "Put it on speaker, please."

She did, and they sat together at the kitchen table.

"You've spoken to Mr. Taggart?" Agent Frank asked.

"First, let me tell you that my bodyguard is here with me."

"Donley," Jon said. "I'm also a private investigator. I've been—"

"We don't need any PIs involved."

Jon glowered at the phone.

Frank moved on. "Miss Masters, did your agent send you the copy of the package he received?"

"We have it here."

"Then you're up to speed. Any idea who might've left that for you?"

"I'm sorry, I don't."

"Any fans bothering you lately? Strange fan mail?"

"Bruce's office filters my mail for me. They don't forward anything they deem inappropriate. You can talk to them about—"

"Did that," the special agent said. "What about people lurking around your house? You live in Beverly Hills, right?"

"Haven't noticed anybody unusual. I don't know if Bruce told you, but I'm not in California right now."

"But before you left... Anybody new in your life? New neighbors, new friends?"

One name came to mind. "There's my house sitter, Monroe Huxley. I know him from church. I've known him maybe six months, a year? So he's sort of a new friend, I guess."

"What can you tell me about him?"

"He's a nice guy. A Christian. Wants to be an actor. He's house-sat for other actors and one of my neighbors, and they said he did a good job, so—"

"Phone number?"

She found it and read it to him. "Do you really think these murders are somehow related to me?"

"Somebody left that package."

Jon tapped her wrist, and she guessed he wanted to say something. She nodded for him to go ahead.

"Have you determined yet when the package was dropped off?"

"No way to know," Frank said. "The agency's rear lot is accessible by an alley that has no CCTV coverage. We've been studying the nearest cameras but haven't picked up anyone carrying the envelope. Guy probably had it in a backpack or something."

"It could've been left before Shannon Butler's murder or after," Jon clarified.

"Even if it was after," Frank said, "we kept the story under wraps until nearly six a.m. If the person who dropped it is just a weird fan of murders and Miss Masters, he'd have to have learned about the murder, printed out the newspaper article, stuck it in an envelope, and dropped it off at Taggart's office, all before Taggart arrived at seven thirty. And since he didn't print the *Times* article about the murder but an earlier article..."

"Got it," Jon said.

Denise closed her eyes, letting the truth of what he was saying settle itself in her mind.

"Our working theory is that the killer left that packet, or it was somebody close enough to him to know who his next victim would be."

"An accomplice?" Jon asked. "Do you have reason to believe—?"

"No evidence he's working with somebody. Most serial killers work alone."

Serial killers.

How were they talking about a *serial killer*?

A serial killer who'd singled out Denise. Why?

"Anything peculiar happen recently, Miss Masters?" the agent asked. "Weird, unusual, out of the ordinary?"

As if she didn't know the definition of *peculiar*. "I can't think of anything. My life is pretty dull, to be honest."

"Oh, right. The poor, bored Hollywood starlet."

Did she hear contempt in his voice?

What was that about?

Jon shot her a look and said, "Somebody took a shot at her at the park today. Long range from a boat."

"What park? Where?"

"Coventry, New Hampshire."

"Oh." The agent paused a moment. "Any leads? Do the locals think it's related?"

"We didn't know about the connection to the serial killer when the detective was here," Jon said.

"Yeah..." Frank was quiet for a long moment. "These killings have been going on for a year now, and none of them have involved shootings. They've all been up close and personal. Thinking it's not related. Ms. Masters, maybe something from your past. Somebody with an obsessive attraction to you? Somebody who has something against you?"

Reid had something against her. But her ex-husband, as much as he hated her, wasn't violent.

And anyway, he was here. The murders had happened in Los Angeles, and even Frank thought they were unrelated to the shooting that day.

"I've had my share of obsessive fans," Denise said. "A few years ago, there was one guy who wrote me every single day. Sent me gifts. Expressed his undying love. I guessed he was pretty young, maybe even a teenager."

"Name?"

"Bruce could tell you."

"What happened to him? Did you ask him to stop writing or—?"

"He just stopped one day. The letters came every day, and then, nothing."

"Just that one fan?" Frank asked.

"That guy's letters got pretty...graphic. That's when I started having Bruce and his team filter them for me. You'd have to ask him."

Jon said, "Detective, did the murder victims receive similar packages with information about the previous murders? Should we be worried that Ms. Masters is this guy's next target?"

"Should you be worried? Heck, yeah. But did they receive

anything like this?" He paused, probably for effect. "They did not."

"What do you think it means?" Jon asked.

"That's the million-dollar question. Miss Masters, can you think of anything you have in common with the victims?"

"Besides the obvious, that we're all women actors living in California? No. Can you?"

He ignored her question. "Can you think of anything they have in common with each other?"

"I'd only ever met one of them," she said. "How would I know?"

"There's some connection," Frank said. "You must know something, and unless you're in favor of somebody killing off your competition—"

"They're not my—"

"—I suggest you start talking."

She started to toss out a retort, but once again, Jon's finger tapped her wrist. Apparently, he didn't want her to get into a confrontation with this guy. Or maybe he didn't see the point, and he wasn't wrong. Being in the public eye, Denise had gotten used to people worshipping her, admiring her, criticizing her, and loathing her. But those people didn't know the real her. She tried not to let their opinions—good or bad—affect her self-image.

It wasn't as easy as it sounded.

She kept her mouth shut. Jon didn't say anything, either. They just let the agent's remark hang between them.

Frank said, "It could be that whatever you're hiding is the connection to the other victims."

"I'm not hiding anything," Denise said.

"Could be something we haven't considered."

"Could be," she said, "but since I have no idea what you *have* considered, I wouldn't know."

Jon nodded as if he approved of her answer, though he didn't look her direction.

"Anything in your past you'd prefer not be made public?"

Of course there was. Everybody deserved a private life, didn't they? In Denise's case, her privacy was vital to signing her next contract. "Did the victims have secrets in their past, secrets that linked them?"

"Hard to know since they're all dead. You're the only potential victim we've been able to interview."

"If I knew what kind of information you were looking for—"

"Anything somebody might kill over."

She looked at Jon for help, but he was staring at the phone. Maybe *glaring* was the right word.

"I'm sorry, Detective," she said, "but I don't know what to tell you. Are there things about my life I haven't made public? Of course. Aren't there things about your life you wouldn't want made public? But is there anything in my past worth killing over? Absolutely not."

"It's possible you just don't know—"

"If you gave me a hint about what kind of information you're looking for, I'd be happy to help you. Or do you just want me to tell you everything I've ever done?"

"Wouldn't hurt."

This was ridiculous.

Agent Frank didn't speak for a long moment, and she certainly didn't have anything else to say.

"If you think of anything—"

"You'll keep us informed," Jon said. "And we'll do the same."

"I expect you will. I'll be in touch."

The call disconnected.

She stared at the black screen, processing.

Jon faced her. "Is there some connection you didn't want to tell him?"

"There's a whole lot of stuff I wouldn't want to tell him—tell anybody. But if I have a connection to the victims besides the obvious, then I'm not aware of it."

He nodded. "If you think of anything that might connect you to even one of them—"

"I have nothing to hide."

Not entirely true, but she couldn't imagine how her secrets —which were relatively tame, considering the trouble a lot of actors got into—had anything to do with the murders.

Denise didn't want to think about that anymore. It wasn't as if she could solve the crimes, and she'd come to New Hampshire to get away from all that madness.

It was time for dinner. Time to shift her attention to something less disturbing.

She stood and scoured the cabinets for ingredients.

She was no gourmet, but she liked to cook. Back in California, she fixed dinner for herself a couple of times a week. Nights she didn't cook, she usually had meals delivered. People who didn't know any better figured a so-called movie star would have friends galore and invitations every night. Maybe other people did, and Denise used to, but now she spent the majority of evenings at home by herself. Most of her friendships had proved to be pretty shallow over the years, people who loved her for her position and money. She liked the people she worked with, other actors on the set, even the professionals who worked backstage, but she mostly saw them during filming. Usually, if she socialized at all, it was with friends from church, but most of them were married with children. Though she knew she could count on them in a crisis, they lived busy lives.

She'd had one good friend who'd moved with her to LA eight years before, but after Brittney tried for years to break into the movie business and failed, she'd moved back to New Hampshire.

Denise had come home to establish a relationship with her daughter. She'd also come to rekindle old friendships. She and Cassidy kept up, and Cassidy had convinced her she would be accepted in her friend group, even by Reid's wife, Jacqui.

But had she brought a killer with her?

She found a recipe on her laptop, browned the meat, drained the fat, and added the rest of the ingredients while Jon pored over the articles spread across her dining room table.

The man was too quiet. It was disconcerting. And shouldn't he be standing at a door? She'd never known a private security guard to investigate. She'd have to ask him about that.

Once the taco soup was simmering, Denise started a fire in the fireplace, something she'd rarely gotten to do in California, then ran upstairs to change. Jon—and the rest of the bodyguards —would have to get used to seeing her in cozy loungewear. She wasn't going to walk around in skinny jeans and fancy blouses in her own home.

She puttered in her bedroom for a while, unpacking some of the boxes she'd had shipped from California and those filled with clothes she'd ordered online, warm sweaters and boots she had little need for back in LA.

Mostly, she was avoiding the man downstairs. It had been strange earlier to have the two bodyguards. With just Jon, it was beyond awkward. Not that he wasn't attractive. He was, very. He was the quintessential strong, soldier-type, broad and barrel-chested, the kind of guy who could star in a Navy SEAL movie or something. But it wasn't his looks that drew her. His protectiveness tweaked a desire she'd let go dormant a long time before. It'd been years...*years* since she'd had a man—had anybody—take care of her.

She liked it.

Which was ridiculous. He was a bodyguard, paid to protect her. His care for her was no less mercenary than her agent's. Maybe she should give up her dream of forming real relationships and hire a few friends while she was at it.

Anyway, Jon didn't seem to like her. She was used to people fawning over her, not scowling at her.

When she figured the soup had simmered long enough to be palatable, she returned downstairs. Jon was still hunched over the papers on the kitchen table. He was making notes on a pad of paper but looked up when she scooted around the bar into the kitchen.

She waited for some comment—about her clothes, about the scents coming from the stovetop—but he said nothing, just returned to his work.

"Anything interesting?" She removed the soup pot from the heat and stirred.

"Just familiarizing myself with the case." He didn't even glance her way when he spoke. And again, she was struck by how different this man was from most she met. If he found her the least bit attractive, he was a master at hiding it. Most men looked longer than they needed to. This guy seemed utterly unaffected. Which was good. The last thing she needed was to fend off advances from people staying at her house.

That'd be a great way for Jon to get himself fired.

"Were you hired to investigate or protect me?"

"Both." He looked up, caught her staring, and returned his attention to the papers.

She swiveled to the refrigerator and pulled out an avocado, a block of cheddar, and sour cream. She set to work slicing the avocado, then grating the cheese.

What else?

She returned to the pantry and found a bag of tortilla chips.

Back in the kitchen, she asked, "You hungry?"

This time when he looked at her, he wore a polite smile. "If you don't mind. It smells delicious."

Pleasure warmed her cheeks. Ridiculous. "Of course. We can eat at the bar so you don't have to move all that stuff."

He stood. "Can I help?"

"There're bowls around here somewhere." She waved at the cabinets. "You find them, and I'll see if I can locate napkins."

She searched the pantry, to no avail. She headed back to the kitchen. "We're going to have to—"

"Found them." He held them up.

She moved the soup pot to the wide bar, beside the fixings, then spun to survey the kitchen. She sang, "Ladle, ladle, ladle-le-he-hoo."

He chuckled, the sound deep and warm, and her cheeks burned for the second time in three minutes. What was wrong with her? She knew, though. She always fought awkwardness with humor, or tried to, anyway.

He snatched one from a drawer, then grabbed two spoons. "How is it that I know your kitchen better than you do?"

"More observant, better memory. I have an excellent memory for lines in a script—and very little else."

She scooped about a half a cup of soup into a bowl, added avocado slices, a tiny dollop of sour cream, and two crunched-up tortilla chips. "I don't have a lot to drink. Lemonade—it's Ella's favorite—and flavored water."

"Plain water's fine."

She fixed two glasses while Jon filled his soup bowl, then piled sour cream and cheddar on top. He stuck a handful of chips in another bowl and slid the whole thing to the opposite side of the bar.

"Are you going to have enough there?" She stared at a week's worth of calories.

He eyed her smaller portion, then lifted one eyebrow. "Are you?"

"I'm trying to keep my figure."

"You're doing a fine job."

That earned a look. This time, it was Jon's cheeks turning red.

She barely suppressed a laugh, instead digging into her dinner.

He did the same. They ate in silence for a couple of minutes.

She nodded with her chin to the table adjacent to them. "So, what'd you learn?"

"Just looking for patterns."

"And?"

"Probably didn't see anything the cops haven't already seen, and they have more information than I do. Victims are all between twenty-five and forty. All women, and all relatively successful actors. At least I'd call them successful. Would you?"

She recalled what she'd read of them. "Most of them, yes. It seems at least one hadn't worked in a while, but she'd been successful."

"Enough to be called starlets."

She scoffed. "That's a silly term."

He wagged his head back and forth. "I guess. You Hollywood people—"

"That is *not* a Hollywood term. We're actors. Professionals. A starlet sounds like...like some prissy puffed-up prima donna."

He smiled and looked away.

"What?"

"This is really good. Do all starlets know how to cook?"

She scowled at him, and he laughed.

It was...strange sharing a meal in her kitchen with a man she'd just met. In New Hampshire. Talking like normal people.

A half hour before, she'd wondered if he even liked her. She'd guess now that maybe he did, at least a little. The thought warmed her as much as the fire crackling in the fireplace.

She couldn't remember the last time she'd enjoyed a bowl of soup so much.

And seriously. How pathetic was that?

CHAPTER SIX

Denise couldn't help a jubilant feeling as she settled into the backseat of the bodyguard's SUV the following day. She'd wanted to drive herself to church, but this guy was as stubborn as Jon. The changing of the guard had happened at some point after Denise had gone to bed. The new guy—older than Jon by at least a decade and built like a Hummer—was even less chatty than her dinner companion the night before. And that was saying something.

She glanced at her watch, afraid they might be late. But there was plenty of time. The little charm hanging from the chain wristband caught her eye, and she lifted it. It was a circle, so small it could easily be a logo tag. Jon had given it to her the night before. It had some sort of tracking device in it. "Just in case we lose you. Not that we will, but I've learned to be prepared."

She wasn't sure how she felt about being tracked, but she hadn't been able to come up with any reason why it wasn't a good idea.

A trip to church ought to be safe enough.

She'd been tempted to wait until the service started and slip in the back, but she had as much right to be there as anybody else. Why should she hide?

So, she'd texted Jacqui that morning—the woman was much more polite than Reid—and asked if she'd please save a seat for her.

Jacqui had responded immediately. *Happy to! We usually sit in the third pew from the front on the right side, so you can come down the side aisle, if you want. Ella is going to be thrilled to see you.*

Denise appreciated her ex-husband's wife. She seemed a little on the shy side, but she was kind and genuine, and she was good to Ella.

And maybe Denise could admit a little jealously, not because Jacqui was married to Reid but because of the relationship she had with Ella. But that was Denise's problem, not Jacqui's.

They pulled up to the door of the old white church a couple of blocks from the lake in downtown Coventry, and the bodyguard walked her inside while another parked the car. There were four of them that morning. Overkill if she'd ever seen it.

But the conversations from the night before were fresh. As if the Starlet Slayer weren't enough, there had been the shooter at the park.

Surely the Starlet Slayer couldn't be in Coventry, right?

Even Jon had seemed skeptical when she'd floated that idea.

But it was either that or there were two killers out there, one of whom might even know where she lived. Which meant he probably knew about her connection to Ella. Which meant...

Her daughter was in danger.

The night before, she'd considered leaving Coventry. She was not willing to risk Ella's safety for anything. But Jon had talked her off that ledge.

"It's very likely that the shooter is a local, and if he is, he already knows Ella is your daughter. Which means she's no more and no less in danger now than she was before you came. With two full security teams, we can keep you both safe."

She'd allowed herself to believe him, maybe because he was right. Maybe because she wanted to stay.

The church had changed in the years since she'd been there. They'd built an addition that connected the sanctuary to the class-room building adjacent to it, and most people entered the doors into that addition. The bodyguards had parked outside the main entrance, though, so she entered through the wide double doors, the way she had as a child. When she stepped inside, the familiar scents hit her—a musty combination of old books and dust and age. She wanted nothing more than to stop and take it in, but the man at her elbow urged her forward, skirting most of the crowd.

"Find your seat, ma'am. Try not to stand out."

Despite her profession, in recent years she'd done her best not to stand out. Didn't often succeed. The service hadn't begun yet, and people streamed into the foyer from the long hallway to the left. Some recognized her—she knew by the way their eyes widened in surprise—but most paid her no mind.

Denise pretended she was just another parishioner, pretended there wasn't an oversize bodyguard at her side eyeing everybody with suspicion, and followed the crowd into the worship center.

She'd always loved this building, the pretty stained-glass windows, the sloping ceiling, the dark podium on the stage, and the simple cross that hung behind it. There was nothing ostenta-tious or ornate about the church, and yet she'd always felt close to God here. If only she and Reid had kept coming through college. If only they hadn't let their faith slip away when they'd sacrificed their purity on the altar of desire. Maybe everything would be different now.

Denise wouldn't be a successful actor. But she'd give all that up to have the years back. The time with her daughter. Even the marriage. Not that she wanted Reid now, but they could have made it work. They could have been happy.

Maybe that other life would have been better. Maybe not. That was the thing about regret. You looked back and assumed different decisions would've been *better* decisions, which would have led to a better life. But maybe different decisions would've only led to a different life, one with just as many trials and troubles.

Regret was pointless.

She was forgiven.

God was good.

Sometimes it was that simple.

She rounded the pews and walked down the aisle on the far right to the third row, where Reid and Jacqui were standing and talking to a couple in front of them. Reid was smiling, even laughing. She hadn't seen that side of him in many years. Jacqui's baby bump was pronounced beneath the fitted top, and Denise felt a sharp pang of jealousy. No, she didn't want Reid, but she did want what Jacqui had found. A man who loved her, a beautiful, precious little girl who lived under her roof, and a child on the way.

All that mattered now was the little girl sitting on the pew, drawing on a notepad while her legs swung beneath the wooden seat.

Denise scooted in to stand beside her. She kept her voice low and leaned down to her level. "Surprise."

Ella glanced her way, then looked again, brown eyes as wide as quarters. "Mommy!" Unlike Denise, she made no attempt to keep her voice low. She scrambled to her feet and launched herself into Denise's arms.

Denise lifted her daughter, whose little legs curled around her waist like she was four, not eight, and fought a wave of tears.

How had she ever left this child?

Regret might be pointless, but sometimes it was as real as the girl in her arms—and twice as heavy.

"What are you doing here?"

Denise leaned away so she could look into her daughter's face. Her skin was milky white, showing off the faint freckles on her nose. Her lips were rosy red and stretched into a smile. She'd grown since Denise had seen her. Every time she held this precious child of hers, she was struck by how much she was missing.

Not anymore. She wouldn't miss any more of Ella's life.

But it was too soon to say that. One step at a time. "I came to see you."

"How long are you staying?"

"I'll be here at least through Christmas."

Ella's eyes widened even more. "Christmas? That's a whole month away!" She released her legs from around Denise's waist and stepped onto the pew again, facing her father. "Daddy, look!"

Reid turned from his conversation, saw Denise over Ella's head. His easy smile slid away, replaced with the tight, polite one he always wore when he was looking at Denise and Ella was watching. He shifted his focus to his daughter. "What a fun surprise."

"Did you know she was coming?"

"She asked me not to tell."

"It's the best surprise ever!"

Reid pressed a finger over his lips. "Let's use our inside voice, okay?"

"Sorry, Daddy." She turned back to Denise, beaming.

The music started, and Denise held Ella's hand and sang

along with the worship music, trying and failing to focus on God. Seemed Ella was having the same trouble because every time Denise glanced at her daughter, she was looking back, love and joy in her expression, making Denise's heart expand.

She wasn't worthy of Ella's love. She wasn't worthy of God's, either, but she had it. And His forgiveness. She didn't deserve the righteousness He said was hers, the freedom from shame. She'd learned that she had to embrace God's promises and believe them before she could experience them. She had to trust His promises despite her feelings.

She was learning. With Ella at her side, it was easy to believe in a God who loved her. What else would explain the love of a precious little girl directed at a woman as unworthy as herself?

In the backseat of the bodyguard's SUV, Ella bounced at Denise's side. "I can't believe you're really here! This is the best surprise ever! Daddy didn't say anything. And Jacqui either. I saw the black car and all the people, but Daddy said to ignore them. Are they bodyguards too? Why are they at our house? Why didn't you tell me you were coming?"

"I wanted—"

"To surprise me, I know. And it was awesome! Where are we going? Omigosh, I'm in a school play. Maybe you could come. Would you? That would be *so cool*! I don't remember when it is, though. Not for a couple weeks, I think. Jacqui would know. I'll ask her."

"I'd love to see it." Denise's smile was so wide, her cheeks were starting to hurt.

"Is this your car? Are these your normal bodyguards?"

"Not exactly." Denise had never told her daughter that she

only had bodyguards when Ella visited. She'd never been that concerned about her own safety.

"What are we going to do today? Can we get pizza?"

"If you want." That wasn't Denise's plan, but she didn't want to disappoint her daughter. "Maybe we could go to that place in town."

In the front seat, the bodyguard cleared his throat. Smitty, she remembered. She caught his expression in the rearview mirror. He shook his head.

Not that he got to decide how Denise spent her time, but she understood his concern.

"You know what?" Denise said. "If you want pizza, we can have it delivered, but I have another surprise for you first."

She hoped, prayed, Ella would be more excited than her father had been. Before when Denise came to town, she'd stayed in one of the little hotels downtown. It wasn't the nicest place in the world, but at least the innkeeper didn't judge her life choices the way her parents did. And anyway, she'd never stayed very long. Normally, Ella visited her in California. Denise only came here when she had a break in her schedule and the longing to see her daughter was so strong that she couldn't wait for their next planned visit.

Reid hated it when she popped in like that, always telling Denise how her visits disrupted *his* daughter's routine, as if Denise had no claim on her. He was amicable as long as Denise stayed in the box he'd built for her—on the West Coast, only visiting after gaining his expressed permission.

He was probably cursing her even now as he drove home from church.

Would he see the irony in that?

"What surprise?" Ella asked.

"You'll just have to wait and see."

The bodyguard wound up Rattlesnake Road, another bodyguard at his side. They followed an SUV with two more guards in it, and another followed with three more. Ella's team and Denise's team would both be available to protect them when they were together.

Denise was so glad she'd had the pool house built. There'd been a detached garage on the property, but for some reason its foundation had been destroyed. She'd had a fresh foundation poured, this one larger. The two-car garage was still there, but now there was also a small apartment with two bedrooms. She hadn't furnished it yet, but Jon had assured her he'd get some air mattresses for the team. It would be their headquarters as long as she needed protection.

Ella kept up a stream of chatter until the bodyguards pulled into the driveway.

The house wasn't huge, but it was charming, especially pretty against the backdrop of pine trees that surrounded it. There was a black SUV—seemed the bodyguards had an endless supply—and a white van that hadn't been there earlier. It had the words *White Mountain Security* on the side.

Jon had told her he'd be upgrading her security system. He hadn't wasted any time.

Ella had quieted beside her. "Where are we?"

Denise didn't answer right away. She waited until the body-guard parked and opened the door for her. She stepped out, and Ella scrambled behind her.

Denise took the child's hand in hers and gazed up at the two-story structure. "Do you like it?"

"It's pretty," Ella said. "Do you know the people who live here?"

Denise smiled down at her daughter. "I do. And so do you."

"Ma'am." The bodyguards had gathered beside and behind. "We should get inside."

"One second." Denise crouched down. "I bought this house, love. It's mine."

Ella's eyes got wide again, and her jaw dropped. "It's *yours*? You *live here*?"

"I still have my place in LA," she said quickly. "But I'm going to try to spend as much time here—"

Ella threw herself into her arms, cutting off Denise's words.

Emotion pricked her eyes. When she backed up so she could see her daughter's face, she saw tears streaming down her little cheeks, and her own fell.

"I didn't mean to make you cry."

"I'm not crying," Ella said through her tears. "I'm happy."

"Me too."

"Ma'am," the man said again. "Inside, please."

Denise straightened and took Ella's hand, and they walked with the throng of bodyguards. The one who seemed to be in charge opened the door for her, and she and Ella stepped inside.

He didn't. None of them did, just let them go in alone.

Denise appreciated that more than she could express.

Ella froze in the entrance and took in the room. Her gaze didn't get farther than the Christmas tree in the corner. "It's ginormous!"

"I was hoping you'd help me decorate it today."

The joy on her daughter's face filled Denise's heart with praise.

Thank You for this, Lord. I don't deserve her. Help me do right by her. And please keep her safe.

CHAPTER SEVEN

J on had stayed alert and on guard until after two a.m. when reinforcements arrived, at which point he'd left to try to get some sleep. Ms. Masters had suggested he and his team use the little apartment in the building out back, and they'd gotten the heat on early enough that the place had been decently warm by the time he'd made it out there. It had no furniture, so he'd slept on the floor with blankets she'd pulled off one of the extra beds in the main house.

He'd already ordered some blow-up mattresses and bedding. The boss had sent ten guards to join Jon and Lake. They would sleep in shifts, all of them in that little house out back. Fortunately, the Cotes only lived a few miles away.

Jon had awakened just after the team left with Ms. Masters for church. He'd been tempted to join them, but he trusted his coworkers to keep her safe. Instead, he'd contacted an alarm company and arranged for them to come to the house immediately to set up a top-quality security system. They were on the property now, putting cameras all around the perimeter. A security fence would be installed on Monday. Mr. Taggart had told them to spare no expense in protecting their client. It was amazing the service money could buy.

While they worked, Jon had dug more into the Starlet Slayings, gathering as much intelligence as he could from the Internet and his sources in law enforcement. He didn't know anybody in the CBI, but he did have a friend in the FBI who'd promised to find out what he could. Since all the murders had taken place in California, there was no federal element to it, so the FBI wasn't technically involved. But they had resources. His friend would be able to learn more than Jon could.

What he'd discovered so far hadn't exactly soothed his worries.

The first victim had been stabbed when she'd gone for a walk in her Brentwood neighborhood. At the time, the police had thought it was a random attack.

The second victim had been at her beach house in Malibu. She'd gone for an early morning jog. Her husband had found her body floating on the tide a couple of hours later. She'd also been stabbed.

It wasn't until the third victim, a month later, that the police linked the murders. She'd been filming on location in San Francisco, had only stepped away for a few minutes to take a call. While her friends and coworkers ran through the scene just a few yards distant, she was stabbed in the heart.

It was then that the reporter first dubbed the murderer the Starlet Slayer.

Some of the most famous and wealthiest female actors in Hollywood hired bodyguards. Others wouldn't leave the house without a companion. Studios paid drivers to take their stars back and forth to work. Upscale neighborhoods put together teams to patrol.

For three months, nothing happened.

And then the fourth victim. She'd had bodyguards. She'd

been careful not to leave her house alone. But she'd thought she was safe behind the walls of her property.

She'd been wrong.

Her body was found floating in her own pool, facedown.

All the victims had been stabbed, but the circumstances had been different with every murder. The killer had hidden in the backseat of one victim's car, stabbed her in the neck from behind. He'd killed another after breaking into her home.

The latest, Shannon Butler, despite her bodyguards, had been murdered in the bathroom at a swanky restaurant.

The killer was getting more daring.

And for some reason, he'd sent Ms. Masters information on his victims. Why?

At the sound of cars in the driveway, Jon bundled up the paperwork he'd been poring over and put it away.

He'd done a final sweep of the house when Grant told him they were leaving the church. Now, he stood against the back wall as Ms. Masters and her daughter stepped in.

The girl was beautiful, like her mother, and though she had tear streaks on her cheeks, she seemed happy.

Ms. Masters took her on a tour of the house, starting upstairs, then down the hall to the office and bathroom, then into the kitchen. "This is Mr. Donley," Ms. Masters said. "Jon, my daughter, Ella."

The girl looked up at him with wide, fearful eyes. He couldn't blame her. Everything about him was oversize. His left leg probably weighed more than this little bird. He crouched down and held out his hand. "It is a pleasure to meet you, Miss Cote."

She giggled. "Only Mrs. Brooks calls me that. She's my teacher, and when she gets mad at you, she calls you by your last name."

"I can't imagine anybody getting mad at you," Jon said.

The child giggled again, a beautiful sound. "Only when I talk too much. Not like Janson. He's *always* in trouble. He likes to pull hair and push people."

"Is he a bully?"

Ella shrugged. "I guess, a little."

Jon glanced at Ms. Masters's face long enough to see the concern there. "If he ever pushes you around," he said, "you let me know. I'll have a talk with him."

Ella's grin stretched across her face. "I bet you'd scare the mean right out of him."

Jon couldn't help but smile. If only *the mean* were that simple to scare out of adults.

Ms. Masters tugged her daughter's hand, and they started for the door beneath the stairs. "I'm going to show you the basement. There's a special room down here you can run to if you ever get scared of anything."

Jon had discovered the basement apartment the night before after Ms. Masters went to bed. It had a bedroom, a bathroom, and a living area that included a small kitchen. If the door to enter hadn't been hidden behind a wall of shelves, he'd never have known it was a panic room. But the door and jamb were made of reinforced steel. Someone had already installed electronic locks. He'd make sure that both a wired phone and a satellite phone were kept behind that door. By the time he and the company he'd hired were finished, it would be a perfect panic room, the kind of place a person could hole up safely for days.

Strange thing to build into a home in a vacation town in New Hampshire, but he wasn't complaining.

Ms. Masters and Ella returned after a few minutes and retrieved a couple of boxes from the office. He'd noticed the stack the night before, so he went down the hall and grabbed the rest.

He set them in the living room, where Ms. Masters was already digging into one that looked old and worn. "These are my favorite ornaments," she said.

Ella pulled out a bundle of tissue paper and unwrapped it, then beamed. It was a little foam reindeer with google eyes and a drawn-on face. "I made this!"

"I know. That's why I love it."

Jon watched as mother and daughter unpacked, sometimes laughing at ornaments Ella had made over the years. When Ella suggested the one shaped like a tiny hand and scribbled all over was "too ugly for that pretty tree," Ms. Masters pressed it to her chest lovingly.

"Don't say that about my favorite one!"

"That can't be, Mommy. It's horrible."

"You made it when you were two years old. It's a treasure, just like you."

Ella beamed.

Ms. Masters might not have been the girl's custodial parent, but she seemed to not only know her daughter very well, but to adore her and connect with her.

When there was a break in the conversation, he cleared his throat. "Ms. Masters, I saw a ladder in the garage last night. Want me to bring it in?"

"Call me Denise, please," she said. "Would you mind? That would be so helpful."

Denise? He preferred to keep things professional, but he wouldn't say so now. "Not a problem."

After he set the ladder up beside the tree, he returned to the kitchen and tried not to watch as mother and daughter covered it with ornaments. Christmas music played in the background, and when Ella wasn't chattering, they sang along.

Ella was filling a tiny area of the tree, stacking the decorations on top of each other, but her mother never said a word, just worked around her. She'd purchased boxes of glittery balls and ornaments of every shape and color, and within a few minutes, the bottom half of the tree was heavily laden.

Jon wished he could give them privacy, but he wasn't comfortable leaving them alone. Instead, he took out the paperwork he'd been perusing earlier, leaving it on the counter away from where Ella might see, and looked again for patterns. It was surreal, reading about murders while *Let it Snow* played in the background.

It was past noon when Jon heard a voice in his ear.

"Car pulling in," Grant said.

Jon moved to the front window to look, prepared to usher Ms. Masters and Ella to the basement.

But a moment later, Grant spoke again. "Guy says she ordered pizza."

"I'll check."

He cleared his throat, but neither mother nor child paid him any attention. He turned down the music, and Ms. Masters's voice lingered after the song faded.

"'...in a winter wonderland.'" She turned to him. "Aw, now you know what a terrible singing voice I have."

Ella said, "Mommy, you have the prettiest voice in the whole wide world."

The girl obviously loved her mother, because that was *not* true.

He fought a smile. "Ma'am."

She glowered at him. Was she trying to be intimidating? Because it was more cute than anything.

"Ms. Masters, did you—?"

"I told you to call me Denise."

This wasn't the time to argue that point. "Did you order pizza?"

"Yay, it's here!" Ella jumped and bolted to the front door.

She almost got it open, but Jon beat her to it and pressed his hand against it above her head.

He leaned down. "Can you let me open it, please? And maybe you can go stand with your mommy?"

Ms. Masters called, "Come on, baby. Help me get out plates and napkins."

The child skipped away, utterly unconcerned.

To Jon, Ms. Masters said, "I already paid and tipped him."

"Great." Jon opened the door to find Grant standing on the stoop with not one pizza box but...eight?

She'd ordered eight pizzas?

He took the stack and carried it to the kitchen. "Hungry?"

She settled a stack of paper plates and napkins on the bar. "Obviously, I ordered enough for you and your team." When he set them down, she opened lids, filling the room with the scents of pepperoni and sausage and onions and tomato sauce, until she came to one that had no toppings but cheese. "Grab yourself a few slices of whatever you like and take the rest to your friends."

She slid slices onto two plates and carried them to the table. "Go wash your hands, love. You want lemonade or water?"

"Lemonade, please!" Ella dashed past him to the hallway. The bathroom door slammed behind her.

"What can I get you to drink?" she asked.

"I have water," he said. When she didn't look up, he said, "Ma'am?"

She was filling glasses with ice. "Jon, please don't call me ma'am."

He took a deep breath. "Ms. Masters."

She poured water into one glass and lemonade into the other before facing him. Her brows lowered. "What's wrong?"

"Two things. Actually...three things."

She crossed her arms. "Go ahead."

"One, you need to let us know when you're expecting company or a delivery so we can be prepared."

"I can do that."

"Two, I stocked the refrigerator in your guest house with food. We can feed ourselves."

"Are you offended by pizza?"

"What? No." She must have seen something in his expression he didn't mean to convey. "We appreciate the pizza. I'm sure we'll devour every slice. I just want you to understand that you don't have to feed us. That's not your responsibility."

"But if I want to, I can. Right?"

"I mean...yeah, I guess, but—"

"And three?"

"Call me Donley. Nobody calls me Jon."

Her eyebrows hiked. "Nobody?"

"Well, my parents. My sisters." *Me*, he thought. But he didn't say that. "But otherwise—"

"Your coworkers call you Donley?"

"They do."

"Your friends?"

Most of his friends were coworkers or old comrades from the Army. They all called him Donley.

"Do you not have close friendships?" she asked.

"You and I are not friends, Ms. Masters. I work for you."

"Denise."

"Ms. Masters. And I'm Donley."

If he wasn't mistaken—and he had to be mistaken, didn't he? —he would've sworn he saw hurt cross her expression.

Before she could say anything else, Ella returned to the room and practically dove into her chair. "Cheese! My favorite!"

Ms. Masters joined her daughter at the table, ending their discussion.

He opened the pizza boxes until he found one covered with meat and slid four slices onto a paper plate, then radioed Grant to come get the rest, leaving only the remaining cheese pizza in the house.

Hopefully, he and Ms. Masters had come to an understanding. He was there to keep her safe and help figure out who was threatening her. He was not there to be her friend.

If only he could wipe that look of hurt from his memory.

CHAPTER EIGHT

D enise shook off her bruised feelings. Of course she and
Jon...*Donley* weren't friends. They'd just met, after all,
and he was here because he had a job to do. So what if they'd
enjoyed a nice meal together the night before? That was no
reason to let herself believe they could form a friendship.

Apparently, he thought they were already too familiar.

"This is the best pizza ever!" Ella shoved a huge bite into
her mouth.

Denise should probably tell her to take smaller bites. She
should probably remind her to chew with her mouth closed.
Eventually, she'd get around to doing those things with Ella, to
being a parent, not just a vacation destination. But today was
about fun. It was about reconnecting and forging a stronger
bond.

She'd leave the hard parts of parenting to Reid and Jacqui
for one more day.

No wonder Reid despised her.

"Don't you like it?" Ella eyed the untouched slice on
Denise's plate.

She lifted it, took a bite, swallowed, and said, "Mmm. It's

really good." It was, too. The pizza place had been in town since Denise was in high school. It wasn't the fanciest place in the world, and it had evolved a little, offering unique flavor combinations that certainly hadn't been on the menu a decade before. But the crust and sauce were the same as they'd always been. This was the pizza she compared every pizza to, no matter where in the world she was.

Ella said, "I can't wait to tell my friends you're here. You're coming to the play, right?"

"Just tell me when and where, and I'll be there."

"Oh!" Her eyes, already bright, lit up. "And there's a class Christmas party, and we're all gonna show off our wreaths. I invited Daddy and Jacqui, but you can come too."

Reid would love that. Hopefully he'd be civil in front of witnesses.

"What kind of wreaths?"

"We're supposed to decorate them. But I don't know what to put on mine. Daddy's not very good at crafts, and Jacqui..." Ella lowered her voice as if her stepmom might hear. "She's even worse."

Denise couldn't help the smile. "You know who *is* good at crafts?" She tapped her chest. "This girl right here. I used to kill it in art class."

Ella's eyes lit up. "Really? Will you help me?"

"I'd love to. Tell me what you're supposed to do."

Between bites, Ella told her about the assignment to create a gratitude wreath. "We're supposed to cover it with stuff that shows what we're thankful for. But not like the actual stuff. Like, if I'm thankful for my new bike, I could put a picture of the bike."

"It would be hard to attach a bicycle to a wreath," Denise said.

"But so funny!" Ella's smile morphed to a frown. "I bet if

Clara could attach her horses, she would. She'd march them right into the classroom if Mrs. Brooks would let her."

"You don't like horses?" Denise asked.

"I *love* horses. But Clara's always bragging about hers. Her parents own like a hundred of them or something. One of them is hers. His name is Chestnut."

"Have you seen him?"

"Just pictures. She brings pictures all the time. I bet her wreath will be all pictures of Chestnut. She thinks having a horse makes her the coolest kid in class, even though my mommy is a movie star." Ella's eyes brightened. "Oh, my gosh! I could have all pictures of you in all your different movies. Maybe I could even get action figures, and pictures of us together, and other, like, movie stuff. Like popcorn and soda and movie tickets. And Beverly Hills stuff, like maybe palm trees! And if you're there and all my friends could meet you, that would be so cool!"

Denise was tempted to feel flattered by her daughter's words, but she guessed the sentiment behind them.

The guess was solidified when Ella added, "Clara would be so jealous!"

Oh, man. This was one of those hard parenting moments she preferred to leave to Reid. She tossed up a quick prayer for wisdom. "Is that the point of your gratitude wreath, to make the other kids jealous?"

Ella's face fell. Denise loved how her daughter's feelings showed so clearly in her expression. She loved that Ella didn't feel the need to hide her true self behind a mask.

Reid had given her that confidence. Reid had created this amazing child.

Maybe, though...maybe some of Ella's kind, unique personality came from Denise's genes. Maybe she could take a *little* credit.

"No." Ella's little shoulders slumped.

"What is the purpose again?"

"I think it's to remember to be thankful. Jansen said that Thanksgiving is supposed to be the thankfulness holiday and Christmas is supposed to be the presents holiday, but Mrs. Brooks said we should be even more thankful at Christmas, 'cause Jesus came to earth like a present just for us."

"I love that." And she loved that her daughter went to a school where the teachers weren't afraid to talk about Jesus. "What are you most thankful for?"

"You, because you're here."

Not because Denise was a movie star who gave Ella bragging rights, but because she'd come home.

She didn't relish the idea of the wreath being about her. She didn't deserve that recognition. Good mothers stayed with their children.

"What else are you thankful for?"

Ella shrugged. "I don't know. My house, I guess. But Mrs. Brooks said we should try to have a...a like, where everything goes together. I forget the word."

"A theme?"

"Yeah. A theme. Clara's will probably be horses."

"Don't worry about what Clara will do." Denise was tempted to buy Ella a horse so she could compete with the other child. But that was Hollywood Denise.

Coventry Denise needed to learn to be a year-round mother, not a month-long mother. Not a mother who showed her love through gifts instead of time.

"Clara's wreath can be beautiful in Clara's style," Denise said, "and if it's covered with horses, then good for Clara. But what are *you* most thankful for?"

Again, Ella shrugged, and Denise guessed it wasn't because

she didn't have an answer but because she didn't want to say it. "I bet you're thankful for your daddy."

Ella's head bobbed. Did she feel like she couldn't say so in front of Denise?

"I'm thankful for your daddy too," Denise said. "He's the very best daddy, isn't he?"

Again, Ella's head bobbed. And then her eyes popped wide. "Omigosh, Daddy told me I could tell you and I forgot. Jacqui's gonna have a baby! I'm gonna have a little brother. Isn't that the coolest thing?"

"That is *so cool*," Denise said. "You must be excited."

"Uh-huh. Me and Jacqui have been working on his bedroom."

"Jacqui and I," Denise said gently.

Ella either didn't hear or pretended not to. "We painted the walls blue and got a rug to go over the carpet with all space stuff on it, like planets and rocket ships, and there're stars on the ceiling that glow in the dark!"

"I bet you're thankful for your brother already, aren't you?"

"Uh-huh. And you know who else? Grammy and Gramps. They're in Florida, but they'll be back before Christmas. They take me to the movies every weekend when they're here."

The mention of Denise's parents had her heart aching. She both anticipated and dreaded their return. Would they be happy she'd bought a house in town, or would they see it as too little, too late?

The way Reid saw it.

Ella added, "And of course Mimi and Poppy."

Reid's parents, who hated Denise almost as much as Reid did.

"That's a lot of people who love you. No wonder you're so thankful."

Ella looked down, chewing her fingernail. She'd eaten about half her slice of pizza, but she didn't seem inclined to eat more.

"What about Jacqui?" Denise suggested. "She's pretty awesome. She's smart and nice, and she takes good care of you."

Ella looked back up, seeming almost nervous. "She works a lot, but when she's not working, we play games and have fun. And she brushes my hair and puts it in braids sometimes."

"She's a good stepmom, isn't she?" At Ella's nod, Denise asked. "And her parents? Are you thankful for them?"

"Grandmother and Granddaddy. I don't see them very much, but they always buy me presents. They're nice to me." She met Denise's eyes, then looked away. "You're not mad?"

"About what?"

"That I love Jacqui and Grandmother and Granddaddy? Because Jansen's mommy and stepmommy hate each other, and he says he's only allowed to like one of them at a time."

Wow. No wonder the kid had issues. Still, if he ever bullied Ella, Denise would send Jon...Donley to have a talk with him. That ought to straighten him out.

She turned her chair to face her daughter. "Beautiful girl, I am thankful, just like you are, that you have an amazing family. You have a daddy and a stepmother who love you, *six* grandparents who adore you, and you're about to have a baby brother, who'll probably idolize you. And you'll always have me."

Ella's little feet were swinging below the table as she smiled. "And now you live here. I have the best family in the whole wide world. Do you think I can make it about that?"

"I can't think of a better theme for your gratitude wreath."

Denise hadn't been to the Christmas store in North Conway since she was Ella's age, but she'd never forgotten it. Now, as she and Ella walked toward the front doors, anticipation had her heart fluttering. She couldn't wait to share this with her daughter.

She could practically feel Jon...Donley—would she ever get accustomed to calling him that?—scowling beside her. He hadn't been happy about their spontaneous plan to go shopping, but he'd managed it nevertheless.

Four bodyguards, including Jon and Lake, accompanied Denise and Ella. Another four would place themselves around the property at strategic locations. Where those locations were, Denise couldn't venture to guess.

On their way to the front door, they passed glittering Christmas trees, blow-up yard decorations, and a few motorized reindeer.

Ella stopped about two feet inside, eyes wide. Christmas decor took up every inch of merchandising space. *Jingle Bells* played on the speakers overhead. The scent of pine was overpowered by chocolate and cinnamon from the station nearby, where teens dressed as elves offered hot chocolate and apple cider.

Santa Claus sat in an oversize armchair, a kid on each knee and a third standing beside. They were all posing for a photograph.

"Mommy, it's beautiful." Ella's tone was reverent as if she'd just stepped onto holy ground.

"Do you want to sit on Santa's lap?"

Ella looked from the man in the red suit back to her mom. "Is it okay? There's a long line."

"Let's do it."

The line took almost an hour, and Denise enjoyed every minute of it, asking Ella what she wanted for Christmas, finding out special presents she'd been given in years past, learning her favorite traditions. She'd only spent one Christmas with her daughter, the previous one, but she intended to never miss another. Reid would have to learn to share.

After Ella had her picture made with Santa, she asked, "Can we get hot chocolate?"

"How about we shop first and then do that after?"

Ella agreed and started wandering from display to display, touching ornaments and pointing at decorations she loved.

Denise was tempted, so tempted, to tell Ella to pick out anything she wanted. Denise could afford to buy every item in the place. But that wasn't a good lesson to teach her daughter. Instead, she said, "Why don't you get out your list?"

Ella dug into her pocket, pulled out the paper they'd written their notes on, and looked for ornaments to represent each of the people she was thankful for. This place boasted ten thousand ornaments. Surely they'd be able to choose something for everybody.

Ella found an ornament shaped like a lab coat to represent Jacqui, a research scientist. A man in scrubs represented Jacqui's physician father. Ella picked a needle-and-thread ornament for Denise's mother, who loved cross-stitch, and golf clubs for her dad. An airplane would work for Reid's father, who'd repaired airplanes for years, and an ornament depicting flowers represented Reid's mother, a gardener. Ella was stuck on Jacqui's mother, who didn't have a job outside the home.

"Does she play golf or tennis?" Denise asked. Based on what Ella had said about her step-grandparents, Denise assumed they were wealthy. It seemed as good a guess as any.

Ella scrunched up her face. "I don't know." She was distracted by a miniature Christmas village with all sorts of motorized displays. Reindeer lifted their heads and looked around. A Santa figurine waved at children. A carousel rotated.

"When you go to see them," Denise asked, "does she take you to do anything?"

Still staring through the glass at the display, Ella shook her head. "She's always busy cooking."

"Do you ever help?"

Ella looked at Denise and nodded. "Uh-huh. We made cookies last time I was there. And I helped with the lasagna. I got to lay out the noodles and spread the icky white cheese stuff."

Denise wasn't a fan of ricotta either. "Maybe you could find her something that represents how you cook together."

"That's a good idea! I think she'll like that." Ella scurried to another ornament display and found one depicting a red apron with cooking utensils in the pockets.

A blue cradle represented the baby.

Denise picked out a *World's Greatest Father* ornament for Reid, and Ella beamed. "That's perfect!"

Of course it was.

"That just leaves you," Ella said. "Hmm..." She wandered from tree to tree, looking at and then rejecting ornament after ornament. She found a palm tree—"Like where you live"—and then left it there. "'Cause you don't live there anymore, right?"

"But I will have to go back sometimes."

Which was true, but only for short periods of time, and only if they weren't filming on location, and all that only assuming the studio renewed her contract. She didn't actually have to live in LA. But to sell the house there, to plan to relocate here indefinitely...

She wasn't ready yet.

Maybe this would go well. Maybe not. Maybe, once Ella got to know her better, she'd decide she didn't like her mother any more than everyone else who used to love her. Maybe Ella wouldn't want her around forever, no matter what she said now.

Denise would keep the Beverly Hills house for the time

being. She needed to have a place she could call home if this didn't work out.

Ella found a tree with superhero characters and searched until she located an Ember Flare action figure. She studied that ornament a long time.

"You like that one?"

"It doesn't...it's not exactly right."

Denise was glad when Ella left the action figure hanging on the tree. That wasn't who Denise was, even if it was how most of the world saw her. She was about as close to a superhero as a little boy with a ten-gallon hat was to a real cowboy.

She also didn't deserve a *World's Greatest Mother* ornament, even if she wished she did. Reid had earned his title. No matter how good a mom Denise learned to be, she'd never compete with him.

But it wasn't a competition. She just had to be the best mother she could be going forward. Which meant not giving in to the regret that bombarded her daily.

Fingers skimming the ornaments, Ella moved to another display, a mishmash of things. Ella studied each until she finally reached out and took one.

A vintage movie camera.

"What about this?"

"I think it's perfect," Denise said. "It represents me like the lab coat represents Jacqui, right? It's what I do." Even if it wasn't who she was.

Ella didn't seem as pleased with the selection as she had the others.

"If you don't like that, we can find something else," Denise suggested.

"But what?"

The problem was, Ella didn't know her mother the way she should. Denise could think of fifty images to describe her own parents, but she'd spent her childhood with them. She knew them, knew what mattered to them.

Ella simply didn't know Denise. The thought brought familiar shame.

She scanned the room until her gaze landed on something on the far side. She took Ella's hand and walked across the space, dodging other customers and ignoring the bodyguards who hadn't strayed more than a few feet away. She crouched in front of the tree.

Hanging there was a simple red heart-shaped ornament. Denise lifted it and turned to her daughter. "This represents me. No matter how far away I've been, no matter how distant a mommy I've been, you have never, ever left my heart. I have loved you every single second of your life."

Ella's gaze flicked from her mom to the heart and back. "Really?"

"Yes, really." Denise wanted to hold her daughter, to assure her of her love. But now wasn't the time. She didn't have to cram it all into one visit.

Denise replaced the heart on the tree carefully. "But I think, for your wreath, the movie camera works. It matches the theme, right? Almost all of your ornaments are about what the people in your family do, either for jobs or for hobbies."

Ella looked into the little basket Denise had set beside them. She lifted her dad's ornament. "This doesn't represent what Daddy does."

"I think it does. You have been your daddy's number-one priority since the moment he laid eyes on you. It does represent how Daddy spends his time."

Ella fingered the little glass heart again. "I like this better than the camera."

Denise almost choked up at the thought, but she kept the emotion at bay. "You know what? I do too."

Satisfied, Ella dug out the vintage camera, hung it on the tree, and set the heart-shaped ornament in the basket.

"Did we get everybody?" Denise asked.

Ella studied her list carefully, then looked up, beaming. "Can we start working on it today?"

Denise glanced at her watch. It was nearly five o'clock, and they had an hour's drive back to Coventry. "Daddy wanted you home for dinner. We should—"

"Could you ask him if I can stay with you tonight? You can take me to school tomorrow."

As much as Denise would love that, she already knew how Reid would react. She didn't think it was a good idea to push it tonight.

One step at a time.

"How about this?" she said. "How about I ask if you can sleep over another night this week. I think your daddy wants you home tonight."

Ella's face fell, but she didn't argue as they made their way to the checkout counter.

The line was long. Though Reid hadn't given her a specific time to have Ella home, she guessed he expected her by six. She'd call from the car and let him know what time they'd get there.

"Don't forget, you promised we could have hot chocolate."

"Of course!" She had forgotten, which meant she'd get Ella home more than *a little* late. But six thirty would still leave plenty of time to eat, and if Reid and Jacqui didn't want to wait, Denise would happily feed her before she dropped her off. It should be fine.

They were next in line when she heard a familiar voice with a familiar tone. "There you are!"

Denise took a deep breath and turned as Reid stomped toward her.

Others looked, too, not just at Reid but at Denise. Because of the low lights in the store and her nondescript clothing, nobody had paid her any attention, but now she saw sparks of recognition in faces around her. People turned to gawk.

Jon shifted beside her as if Reid were an ax murderer, not an irritated ex.

She braced herself and plastered a smile on her face. When he got close enough to speak to with a low voice, she said, "I was just about to call you."

"Sure you were." Reid held out his hand toward Ella. "Come on, sweetheart. We're going to be late."

Ella scooted behind Denise. "I don't wanna go. I wanna stay with Mommy."

Reid's face, already red with anger, contorted as he glared at Denise. "I told you we had dinner plans."

What? No, he hadn't.

She didn't want to have this conversation, and she certainly didn't want to have it in front of a store full of witnesses. She stepped out of line, handed her basket to a clerk behind the counter, and said, "I'll be right back for that." Holding Ella's hand, she stalked past Reid and out the door, then around a giant Christmas tree with multicolored twinkle lights to a relatively private spot. It was chilly outside, but her anger kept her warm.

Reid followed on her heels—along with six bodyguards.

"It's five o'clock, Reid. You didn't give me a specific time, so I figured six or six thirty."

"There's no way you'd have had her home in time. Thank God I checked in with Lake."

Denise wanted to scowl at the bodyguard. It might not've been Lake's job to keep Ella's whereabouts from her father, but she could have at least warned Denise that he'd called. "In time for what?"

"I told you we had plans. Jacqui's business is having a Christmas party tonight for the staff. I'm supposed to be in Plymouth at six. As it is, I had to send Jacqui to set up by herself."

"You didn't tell—"

"How dare you take her out of Coventry without my permission?"

"I don't need your permission, Reid. I'm her mother."

"You have no rights here."

"I don't think a judge would see it that way."

He glared at her. Then to Ella, he said, "Let's go, sweetheart."

Ella gripped Denise's hand harder. "I don't wanna go to the stupid party."

Reid shot Denise a scathing look before crouching down in front of their daughter. "Santa's going to be there, remember?"

"I sat on Santa's lap already."

If Reid had looked angry before, now he seemed ready to explode as he stood and faced Denise. "You took her to see Santa?"

"He was here." She winked at Ella, hiding the embarrassment and fury simmering beneath the surface. "He had to leave, though. Now we know he must've been headed to Jacqui's party, right?"

"Probably." Ella didn't smile as her gaze flicked between her parents.

Couldn't Reid see what their arguing was doing to her?

"How about this?" Denise leaned down to Ella. "Why don't you go to the party with your dad, and you and I can get together tomorrow to start the wreath."

"She has dance tomorrow," Reid said.

Denise kept the smile on her face, though it felt as fragile as dried clay. She squeezed Ella's hand. "After dance?"

"Dinner and bath and bed," Reid said.

Denise looked up at him. "What day works for *you*, Reid?" Because this obviously wasn't about Ella but about him.

"I'll have to get back to you." He reached for Ella's hand. "Let's go."

"No!" She burst into tears and clung to Denise.

Denise's eyes prickled with emotion. So much for the world's greatest daddy. She took Ella in her arms and whispered in her ear. "I'm not going anywhere, beautiful girl. I'll be right in my house. Your daddy and I will figure out a time for you to come over. I promise."

"I wanna stay with you."

Never, in all the times Ella had gone to California to see her, had she expressed a desire to stay longer. She'd always looked forward to returning to her father. That she wanted Denise brought such a rush of joy, she could hardly contain it.

She squelched it and forced herself to be sensible. "I want that, too, but your daddy wants you to go to the party with him and Jacqui tonight. I bet it'll be fun."

Ella's arms just tightened around Denise's neck.

She could smack Reid for doing this. To him, she said, "How about I take her to dance tomorrow?"

He seemed to search for some reason that was a bad idea but came up short. "Fine."

She backed up and met Ella's tear-filled eyes. "I'll stay and watch you dance. Okay?"

Ella sniffed and nodded. "Can I come over after?"

"Your dad and I will discuss it. I had so much fun with you today. I'll go inside and buy all that stuff, and it'll be ready for us the next time you come over."

"Will you buy everything else we need?"

They discussed a shopping list—wreath, ribbons, and other

decorations. Finally, Denise set her daughter down to let her go with Reid.

But he wasn't there.

She spied him a few feet away in a quiet conversation with Jon. Neither man looked happy.

CHAPTER NINE

I f Reid Cote didn't watch himself, he'd get more than a stern lecture.

Jon squared off with the man a few yards from where Denise and Ella were talking. "We have a problem."

Cote rubbed his arm where Jon had grabbed him, the same spot he'd gripped the night before. "We're gonna have a problem if you ever grab me again."

Jon ignored that. "Our job as bodyguards is to protect. One way we do that is by staying close without drawing attention to ourselves or our clients. Ms. Masters and your daughter managed to spend hours here surrounded by bodyguards without anybody giving them a second glance. As far as I know, not a single person recognized your ex-wife. And then you barreled in and drew attention to yourself—and to her. Suddenly, people lifted their phones. They took videos. Do you think that made her more safe—or less safe?"

"That's not my problem."

"Maybe you don't care about *your child's mother*." Cote flinched at the implication, because of course the man should. "But Ella's safety *is* your problem, and a whole bunch of people just got photos and videos of her with a famous actress, a woman whose life might be in danger."

Realization dawned slowly, and color leached from Cote's face. He ran a hand from forehead to chin. "I didn't... That never occurred to me."

"Maybe you should try to think past your anger for two seconds before your next encounter with Ms. Masters." Jon took a step closer. "In fact, you should more than try. You pull another stunt like that, you'll have more than a bruise on your arm to show for it."

"Are you threatening me?"

He gave the man a long look. "I'm warning you to stop being an idiot." He stepped back, almost far enough that Cote could pass him and return to retrieve his daughter. But not quite. "And for the record, you didn't tell Ms. Masters about your plans tonight. You said to have Ella home by dinnertime because it was a school night. You owe her an apology."

He wasn't sure why he'd said that. As Ms. Masters's bodyguard, it was his job to keep her safe. It wasn't his job to get involved in interpersonal conflicts. But the way this jerk had barreled in and started hurling insults had Jon itching to defend her.

Cote shouldered past and returned to where Ms. Masters and Ella stood waiting for him. Jon stayed close enough that Cote had to know he was there. Which was the point.

He was lucky Jon hadn't throttled him.

Cote stopped a few feet from his ex-wife. "Your, uh..." His voice was calm, at least. "Donley told me I didn't tell you about tonight's dinner. I thought I had. I'm sorry for yelling at you. That was uncalled for."

Ms. Masters's eyes widened. "Oh. That's..."

Jon braced himself, waiting for her to tell the rude man it

was all right that he'd treated her that way when it was absolutely not all right.

But she surprised him.

"I appreciate the apology, and I forgive you."

Jon wished he could see Cote's face.

Ms. Masters continued. "I'll pick up Ella from school tomorrow and take her to dance. Will you text me the details, please?"

"Fine." He held out his hand. "Tell your mom goodbye."

Ella did and then went with her father.

Ms. Masters watched until they and their bodyguards disappeared into the parking lot, then spun and returned to the store.

Jon stayed by her side as she waited in line to pay for her things. He doubted she'd noticed what any of them cost, but the tally was north of two hundred dollars.

All for a basketful of ornaments, many of which would honor Cote and his family. Jon had heard the things Ms. Masters had said about Ella's stepmother, his parents and hers, even Ella's father, about what a good man he was.

Maybe he was.

By Ms. Masters's admission, she hadn't been a good mother. She hadn't been available for Ella. She hadn't made Ella a priority. Maybe that was true. Ella certainly hadn't argued.

But watching Ms. Masters and Ella today, and then watching the two parents interact just now, Jon would pick Ms. Masters's brand of parenting over Cote's any day of the week.

CHAPTER TEN

R eid had apologized. Actually apologized.

Settling into bed for the evening, Denise was still amazed.

She'd imagined the day ending with her walking Ella to Reid's door, saying hello to Jacqui and congratulating her on the baby, getting a glimpse of the house Reid and Jacqui had bought together. She'd imagined a goodbye hug on the doorstep, her daughter going inside but glancing back for one final look at her mother.

It was possible Denise had spent a little too much time imagining the perfect day with her daughter. And no, it hadn't ended like she'd hoped it would. But other than that, it *had* been perfect.

She had no doubt that the heated conversation between Jon and her ex had led to Reid's apology. Even so, he'd done it.

Maybe there was hope. Maybe Reid and Denise could forge a new relationship, one built on mutual respect, mutual love for their daughter. Maybe Denise could really build a life here.

She opened her devotional and read that day's message, which reminded her of her freedom in Christ. She was free now. She might not always *feel* free, but feelings weren't a gauge for the truth. She'd made so many mistakes, endured so much hurt—not all of it self-induced. But she'd arrived on the other side of those trials a better person. A stronger person.

She could be Ella's mother, even be a positive force in her life. She could do this. She *would* do this.

Meditating on the verse in her devotional, she shut off her light and snuggled beneath the covers in the chilly room. She had been set free from sin. All her life she'd been a slave—of attention, of fame, eventually of substances—but now she was a servant of God. And the benefit God promised was holiness. Holiness and eternal life.

That the perfect Creator God could have chosen her out of the world and made her clean, that He promised her holiness and forever with Him... It was astonishing.

Like she did most nights, she fell asleep with scripture on her mind.

Shattering glass yanked her awake.

Before she could process what had happened, a man filled her doorway. He crouched low and crossed to her bed.

Terror built in her chest and escaped on a scream, which exploded into the silence.

"It's me." Jon yanked the comforter off her bed and laid it on the floor. "Come on. Stay low."

It was Jon. The bodyguard. Not... She shook her head, but the face she'd imagined wouldn't shake off. "What happened."

"Ms. Masters, come on." When she didn't move, he said, "Come with me. Now, Denise."

His use of her name snapped her out of her fog. Cold air wrapped around her, raising goose bumps on her skin.

The light coming through the doorway illuminated a broken window. On the other side of the room, something protruded from her wall.

What was that?

He tugged her hand. "Come on. And stay down."

She slithered off the bed onto the floor, realizing then why he'd tossed her blanket down. Beyond it, shards of glass glittered across the carpet in the low light. As soon as she started crawling, Jon shifted behind her, almost *over* her. But the closeness of his body didn't bring the terror it should have. He wasn't threatening. He was protecting.

Outside the window, shouts rose in the darkness.

"That way!"

"Stay low!"

"No, no. Protect the front!"

All she could think was *Ella!*

Thank God, Ella wasn't here.

In the distance, an engine roared to life, and then the sound faded.

She reached the end of the comforter and started to stand, but Jon pressed a hand to her back. "A few more feet. All the way into the hallway and out of sight of the windows. Watch out for glass."

She kept moving until the pressure of Jon's hand let up. She cautiously stood, turning to peer back into the bedroom.

Jon stopped her from looking and gently urged her against the wall. "Stay here." He continued down the hallway, closing the doors to the other bedrooms, then returned to her. He gripped her arm gently. "Come on."

She allowed him to support her as she descended the steps.

Her window had shattered. She pictured the thing she'd seen protruding from her wall.

Someone had shot an *arrow* through her window?

There had been three bodyguards on duty—and more asleep in the apartment on the property—but someone had gotten close enough to fire an arrow through her window.

Close enough that it shattered the glass and embedded in her wall.

She aimed for the couch, feeling dizzy and confused, but Jon urged her to the door leading to the basement.

"Where are we going?"

"Just until we know it's safe." He ushered her down the creepy staircase. She'd only been in the basement twice, once when she first moved in and again to show the room to Ella. She didn't relish the idea of returning. But Jon wasn't asking her opinion as he led her across the freezing concrete floor and through the hidden doorway at the back. He entered the safe room with her, flipped on the overhead light, closed the door, and locked it.

"We're in," Jon said, obviously not to her.

They stood in the center of the empty space, him in a sweat-shirt, jeans, socks, shoes.

Her in a fitted pink tank top and skimpy short-shorts. Shivering.

The floor and walls were concrete. The door was steel or something equally cold and uninviting.

"There's a bed, through there," Jon said, nodding toward another door.

A bed? She hadn't seen that, and its presence didn't make her feel better. It just doubled-down on the creep-factor.

Her stomach was churning. She feared she might be sick if she moved. And anyway, she didn't want to go further into this terrifying space alone. She'd just stand there and freeze.

He spoke again to his teammates, his voice low and no-nonsense. "Every inch of the property. I understand that, but..." A long pause. "Get Randall on those cameras. Now." He glanced her way, then paused for a better look. "You okay?"

"Um...no?"

He moved into the other room and came back with a blanket, which he draped around her shoulders. She gripped the edges and pulled it closed at the neck. The warmth helped.

He stayed behind her, close, holding the blanket in place. His hands, so sure and strong on her shoulders, calmed her just a little.

"They've searched the entire property." His voice rumbled in her ear and sent fresh shivers across her skin—only she didn't think those came from a chill but from something else entirely. "As soon as they clear the house, we'll go upstairs."

"Okay."

He backed away, and she missed the heat of his body, the comfort of his closeness. He stepped around her and leaned back against the door. "Next time I tell you to come, you come."

Was he *annoyed* with her? "I was half-asleep, disoriented."

"All the more reason to do what you're told."

She wasn't about to apologize for not obeying his orders one second after she woke up. But...she got his point. "I'll do my best."

Footsteps pounded overhead. A moment later, Jon must've gotten the all clear because he said, "We're coming up." He followed her out of the basement and settled her on the couch, where she snuggled beneath her blanket. The lights had almost all been off when they'd hurried through before, but somebody had turned them on. The room was bright. The front door wide open, probably the back door too.

She was so cold.

"Stay there, okay?"

She nodded, and he went to the kitchen, leaving her alone.

Well, not alone. A guard stood at the front door. Another stood at the back. Nobody was getting past those guys.

Jon spoke to the one behind her. "Anything?"

The man answered in a low tone that Denise couldn't hear.

The clock on her wall told her it was nearly one a.m. From

her vantage point, she could see that the light was on down the hall in the office. Had Jon still been working? When she'd tired of seeing police reports and gruesome photos spread out on her kitchen table, she'd encouraged him to set up back there. When did he sleep?

Not that she was sorry he had been here. It was bad enough having been awakened in such a terrifying way. She couldn't imagine if it'd been a stranger standing over her. Sure, she'd met everybody on duty, but would she recognize them in the dark after being so shockingly torn from sleep?

Embers in the fireplace glowed. If she weren't so cold, she'd get up and stoke them, add another log.

Jon returned and crouched in front of her. "Are you all right?"

She was, thank God. Scared, but alive.

But if Ella had been there... The shattering glass, the shouts, the activity. She would have been terrified.

Jon was waiting for an answer.

"I'm okay."

He looked her over, but most of her was hidden beneath the blanket. "No cuts?"

She checked her hands, then peeked under the blanket at her knees. A normal person would wear long pajama pants in the winter in New Hampshire, but she'd always hated sleeping in much more than a T-shirt and shorts. She relied on her down comforter to keep her warm.

Seeing no blood on her legs, she said, "Quick thinking with the blanket to cover the glass."

"It's not foolproof. You sure?"

"I'm fine, Jon."

His eyes narrowed the slightest bit, but he didn't chastise her for the use of his name. Instead, he stood and stoked the fire.

"Let me get this going. And maybe something else to wear? Something more, uh..."

"I'd appreciate that."

"Do you have clothes anywhere but in your bedroom? I'm sure the police won't want us disturbing that room until after they've had a look at it."

"Weirdly, I keep all my clothes in my closet."

He glanced back at her, and maybe the tiniest smile graced his lips. "You are an odd duck." He peeled his sweatshirt off, leaving him in a T-shirt that hugged his muscles just right. He held it toward her. "Until we can get you something else."

"But you'll be cold."

"I'm fine, ma'am."

She'd started to take it but dropped her hand. "I can't wear the sweatshirt of a man who calls me ma'am."

He blew out a long breath. "Please take it, *Denise*." Heavy emphasis on her name. "The police will be here any second, and I'm sure you'd like to wear something more than that...that..." He waved toward her, though her tank top was hidden beneath the blanket.

She took the sweatshirt and slid it on. It was still warm and smelled like him, like pine and a wood fire. She let the blanket fall to her lap and pulled the sweatshirt over her hips. If she stood, she figured it would reach almost to her knees, certainly beyond her flimsy shorts. Still not as much coverage as she'd like, but better than before.

He put a log on the embers, and they sparked to life.

"What happened?" she asked.

"Somebody shot an arrow through your window."

"Worked out that much myself. Did they catch him?"

The scowl on his face told her the answer before he uttered a low, "Guy escaped on a four-wheeler."

"How?"

"There're four-wheeler trails"—he gestured with his chin toward the backyard—"but the closest one passes quite a distance from your house, and the way between is overgrown and thick with brush. We installed a camera on the trail where it passes. I don't know yet if he came from a different direction or if we just missed it on the video feed. We should have seen him coming. He never should have gotten so close."

Jon looked furious.

"The police are watching the trails' different access points, but I'm guessing this guy had a way out of the woods."

"He didn't hurt me," she said. "You did everything you could."

"Did I?" He turned away, obviously not expecting an answer.

Before she could remind him that she was safe, that nobody had gotten hurt, Jon tapped the contraption at his waist, said, "Okay," and stalked toward the front door. He swung it open.

Detective Pollard stepped inside, a uniformed officer right behind him. The detective crossed to Denise on the couch and crouched in front of her. "You all right?"

She nodded. "They took care of me."

"Good, good." He stood and turned to Jon. "Show me."

Her bodyguard led the detective and the uniformed officer up the stairs. She knew Jon expected her to stay where she was, but this was her house. That was her bedroom.

She scrambled to her feet, yanked the sweatshirt down, and hurried up behind them. The higher she climbed, the colder it got. She'd need to cover that window with something until she could have it repaired.

She watched her step, careful of her bare feet with the glass, and stood at the threshold of her bedroom.

Inside, Jon and the detective studied the arrow that had lodged in the wall opposite her bed.

"Angle's not steep enough," Jon said.

Detective Pollard glanced at the arrow, then at the window. "Meaning?"

"Meaning he's either twenty feet tall or he climbed a tree to take the shot." Jon's voice pitched low, almost a growl. He stalked to the window and looked out. "Meaning the guy crept onto the property, climbed a tree, fired that arrow, climbed back down and took off, and we still didn't catch him."

The detective turned toward the window, catching sight of her on the way. "You shouldn't be up here."

"This is my house."

"You're going to cut your feet."

Jon snatched her slippers from the closet and held them out to her.

"Thanks." She dropped them on the floor and put them on. "He was in a tree?"

"Had to be," Jon said. "How's your ex with a bow and arrow?"

The words had her backing up a step. "Reid didn't do this. He wouldn't."

Jon regarded her a long moment. "Lake said he hasn't left the house all night, but he could have slipped by the bodyguards."

"It wasn't him."

"You're sure about that?" Jon asked.

"Positive."

Clearly displeased with her answer, he returned his attention to the detective, who was pointing outside and calling to someone on the ground.

Denise watched as the uniformed officer snapped photos of the arrow, the glass, the gaping window, the room. He measured the angle and the distance to the window.

She hadn't known about the trails, but even if she had, that wouldn't have stopped her from buying the property. When she'd chosen the house, she'd been thinking of its seclusion and its proximity to Ella. She hadn't been thinking of arrows and gunshots and murderers.

Would any place be safe from those, though?

Finally, the police officer pulled the arrow from the wall and set it on her bureau. He snapped another photograph of it. From where she stood at the room's entry, it looked thicker than any arrow she'd ever seen. Not that she'd seen any since the archery unit in elementary school gym class.

"Look at this," the cop said.

Jon and the detective moved closer, and she crowded in beside them.

The cop pointed to what she'd thought was a thick white stripe on the black shaft. Looking closer, she saw it wasn't a stripe at all. Something had been affixed to it, held down and glossy with tape.

Jon pulled out his utility knife. "Do you mind?"

The detective said, "I'll do it. You're not wearing gloves."

He took the knife and sliced the top and bottom of the tape. He moved his fingers gently along the width of it. Finding a seam, he slid the skinny knife along the spot, then picked at the edge.

A piece of paper unfurled, and he straightened it out. She couldn't read it from her vantage point, but by the look on Jon's face as he huddled close, she wasn't going to like it.

He shifted the paper so she could see. Words were written in all caps across the top in thick black ink.

GO HOME. YOU AREN'T LOVED HERE ANYMORE.

· · ·

Jon's gaze met hers over the paper. "You're sure your ex—"

"You said yourself he's at home."

He grunted. "We think."

"We'll check him out," the detective said.

"Reid was at the park the day that man shot at me," Denise said. "I saw him there."

Jon's lips pressed together as if he wanted to argue. But he said, "Right. Okay."

The detective gave the room one more visual sweep. "Let's go back downstairs."

The cold air from outside had her shivering, but maybe not as much as the chilling words on that note.

You aren't loved here anymore.

She could see why Jon suspected Reid. Whoever'd written that note had, at some point, "loved" her. An old friend? Her closest friends from high school were Reid, James, and Cassidy. As far as she knew, James had nothing against her. She and Cassidy had reconnected.

Reid would never hurt her. None of them would do this.

She couldn't think of a soul who would—not anybody she knew, anyway. On the other hand, she was *loved*—and *hated*—by a whole lot of people who didn't know her at all.

She led the way to the living room, sat on the sofa, and pulled the blanket over herself again.

Detective Pollard asked her the same questions he'd asked the night before. Did anybody in town hold a grudge against her? Could she think of anyone who'd want her to go away?

Besides Reid? Maybe his parents? But none of them would resort to this. None of them hated her this much.

While the cops and a few bodyguards talked, another guard jogged up the stairs holding a blanket and a toolbox. A moment later, she heard pounding.

What in the world?

Jon must've seen confusion on her face. He turned away from the detective, lifting a hand to silence the man, and said, "They're covering your window, trying to keep out some of the chill."

"Oh. I appreciate that."

He turned back to Pollard. "We'll clean up the glass, unless that's a problem."

"We got what we need. Go ahead."

Jon spoke into his microphone, and a moment later, the vacuum cleaner purred overhead. They were cleaning? Seemed they were a full-service private security agency.

The detective shifted his attention to her. "Ms. Masters, I'm sorry this happened. We'll do everything we can to find who did this and arrest him."

"I'm sure you will. I'm grateful."

"If you think of anything else..."

She promised to be in touch, but she couldn't imagine what she could tell him that he didn't already know.

She was famous, and people hated her for reasons she couldn't comprehend. At least in Beverly Hills, she'd been one of thousands of famous people. Here in Coventry, she stood out. Apparently, somebody didn't like that.

CHAPTER ELEVEN

J on sent Pollard to the guest house. He'd already directed a teammate to make a copy of all the video recorded that afternoon and evening, but Pollard wanted to see the setup himself.

Between the police and the security team, eventually they'd figure out how the shooter had gotten so close. Jon wouldn't rest until they did.

The guard whose job it was to monitor the cameras had missed something, obviously.

The perimeter fence would be installed the following day or —he glanced at the time—later that day, he supposed. Ms. Masters might not like the eight-foot-tall chain link, but she'd get over it. Not that it would have changed anything in this case.

Ever since he'd heard the crash of glass breaking, he'd been working on adrenaline and fury. Now he imagined what had happened. Somebody had fired an arrow through the window, likely with a crossbow, a weapon powerful enough to launch an arrow a long distance. He wasn't a crossbow shooter himself, but he knew an expert could hit a target from eighty, maybe a hundred yards away. Which meant the shooter might not have been on Ms. Masters's property at all.

Would they need to keep all the blinds closed in the house now? He hated to do that and figured his client would hate it even more. She should be able to feel secure in her own home.

Finally, he shuffled everybody out. As much as he wanted to pore over the footage himself, his primary responsibility was keeping Ms. Masters safe. Somebody needed to remain in the house at all times, and she seemed to trust him. He'd stay connected via his earpiece, but for the time being, he wasn't leaving her alone.

She'd snuggled up in the corner of her sofa, the blanket tucked around her, staring at the Christmas tree.

Tears streamed down her cheeks.

He'd seen this woman manage a lot already in their short acquaintance. She'd opened a package likely delivered by a serial killer. She'd been shot at and tackled and had feared she was being abducted. She'd been yelled at not once but twice by her jerk ex-husband. Despite all that, this was the first time he'd seen her cry.

Instead of opening his mouth and saying something stupid, he went to the kitchen and turned on her electric kettle. She kept the house cool at night, and with the gaping window upstairs, the temperature probably hovered in the sixties now.

He lowered the volume on the chatter in his ear. If his team discovered something he needed to know, they'd get his attention. He found a tea bag that seemed appropriate—what flavor was *Sleepy Time*?—and dropped it in a mug of hot water, then stirred in honey like he'd seen her do the day before.

With the cup and a box of tissues, he approached her cautiously. "I bet you don't get this much excitement in LA."

She lifted her gaze, which showed him red-rimmed eyes and bone-deep sadness. "Thank God Ella wasn't here."

Not that the girl would have been in any danger. Ms. Masters hadn't been, either. Not really. All the windows in the house had curtains or blinds, so it wasn't as if the shooter had aimed to kill. He'd just aimed to send his message.

"She would have been so scared," Ms. Masters added.

He set the mug and tissues on the coffee table. "To warm you up."

"Thanks." She snatched a tissue and wiped her eyes, but the tears continued.

"You're safe. I'm sorry that happened, and I know it seems scary. It was definitely intended to frighten you. Going to the safe room was just a precaution. I don't think he actually set foot on your property—"

"I don't care about that."

He must have looked shocked because she added, "I mean, I do. Of course, I do. But an arrow in my wall can't hurt me. A stupid note from some jerk can't hurt me. But Ella... She asked if she could spend the night." Her voice pitched high. "Thank God I said no, but only because I knew Reid would refuse. I didn't want to put him in that position."

Why would she worry about that?

"But if I'd said yes. If Reid had said yes..."

"Your daughter would have been safe."

"She would have been terrified. First the breaking glass, then all the guards and cops. And it's not safe." Her voice rose and cracked on the last word. "It's not. A man shot an arrow through my window."

"He couldn't have been aiming—"

"Someone shot at me the other day."

At least she finally seemed to understand that the rifle shot hadn't been a random event. Until that moment, he hadn't thought she'd taken the threat to her life seriously enough. If nothing else, the arrow had driven that point home.

He kept his voice low and confident. "We're going to protect you."

"I'm not worried about me!" She shot to her feet, dropping the blanket. She still wore his sweatshirt, and the sight of it, the way it fell to her thighs, hiding the short-shorts she wore and highlighting those shapely legs...

He lifted his gaze to her face and was very careful to keep it there, where fear and sadness reigned.

"If I'm in danger, then I have to stay away from her. Don't you see? I came here to be with her, but if somebody's trying to kill me, then I obviously have to avoid her. I promised her, and..." She slumped onto the couch and ran a hand through her unruly hair. "I'm going to have to disappoint her. Again. Prove to Reid I'm a lousy mother. Again."

He settled in the chair catty-corner to her. "What happened was not your fault."

"Of course it's my fault. How many"—she seemed to falter for words—"*not* famous people do you get hired to protect?"

"They're not all famous, ma'am."

She glowered at him, and he realized his mistake.

"They're not all famous," he repeated—without the offending title. "Sometimes they are, but often they're people in powerful positions who've made enemies. People the average person wouldn't recognize."

Ms. Masters pulled the blanket over herself again. "But fame...that's why *I'm* in danger. Because I'm an actor. Because people think they know me. They form opinions about me based on nothing. They love me or hate me based on *nothing*."

He'd brought her the tea to calm her down, but her voice was rising with her irritation.

"Ms. Masters, I didn't mean to—"

"Oh, for the love of all that's holy, stop calling me that!" She swung her feet to the floor and straightened. "It's Denise.

Denise. I'm not your elder. I'm not your boss. I'm just a normal person. Do you call everybody you meet by their last name?"

"In my work, yes."

She blew out an exasperated breath. "Well, I don't like it. I'm tired of being 'Ms. Masters' and 'ma'am.' I'm tired of being treated differently because of my job. I'm just an ordinary person who happens to be a halfway decent actor and got really, really lucky with a part, and now I'm... Masters isn't even my real last name. Did you know that?"

"Uh..."

"I just want to be Denise. Ella's mother. And now I can't even have that because of some...some nut job who doesn't want me in town for who knows what reason. And that nut job is going to steal my daughter away."

You aren't loved here anymore.

As if she had been at one time. If not Reid, then who?

He'd wait to ask that question when she was in a less volatile mood. Instead, he said, "We can keep both you and Ella safe."

"Right. I feel so safe. I can't even go into my bedroom."

He cringed at the accusation but tried to hide his reaction. If he'd done his job well, it wouldn't have happened. This was his fault.

She glared at him, then seemed to force a breath. She lifted the mug and sipped her tea and stared at the Christmas tree.

"You had quite a scare," he said. "Maybe you should try to rest."

"I'm not as fragile as I look. I'll be fine."

"Who said anything about fragile? You seem pretty tough to me."

She uttered a half laugh. "Right. Nothing says tough like a pink tank top."

The memory of the getup she slept in had him swallowing.

He shifted his gaze to the fire. "You're not fragile. You're impressive."

A beat passed before she spoke again. "Why do you say that?"

"You spent hours at the store today picking out ornaments for your daughter, one of which honored her father, who then attacked you."

"He didn't *attack* me. He was just angry."

"Whatever you want to call it"—he faced her again—"if someone had told me what was coming and asked me to predict your response, I'd have put money on your breaking down in tears."

"Do I seem that delicate to you?"

He took her question seriously, considering it. "Not now that I know you. If not tears, I'd have guessed you'd get into a shouting match with him. But you didn't. Seemed to me that the angrier he got, the calmer you got."

"I was more concerned with how our fighting would affect Ella."

"Like I said, impressive. You put her needs before yours all day long. You were the one to pick out that ornament for her father, even though he's been treating you like he's the world's greatest jerk."

She seemed surprised that he'd paid that much attention to the ornaments.

"You encouraged her to express her gratitude for her step-mother and step-grandparents," he added. "I don't know what sent you away, but it's obvious you love your daughter. And that much love..." He shrugged. "Nobody can deny it forever. Not even your idiot ex-husband."

The faintest smile graced her lips. She lifted her mug. "Do you want some?"

"No, ma'am."

She quirked one eyebrow.

He cleared his throat. "It's not appropriate for me to call you by your first name."

"You did earlier."

"To get your attention. But it'll be Ms. Masters from now on. And I'd appreciate it if you'd call me Donley."

"So I have to respect your wishes and call you by your last name, but you don't have to respect my wishes and call me by my first?"

How to argue with that logic? "I mean no disrespect."

She just stared at him with those dark eyes. A man could get lost in those eyes.

He forced his gaze away. "Why do you care?"

"Because you're here, witnessing all the ugliest things about me. What a terrible mother I am."

"You're not—"

"I am. I'm trying to fix that, but my daughter couldn't think of one thing about me today except that I'm in the movies and live in LA—what does that say about me? You get to witness how much my ex hates me. You get to see the absolute worst things in my life. For crying out loud, I have people who want to kill me on two coasts. And yet you and I can't be on a first-name basis? You get to stand in the corner and watch, and judge, and I can't even call you by your first name? It's just... I feel..."

What? Because the only thing he wanted her to feel in his presence was safe.

Did she not? How would calling her by her first name change that?

And how had he gotten into this conversation? He'd worked in private security for years, and he'd never had any trouble keeping a professional distance. But it was the middle of the night, and Denise...Ms. Masters was alone and vulnerable and feeling...

Exposed.

Ah. He tried to imagine what it would be like to have the worst things in his past exposed.

It would be bad enough to feel that way, but to feel it with a total stranger, someone determined to keep his professional distance... Maybe that made it worse.

Maybe he could understand how she felt, to a degree anyway.

"I'm not judging you."

"Sure you are. You might not find me wanting—yet—but you're judging. How could you not?"

"Let me rephrase. I am judging you, and I'm finding you sort of...amazing."

Her eyebrows hiked, and her mouth opened the slightest bit.

Oh, man. He shouldn't have said that. How did *professional distance* and *I find you amazing* go together?

But she was watching him with those mesmerizing eyes, those full lips parted in surprise, and he couldn't seem to get the shut-up message to his brain.

"I expected you to be a prima donna," he said, "demanding we wait on you, jump at your every command. Instead, you bought us pizza and apologized when you wanted to go shopping without giving us more notice. When your ex acts like a braying jackass, you make excuses for him. You keep your cool. You dote on your daughter. You're"—beautiful, kind, gentle... amazing—"not what I expected."

What was wrong with him? He needed to sleep. He needed to get away from this gorgeous, vulnerable creature.

She regarded him through squinted eyes as if trying to decide if he was being honest or blowing smoke. Granted, he'd been known to blow his share of smoke to soothe irritable clients. But that wasn't what this was.

This was something completely different, something he'd never experienced with a client.

This was a problem.

He swallowed hard, cleared his throat. "Anyway, it's obvious your daughter loves you," he said. "Just keep doing what you're doing."

"How, when I can't even spend time with her? I won't put her in danger. I won't."

He appreciated how worried she was about protecting her daughter. What bothered him was that she didn't seem as concerned about protecting herself.

"I promise you, we'll keep you both safe. We'll get your perimeter fence erected today, and I plan to install more cameras. You each have three guards at all times, four when you go out in public. That's more than—"

"Maybe you could assign more to Ella and fewer to me."

"You're the one in danger." If it were up to him, they'd do just the opposite.

"But I'm... She's the one who matters."

He pushed to his feet. "I can't tell if you're serious or if you're being melodramatic."

"I'm not melodramatic." The vehemence in her words surprised him.

"Either way, knock it off." He didn't temper the anger in his voice. How could he protect somebody who had so little sense of self-preservation?

Her eyebrows lifted high. He'd shocked her. Good.

"Are you a Christian," he asked, "or did you just go to church because Ella would be there?"

"I'm a Christian." She practically spat the words.

"I don't get you people." He stalked across the room, where he peeked out the window. All but one of the police cars was gone. The chatter in his ear had quieted. Guards were on duty, and aside from the broken window upstairs, things had gone back to normal.

He turned back to face her. "Your ex-husband is a hypocrite, and you clearly don't believe what you claim to believe."

"He's not a hypocrite." Her words were infuriatingly confident. "Knowing what you should do and doing it are two different things. Being a Christian doesn't make you perfect."

Obviously.

"And I know what I believe," she added.

"Is that so? Because you're acting like your worth is measured in whether or not people love you. Is that what the Bible says?"

"Oh." She didn't add anything to that helpful comment.

"I'm *not* a Christian," he said, "but I've been reading the Bible, and—"

"Why?"

He took a few seconds before answering. Some of the anger had drained out of his voice when he did. "I like to understand things. I like research."

"Huh." She tilted her head to the side and studied him.

"I know I don't seem the type."

"I didn't say that."

She didn't have to. He knew what he looked like. Physically, he was his father's son. Dad was a cop—tall, broad, strong. But Mom was a high school history teacher who loved reading, research, and learning. He'd gotten that from her.

When Jon had still been in the service, he'd studied the history and political systems of the nations where he was stationed and where he ran ops. In his life as a private security guard, he studied his clients' professions—and their enemies. Which meant he'd studied the music scene, politics, various enterprises, and organized crime.

And because of the job he'd done that summer, religion.

He didn't explain all of that, though. "All the stuff you hate yourself for—"

"I don't hate myself."

"Whatever you want to call it," he said. "Aren't you supposed to be forgiven?"

"Well, yeah. I am. By God."

"In your religion, is your ex—is anybody—more important than God?"

"Of course not."

"Then why do you act as if Cote's, or anyone's, opinion of you is all that matters? It seems to me that if God loves and forgives you, then you're valuable because He says so. Right?"

She stared at him until he wanted to squirm.

"Are you sure you're not a Christian?" she asked.

"Am I misunderstanding something?"

"No. You're spot-on."

"But you don't believe it, obviously."

"I do." She blinked a few times. Was that moisture in her eyes again?

She'd finally stopped crying, and he'd started her up again. Great.

"I'm trying." She uttered a humorless laugh. "It's not as easy as it looks."

The way she stared at him with that tender, honest expression had his heart thumping wildly. "I don't understand. If Christians don't believe the Bible, why should anybody else?"

Her lips parted, then spread into a smile. "You know what? You're right. You're absolutely right. I do need to live as if I believe it. I've been working on that. Being back here just reminds me of everything I've done wrong."

He let that sink in and thought maybe he understood. "I guess being forgiven doesn't make you forget the past." If it did, he might become a believer himself.

"As if anybody would let me."

Jon settled on the chair again. "If Cote is half the man his daughter thinks he is, he won't be able to keep hating a woman who loves her so much."

She tilted her head to one side as if really considering what he'd said. "Don't judge him too harshly. I deserve his wrath."

Jon scowled at that. "I doubt it."

"That's because you don't know."

Jon stood and stoked the fire. He should really encourage her to go to bed, but if she wanted to talk, he'd let her. Maybe she'd shed some light on who wanted her to leave town so badly, assuming she was right and it wasn't Cote.

And maybe Jon was curious. More curious than he should be.

"When Ella was four," Denise said, "she was kidnapped."

His gaze snapped to her, but she was staring at the mug on her lap.

"And I didn't come home. I couldn't. I wanted to, so badly." Tears filled her voice. "It was torture, pure torture. But I couldn't come."

He settled the fireplace screen in place. "Why not?"

"I was in...the hospital because..." She looked up, tried a smile that looked more like a grimace. "It's a long story. But, anyway, I deserve their contempt. Can you imagine? What kind of a mother doesn't come home in a situation like that?"

"One who can't because she's in the hospital. Who could blame you for that?"

"I only told Reid, but I don't think he believed me."

"Why?" He shouldn't have used a demanding tone, but he was confused. He didn't understand, and he hated when he didn't understand.

"Because I wouldn't tell him what I was in the hospital for." She looked down again, shook her head. "It's hard to explain."

Something had her in a hospital that she was so ashamed or embarrassed about that she'd rather her daughter think she hadn't cared enough to come home.

He couldn't imagine.

She didn't seem inclined to explain.

Which was incredibly frustrating.

She yawned, and he glanced at the clock. Quarter till three. As tempted as he was to grill her until he got the answers he wanted—and didn't deserve—he said, "You should get some sleep. Are you going to stay in one of the rooms upstairs?"

"Is it okay if I sleep right here?" She swung her feet back onto the sofa.

"It's your house, m—" He shut up before he spoke the dreaded word. "I have an idea. Why don't I call you Denise and you call me Jon when we're alone, but when we're with other people, including my teammates, we'll be Ms. Masters and Donley. Would that work?"

A smile crossed her lips. "If it's okay with you."

He chuckled. "Considering you've been calling me Jon all day, and you've glared at me every time I've called you anything but Denise, my feelings seem irrelevant."

She dipped her head to one side. "Is it that bad, being on a first-name basis?"

Calling this woman by her first name was anything but bad. But he didn't say that. "I'll get used to it." She seemed to have everything she needed, including a pillow, a blanket, and a flickering fire. "Okay...Denise..." He tripped over her name but recovered fast. "Settle in. I'm going to be in the office, so—"

"Oh. No." She started to sit up. "If you plan to stay in the house, you can sleep here. I'll go upstairs."

"You stay where you are. The office is fine. I have men posted at both doors and two more patrolling the property. You'll be perfectly safe. Okay?"

"Do you need blankets? Help yourself to whatever you can find."

"I'll manage. Good night."

He shut off all the lamps, leaving the room lit by the glow of the fireplace and the Christmas tree lights, and she stretched out on the sofa while he went upstairs to grab a pillow and blanket.

Not that he'd sleep. He'd check in with the team, learn if they'd figured out how the shooter got so close without being seen.

Somebody'd sent that message. He needed to figure out who.

It was after five a.m. by the time Jon closed his eyes. His teammates had discovered the shooter's nest in a tree near the trail, seventy-five yards from Denise's house. They'd finally found a camera angle that showed him army-crawling through the woods on Sunday afternoon. Denise and Ella had been in North Conway at the Christmas store at the time. The man had climbed into a tree and then waited for nine hours before firing his crossbow.

Nine hours.

The skill to get on the property without alerting guards, to make a shooter's nest in a maple tree, and to fire through the center of the window—all of that told Jon the enemy had military training.

The patience to wait nine hours, though. That was what terrified him most.

If it was the same person who'd taken a shot at her from the boat, then Jon had no doubt he'd been trying to scare her at the park, not kill her. But what would he do when Denise didn't leave town like he demanded?

WREATHED IN DISGRACE   117

Would he send another warning? Or would he shoot to kill next time?

Thanks to Jon's own military training, when it was time to rest, despite all the unanswered questions, he lay down and fell instantly asleep.

A voice in his ear woke him up. The sun was bright outside. He glanced at his watch—eight thirty.

He tapped the mic. "What is it, Hughes?"

"The ex is here."

"I'll get back to you." He'd slept in his jeans, so he slipped on yesterday's T-shirt and headed for the living room.

Denise was sitting on the sofa, a steaming mug in her hand. The sleeves of Jon's sweatshirt bunched around her wrists. The blinds were closed. Based on her relaxed expression, she had no idea Cote was outside. She smiled when he entered. "Did you get some rest?"

"Enough. You?"

She nodded. "There's coffee. Help yourself."

"In a minute. Your ex is here."

She slumped against the sofa. "Of course he is."

"We can send him away."

Her expression brightened as if she considered it. "Does he know about last night?"

"I assume so, yes."

"How?" She pushed to her feet, then tugged his sweatshirt down. "It doesn't matter. I need five minutes." She hurried up the stairs.

Figured she wouldn't deny the man. Cote probably wasn't happy. Maybe Jon could help dispel some of that fury before Denise faced him.

Not that protecting her from an angry ex was his job, but... Well, he'd figure out his motivations later.

Prepared for a confrontation, he yanked open the door and

stepped onto the porch. The clouds that had hung low all weekend had blown away, leaving bright blue skies and colder temperatures.

Cote stood on the walkway. It wasn't the man who caught Jon's attention, though.

At his side stood a pretty redhead wearing a tentative smile. Her jacket was open around her rounded belly.

"Will she not see us?" Cote's words, carried in a puff of vapor, seemed calm enough, though Jon heard anger beneath them.

Jon ignored him as he descended the three steps. He held his hand out to the redhead. "I'm Donley."

"I remember you from this summer," she said, shaking. "Jacqui Cote."

"It's a pleasure, ma'am."

Beside her, Cote surprised him by holding out his own hand. "We haven't met properly. I'm Reid."

Jon gripped it. "You always stop by people's houses this early without calling first?"

But Mrs. Cote answered. "It's my fault. I need to get to the lab, but I wanted to make sure Denise is all right."

He stepped back and smiled at the woman. She seemed genuinely kind.

Cote said, "It was a last-minute decision. We dropped Ella at school and then took the chance Denise would be awake."

"She had a long night."

"So she won't see us?" His words *sounded* cordial enough, but Jon didn't miss the tightness of the man's jaw. Apparently, he was on his best behavior for his wife.

"Be patient. She'll see you when she's ready."

Reid wrapped his arm around his wife. "Awfully chilly out here."

"You're welcome to wait in your car."

"We're fine." Mrs. Cote pulled her jacket closed, though the fabric barely reached around her belly. "It's not that bad."

Jon wrestled with saying more. It was none of his business, but Denise had had enough grief without this guy piling on. "You heard what happened last night."

"At two o'clock in the morning," Cote said. The barely controlled fury was back. "Apparently, my ex thought I might be responsible."

"I'm the one who told the police to check your whereabouts."

Cote's jaw dropped.

Mrs. Cote's smile faded. "Why?"

He turned his attention to the woman and tried to soften his expression. "Your husband has made it clear that he doesn't want Ms. Masters here. He was the most likely suspect."

"It wasn't me." Cote sounded indignant. "I would never—"

"I heard you were cleared." Jon had gotten that bit of news before he'd gone to bed. "Any idea who might've taken that shot? I'm guessing the guy's former military, maybe a sniper or a hunter, great with a crossbow. Knows the mountain trails."

Cote seemed to consider the question seriously. "I can't think of anybody around here who'd threaten her. You're sure it was... I mean, Denise can be sort of melodramatic, so I thought maybe she—"

"Jumped out her second-story window, ran through the woods, climbed a tree, fired a crossbow eighty yards into her own bedroom, climbed down from the tree, ran back, scaled her house, and was in her bed when I went in there to bring her to safety seconds later?"

Cote's mouth pressed closed, the corners turning down-ward. "I get it."

His wife was giving him a look he must've recognized, because he seemed chagrined.

To Jon, she said, "She must've been terrified."

She *should* have been terrified. "She handled it." He'd said what he wanted to say. Now, he was ready to be done with this conversation. He was turning to step back into the house—leaving the Cotes outside—when the door opened.

They looked past him.

Mrs. Cote said, "Sorry to intrude."

"No problem. Sorry for the wait," Denise said. "Come on in."

Jon led the way. The living room had been set to rights, the blanket and pillow Denise had used the night before stowed somewhere. She'd even stoked the fire.

She wore a pair of jeans, a purple hooded sweatshirt, and tennis shoes. Her hair was swinging in a ponytail, which made her look years younger, more girl-next-door than movie star. "Coffee? Tea?"

"We're fine," Reid said. "We heard what happened. Are you all right?"

She angled back, eyes wide, as if the question surprised her. It surprised Jon, that was for sure. "I wasn't in any danger, though the sound of shattering glass will yank you awake fast."

"I bet." Reid nodded to the sofa. "Can we sit?"

"Please."

The Cotes settled on the sofa, Denise in the chair where Jon had sat the night before.

He pressed his back against the wall where he could observe all their faces. Reid might not have fired that arrow, but that didn't make him safe.

"Do you have any idea who it was?" Reid asked.

"None," she said. "Do you?"

"How would I know?"

"You live here. Maybe somebody said something to you about me?"

He shook his head and turned to his wife. "How about you?"

"Nothing bad." She smiled at Denise. "Cassidy only has kind things to say about you. I didn't tell her you were in town, and she wasn't at church yesterday, but I'm sure she'd love to hear from you—and introduce you to little Hallie. The baby's darling."

Denise gave Jacqui a warm smile. "I'll call her today."

"A little group of women from our church get together every Monday," Mrs. Cote added. "Would you like to join us tonight?"

"Oh. I was hoping..." Her gaze shifted to Cote. "I guess you probably don't want me anywhere near Ella after what happened." Her voice cracked, but she kept a brittle smile in place. "I would love to be able to explain to her myself. The last thing I want is to let her down again."

Cote glanced at his wife, who was giving him a look Jon couldn't decipher. "Um... Maybe you could come over after dance and explain—"

Jon cleared his throat, and Cote glared at him.

But Denise said, "Go ahead, J-Donley."

"When Ms. Masters is in the open, there's a chance *she* could be in danger. The man who shot that arrow is obviously well trained. But inside, with blinds drawn, nobody will get close to her or your daughter. There's no reason that she shouldn't be able to spend time with Ella."

"I'm not going to put my daughter in danger to satisfy her whims."

Denise seemed stunned, but it was Mrs. Cote who spoke.

"She's her mother, Reid. Love isn't a whim." Her voice was gentle but firm.

Denise gave the woman a grateful look before speaking to Jon. "You really think you could protect her?"

"Both of you. Absolutely. She's so little that all we have to do is surround her. Nobody could take a shot at her or get anywhere near her." He turned to Reid. "I'm confident."

"And I'm supposed to trust you?"

Jon crossed his arms to keep from throttling the guy. "Yes."

Reid glared but said nothing.

"Okay." Denise's voice was calm, though he could see the hope in her expression as she faced him. "So I could pick her up from school like I promised?"

"Sure—"

"—No!" Reid started to stand, but his wife seemed to hold him in place with a gentle hand on his arm.

"You really want me to break a promise to her, Reid? For no reason?"

"You're in danger. Anything could happen when she's with you."

Denise leaned forward and lowered her voice. "And nothing bad's ever happened when she was with you?"

His mouth opened and closed. "That's not fair."

"Perhaps," Denise said. "But, under your protection, Ella was kidnapped."

Reid's face paled, his jaw tightened.

"She could have been kidnapped a second time in Boston."

"I would never—"

"I know." Denise held up her hands to quiet him. "I know what you did. I know you launched yourself over the seat and guarded her with your body." Her voice shook with the words. "I know they would've had to kill you to get to her."

Jon tried to imagine the scene. Cote didn't have Jon's width, but he was tall and broad enough. Amazing the things a person could do when someone they loved was in danger.

"I would not have let them take her."

"I know that. Here's what you need to know." Denise

leaned toward him, propping her elbows on her knees. "This might be hard for you to believe, and I haven't always shown it, but I love her that much, too, Reid. I will do everything in my power to keep her safe, just like you did. Maybe I'm not as strong as you are, but I don't have to be because I have..." She waved her hands toward Jon, and his heart did a little flip.

He'd analyze that later.

"You can't promise Ella total protection at all times," Denise said, "and neither can I. But I can promise you that I will take very seriously the need to keep her safe, including having Donley and the rest of his team involved. And if he tells me he can protect her, then I believe him."

Reid pressed his lips together. Jon couldn't tell if he was considering her words or formulating a scathing reply. Before anything came out of his mouth, though, Denise continued.

"We'll be surrounded by bodyguards. The very last thing I want is to put her in danger, but whoever this guy is, he's after me, not her. If he were after Ella—which he isn't—being with me or not being with me would make no difference. If it will make you feel safer, I can keep my distance when we're moving from building to car and vice versa. She'll be surrounded by bodyguards, like Donley suggested. I'll make myself a target elsewhere."

Jon barely suppressed a growl of frustration. "This isn't an either/or proposition, Ms. Masters. We will keep you both safe."

She aimed a smile his way, and he realized she was just trying to placate Cote. She trusted Jon with her safety.

More than that, she trusted him with her daughter's.

Mrs. Cote angled to face her husband. "Ella would be crushed if she couldn't spend time with her mother. You don't want that, do you?"

Based on the expression, he wasn't sure. He focused on

Denise. "When you're outdoors, you'll keep your distance from her."

"I can do that," Denise said.

"When you're indoors, you'll keep the blinds closed."

"Of course."

"School, dance, here," he added. "No restaurants or shopping or anything else."

Jon cleared his throat again, and again, they turned in his direction. "Just to be clear, we can protect them wherever they choose to go, as long as we're given enough lead time."

"For today, though," Denise hurried to add, "we'll come back here. We'll deal with next time...next time." She turned her attention to Mrs. Cote. "We want to work on the gratitude wreath." Suddenly, Denise sounded unsure of herself. "I hope that's okay. We got most of the supplies for it yesterday. Maybe I should have checked with you."

But the woman's expression brightened. "I would love that. Crafts are definitely not my thing." She turned to Reid. "Unless you wanted to do it with her."

"Uh..."

Jon enjoyed watching the man wrestle with his answer. On the one hand, he didn't want Denise doing anything special with Ella. On the other, he probably didn't relish the idea of messing with ribbons and glitter and glue.

"It'll be nicer if you do it," he finally conceded. "You always were good at that kind of thing." He glanced at his wife, eyes wide, but she just smiled at him.

Jon liked Mrs. Cote about as much as he loathed her husband.

Denise asked the details about dance class, typing them into her phone. "I'll feed her dinner. What time do you want her home?"

"Seven," Reid said.

"I think seven thirty will work," his wife said. "That gives her time to take a bath and get to bed by eight thirty."

When Cote didn't protest, Denise pushed to her feet. "Seven thirty it is then. I'll drop her off."

"Maybe I should pick her up."

Cote's remark had Denise's cheerful expression dimming. "Okay, if that—"

"We'll deliver her safely at seven thirty."

Jon should have kept his mouth shut. He knew that. Maybe he should give Cote more credit. What did Jon know about being a father? But he did know about protection, and he knew how to keep the child safe.

He knew, no matter how much a person might want to, that it wasn't right to lock people away until all danger had passed.

People had the right to live their lives. The duty, in fact, to not cower but to boldly go on in the face of danger. Otherwise, the tyrants won.

Looking at Denise, Cote said, "Fine. You can drop her off." He stood and helped his wife to her feet.

"Congratulations, by the way," Denise said.

The woman beamed, rubbing her belly. "We're so excited. He's due in February."

"I'm happy for you. Ella seems thrilled."

"She'll be a good big sister."

Jon beat them to the door, tapping his mic. "Coming out. All clear?"

"Clear," Hughes said.

Jon pulled open the door.

Cote was about to step out when he turned. "I...uh..." His gaze flicked to Jon but settled again on Denise. "I understand Donley thought maybe I was behind last night's...event."

"I never thought that," Denise said, "not for one moment.

You and I have had our differences, but I know you better than that."

He ran a hand over his short hair, his Adam's apple bobbing. "Good. I think... I'm not sure I deserve that but...thank you."

She seemed at a loss for words as the couple walked out.

Jon closed the door behind them. "You okay?"

"Yeah. That was...yeah."

Surprising, no doubt. Maybe the world's greatest jerk wasn't as bad as Jon had first believed. Or maybe he was just really good at pretending in front of his wife.

CHAPTER TWELVE

Word traveled fast in Coventry. For all the gossip rags and the scandals whispered behind hands in Hollywood, nothing could beat the speed at which a rumor spread in a small town.

Which explained how Cassidy had heard the news by nine a.m. She called a few minutes after Reid and Jacqui left, voice filled with a combination of concern and irritation.

"Someone shot at you?"

Denise snuggled beneath the comforter in her bedroom. The broken window meant the room was freezing, but she'd been about to shower when the phone rang. She explained to her friend exactly what had happened the night before, then added, "I should have let you know I was in town. I planned to come find you Saturday at the park, but..." She decided against telling her about the gunshot. "Things have been crazy."

"I heard you bought Aspen's old house up on Rattlesnake. It's a beautiful place. Garrett McCarthy—you remember him? He did a great job remodeling it."

"I don't remember him from when we were kids, but I

worked with him this summer. He built a guest house for me out back. He's definitely talented. But Aspen...should I know her?"

"She's new to town. I'll introduce you. That is... How long are you staying?"

"Through the holidays at least." And longer, but she'd fill Cassidy in on her plans later.

"Yay! That's great." Cassidy giggled into the phone, and the sound transported Denise back to high school, to a million sleepovers. She and Cassidy had done a lot of giggling and squealing and planning together. "Ella must be thrilled."

Denise felt her own giggle trying to rise. "I think so. I'm spending the evening with her."

"Oh, bummer. I mean, that's great. But I was going to invite you to girls' night. Do you remember Tabby Eaton? It's McCaffrey now. She was younger than us. Anyway, she hosts. Sometimes Chelsea O'Donnell—Hamilton—comes. You remember her?"

"Everybody knows the Hamiltons."

"Carly's from Boston. Grace is from Washington State, I think. Our newest member, Josie, moved here from DC. She used to work in politics. She and Thomas Windham— remember him?"

"Cute, winsome?"

"Yeah. He's going to be the mayor come January. Anyway, he and Josie are together. Not engaged yet, but soon, I think. Of course you know Jacqui... Would that be awkward?"

"She invited me this morning, so I guess she wouldn't mind."

"She doesn't come very often, anyway, what with her business and the pregnancy and Ella."

Denise didn't know this grown-up Coventry world. Cassidy had told her about the girls' nights during one of their phone calls, but she hadn't mentioned the names of the women who went. Now Denise wanted to know them. She wanted to have friends here, believers to do life with like she had back in LA.

If she was going to build a life here, she'd need that.

"Anyway," Cassidy said, "if you can't come tonight, how about lunch? I know James would love to see you."

"Would he, really?" She couldn't help the skepticism in her voice. James was Reid's best friend, after all.

"He doesn't hold grudges like Reid."

"*Nobody* holds grudges like Reid."

Cassidy didn't argue with that. "So what do you say? Noon?"

Should she ask Jon first?

No. Jon had said he could keep her safe anywhere, as long as he had enough notice. "I can't wait."

After she hung up, she hurried downstairs to tell Jon, but it was another guard standing in her living room. She couldn't remember his name. Humphrey? Hayes? Rather than ask, she told him her plans.

He nodded. "I'll let the boss know."

After her shower, Denise was slipping into some of her warmest new clothes when Jon called up the stairs.

"Ms. Masters, there's somebody here to see you."

It was stupid, but she was glad it was Jon and not that other guard. Not that it mattered. It shouldn't, anyway. But she trusted Jon.

She liked him. He made her feel safe.

And so what if he was handsome and kind? She wasn't attracted to him.

She pretended she didn't hear the voice in her head calling her a liar as she shoved her feet into her favorite leather booties, closed the bedroom door against the chill, and hurried to the top of the stairs. "Who is it?"

One hand on the newel post, Jon looked up at her. "Jack and Harper Rossi. They own the company that manages this house."

"Oh." She descended the staircase. "Why are they here?"

Jon stepped back as she neared. "I assume it's related to last night. Pollard said he was going to get a list of everybody who knew you were in town. Maybe they have some information for us."

"Why not just tell the detective?"

Jon's broad shoulders lifted and fell. "I guess we'll have to ask him. Should I let them in?"

It was a lovely day, and she was dressed warmly. "Let's talk outside."

His brows lowered. "Too exposed."

She wasn't used to so much inside-time. Back in California, she lived half her life outdoors, opening the oversize sliders that led from her great room to her deck and leaving them open nearly every day. She longed for fresh air and sunshine.

But she didn't want to be difficult. "Fine. Let them in."

Jon spoke into his earpiece, then opened the door.

A moment later, a gorgeous blonde stepped into the room, followed by a tall, handsome brown-haired man. They both froze in the entry and gaped.

She smiled and held out her hand. "Hi. Denise Masters."

The woman recovered first, shaking it. "Harper Rossi. You're... Sorry. We didn't know."

Denise had assumed they'd come because of who she was. But no, they gave this level of service to all their clients. She liked that.

The man held out his hand to shake. "Jack Rossi. We didn't realize who you were. Your paperwork is signed Denise Masterson."

"That's my real name. Masters is my stage name. Come on in." She led the way into the living room, which had been the scene of so many conversations in the last twelve hours. "Have a seat."

When they were all settled, Jack said, "We heard you had some trouble last night. The police believe whoever broke your window could have found out you were here through my company. I came up here to speak with the detective and turn over our employment records. I've met everybody who works for me, but I'm less familiar with the ones in this neck of the woods. We're located in Nutfield."

"I've been there," Denise said. "Cute town."

"So is Coventry." Harper glanced at her husband. "We're thinking we need to bring the kids back in the summer."

"You'll like it. Lots of activities for children."

"Anyway." Jack shifted in his chair. "I wanted to apologize. If anybody in our company passed information about you along to anyone else or..." He shook his head, glanced at his wife. "God forbid, if one of my employees shot that arrow, I'll work with the authorities to have that person prosecuted. I'll take full financial responsibility."

"That's very kind of you."

"The least we can do. Well, that and... I have a crew prepared to repair your window. If you'd prefer to hire your own people, I completely understand. Just send me the bill. But with the labor shortage, I thought it might be easier if we took care of it for you."

Denise glanced at Jon, who spoke to Jack. "You know these people?"

"They're trusted employees from Nutfield. They have nothing to do with the contracts this far north. You can trust them."

Jon nodded to Denise.

"I would really appreciate that," she said.

The man pushed to his feet. "Is it okay if I get measurements?"

She waved him toward the staircase. "Just walk toward the Arctic."

Ten minutes later, Jack and Harper left after promising to send their crew back that afternoon.

As soon as they were gone, Denise turned to Jon. "Lunch is okay?"

"You don't need my permission." Amusement flicked the corner of his lips, and her heart swooped as if she were riding a roller coaster. What was wrong with her? Was she so starved for attention that she'd fall for the first guy who listened to her?

Jon was being paid to listen to her. Who cared if he was handsome in that rugged *American Sniper* sort of way, tall and broad and gorgeous? He wasn't a romantic possibility. He was an employee.

"I've got some work to do," he said. "We'll load up at quarter till." He marched down the hall toward her office.

She watched his broad back until he disappeared through the door.

She needed to get a grip. It was bad enough being so far from the church friends who'd become her family in California, but with Reid's anger and the death threats, not to mention the serial killer out there somewhere...

She was feeling vulnerable, and when she felt like this, she *was* vulnerable—to anybody or anything that could make her feel like she mattered. Like she was worthy.

She moved into the kitchen and settled at one of the barstools, closing her eyes. *Father, I am worthy because You say I'm worthy. I don't need Reid or Ella or anybody else to love me to know I'm loved. Your love is enough. I don't need alcohol or drugs to fill me. You fill all my empty places. I don't need the adoration of fans to know I matter. You say I matter. I am Yours.*

Help me remember, Lord. Despite everything, help me hang onto You.

She breathed in the truth in her prayer, breathed out all the insecurity that had no place in the heart of a believer. Jon was right about that. If she didn't believe what the Bible said, why should anybody else?

～

Settled in the backseat of the SUV, Denise scrolled through her phone. Bystanders had taken videos of her argument with Reid at the Christmas store the night before and posted them on social media. She watched a few, scanned the comments.

As usual, people who hated her excoriated her, and people who loved her defended her. There seemed plenty on both sides of the argument.

Neither the praises nor the criticisms were true. Neither mattered in the grand scheme of things, and she ought not to waste a single moment reading their comments. With that thought in mind, she closed the app.

There'd been a time when she'd lived for the praise of the public. When she was loved, she was on cloud nine. When she was hated, she sank into depression. She didn't have to live like that anymore. Now she was God's, and His opinion of her mattered more than anybody else's.

Jon had reminded her of that fact. A man who wasn't even a believer had picked up on her faithlessness.

Lord, use his curiosity to bring him to You. Speak to him as he reads Your word.

"Ma'am?" Jon reverted to the respectful title for the sake of the guard driving.

"Yes, Donley." She smiled as she played along.

"Since your ex has been cleared, I wondered if you have any other former boyfriends around."

"Reid was my high school sweetheart. There weren't any other boyfriends in New Hampshire."

"Other guys who took an interest in you? Maybe somebody you rejected? Maybe someone younger or older?"

Closing her eyes, she considered the question. Truth was, most people wouldn't recognize the Denise of elementary and middle school. She'd been an awkward kid, all arms and legs. Gangly and insecure, tomboyish, not girly. She'd had friends, of course, but none as good as Cassidy, who had moved to Coventry in high school, and Reid and James, who'd been her friends since kindergarten.

She opened her eyes to see him watching her. "I don't think so."

"How about older guys, men with an...unhealthy attraction to you. Teachers, coaches..."

"Gross. Not that I know of. How do you know it wasn't a woman?"

"The person on the surveillance video looked like a man. Could have been a tall woman, but most shooting crimes involve men. Why, can you think of a woman who might have done this?"

"No."

He blew out a long breath. "Somebody wants you to leave town. Try to think."

"I am thinking," she snapped. *Try to*, as if it were an effort. As if smoke might come out of her ears with too much brain work.

Jon said nothing.

The other guard said, "Maybe fathers of friends? People you babysat for?"

"I had a very normal childhood. I was just an ordinary girl.

And this is an ordinary town. That sort of thing doesn't happen in Coventry."

The guards shared a look. Jon said, "All due respect, that sort of thing happens everywhere."

"Well, not to me."

Jon faced forward until they reached the intersection with the road that led to town. Then he turned toward her again. "We're just trying to jog your memory. We don't mean to offend."

Of course. She was being too sensitive.

Melodramatic, Reid would say.

She hated that word.

She plastered on her *all is well and I'm as happy as can be* smile. "No problem."

Her acting skills could be useful in all sorts of situations.

Though, by the way he squinted, he wasn't buying it. "Would you mind if I asked your friend some questions? Maybe she heard something or remembers something you've forgotten."

"After we eat, I guess."

When the guard double-parked in front of The Patriot, Jon said, "Wait there," and stepped out.

Traffic bunched up behind them. More than one person glared as they inched by, though, because of the tinted windows, they couldn't possibly see her.

The other SUV had parked just ahead, and one guard walked inside. A moment later through the car door, she heard Jon say, "Coming in." And then her door opened.

Sheesh. How to make a scene. When she stepped onto the asphalt, she was immediately surrounded by a ring of tall, broad-shouldered men.

Directly in front of her, Jon led the way inside, through the restaurant, and toward the back. Finally, he stepped to the side.

Cassidy was standing beside a booth. The moment she saw Denise, her arms opened.

Denise stepped into them and hugged her old friend. "It's so good to see you. Sorry about the fuss." She waved toward the four guards as they retreated to various areas in the restaurant.

Unlike in LA., where bodyguards wore dark suits, these dressed in everyday clothes—jeans, sweaters, windbreakers. If not for the strange way they'd entered, nobody would peg them for guards.

Oh. Maybe that was the point.

Denise said, "You look fabulous."

Cassidy was beautiful, with her dark brown hair and those enviable blue-green eyes. She'd always been the prettier one, and now she looked radiantly happy.

On the table, a beautiful little girl with eyes that matched her mother's beamed up from a bouncy seat.

"Oh, my word. She's gorgeous."

"Right?" Cassidy slipped into the booth, and Denise sat across from her and grabbed the baby's socked foot. "Aren't you precious? I'm your Aunt Denise."

The baby giggled. To Cassidy, Denise said, "I'm in love. Two seconds, and I'm a goner."

Cassidy beamed at her baby. "Me too."

Denise saw James approaching and said, "You're lucky she looks like you and not that troll of a husband."

"Hey, now," James said, mock scowl on his face. "It's true, but you don't have to say it."

Denise stood again, and James gave her a quick hug, then set her away to look at her. "I'm glad you're home."

Clean-cut, athletic James had grown his hair long and scruffy after his sister died and Cassidy disappeared. Without the grief that'd been etched on his face for years, with his long hair pulled back in a ponytail, he looked good. Not just good but, like his wife, happy.

"I'm glad to be here. Truly."

"How long are you staying?" he asked.

"A month or so, maybe longer."

"That's wonderful."

"I don't think Reid agrees."

James's smile faded a little. "He'll be okay. He can handle a little competition for Ella's attention, even if he doesn't want to."

"There's no real competition, James. She adores her daddy."

He squeezed her elbow. "She adores her mommy too." He stepped back to include Cassidy. "I just came over to say hi. Hopefully we can catch up more later." He shot his wife a broad smile, waved at Hallie, who giggled and kicked her chubby legs, and walked toward the kitchen.

Denise sat again. "I haven't seen him that happy since high school."

"Amazing what God can do, isn't it?"

They caught up over clam chowder and fried haddock and french fries. The food was good, if a little greasier than she was used to. But the conversation was the best she'd had in a long, long time.

There were a lot of hard things about being in Coventry, but reconnecting with Cassidy wasn't one of them. Despite the years that stretched between them, their friendship felt as strong as it'd been before Cassidy'd disappeared when she was eighteen.

The dishes had been cleared, their drinks drained, refilled, and drained again, when Jon caught Denise's eye from his post against the wall. She saw the silent question in his gaze.

She didn't want this to end, but Cassidy had things to do, and Denise needed to get the supplies for the wreath. "Do you mind if my bodyguard asks you some questions?"

Her friend looked surprised but said, "Sure, no problem."

Denise waved him over, and he approached and shook her hand. "Donley."

"Cassidy Sullivan. Join us."

Denise slid to the end of the booth, and Jon sat beside her. "We're trying to think of anybody who might have something against Denise. She couldn't think of anyone, but I thought maybe, since you live here, you might have heard of someone with a grudge against her. Maybe someone who used to like her but now doesn't? Someone with hurt feelings?"

Cassidy was shaking her head. "I'm sorry. I can't think of anybody. I left a long time ago, though. I've only been back a few years."

"From school? Old boyfriends? Maybe guys who had crushes she never knew about?"

"No. Sorry."

He asked her all the same questions he'd asked Denise in the car, and Cassidy had no more insights.

"You should talk to James," Cassidy finally said. "He owns this place, and he's been in Coventry all his life."

"James is—?"

"My husband." She pointed behind the lunch counter. "He hears everything that goes on in Coventry. Hold on." She shuffled out of the booth and headed James's way.

When she was gone, Jon said, "She's nice, your friend."

"The best."

He smiled at the baby, who was watching the scene with wide eyes. "What a cutie."

Denise had left when Ella was only four months old, so she'd missed this stage with her. For the thousandth time, she asked herself how she could have done such a thing. No matter the depression, no matter the terrible, terrible thing that had happened to her, she should have stayed. She should have stayed and dealt with it. Learned to be a mother.

People assumed that, considering the level of success she'd enjoyed, she probably had no regrets. They were wrong. Denise's adult life consisted of one long stream of regrets.

Cassidy and James returned, and Jon stood. After the men introduced themselves, they all sat again, and Jon began round three of the same tiresome questions.

As expected, James didn't know of anybody who'd had a crush on Denise in high school. "Besides Reid, of course. He was head-over-heels back then." James rolled his eyes as if he found it amusing.

Jon was all business, though.

"How about in the last few years?" Jon asked. "Anybody give you the impression they disliked her or liked her too much? Anybody overly interested?"

James sat up straighter. "Actually, there was a kid a few years ago. Forget his name. He was with his dad and a group of guys on a backpacking tour I led."

Jon leaned in. "Tell me about him."

"Teenager—seventeen or eighteen? He mentioned Denise multiple times in the first couple of hours of our hike. Her movies, mostly, but it was obvious he was a fan, so I told him, bragging a little"—he shot Denise a wink—"that I'd been friends with her in high school. That was a mistake. He didn't stop peppering me with questions for the rest of the trip." James smiled at Denise. "The *three-day* trip."

"Torture," Denise said.

"You have no idea," James deadpanned.

But Jon wasn't amused. "Any idea why he was so enamored with her?"

To Denise, James said, "He claimed he changed a tire for

you once. It seemed unlikely because you didn't come home a lot back then, but maybe I just didn't know you were here."

She remembered. "I came to visit my parents. I was going to see if Reid would let me see Ella, but then..."

Then her parents had been so unkind. *What kind of mother leaves her child?*

What kind of mother chooses money and fame over family?

What kind of mother...?

The words had become Mom's mantra.

Her father never joined in, but his disapproval was obvious enough that he didn't need to add words.

She'd come home desperate for help with her addiction and desperate to see Ella. But they'd started in the instant she'd walked through the door. Ultimately, instead of asking for help, she'd popped a few pills, downed a few shots, and in that inebriated state, decided to go for a drive.

After years of counseling, she could admit now that she might have had a death wish. She hadn't actually thought it through, but there'd been that tiny voice in the back of her mind...

Nobody would miss you.

She'd just turned toward the road that wound up Mt. Ayasha, headed for a place where the trees were sparse between the road and a steep drop-off, when the tire on her rental blew out.

That instant terror—the feeling like she was no longer in control of the car—had sobered her up.

She'd had no reception on her cell and had no idea what she would have done if that kid hadn't happened by. He'd changed her tire, then offered to follow her home to be sure the skinny spare held up. And maybe because he'd figured out she wasn't entirely sober.

She'd decided then that she had to quit the drugs and

drinking before she killed herself. She'd decided that many times before she actually did it.

The silence might have stretched and become awkward, but Jon filled it, his focus on James again. "You know the kid's name?"

"I can go through old records," James said. "It'll probably take me a couple of days."

Jon stood, pulled a business card from his jeans pocket, and handed it to him. "Call me when you get the name or if you think of anything else."

James pushed out of the booth and took the card. "Will do."

Both men seemed to think they'd come across an important clue, but surely that skinny teenager hadn't shot at her. He'd liked her, right? Could that morph into hate so easily?

CHAPTER THIRTEEN

While he'd stood guard at the restaurant, he got a call from his FBI contact, who'd gone over Agent Frank's head to the higher-ups in the California Bureau of Investigation and convinced them to send copies of the Starlet Slayer files.

He'd forwarded the information to Jon's inbox.

After they left The Patriot, Denise had wanted to go to not one but two different craft stores so she could find the perfect wreath and ribbons for Ella's project. All the while, Jon had itched to get home and look at the files. But from there, they'd picked up Ella, taken her to dance, and then watched the class.

Though he'd enjoyed Denise's company—more than he should have—he couldn't wait to get back and study what the police had learned about the murders.

Now, he stood in Denise's office and stared. He'd removed the bland artwork from the largest wall and taped up long strips of butcher paper—a lucky find at one of the craft stores. He'd affixed images of the victims and then written down all the details he knew about each murder.

It helped to have it laid out like this. He gazed at the wall where he'd taped up a map of the Los Angeles area. He'd marked it up with three locations for each victim—home (blue), work (green), scene of the murder (red).

Aside from the facts that all the women were well-known actors, and all had been stabbed, there were no discernible patterns.

The victims ranged in age from twenties to forties. They lived from Malibu, west of LA, to Laguna Beach, south of the city along the coast. When they worked, they mostly did so in LA.

Their murders were spread all around the area.

Five were killed at or near their homes, one while filming on location, one in her car, and the most recent in the bathroom at a restaurant.

Some, like the latest victim, had been wildly successful, A-list actors. Most had been actively working, but two hadn't worked in years. A blog post described one as washed-up.

They worked for all different studios, some in movies, some in TV. Some were known for comedy, others for drama. One was popular in action films.

Some were single, some were married, some were divorced and remarried. Some had children, some had stepchildren, some had no children.

Two went to church regularly, though not the same church. The rest didn't attend any religious services.

Some had memberships at fitness centers, but not the same fitness centers.

The police had checked for common doctors, diet gurus, chiropractors, personal trainers, clothing stylists, hair stylists, manicurists. Some had a few of those in common, but none had them all in common.

Police had checked for similar banks and other financial institutions.

Favorite grocers.

Mechanics.

Delivery services.

Nothing, nothing, nothing.

As far as Jon could tell, the only thing these women had in common, besides where they lived and what they did for work, was that they'd all been victims of the same killer.

And what did Denise have in common with the women? Why had the killer singled her out?

He kept the office door open just in case there should be another attack, though the evening team was protecting her now. He'd traded his private security hat for his private investigator hat.

He didn't have much investigating experience. This would be good practice.

Denise's laughter rose above the Christmas carols drifting from down the hall. Ella was chattering excitedly, adding her giggle to her mother's. He smelled garlic and chicken.

They must have set aside the crafts to make dinner. Good for them.

He forced himself to concentrate. There had to be a clue he was overlooking. He'd just turned his attention back to the wall when the sound of footsteps approached, fast. He got to the door just in time to head off little Ella before she charged inside, saw the murder wall, and started asking questions. He hadn't been dumb enough to tape up crime scene photos, but still, he'd rather not have to explain to to an eight-year-old what he was doing.

"What's up, little bit?"

"Mommy says you have to come and eat dinner with us."

"I have to, do I?"

Her head bobbed. Any shyness she'd felt with him at their first meeting had fled entirely. She slipped her tiny hand around his fingers and tugged. "Come on. It's fettuccine Alfredo, my favorite. And Mommy makes it the very best."

He probably shouldn't, but the scents were calling him. And how did anybody say no to this kid? She was too cute for words.

After shutting off the light and closing the door, he allowed Ella to drag him—pretending to struggle, which elicited more giggles—into the kitchen.

"I got him, Mommy."

Denise turned from her place at the stove. She'd pulled her hair back in a ponytail, and she wore an apron over her jeans and sweater. "I hoped you might join us."

He thought of the other guards on the property—all eleven of them. There were six on duty right now, Ella's three and Denise's three. Surely she hadn't made enough for them all.

Which meant she'd singled him out.

Which he didn't mind one bit. But... "I don't want to intrude."

"Don't be silly. I made enough for an army. Well, not really. Not even enough for your whole team. Will they be offended if I don't share?"

"I told you, you don't have to feed us."

After giving him a look he couldn't quite identify—shyness, maybe?—she stirred the bubbling pasta. "Is it okay if I only share with you?"

"I won't tell." Crap. Did that sound like he was flirting?

Her eyes twinkled. "It'll be our secret then." She turned to Ella, who'd climbed onto one of the barstools. "Can you keep a secret, love?"

Her head bobbed. "Uh-huh. I didn't tell anybody when—" She clapped her hand over her mouth, eyes wide. "I almost did!"

He chuckled. "You kept those words in. Good job."

She beamed. Wow, she was adorable with those dark brown eyes. "Have you been helping?"

"Uh-huh. I buttered the bread and put on the garlic salt." She pointed to a short baguette that had been cut lengthwise. "We're gonna boil it."

"*Broil* it," Denise said. "You broil food in the oven. You boil food in water on the stove." She pointed to a pot where steam rose. "The fettuccine is boiling."

Ella shrugged like she couldn't care less.

To Denise, Jon said, "What can I do?"

"Put the bread in?"

"To boil?"

She shot him a look, and he laughed as he grabbed it and did as she asked.

"Set the timer for one minute."

He set his phone timer, then turned to see what else he could do just as Denise was preparing to lift the huge stockpot. "Whoa, let me get that for you."

"I can do it, but if you insist..." She stepped back and handed him the oven mitts. "It's hot."

He poured the pasta and water into the colander in the sink. Steam rose and heated his face, and he stepped back, bumping into Denise. "Oh, sorry."

"Just supervising. Gotta make sure you don't screw it up." She winked at her daughter, who smiled in return.

"Mommy's the best cook. Daddy and Jacqui are okay, but nobody's as good as Mommy."

"Is that so?" Jon asked.

The woman in question turned back to the stove and gave the white sauce a quick whisk. "Not really."

"What's next?" By the time the words were out of his mouth, his timer was going off. He removed the bread from the oven—it was bubbly and golden brown on top. The scents of butter and garlic had him itching to tear off a bite.

While Denise chopped chicken she must've cooked on that

little indoor grill on the counter, she nodded at the loaf and said, "Slice that sucker up."

"On it."

Five minutes later, they settled at the kitchen table with plates of food in front of each of them. Not only had Denise made the Alfredo sauce from scratch, but she'd also chopped up a Caesar salad.

"Do you want to pray?" she asked Ella.

"Okay."

Denise and Ella held hands, each holding their other out to him.

He took them both, relishing the feel.

This was not where he should be. As a professional, he shouldn't get emotionally involved with his clients. But as a human being, as a man...

He didn't want to keep his distance. And he didn't believe for one second that caring about the people he was protecting would make him less effective. If anything, it should make him more effective.

"Dear Jesus," Ella said. "Thank You for this yummy food and for Mommy who made it and for Mr. Donley who helped. And for Daddy and Jacqui and the baby. Let him be big and strong and not bite me. Amen."

Jon stifled his chuckle. "Amen."

Denise cleared her throat, and he guessed she, too, was trying not to laugh. "That was a nice prayer."

Ella twirled her fork in the creamy pasta. "Jasmine at school has a little brother, and she said he bites her all the time. He even got in trouble at church for biting other kids."

"I see," Denise said. "Smart to ask God for a brother who doesn't bite."

The child had shoved a huge bite of food into her mouth, so she just nodded.

Jon didn't say much during the meal, content to listen to Denise and her daughter chatter. Denise seemed so...light-hearted with Ella. She'd seemed that way with Cassidy, too, for the most part.

There'd been that one moment, though, when James had mentioned the kid who'd changed her tire. Denise's open expression had shifted to something he wasn't sure he could name. She'd lost a little color. Her eyes had dimmed. She'd even inched back a little in her chair and crossed her arms as if she'd felt...attacked. Or ashamed.

Why?

Had something happened with that kid, something she didn't want to talk about? Had he hurt her? Assaulted her? Or maybe she felt embarrassed about what had happened that day. Not that having a flat tire was anything to be embarrassed about.

There was more to the story, and maybe the *more* would lead to the man who was trying to run her out of town. As much as the Starlet Slayer had consumed his attention that afternoon, the greater danger right now was the shooter here in Coventry. Was it the same person? Or two different killers?

Either way, Jon needed to get to the bottom of what Denise had been thinking back at the restaurant.

But, based on the way she'd reacted, she wasn't going to share that *more* very easily.

Jon gathered dishes from the table and carried them to the kitchen. Least he could do was clean up after she'd served that delicious meal.

"Mommy, can we show Mr. Donley what we did?"

"You want to see it, Jon?"

Ignoring the warm feeling his name on her lips elicited, he

said, "Sure." He set the plates in the sink and followed the girls into the living room. Denise had draped a cloth over the coffee table. He'd seen it earlier, covered in needles from the wreath and metal ornament hooks. The ornaments had been strewn across the white sofa. Now, most of the mess had been cleared away.

While Denise perched on the sofa, Ella stood by the table and lifted the wreath for him to see. He sat on the chair to get a good look.

The evergreen circle was covered in brightly colored ornaments, not to mention some fake little red berries. "Wow. It's beautiful."

Ella beamed. One by one, she pointed to all the ornaments and told him who each represented. They'd added one he hadn't seen before, a small nativity scene, and she pointed to it last. "Of course I'm thankful for Jesus, because without Jesus, there'd be no Christmas!"

He chuckled. "Christmas is pretty awesome." He leaned forward and studied the wreath closely. "And this is what you're most thankful for in the whole world?"

"Uh-huh. My family and Jesus. They're the best presents ever."

"You, little bit, are very wise."

"'Cause I have a God who loves me, and He gave me all these people. Did He give you a good family too?"

"I have a great family." Jon wasn't sure yet about the God part. "I have two big sisters."

"They're not bigger than you, are they?" Her voice held a tinge of awe.

He laughed, sharing a look with Denise. "No, not bigger, just older. Julie is six years older. She has two teenage boys, my nephews, and I get to take them to movies sometimes. Jenny is four years older. She's married and has little kids, but they live in Florida, so I don't see them often. And of course I have amazing parents, just like you do. And I have cousins. One of them is like a little sister to me."

"I have cousins, too," Ella said, "but I don't see them very much. Do you see yours a lot?"

"One of them. And you want to hear a secret?"

At Ella's nod, he lowered his voice and said, "You get to see her too."

Her eyes widened. "I do?"

"Yup. Miss Lake is my cousin."

Her mouth formed a little O. "Cool."

"Is that right?" Denise's head tilted to the side. "Actually, now that you mention it, I can see some resemblance. Obviously, you're both really tall. But also, around the mouth, maybe?"

"Don't tell her she looks like me. She'd cry herself to sleep."

Denise laughed.

Ella said, "Nuh-uh. You're cute."

Heat filled his cheeks. He'd never been complimented by an eight-year-old. "Thank you. Not as cute as you though." He tapped her button nose.

"Their family must have lived near yours if you spent that much time together."

He turned to Denise on the sofa. "Her family wasn't as... stable as ours, so she stayed with us a lot when we were kids. I'm as close to her as I am my sisters. Actually, now that we work together, I'm closer to Lake."

"So, did she follow in your footsteps? Is that why she's a bodyguard?"

"Not...exactly." He wasn't about to explain how Lake had come to work with him. That was her story to tell.

"Wow," Ella said. "You have lots to be thankful for too."

"I do," Jon said. "Lots and lots."

She turned to her mother. "Can we do the ribbon now?"

"Sure." Denise pulled spools from a sack—red, gold, and red-and-green checkered. "Which one do you like best?"

Ella studied the options, then turned to Jon. "Which one do you think?"

"Uh..." He looked to Denise for help. He didn't have a clue. "They're all pretty, but I think maybe the gold?"

Denise smiled. "I'm partial to the gold too. And not just because it'd be pretty."

Ella said, "How come?"

"Gold is special," Denise said. "Real gold, that is. It's valuable today, and it was valuable even back when Jesus was a baby. Remember the gifts the wise men brought?

"Gold, frankincense and myrrh."

"Frankincense and myrrh are some sort of scented...something," Denise said. "But gold—"

"Everybody knows what that is!" Ella said.

Denise ran a hand over her daughter's hair. She touched her often, like it was her way of showing love, of connecting. Or maybe, after a long separation, she just couldn't help herself. "Gold is one of the most valuable metals on the planet. It's been used as money for thousands of years."

"Really?"

"And it's an interesting metal because it's very malleable."

Ella squinted, her question obvious.

"Malleable means it can be shaped. In the case of gold, very easily." Denise slipped a ring from her right hand and handed it to Ella. "See how it's not an exact circle? It's a little tight, and over the years, it's molded itself to my finger. And that's not even pure gold. They have to combine it with other metals so it'll keep its shape."

Ella studied the ring, then handed it back. "Is that why you like gold?"

"All girls like gold." Denise winked. "And diamonds. But the point is, I think it would represent something important about your wreath. Real gold can be stretched and molded, like a family. See, when your daddy and I first got married, it was just us, and of course our parents were our extended family. But then the family stretched to include you. And now, it's stretched even more to include Jacqui and her parents, and pretty soon—"

"A baby!" Ella said. "It's gonna have to stretch even more."

"That's right. So, to me, gold is the right color because real gold can shape itself to cover any family, no matter how big or unique it might be. It's sort of like the family of God. When you give your heart to Jesus, you get to join God's family along with all the other people who love Jesus. And then you have brothers and sisters all over the world. They're all different colors and shapes and sizes, they speak different languages and come from different cultures, but they're still your brothers and sisters in Christ."

It was clear Ella didn't fully comprehend what her mom was saying. Rather than ask for clarification, she said, "Cool," and picked up the spool of gold ribbon. "Can you show me how?"

"We'll do it together."

Jon probably should have excused himself, done the dishes, and returned to the office-turned-murder-room. Instead, he watched as Denise instructed Ella in attaching the ribbon to the wreath. He would've just wrapped it around, but what Denise had in mind was more creative.

Beautiful.

Even more so because she didn't do it herself. Rather, she directed Ella. "Maybe pinch it there."

"Twist it here, see."

"Let's put a dab of glue…"

Ella followed her instructions. When they were done, the simple wreath looked like a work of art.

Ella lifted it for him to see.

"Wow, that's amazing," he said.

Her grin stretched wide, pure joy. "I can't wait to show Dad."

The contentment on Denise's face faded, and she pushed to her feet. "I'll put it in a plastic bag to protect it for the ride."

Ella set it back on the table. "Can I leave it here? Daddy can see it at the Christmas party at school."

"You don't want to take it home?"

"I thought... Can we hang it up here?"

If Jon weren't mistaken, he caught the sheen of tears in Denise's eyes. "Of course, love. Where do you want to put it?"

Ella decided it should go on the back of the door, and Denise didn't bat an eye when she asked Jon to drive a nail into the glimmering wood. After they'd hung it, they enjoyed home-made peanut butter cookies—the kind with chocolate kisses pressed onto the top—and hot chocolate in front of the fire while Christmas carols played in the background. Everything about the space, from the sparkling tree to the crackling fire to the scents of chocolate and pine, drew him in.

Denise and her daughter completed the perfect holiday picture.

Again, Jon didn't contribute much to the conversation. An irritating voice kept telling him he should leave them alone, but he ignored it. This house was completely different from the colonial he'd grown up in, the tree more subdued than his parents' flashing multicolored one, and the family smaller. But the sense of it, the feeling of comfort and home...

He liked it. He liked little Ella. He liked Denise—more than he should.

Ella's gaze strayed often to the wreath, and each time, she smiled.

Denise had claimed more than once that she wasn't a good mother. It was clear by the way Ella watched her with admiration and adoration that nobody had told *her* that.

If Jon wasn't careful, his own expression would reflect those same feelings, feelings he had no business having about a client.

CHAPTER FOURTEEN

I t had been a perfect afternoon. Denise hated for it to end, but as she waved to Ella, she felt not sad but buoyed. This wasn't goodbye, it was see-you-soon.

She'd call Reid to find out when she could see her again. Probably not Tuesday, but Wednesday or Thursday at the latest.

Reid wouldn't be happy, but he'd learn to share.

Like her daughter had been, Denise was surrounded by bodyguards for the short walk from the driveway to her front door. When she stepped inside, only Jon followed.

Usually, bodyguards got on her nerves. She'd learned to tolerate them when Ella was visiting but was always happy to see them gone. But Jon was different. She liked having him around. He made her feel safe, but it was more than that. His presence was calming. Gentle. And if he judged her, it wasn't harshly.

In fact, the way he'd joined them for dinner and then stayed to look at the wreath... He could have easily made an excuse after the meal and disappeared, but he hadn't.

It was almost as if he *liked* her. Denise had fair-weather

friends, fake friends, and fans. She had a few genuine girlfriends at church, and their husbands were cordial enough.

But she couldn't remember the last time she'd been with a man who simply...liked her. Not because of her fame or her looks but just because of who she was.

Inviting Jon to dinner had been Ella's suggestion, but Denise could admit, in the privacy of her own mind, that her heart had leapt at the idea. Maybe Jon liked her, maybe he didn't, but she definitely liked him.

Too much.

And now she sounded like a middle-schooler with a crush.

When he closed the front door, he said, "You did a great job with it." He was admiring the wreath.

"I think it came out pretty well."

"You're a woman of many talents."

Arts and crafts had always come easily to her. As had cooking. And acting. And...that was about it. "Not 'many' talents," she corrected, heading for the kitchen. "I've learned to focus on things I'm naturally good at and ignore the things I'm not."

"Like singing."

She laughed. "It's not that bad."

"It's not that good."

"Okay, then. How about you?" She started clearing the table they'd ignored earlier. "Can you sing?"

"I can carry a tune, but I'm no Bing Crosby." He turned on the water.

Hmm. With that deep, soothing voice, he could knock *White Christmas* right out of the park. "Let me be the judge of that. Sing something for me."

He squirted dish soap into the sink. "I don't think so."

She transferred the leftover pasta to a storage container. "Come on. One little line. A carol."

"Nope." He started rinsing dishes.

"How about this," she said. "I'll sing, and you can join in."

"Please don't. I just got my ears to stop bleeding from the last time."

She smacked him with a kitchen towel.

He chuckled. "Was that supposed to hurt?"

"Oh, but you've told me how to hurt you." She belted out the first line of *Jingle Bells*.

Her singing voice really was atrocious.

He covered his ears with soapy hands. "Stop. It burns!"

Her song morphed into a laugh. "Come on, coward. Sing for me."

When he didn't, she picked up her song where she'd left off.

His eyes were mirthful when he glanced her way, shaking his head.

And then he joined in.

She wasn't wrong. Jon might not've had Bing Crosby's voice, but he had talent.

She quieted so she could hear him better, though he didn't seem to notice, switching from *Jingle Bells* to *Winter Wonderland* smoothly.

Finally, as she stowed the remainder of the food and wiped the counters, she let her voice fade entirely, not wanting to ruin his song. He sang a low tenor, smooth as cream pie.

When everything but the dishes were done, she grabbed a clean towel and dried the pots he'd propped on the counter.

Finished washing and the song fading, he held the colander toward her to dry. "Well, what's the verdict?"

She took it, accidentally—or maybe not—brushing his fingers with her own. "Not bad." And then she smiled. "Really good. You should sing more often."

The shy look he gave her made her heart flutter. She swallowed and focused on the task. What was she doing? Flirting with her bodyguard?

Stupid. This man was staying in her house. What if he got the wrong idea? What if he took advantage?

He wouldn't. Would he?

No. He was a protector. She'd stayed in the same house with Jon for two nights, and he'd been nothing but a perfect gentleman. That she feared anything else had nothing to do with his character and everything to do with her own demons.

"You did a great job with Ella today." He dried his hands.

"You think so?" Warmed by the compliment, Denise opened and closed a couple of cabinets before she found where the colander went.

"The way you used the gold ribbon to talk about your family... That was really insightful. It made me think of my own, with my sisters and their husbands and kids, and of course Su...Lake."

"Sue? Is that her name?"

"No." He lifted the dirty towel. "Where do you want this?"

Denise grabbed it. "Susanne? Suzette?"

"No and no."

"Sully?"

He just raised his eyebrows.

"Come on. Now I have to know."

"She'd kill me. And don't let my superior size fool you—she could do it."

"Only because you wouldn't fight back."

His lips tipped up at the corners. "True."

"Sabrina? Savannah?"

"You aren't going to let this go, are you?"

"It's just a name, right?"

"She doesn't like people to know."

"Why?"

He grabbed a cookie from the bowl and leaned against the counter. "Not my name. Not my story."

"There's a story about her name?"

He blew out a long breath. "You're annoyingly persistent."

"It's another of my talents."

He just shook his head, though she saw amusement in those dark eyes. "I'm going back to work. Thanks for including me for dinner and the wreath and...stuff. It was fun."

"Next time, I'll let you play with the glue gun."

Chuckling, he rounded the island, but she wasn't ready to be alone yet. It was too early to go to bed, and she was too hyped up after the day with Ella to watch TV or read.

She followed him. "What are you working on?"

"I got the files from Agent Frank." He stopped at the entrance to the hallway, and she froze halfway across the living room, feeling like an irritating little sister. She should leave the man in peace.

And then she realized what he'd said. "On the murders? Anything interesting?"

"I've been perusing them. When you have a chance, I want to show you. Maybe something will jump out at you."

"Why can't we do that now?"

He made a show of looking at his watch, one of those giant things that probably worked a thousand feet underwater. "It's a little late to be thinking of serial killers, isn't it?"

"Isn't that what you're about to do?"

"It's my job."

"It's my life."

He conceded that with a nod. "If you want."

She wasn't sure she wanted to think about the Starlet Slayings tonight, but she did want to keep talking to Jon, so she followed him into the office.

One wall was covered with butcher paper. He'd bought a roll at the craft store, but she hadn't bothered to ask why. Now she knew.

He'd taped pictures of the victims across the top. Beneath each one, he'd written facts about them. Some of those facts were circled or underlined, and she realized he was indicating similarities. There were very few.

None of them had everything in common except the obvious—they were all female actors. Otherwise...

"What am I missing?" He leaned against the front of her desk.

She gazed at the facts as he'd laid them out, then at the map on the adjacent wall, and tried to think of something, anything he hadn't covered.

"Studios they've worked for?"

He pointed, and she saw he'd written those nearer the bottom of the paper.

"People they've worked with? Actors, directors, producers."

"The police complied that list."

She remembered something she hadn't thought about since the first victim. "I know someone who worked with Lauren Lahey." She nodded to the photo of the sitcom star. "She was an aspiring actress, but she worked as a makeup artist at the studio. She and Lauren bccame...not friends, but they were friendly."

His expression perked up. "Could you reach this woman?"

"Yeah. She went to college with me, and when I decided to go to LA, she came too. We shared an apartment for a couple of years. She never was able to land a meaningful role. She did some stand-in work, a couple of commercials, but not enough to pay the bills."

"She still in LA?"

"She gave up a few years back. I think she lives here now."

"Here as in—"

"New Hampshire, somewhere."

"Do you think she'd talk to us? Maybe she knows something about the victims we don't."

"Can't hurt." Denise found Brittney's contact information. She sent a text and got a response almost immediately. "She's available tomorrow. Should I set it up?"

He smiled. "That'd be great. Good idea."

It was stupid, the rush of pleasure that came with his offhand remarks. She texted Brittney back. After her friend replied, she said, "We're going to meet her at four in Portsmouth."

"Good, good." He seemed genuinely pleased. "It's good to have a next step."

Denise leaned against the door jamb. "Maybe she'll have some insights for us."

"Any information is helpful. The more pieces of the puzzle we get, the clearer the image will be. Speaking of..." He pressed his hands against the desk behind him and angled back. "Can I ask you something?"

The seriousness in his voice had her worried. "I guess."

"Today at the restaurant, when you were talking about that kid who changed your tire..."

She crossed her arms. "What about him?"

"You seemed"—he shrugged—"almost nervous."

Realizing he was watching her closely, she uncrossed her arms and settled into a relaxed stance.

But Jon seemed to miss nothing, just watched her try to pretend all was well. "Did he hurt you?"

"What? No. Nothing like that."

His eyebrows hiked. The man could speak volumes with those eyes.

"When you were hired, did you have to sign some sort of nondisclosure agreement?"

He leaned farther back. "I did. Even if I hadn't, I wouldn't tell anybody anything about you without your permission."

Should she believe him? She'd worked so hard to keep her

secrets to herself. Part of her—a big part of her—wanted to tell somebody besides her counselor the truth.

Not just somebody, though. Jon.

"It's just that...I was... I wasn't exactly sober."

"Oh." He dipped his head to the side and squinted. "How... not sober were you?"

"Very."

"Is that a regular thing for you? Drinking and driving, or just—"

"Not anymore. But back then... Not the driving, usually. In LA, I would hire a driver or ride with friends. But here..." She sighed. "I'd gotten into an argument with my parents. I had a rental car, and I just took off."

"Drunk," he clarified.

"And...I'd taken some pills."

His head bobbed a couple of times, all amusement erased. "That something you still do?"

"Never. Remember I said I was in the hospital when—"

"Ah. You were in rehab when your daughter was kidnapped."

The offhand way he said the words—words she'd never said to Reid or her parents or Ella—had her heart thumping. "I wanted to be here. Everything in me wanted to check myself out and get on a plane. I was so scared. I thought, if she died... If she'd died, I'd have probably joined her. I would not have survived it. And if she'd just disappeared, was never found?" She swallowed the emotion rising with the memories. "I still have nightmares."

He nodded but said nothing.

"But I'd just finished detoxing. I wasn't strong enough to leave. I definitely wasn't strong enough to handle the pressure, the fear. And this place...this is the hardest place to be because of my parents and Reid... All the reminders about how I let them all down."

"Which they won't let you forget."

"I deserve their contempt."

He scowled at that.

"My counselor at the rehab hospital told me that if I came home and relapsed, I would take focus off finding Ella and put it onto me. Nothing good could come of that. It wasn't as if I'd be able to find her, and definitely not if I wasn't sober. Reid and our parents didn't need to deal with my issues. So I stayed. It was the hardest thing I've ever done." Her voice cracked with emotion. "I swore that if God saved Ella, I'd never take another pill, never touch another drop of alcohol."

"I take it you've kept that vow."

"I've been sober for four years, four months, and"—she quickly did the math—"seventeen days."

"That's something to be proud of, Denise. Why are you ashamed of it?"

"I'm not."

Again, his disagreement showed in his expression.

"I'm not ashamed of getting clean. I mean, I don't really want Reid to know. It would only give him more fodder to use against me. And I'd prefer Ella not know. But it would be better than them thinking I didn't care enough to be here." She shrugged. "If they knew, it would be fine. God's grace is big enough to cover me despite their opinions."

"God's grace. Is it malleable like gold?" A hint of humor carried in his voice.

"Incredibly. It stretches over the ugliest sins."

Humor fading, he seemed to consider that. "But you haven't told anybody the truth. Wouldn't it be better if they knew why you didn't come home?"

"I have a contract with the studio, and there's a morals clause. I mean, it's a gray area. Addiction is a medical condition, but it's also a choice. One can't get addicted to drugs if one never uses them. And I signed a contract that said I wouldn't. Would the studio have canceled my contract? Probably not. But would they renew it?" She lifted her shoulders, let them drop. "It's not that they care that I used drugs or went to rehab, not really. It's that they don't want my reputation sullied. My work was all I had. I was afraid to lose it. I was afraid that if I lost that... My life was hanging by a very thin strand. I felt like I was always fighting a death wish, fighting the belief that the world would be better off without me. If I lost my job—"

"Surely your family wouldn't have told anybody."

"Maybe."

"Why can't you tell them now?"

"My contract is up for renewal, so it would be better if it doesn't come out. But I'm stronger now than I've been in a long time. I could handle losing my job, losing Ember Flare." She felt silly using the name of the superhero she played. "Unlike before, I know who I am. I can differentiate between who I am— a child of God, loved and forgiven—and what I do. I'd rather *not* lose my job, but..."

"You don't trust Reid not to tell anybody."

"Do you think I should?"

"Well, if your contract were canceled, you could stay here full time. Maybe if he knew that—"

"Ha. Good point." She laughed. "There's the incentive he'd need to keep his mouth shut."

"That's all I'm saying." His eyes softened, filled with warmth and kindness. "Thank you for trusting me with that." His gaze flitted to the wall beside her, and he sat up. "Maybe that's the connection. Do you think these women went to rehab? Or struggled with addiction?"

She followed his gaze. "I hadn't thought of that. We should find out."

Denise and her cadre of bodyguards left the house the following afternoon under low-lying clouds. Maybe it would snow. She'd always loved snow when she was a kid. It was one of the many things she'd missed living in LA. Today, it was certainly chilly enough, the temperature hovering in the twenties. They had an hour and a half drive ahead of them, and they were giving themselves a little wiggle room to get to the meeting place early.

She was accustomed to sitting in the backseat of the luxury SUV behind two bodyguards, so when Jon opened the passenger door for her, she felt flush with pleasure.

He offered no explanation as he climbed into the driver's seat. The other three bodyguards occupied the second SUV, which followed them down Rattlesnake Road.

Denise had awakened feeling a weird combination of giddiness and embarrassment. Jon had already seen a lot of the ugliness in her life. Now he knew about her addiction as well. He'd already alerted Special Agent Frank to the possibility that the victims had substance abuse recovery in common—without mentioning Denise's struggles—but Frank said they'd already checked out that angle.

Leaving Denise feeling...unsettled. Had she overshared? She could pretend now that she'd told him about the drugs and alcohol because the information might help him figure out the connection among the Starlet Slayer's victims.

But that wasn't what she'd been thinking. She'd been thinking that she wanted him to know. She'd gotten the impression that he liked her, and she'd wanted to know if his feelings, however light and tenuous they were, would last if he knew the truth about her.

Not that she'd told him everything. She'd never told anybody but her counselor everything.

Jon had claimed to believe that her years of sobriety were something to be proud of. Did he still feel that way? Did he still like her?

How silly and childish she was. But it felt good to make a new friend.

And if his feelings went beyond friendship...?

She wasn't ready to face that. Even if he felt something more for her, she had no idea what that would look like or how it would work. And he wasn't a Christian, so she shouldn't even be entertaining the thoughts.

The thoughts were rather entertaining, though.

Jon didn't speak until they'd driven through Coventry. "I wanted to ask you another question, and I thought you'd prefer to answer in private."

"Oh." And here she'd hoped he'd wanted to spend time alone with her. "Okay."

A long silence followed. The longer it stretched, the more her guard went up. And then he said it.

"Why did you leave your family?"

"No." Of all the things...of all the questions. Hot shame and cold fear mixed inside her. Hadn't she already bared enough to this man? Couldn't he wish to know something about her that she'd be proud to share?

But no. He asked the hardest question imaginable.

She had a story she could tell him, of course, a story she'd told everyone. And it was true. It just wasn't the whole truth. She could share it, but even if he bought her pat answer, which she doubted, she didn't want to lie to this man.

She wouldn't. "No."

"I know it's personal," Jon said, "but I've learned that some-times it's the personal things that connect us. Maybe that's the connection—"

"It's not."

He blew out a long breath. "Denise—"

"No. I can't tell you..." Stupid tears burned her eyes, but she blinked them back. Eight years had passed. Eight years, and she still couldn't think about that time without crying. She crossed her arms against the sudden chill in the car.

He adjusted the heat, missing nothing. "I didn't mean to upset you. I just want to put the picture together."

"How could the reason I left Coventry have anything to do with murders in LA?"

"Maybe it has to do with the guy who's taken two shots at you here."

"It doesn't."

"There wasn't anybody else? A man?"

"No, of course not. Never. Reid and I were in love. I would never have cheated on him."

He didn't voice a follow-up question, but he didn't have to. If they were so in love, then why had she left?

"It's complicated."

"Relationships usually are." His voice carried none of the judgment she expected. The judgment he no doubt felt. "Was he as in love as you were? Was there another woman?"

"No! No. You don't..." How could Jon possibly understand what their lives had been like? "None of what's happening now is related to what happened back then."

"Somebody wants you out of Coventry. Maybe it's the kid who helped you change your tire, but my money says it's not."

Not that she'd suspected that sweet, gentle kid, but still she asked, "Why?"

"Because he'd be, what? Twenty-two? Even if he could, at

his age, shoot a crossbow eighty yards with that accuracy, I don't see a twenty-two-year-old having the patience to wait nine hours."

Nine hours? "What are you talking about?"

"Oh." He glanced her way. "I guess I didn't tell you that. We finally found the guy on video. He army-crawled across your property while you and Ella were in North Conway. He waited until he thought everybody was asleep."

Wow. That had taken some planning. And patience.

"Guys in their twenties are cockier than that," Jon said. "More daring. Less disciplined. I assumed the person had military training, but unless this guy enlisted at eighteen and then was discharged early for some reason..." He shook his head. "No. My instincts tell me it's someone older. Considering the personal nature of the note, it's probably somebody who knows you, or at least thinks he knows you. Which means it's probably somebody you know or used to know. If not from high school, then from college or after you were married."

"Reid was faithful to me. I was faithful to Reid. There was nobody else."

"You're certain about Reid?"

"Unequivocally, yes."

"Mind if I ask him?"

"Go for it, but you'll be wasting your time."

Jon nodded, but she could tell he wasn't convinced. "And there was nobody else who wanted to be with either one of you? Rivals for affection?"

"Not that I'm aware of."

Jon drove in silence a few minutes before he asked, "Did Reid ever... Was he abusive?"

"What? No. Never. Why would you even ask that?"

His jaw tightened, a look she'd seen when he was angry. His

lips were pressed closed as if he were debating saying something. Or trying not to. Or maybe debating how. Finally, he spoke. "I've had the feeling a couple of times that you're...afraid."

"Someone's taken a shot at me—twice."

"And you weren't as scared as you should have been, in my opinion. It's not that. It's... Yesterday, when you were talking about that kid on the road."

"I explained that."

He nodded but clearly wasn't mollified. "Sometimes, you seem very self-protective, more so than most. Often when you're talking about Reid."

"He's—"

"Cruel to you. I know. I just wondered if it used to be more than words."

"Look, I know he acts like a jerk sometimes. He needs to forgive me, and he's trying. But what I did to him... It was my fault. I had an infant, this beautiful little girl I loved. But I couldn't... I didn't know how to be happy. I was miserable."

Jon was silent, giving her time to elaborate. She'd told herself she wasn't going to tell him why she'd left, and now she was delving into the story. She needed to shut up.

"Were you suffering postpartum?" Jon asked. "I hear that can be rough."

That was an easy one. "Yeah. In retrospect, I realize it was really bad. *Really* bad. But at the time, I just thought there was something wrong with me. And Reid..." She sighed. "He didn't understand, of course. How could he? He had this new beautiful baby, and this weepy, useless wife."

"Maybe a little compassion wouldn't have hurt."

"We were twenty-two. What did you just say about guys in their twenties? They're rash, yeah. They're also arrogant and... dumb. We were both so dumb, but we thought we knew everything. At least I *had* thought that, until Ella was born. Then it felt like I didn't know anything.

"We were still in college when I got pregnant. We'd had all these plans. Maybe...maybe they were mostly my plans. I'd always wanted to be an actor. I figured we'd graduate, and then I'd start trying to break into the industry. I'd done some community acting, studied theater in college, and I was pretty good. He said he'd go anywhere with me, that he'd support me. But then I got pregnant. We got married. Ella came along, Reid got a job, and we bought a house in Coventry, and it felt like the world was closing in on me. Like my life was over, and all I had to look forward to was years of darkness."

"And so you left?"

There was more to it. So much more. But she hadn't meant to tell Jon as much as she had. She definitely wasn't going to tell him the rest. "None of that has anything to do with what's happening now."

"Okay." After a moment, he said, "I'm sorry. I didn't mean to dredge up bad memories."

"Sure you did."

His Adam's apple bobbed, and he glanced her way. "I meant to get the information. I didn't realize how hard it would be for you to share."

They drove a long time in silence. When they reached Lake Winnipesaukee, she stared at the expanse of gunmetal gray. The water was choppy, and the clouds hid the mountains that surrounded the giant lake. Even still, there was beauty. Beauty in the rough surface that hid the clear waters. Beauty in the spindly pines that stood guard year-round. Beauty in the bare trees that waited patiently for spring.

That was life, wasn't it? Sometimes hard, ugly, choppy. But, like the majestic peaks, the beauty was there, just waiting to be revealed.

There'd been a time in Denise's life when the biggest battle was simply surviving to face another day. When she'd pop any pill or swallow any drink just to shut up the voices telling her she shouldn't exist. That she didn't deserve to exist.

Anybody who claimed there was no such thing as Satan and his minions wasn't paying attention, because that voice—that sneering, snickering, evil voice telling her she ought to end it all —that voice did not belong to her.

Her enemy had almost won. But even in the midst of the ugly, God had shown her beauty. He'd shown her in beautiful sunrises over the canyon.

In good-triumphing-over-evil scripts.

In kind words from costars, friends, strangers.

Mostly, in those days when she woke up hungover, hating herself, she'd see a picture of her daughter, all innocence and light, and think... *For her. Today, I'll be better. For her.*

It had taken years to reach *today*.

But eventually, she'd done it. Now, on the other side of it, she spent her life searching for beauty. Which was why she could look past Reid's hateful comments and angry glares and remember the man he used to be—the man he still was with everybody but her. She didn't want to be judged for her ugliest moments, and she refused to judge others for theirs.

They stopped at a light, and Jon faced her. "I should have trusted you. You told me it wasn't related, and I should have believed you. I shouldn't have pried. I'm sorry."

True regret showed on his face. He watched her, waiting for her response, as if fearing she'd hold a grudge. She'd never been good at grudge-holding, though. Grudges were heavy. They only weighed a person down.

"You're trying to keep me safe," she said. "I appreciate that."

"So we're good?"

She smiled. "We're good. I'm sorry I got emotional."

"You don't owe me anything." His gaze flicked downward. To her lips? Was he thinking...?

But the light turned green, and he accelerated through the intersection.

Of course he hadn't been thinking about kissing her. Ridiculous to even consider such a thing. That she was now thinking about kissing him...

She liked him, too much. She hadn't felt this kind of attraction for anybody since...

Reid.

And she'd been head-over-heels for him.

But that wasn't what was happening now. It couldn't be.

Could it?

CHAPTER FIFTEEN

P rescott Park looked mostly deserted when they arrived. While the bodyguards scoured the area for threats, Denise and Jon waited in the SUV.

"I don't like this," Jon said.

"Nobody knows we're here. It'll be fine."

But his lowered brows and intense gaze told her he wasn't convinced. "You should have told me the meeting place."

She had told him they were meeting at an old haunt in Portsmouth. He'd assumed a restaurant, but that wasn't her problem.

"You should have chosen someplace enclosed. Maybe she can get in the car?"

Denise appreciated that he was trying to keep her safe, but they were an hour and a half from Coventry, and nobody except herself, Jon, and Brittney knew they were going to be here.

"Were we followed?"

"Of course not. We're not amateurs."

"Then what's the problem?"

"It's not secure. Why does it matter, anyway? Why not meet at her place of work or something?"

"She suggested this, and I like Prescott Park. Brittney and I used to perform at the theater here. We have good memories."

"It's freezing."

Jon wasn't wrong about that. The dashboard display told her the temperature outside hovered near thirty. "We're dressed for it. Can we go now? I don't want to miss her."

Obviously not happy about it, he rounded the car and opened her door. "Stay close. Do as I say, okay?"

"Yes, boss."

Not even a smile.

The steady breeze made it feel colder than the temperature indicated. Fortunately, Denise wore a toasty warm fur-lined jacket. She took a knit cap from her pocket and pulled it down over her ears, then slid on her gloves as she headed toward the gate where Brittney had suggested they meet. They passed some of the old houses that made up the Strawbery Banke Museum, which were decked out for the holidays—trees, garland, wreathes galore. She wished it were dark and the holiday lights were lit. Portsmouth had always been extra charming at Christmastime.

They entered the park and were walking beneath the barren trees when Jon asked, "What can you tell me about this woman?"

"She was a theater major, like me. We were friends."

"She's not as good an actor as you, I assume."

"I wouldn't say that. She's taller than average, which limits the number of roles a person can get. She's a good dramatic actor but not great with comedy. She's a very nice person, but kind of shy, which doesn't help her connect with people. There's so much competition. Everything has to work out, and she just never had the pieces fall into place."

"You're good at focusing on the best in people."

She looked down to hide her flush of pleasure. "We celebrated victories together. At first, those were few and far between. More often, we commiserated when we were passed over for parts. We'd buy a couple of pints of Ben and Jerry's ice cream—Cherry Garcia for me, Chunky Monkey for her—and tell each other how all the casting directors were stupid to overlook us." Denise remembered those days as hard and frustrating, but also fun and simple. Things had changed when Denise started getting parts and Brittney didn't.

"I probably didn't treat her very well," she said. "When I got the Ember role, I bought a house, leaving her to find a new roommate. In retrospect, I should have invited her to live with me or given her more notice. I was pretty selfish back then."

Jon stopped cold, gaze flicking around the barren park. A few folks walked through it—probably more to get to their destinations faster than to enjoy the scenery. "Was she angry with you? Did you argue?"

"She's not my enemy, Jon. If she was angry, she never said so."

He started walking again, though he looked even less happy about this meeting than he had earlier.

The other bodyguards hovered nearby. She felt safe, surrounded by all of them.

The guy who'd taken the shot at her at the park in Coventry could have seen her coming. He probably caught sight of her Tesla—she should have bought something a little less conspicuous—and realized she was there. And she'd sat on that picnic table by herself for a long time, plenty of time for someone to get on a boat.

This was different. By the time anybody could get set up to harm her, she'd be leaving. And anyway, Jon had said nobody followed them.

A tall woman approached on the path, still a good fifty yards away. Brittney had put on a little weight, but it only enhanced her features. She'd always been attractive with her light brown hair and dark brown eyes, that perpetually tanned skin that came from her Italian roots.

"That's her," Denise said.

"I'll be close if you need me. I'll ask our questions, so when you're done visiting, let me know, and I'll join you." He added, "If that's okay."

She nodded, and he moved away.

Brittney's smile was probably her most memorable feature. It wasn't Julia Roberts wide, but it was big and inviting.

Denise opened her arms, and Brittney stepped into them and hugged her tight. "How are you?"

Backing away to get a better look at her, Denise said, "I'm happy to see you. I've missed you."

"It's been a long time." They walked along the path, settling into conversation as easily as if it'd been five weeks, not five years, since they'd last seen each other.

Denise told Brittney about playing Ember Flare, about mutual friends and what they were up to, about what she was doing back in New Hampshire.

"How's that going, then, reconnecting with Ella?" Brittney asked.

"Really great. We've spent time together over the past few years, so it's not as if we're strangers, but being here with her, being able to do everyday things with her...I love it."

"I'm so glad. And the stuff you were dealing with back then, the drinking and—"

"Been sober more than four years."

"Wow." The surprise in her voice was almost insulting.

"Didn't think I had it in me, did you?"

Denise expected Brittney to laugh, but she stopped, tilted her head to the side, and studied her through narrowed eyes.

"Honestly, there were times I worried, really worried about you. But you look...great. Like a new person."

"I am. Not just sober, either. I returned to my faith."

"Hmm. Well, good for you." The way she said the words told Denise she wasn't interested in hearing about that.

Denise would have to keep in touch. Maybe she'd have an opportunity to share her faith another time. "Tell me about what you've been up to."

It seemed Brittney had done well for herself since she'd given up the dream of being an actor. She'd returned to New Hampshire and opened an art gallery here in Portsmouth.

"Wow." Denise almost asked how her friend had funded such an expensive venture, but she held her tongue. Considering her success compared to Brittney's lack thereof, it seemed a bad idea to discuss money. "I'm proud of you. I'd like to visit it someday." She quickly added, "But probably not today. I've got other things going on." She really did want to see the gallery, but not surrounded by burly bodyguards who might scare away Brittney's customers.

"Just as well," Brittney said. "I have an appointment this evening. How long will you be in New Hampshire?"

"Through New Year's, at least."

"That long?" She seemed pleased. "We're showing a great local artist in a couple of weeks, Donovan Gilcreast. Ever heard of him?"

"I haven't."

"He's really good. You should look him up. And if you have time, I'd love it if you'd come to the show. I'll send you the details."

"Thanks." It seemed like her friend had found her niche. "I looked you up on social media last night, but I couldn't find you."

Brittney lifted her shoulders and let them drop. "You could

find the gallery, but me? I gave up Instagram a few years ago. I kept comparing my life to everyone else's. It turned out so differently than I'd planned. Looking at everybody else's successes...it wasn't healthy."

"It's funny, isn't it?" Denise said. "Some people look at my life and think how lucky I've been. But I look at yours and think the same thing. I love acting, but sometimes I hate the stuff it comes with. People long for fame, and I long to be a normal person. People long to be actors, and I long for anonymity." She sighed and added, "I long for a family."

"Do you really? Because you had that, and you left it."

Denise wasn't offended or even surprised by Brittney's question. That directness was one of the things she'd always liked about her friend. "I wish I'd stayed. I wish I'd sought help for the depression and stuck it out."

"But you've done such good work."

"The world would have survived if somebody else had been cast as Ember Flare. Nobody else can play Ella's mom. That's the role I should have fought for." She struggled against the melancholy that tried to descend. There'd been a lot of such conversations lately, and each time regret gripped her ankles and tried to yank her down.

She kept her focus on Christ. He held her up.

They passed the fountains—empty of water in the cold-weather months—and reached the stage. Denise paused to gaze at it, remembering the summers they'd both had roles. Because of Denise's terrible singing voice, she'd never been cast as a main character, but Brittney had played a couple of important parts. "Do you ever miss it?"

"Not even a little. When I left LA, I left all those dreams behind, and I've never looked back. Never let myself look back."

"Good for you."

They started walking again and reached the edge of the

park where they could gaze out over the harbor. Brittney stared toward the islands. The wind caught her hair, and with her height, her strength, she brought to mind a stately, beautiful figurehead that would lead sailors to unknown lands.

But Brittney's next remark crushed the image. "I regret ever going, to tell you the truth."

"Oh." Denise hadn't expected that. "We had some fun, didn't we?"

She shrugged. "You started getting roles right away. It was different for me. Frustrating. I felt like I had something to offer, but nobody saw it."

"I'm sorry about that. I wish it'd been different for you." Emotion tightened her throat. "I wish I'd been different for you."

Brittney squeezed her hand, lips spreading into a genuine smile. "You were a good friend. I'm happy where I am now. I'm happy with my gallery. I'm dating this guy, and it might turn into something, you know? I get to travel, meet artists. It's a good gig."

"I'm happy for you." They watched the waves lap the shore. Thanks to all the little islands—so close they were connected to the mainland by bridges—the waves were gentle, though the surface was choppy. The weather still held, but it felt like a storm was coming.

"Anyway," Denise said, "I need to talk to you about something."

"Okay."

"Actually, my bodyguard wants to ask you some questions. Do you mind?"

Brittney dipped toward Denise, lowering her voice. "You mean that hot guy who's been following us?" Her gaze darted toward Jon, who was about twenty feet behind them.

"That's him."

"He's uh…" Her eyebrows waggled. "Hubba hubba."

Denise laughed. "Get a grip. You just said you had a boyfriend."

"Do you? Or do you have a little Kevin Costner-Whitney Houston action going on?"

She wasn't about to admit she'd thought about *The Body-guard* movie more than once since she'd met Jon. "Don't be ridiculous." Her words were vehement, if slightly amused. But she felt her cheeks burning.

Brittney just laughed. Then, she looked around. "I assume the other guys hovering are with you too? I don't remember you being so paranoid."

"That's what we wanted to talk to you about."

Brittney backed up. "Okay then. Fire away."

Denise waved Jon over, and he approached, hand outstretched. "I'm Donley."

"Brittney."

"Do you mind if we start back to the car?"

"Fine by me." Brittney moved toward the road, and they fell into step beside her.

"We're investigating the Starlet Slayings. Ms. Masters tells me you used to work with Lauren Lahey."

Brittney blinked, surprise clear in her expression. "A long time ago."

"We're trying to find connections among the victims. Did you work with any of the others?"

"I did the makeup for the sitcom Monica Brown starred in. And I worked with Shannon Butler once, when she was a guest star."

"Good, good," Jon said. "Can you think of anything the three women have in common? Anything the police might be missing?"

She shrugged. "Geez, I don't know. They were all attractive."

"Were they personable? Short-tempered?"

"They were okay. I mean, Shannon was distracted, barely looked at me while I was doing her face. But she wasn't rude or anything. Monica didn't pay me much attention, but when she spoke to me, she looked at me, which is more than I can say for a lot of people whose makeup I did. Lauren and I were friendly."

"How so?" Jon asked. "Did you see each other outside of work or—"

"No, no. Nothing like that. We just used to joke around a lot. It started when I made a crack about Californians."

"She wasn't from there?"

"I think somewhere in the middle of the country. Omaha? Oklahoma? I forget."

"Okay. Did any of them ever talk about having a stalker, or about someone they were afraid of?"

Brittney shrugged. "Not to me."

"Do you know if any of them went to rehab or had a drug or alcohol problem?"

"Not that I know of." Her gaze flicked to Denise's. "What's this about? Why are you investigating this?"

Jon looked at Denise, giving her the option to answer.

"There's a chance the killer might be targeting me," Denise said.

Brittney gasped, halting in place. She gripped Denise's arm. "Oh, my gosh. What...? How do you...? Does the killer let people know before he kills them? I mean, how do you know that?"

Denise explained about the package that'd been delivered to her agent's office. "It might be nothing. None of the other victims had anything delivered."

"Wow." Brittney started walking again, more slowly this time. "Wow. Is that why you're here? To get away from him?"

"I'm here for Ella. It didn't hurt that there was a killer hunting down actors, though."

"I'm sure." Brittney walked in silence a few moments, then shook her head quickly. "Anyway, rehab? I don't know. Lauren used to talk about partying. She'd laugh about how people all drank fancy drinks—lemon drop martinis and the like. She claimed to prefer beer, but really, she was stick-skinny. How much beer could she have possibly drunk?"

"You don't know if she had a problem with it?" Jon clarified.

"Sorry. I don't." She walked a few steps, then said, "There is one thing, though. I think she had work done."

By the expression on Jon's face, he had no idea what Brittney was talking about. Denise said, "Plastic surgery."

"Oh."

"She had pretty full cheeks when I worked with her, but later, it looked as if maybe she'd had some kind of implants. Her cheekbones seem higher and more pronounced than they used to be."

"Really?" Denise said. "I didn't notice."

"You didn't look at her face for an hour every day."

"What about the others?" Jon asked.

"Maybe, yeah. Monica's nose...the nostrils used to be more pronounced. Shannon—I have no idea. But who doesn't have work done these days?"

Jon turned to Denise. "Have you?"

"No. But it is pretty common. Especially if you consider Botox injections, things like that."

He focused on Brittney again. "That's a great tip. We'll look into it."

Maybe that was the connection among the victims. But it still begged the question—what did that have to do with her?

CHAPTER SIXTEEN

"Isn't it lovely?"

Jon glanced at Denise, who was staring out the window at the storefronts. They were stopped at a light in downtown Portsmouth, so he followed her gaze. It was a cute town, all decked out for Christmas. Wreaths on doors and trees in windows. Candles and garland. A Santa on the corner, ringing his bell. A few flurries danced across the windshield, carried on the breeze.

Denise looked his way, eyes bright and eager. "Let's stop and get something warm to drink. We're not in any hurry, are we?"

She was shivering. Her own fault for agreeing to meet her friend in the park instead of in a nice, safe environment. "Why don't you see if you can find a drive-through coffee shop?"

"That's not what I..." She sighed and looked away, her expression falling. "It's just nice here, all Christmassy and festive. Never mind."

Oh. It wasn't about the warm drink.

"We've been in town for an hour," he said. "The park wasn't as empty as I would have liked, and my guys tell me at least one person recognized you and took your photo. It's possible it's already being shared on social media that you're in Portsmouth. Which means the person who fired that arrow—"

"It's fine. Whatever."

Following his GPS, he turned back toward the state highway. "But maybe we could stop along the route, if you really want to. We passed through that town on the lake—Meredith?"

"Oh, could we?"

The excitement in her voice had his heart melting despite the cold she'd forced him and his team to endure. He really shouldn't care if she was happy. He should care if she was safe— that was his job.

But that he'd made her happy...

"Sure. If you want. Find a place. We'll have to have the guys check it out first, but it should be fine."

She tapped on her phone. "Here we go. There's a diner..."

By the time his team had cleared the little restaurant in Meredith, it was nearing six o'clock. Grant had already secured a table, so the hostess immediately led them through the casual space which was, like everything else, decked out for the holidays. A Christmas tree in the bar area crowded the tables. Garland wrapped in twinkle lights hung along the edges of the ceiling. Cheerful holiday music played in the background, barely heard above the chatter and laughter and clinks of dishes.

The restaurant was busy, almost every table occupied.

The four bodyguards stationed around the room stood out like the Easter bunny at a Christmas parade.

At a table near the wall, Denise chose the seat that had her back to the room. For privacy?

Jon leaned down and whispered, "I'll be right over there." He nodded toward the door to the kitchen.

Her eyes widened. "You aren't going to sit with me?"

He hadn't known if she wanted him to or not. Now, seeing

the hurt on her face, he realized he'd guessed wrong. "I didn't know if you... I mean, we aren't—"

"It's fine. You don't have to."

He slid into the chair across from hers. "I'd like to, though. If you don't mind."

Her expression was shy, and she hid it behind her menu before he could analyze it further. "Should we order dinner? I wasn't thinking about the time when I suggested this."

"I could eat." He lifted his menu as well, trying to study the options. But...

But.

Were they on a date?

No, of course not. She'd just wanted to stop, and he just happened to be with her.

It wasn't a date. It was just two people eating together. Like, a business meal.

Right.

She set her menu down. "Do you want to split something?"

Split? He'd already picked out what he wanted—steak tips in gravy. "Unlike some people I know, I can finish my whole meal. Besides, you're the one who suggested we eat."

She shrugged. "Mostly I'm just not ready to go home. Maybe I could just nibble off your plate."

"Men have died for less."

She laughed, setting his heart racing. "Fine. I'll get my own. But don't be surprised if I don't finish it."

"Don't be surprised if I help."

They ordered—she chose a grilled chicken sandwich—and then settled in to wait.

"Tell me about your life," she said.

"What do you want to know?"

"Where did you grow up?"

"Leominster, Mass."

She lifted one eyebrow, looking very Ember Flare, and let her expression press the question.

After the server delivered the drinks, Jon expounded on his short answer. "Dad's a cop. Mom's a history teacher. They keep talking about retiring, but they both love their jobs."

"And you have sisters."

"Yup. They're older, though. We weren't close growing up. We are now, as much as we can be living such different lives. And of course I have Lake."

"Whose name is...Susanna."

He chuckled, shaking his head. He wasn't sure how he'd react if Denise guessed right. He wouldn't want to lie, but his cousin would kill him if anybody found out her real name. Most of their teammates didn't even know.

"Why private security?" Denise asked. "Or were you a cop at one point, like your dad?"

"I enlisted after high school. I was a Green Beret." Why had he added that? Was he trying to impress her?

Maybe.

Okay, yes.

Denise's eyes widened. "That's like...special forces, right?"

"Yup."

"Wow. Pretty elite."

He shrugged and sipped his drink. "How about you? You went to LA—"

"Nuh-uh. We've talked enough about me." Those sapphire eyes sparkled. "I want to know about you."

So, Jon talked. He told her about his years in the service, some of his assignments, how it had felt to be so far from home, often in very different cultures. He told her about the incredible hospitality he'd found in the Middle East, the easy camaraderie among the people in Africa. He told her about friends he'd made along the way—and a few he'd lost when missions went south.

Their meals were delivered, and while they ate, he talked.

Even as he was sharing, he asked himself why.

Why tell his client so many personal things about himself?

The answer was clear enough that it should have put him on his guard. Truth was, he wasn't thinking about her as his client anymore.

And he wasn't thinking about her as *Denise Masters, movie star.*

He was thinking about her as a woman. A woman he liked. A woman he wanted to get to know better.

A woman he wanted to know him.

It was a problem. He knew that. But knowing it and doing something about it were two very different things.

When he described the time he'd caught frogs at the creek and left them in his oldest sister's bed, he got the reaction he'd hoped for.

"You didn't!" Denise seemed mortified. "That's so mean."

He just laughed. "Nah, she was tough. She could handle it."

"She had to be tough with a brother like you. What did she do?"

"There might've been screaming involved. And crying."

"You made your sister cry?"

He wished that were the case. "No. Julie screamed—to Mom. Mom told Dad. Dad got out the paddle."

"Ah. So the tears were yours."

"Don't judge me. I was six."

Denise just shook her head. He'd eaten his meal, finished hers, and now they were sharing a slice of apple pie, of which she'd taken a single bite.

He nodded to the plate in the middle of the table. "That was your idea, you know."

"I had some."

It was his turn to let his facial expression display his opinion.

"I'm full." She pushed the plate toward him. "Go on. You know you want to. How you don't weigh three hundred pounds, I'll never understand."

He was about to respond when a voice sounded in his ear.

"Huge group coming in," Grant said. "You might want to wrap up your date."

He caught the man's eyes across the restaurant and glared, but Grant didn't seem at all sorry for the remark. Jon nodded, and Grant stepped outside. He'd bring the car around.

"We need to get the check," Jon said.

"Everything okay?"

He got the server's attention and pulled out his wallet.

"I'm buying." Denise sounded genuinely shocked.

"No, you're not."

"But this was my idea."

As if he was going to let her buy his dinner. Maybe this hadn't been *planned* as a date, but it'd sure felt like one. Even if it hadn't, he didn't let women buy his meals.

Rather than argue, when the server came with the check, he snatched it, saw the amount—it wasn't exactly the Russian Tea Room—and dropped a couple of bills on the table. "The car's here. You ready?"

Disappointment crossed her features. He guessed one of the reasons she was a good actor was her communicative facial expressions. Made her a good actor, but she had a lousy poker face. "I guess."

He'd explain in the SUV why they'd needed to leave so quickly. Most likely the party on their way inside was perfectly innocuous, but they couldn't know for sure. If someone wanted to get close to Denise without raising alarms, the best way to pass the guards without being noticed would be to blend in with a group. If Grant mentioned it, they must've made him nervous.

Always better safe than sorry.

As soon as he stood, Marcus, who'd been stationed against the wall on the far side of the room, started toward them to follow them out. A guard in front, another behind. It worked to get through a cramped space.

But an old woman pushed back in her chair, forcing Marcus to stop. He couldn't exactly push the lady out of the way, but there wasn't an easy path around her in the busy restaurant.

Jon's heart thumped. Just bad timing, nothing else. Obviously, that elderly lady wasn't trying to hurt anybody.

Still, he didn't like that nobody had Denise's back.

They were a few feet from the front door when it whooshed open, ushering in frigid air and a huge throng of people.

Jon froze to assess the situation.

Grant hadn't been kidding. There were at least fifteen, maybe twenty people—men, women, kids—all talking, smiling, laughing.

One man stood out. Near the back, six feet. Maybe middle forties. Hard to tell his weight with all the people in front of him. Stood straight, looked serious, unlike everybody else. His gaze skimmed the restaurant, and Jon's instincts kicked in. He spoke into his comm. "Brown hair, plaid shirt."

"See him," Ian said.

Jon took Denise's hand and pulled her toward the bar, shifting so she was in front of him. He urged her past the close tables and chairs and near the Christmas tree against the far wall.

She turned when she reached it, and he blocked her with his body. The space was tight, but she should be safe here.

Her eyes reflected the twinkle lights on the tree behind him. "What in the—?"

"It's okay. Just be still."

"Jon, what did you see?"

"Probably nothing. I didn't like the idea of walking past all those people. We'll wait here until they're seated."

"All of them? That'll take forever."

In his ear, Grant said, "We're right outside."

Jon tapped his comm. "Guy still there?"

Marcus answered. "Yup. Searching the restaurant."

"For her?"

"No way to know. Maybe he's looking for his date."

But Jon had studied every table. There hadn't been a person sitting alone, looking like they were waiting for someone. That didn't mean anything. It was possible the person the guy was meeting hadn't arrived yet. It was possible the guy was just trying to decide if it was worth waiting for a table.

It was also possible that somebody had seen Denise, told their social media followers she was there, and this guy had come to see her.

A fan?

A shooter?

A killer?

"Jon." Denise's voice was stern, and he looked down to find her staring up at him with wide, frightened eyes. Her hair, falling gently around her shoulders, tickled the backs of his hands.

When had he put them on her shoulders?

It was his imagination, of course, that had him thinking he could feel the heat of her skin through her thick jacket.

They were close, too close. He was just trying to protect her. That was all.

But her mouth opened the slightest bit, and his body reacted with such a strong surge of desire that it took every bit of his self-control not to bend nearer and brush her lips with his own.

Realizing what he was looking at, he snapped his gaze back to her eyes, only to find her watching him. She knew. She knew what he was thinking.

Was she thinking it too?

He tried to step back, but the tree was there, hemming them in.

"The crowd moved through," Marcus said. "There's a private room in the back."

Jon tapped his comm device again. "And the man?"

"Went with them. It's clear."

Jon stepped back. "You ready?"

She blinked several times, then nodded.

Taking her hand in his, he hurried to the door and outside. The cold night air blasted him, cooling his desire and snapping him back from that little fantasy. The SUV waited at the curb. Grant was in the driver's seat but started to get out when Jon approached.

"Stay there," Jon said into his mic. "You're driving."

The last thing he needed was to be alone with Denise for one more minute.

CHAPTER SEVENTEEN

It was a long, tense drive back to Denise's house. Silent, except for the chatter of bodyguards in Jon's ear. Beside him, Grant kept his mouth shut—a necessity considering Denise rode in the backseat—but his opinions were clear in his expression.

Marcus, Ian, and Hughes, riding in the car behind, didn't have to keep quiet.

It had started with Marcus's "What the heck was that? Are you two *dating*?"

Of course Jon couldn't defend himself because of Denise's presence.

And because he had no defense. He shouldn't have sat with her. He shouldn't have opened up so much to her.

And he definitely shouldn't have gotten so close to her in the bar, suspicious character at the door or not. But he'd needed to get her someplace where nobody could see her.

What he hadn't needed to do was stand with her, face-to-face. So close.

He hadn't needed to fantasize about kissing her as if they *had* been on a date.

He was glad he couldn't respond to their comments, which started lighthearted but didn't stay that way. Jon was the boss, and the guys weren't stupid. They didn't make accusations aloud, but he knew the questions they weren't asking.

Was there more between Jon and Denise than there ought to be between a guard and a client? Since the answer to that seemed obvious, the real question was *how much more?*

When they arrived at the house, Marcus, Ian, and Grant spread around the premises. They would be on duty for a few more hours.

Hughes and Jon delivered Denise to the front door. She turned once she was inside, as if expecting him to follow.

Without a word, he pulled the door closed, trying not to see the hurt in her expression.

He figured the news of what happened had already spread to the rest of his team. When he stepped into the guest house, the looks on the faces staring at him confirmed his guess.

The guys were spread out on the floor or seated at the table. Some were smiling as if it were all a big joke, but others clearly took it more seriously.

Jon had expected that.

But Lake had been staying at the Cotes house, even when she was off-duty. When she stepped forward, he knew things were about to get interesting. She said, "Upstairs."

"Fine." Jon marched through the room and climbed the stairs to the second-floor bedroom. One guy was reclining on his air mattress, reading.

Jon said, "Give us the room."

"Oh. Sure." He scrambled up and past them and jogged down the stairs.

Jon closed the door and lifted his hand. "I know."

"Do you?"

"It was just dinner. She asked me to join her because she didn't want to sit alone."

"According to the team, it was more than just dinner."

"I never took my eyes off the ball."

She leaned against the wall and crossed her arms. Lake wasn't like other women, never had been. Not just because of her height—she was nearly six feet tall. And not just because of her looks. He was her cousin, but he could admit she was drop-dead gorgeous, despite the severe bun and lack of makeup. But Lake carried—had always carried—an air of fearlessness. As a child, her father had physically abused her mother, Jon's dad's sister. He'd verbally abused her sisters. But he'd always been careful with Lake. It was as if, even then, he knew she was tougher than he was.

Even in the midst of the terrible ordeal she still refused to talk about, she'd remained stoic, strong, and clear-thinking. Which was how she and everyone else had survived.

When Jon and Bartlett had started the private security agency, they'd brought Lake on as a partner. She'd been a newbie, learning as they went. In the first couple of years, Bartlett had been a guard, too, but as Lake's skills had improved, he'd stepped back. Now Bartlett, who was in his fifties, preferred to stay in Boston and run the company. He made administrative decisions, but in the field Lake and Jon were in charge.

She was giving him a look she'd perfected over the years, some combination of curiosity and disdain.

He hated that look.

"There was never a moment that I wasn't thinking about the client's security," Jon said. "I saw every person who walked in, who walked out, who looked her way. There was a boy—about eleven, brown curly hair—who took her picture with his phone. The table at two o'clock debated whether she was who they thought she was. One guy at the table at eight o'clock was dared by his friends to ask for her autograph, but he chickened out. Nobody else paid us any attention."

Lake's eyebrows lifted.

"I can do my job."

"Nobody said you couldn't."

"Then what's the problem?"

"Do you think Ian could have dinner with a client and still watch the room?"

Ian was their newest hire. He was decent, but his skills needed to be honed. His focus, especially.

Jon didn't answer the question because he knew what she was getting at.

"You're the boss," she said. "We make rules for a reason. If you don't follow them, how do you expect anybody else to?"

"There are no rules about eating with a client, and there were four guards. Technically, I wasn't on duty. I went because I needed to question Brittney."

"So you'd planned to take Ms. Masters to dinner?"

"No."

"We agreed to four in public. Why the extra guard?"

"I needed to question De—Ms. Masters's friend."

Lake's eyebrows hiked, but Jon barreled forward. "I knew I'd be focused on the friend for at least a few minutes. It seemed prudent to have an extra guard."

"Denise?"

Of course Lake wouldn't let it go. "She doesn't like to be called Ms. Masters."

"You're the one who came up with the rules."

"I know that."

She studied him a long moment through narrowed eyes as if trying to read something on his face.

He did his very best to keep his expression impassive. But

Lake had known him a long time. All their lives. He'd never been able to hide anything from her.

Finally, she said, "Is it serious?"

"It's nothing."

"Are you lying to me? Or to yourself?"

He blew out a long breath and looked away from his cousin's probing eyes.

The beige walls were interrupted by windows that faced into the forest on three sides. There was space enough for a king-size bed, a bureau, maybe a couple of chairs or a sofa, though none of those things furnished the apartment yet.

Right now, blowup mattresses, blankets, pillows, and various personal items littered the carpeted floor. Frustrated as he was, he managed to not kick anything as he crossed the room to the window and gazed outside.

Snow was falling, heavier than the flurries from that afternoon, but it was still nothing to worry about. A little weather was the least of his problems.

Lake approached, and he glanced her way when she stood at an adjacent window. She was looking outside as well. "You're allowed to be attracted to her. Nobody would blame you for that. If what I heard before you walked in is any indication, you wouldn't be the only one."

He faced her. "Are the guys talking about her? If they're making cracks or being disrespectful—"

"It'd be like every other job."

He focused out the window again, barely suppressing a growl. Lake wasn't wrong, but the idea of anybody disrespecting Denise had his hands clenching.

"Is it more than attraction?" Lake asked.

"Of course not."

"Really?" She leaned one shoulder against the wall and speared him with those dark gray eyes. "Hughes called me on the way back and told me what he witnessed. He's known you a couple of years, and he said he's never seen you talk so much as you did at dinner. And smile. And laugh."

"I'm not allowed to have fun?"

"With a client?"

Lake was right. He knew she was right, even if he didn't want to admit it. He wasn't just attracted to Denise. He was falling for her.

He crossed his arms. "What do you want me to do?"

She sighed. "I'd say we should trade places, but the Cotes trust me at this point. They don't mind me staying there, inside. I can't imagine they'd feel the same way about you."

He barked a laugh. "I guarantee Cote will never feel the same way about me."

"They won't let any man get close to Ella. So...I have to stay there. Which means you have to stay here. And you're investigating, which means you need to be close."

"So...what? What are you saying?"

"You need to put somebody inside with her. Do your investigating here in the guest house."

He made a show of looking around. "Where? It's not something I want the guys involved in. And Ms. Masters is helping me. She knows a lot more about this industry and the victims than I do."

Lake was nodding, thinking it through. "Okay, you keep working in the office, but you can't stay inside with her overnight. And no more dates."

"It wasn't a—"

"Whatever you want to call it. You and Ms. Masters can pursue whatever relationship you want when this is all over. But as long as there are threats, you need to keep your distance. Otherwise, Bartlett's already said—"

"You called Bartlett?"

"—he'll replace you. He can be here tomorrow."

Bartlett could guard Denise as well as Jon could. But Denise didn't know him, didn't trust him. And Bartlett wasn't an investigator. Jon had taken on the new role to keep his mind engaged. Sometimes being a personal security guard could be mind-numbingly boring. Truth be told, he was tiring of the job. He wouldn't mind expanding the personal security agency to include private investigations, but he'd need to prove he had the chops to do it.

Jon didn't want to be dismissed, but if Lake and Bartlett agreed he needed to leave, he'd have no choice. That was the agreement. They all had an equal stake in the company, and majority ruled.

"I'll keep my distance," he said.

Lake allowed a rare smile. "When we first approached her, I thought she was going to be... Well, you know. We've guarded our share of difficult women. But she's not. I can see why you like her. She's...impressive, the way she loves her kid. The way she treats people."

"Even Cote, who's a world-class jackass."

Lake wagged her head side to side. "Just with her."

Exactly what Denise had said. Still, Jon had to fight an urge to deck the guy every time he saw him.

Lake touched his arm. "It doesn't have to be forever. If you really like her, when this is all over—"

"She's a movie star. I'm a bodyguard. She might find me interesting for an evening, but..." It would never be more than that. Jon needed to keep that in mind.

He *would* keep it in mind. And from now on, he'd keep his distance from Denise Masters.

∾

Jon was halfway across the backyard when his phone dinged with a message from James Sullivan, Denise's friend.

Found the name of the kid who was obsessed with Denise. Landon McLaughlin. He came camping with his father, Ken.

Jon stopped and tapped out a reply. *Can you forward that to Detective Pollard?*

Much as Jon would like to look into it himself, he had enough on his plate with the Starlet Slayer and keeping Denise safe.

Already did, James replied. *Just thought you'd like to know.*

Jon responded with a thumbs-up, then stood in the middle of the backyard, centering his thoughts. The snow had left barely a dusting. Now, the clouds were parting, revealing an expanse of star-studded blackness. This far from town, the show was impressive. If it weren't so cold, and if he weren't so focused, he might linger to identify some of the constellations his father had taught him to recognize when he was a kid. Out of habit, he located the Big Dipper and followed the two stars at the edge to the North Star.

Sort of amazing that there was a star so perfectly aligned with the north pole that it never appeared to move.

Jon had a few north-star ideas in his life, beliefs he carried. Even in the middle of missions, surrounded by death and evil, those beliefs hadn't faltered. Like the belief that the strong should always protect the weak. The belief that good and evil weren't just theories but truth—and it usually wasn't that complicated to figure out which was which.

At that moment, things didn't seem so black and white.

Did he have to deny his feelings for Denise in order to do his duty? Would he really be a better bodyguard if he didn't care about the client? Or could his concern for Denise not compromise his abilities but sharpen his judgment?

He didn't know. He did know that there were rules, rules

he'd helped to establish. If he wanted his team to follow them, then he needed to do the same.

Regardless of how little he wanted to.

He rounded the house, climbed the steps to the front porch, nodding at the posted guard on his way, and knocked.

The door swung open. Denise had changed out of the pretty slacks and sweater and into one of the fuzzy, comfortable outfits she wore when she was home for the night. He had no idea what that fabric was, but it looked very...touchable.

Denise hadn't even asked who it was. He considered mentioning her lack of concern for personal safety but discarded the idea as she gazed at him with cautious, guarded eyes.

The way he'd treated her in the car and when he'd walked her to the door—he'd hurt her feelings, that much was clear.

"Mind if I come in?"

Leaving the door open, she moved to the sofa and sat, crossing her ankles on the cushions beside her. The TV was bright in the dimly lit room, the action paused. On the screen, Shannon Butler smiled at her costar. It was a romantic comedy, he thought.

He stepped in and closed the door.

"Every time I turn on the TV," Denise said, "one of her movies is playing. Now that she's dead, everybody loves her."

Jon settled on the chair adjacent to her. "Did people not like her before?"

Denise lifted one shoulder and let it drop. "Some did, some didn't. It's just...it's so sad. She was a nice person. Just a nice, ordinary person. They put our images on the screen, and suddenly we look larger than life. But we're not. We're just normal people who happen to be able to act. And now, because of her job, she's gone."

"I'm sorry for your loss."

"I just..." She shook her head and smiled, though not the wide, joyful expression he'd come to expect. "I'm fine. Being a little maudlin, I guess."

"Someone you know was murdered. It's normal to grieve."

"I try not to be melodramatic."

"You aren't. At all." He clasped his hands together. "We need to talk."

She gave him a wary look. "Am I in trouble?"

"Not you. Me."

"Because we had dinner together?"

He nodded. "And because of what happened...after. In the bar."

"You mean *nothing*? Because nothing happened."

Rather than argue, he said, "My team—"

"They got the wrong idea."

Did they?

Was Denise being coy? Or shy? Or self-conscious?

Or was she serious? Had the attraction he'd felt only come from his side?

As much as he'd like to skirt the question or avoid it altogether, that wasn't the kind of man he was. He was a face-it-and-deal-with-it kind of guy, even if it was awkward. Even if it hurt.

This was probably going to hurt.

He pulled in a deep breath for courage. "I don't think they did...get the wrong idea, that is. At least, not on my part."

She lowered her feet to the floor. "What are you saying?"

"I'm attracted to you. Of course." Of course he was. He was talking to Denise-freaking-Masters, movie star. What was he thinking? "Every man in America is attracted to you, so that's no big thing to you. The point is..." What was the point? He needed to pull it together. "My behavior was unprofessional, and I'm sorry."

There.

That was all he needed to say. Well, that and...

"Obviously, after what happened, it's not appropriate for me to stay in the house with you at night. But you will need someone inside. Grant has the most experience. So unless you have an objection—"

"No. Absolutely not."

"If not him, then—"

"I don't need anybody to babysit me. If you don't want to stay in the house, then I'll stay alone."

"It's not that I don't want to." He kept his voice level, showing none of the frustration he was feeling. "It's not appropriate."

She stood and crossed her arms, but the aggressive stance didn't hide the moisture filling her eyes.

Was she crying?

What the heck was he supposed to do with that?

"I'm not trying to hurt you," he said. "I'm trying to do the right thing."

"To abandon me? That's right?"

He stood as well. "I'm staying on the property, on the case. I just can't stay in the house with you at night anymore. I need to keep my distance."

"Why?" The single word carried such hurt, such pain.

How had a simple conversation gone so awry? "I just told you, I'm attracted to you."

"You also said every man in America is attracted to me. So why would I be better off with one of the others?"

He'd walked right into that, hadn't he?

"I don't know them," she said. "I don't trust them. It's not easy for me to..." She swiped at her tears.

"To what?"

"Trust...people. If they're attracted to me, too, then why should I trust them and not you?"

"You can trust me. That's not the problem. It's that...they're not attracted to you like I am."

"What does that mean?"

"Do I really have to spell it out?"

"Apparently."

He blew out a frustrated breath and sat again. "I like you, okay? More than I should. I...I just... I like you." He didn't know how else to say what he was saying.

"Well, I like you too." She hurled the words like an insult. "So by all means, let's not spend time together. By all means, send in somebody who *doesn't* like me, who *doesn't* care about me. That'll be so much better."

He couldn't figure out if she didn't understand what he was saying or if she did and didn't see the problem with it.

"Please, sit down."

She settled on the sofa again, though *perched* would be a better word, ready to spring up and run.

"Denise." He would have to stop calling her that, even in private. Once they got this awkward conversation over with, he would. "I'm developing feelings for you. Feelings that go beyond friendship."

He expected her to lean away, to be repelled. Maybe to laugh in his face.

But she smiled that easy smile. "Really?'

"It's not okay." His words came out harsh. "For a million reasons, it's not okay. But the biggest reason is that you're a client, and I'm your bodyguard. I need to keep my professional distance."

She opened her mouth, closed it again. Seemed to consider what he was saying. It was a moment before she asked, "You can't guard me if you care about me?"

"It's against the rules. As the lead, I need to be a good example, and I can't do that if I'm sleeping under the same roof with a woman I want to be with."

Her eyebrows hiked. "You want to be with me?"

He let out a groan and pushed to his feet. "You're missing the point entirely."

"What if I want to be with you too?"

That silenced him.

In fact, that remark chased all coherent thought from his mind.

She couldn't mean it, not the way he did. Not that he was planning their future or naming their kids, but...

"I'm not really a casual-fling kind of guy."

Her jaw dropped. "Do I come off as a casual-fling kind of girl?"

"I'm not saying... I'm just saying that, if you were to settle down with somebody, it wouldn't be with somebody like me." How had they gotten here? He wished he were recording this conversation so he could go back and study the transcript, figure out where it all went wrong.

Her head tilted to the side. "Why do you say that?"

"Because you're"—he waved toward her as if to encompass her amazing, beautiful, talented self—"Denise Masters. And I'm—"

"I'm an ordinary human being who happens to have a job that makes her famous. Otherwise, I'm just like you."

Okay. Maybe he could see that. Maybe if he weren't so affected by her, he'd even agree. He'd protected his share of famous people. He wasn't intimidated by fame or money or power.

"Even so," he said, "you're the client, and it's not appropriate. Grant is competent. He'll stay in the office. You won't even have to see him."

"No."

"How about Hughes, then? He's the one with—"

"I know who he is. I can stay by myself."

"After the other night—"

"You guys aren't going to let another arrow come through the window, right? I'll be fine."

"Don't be obstinate."

She reared back as if he'd hurt her. "You think that's what this is? That I let you stay inside..." Her blue eyes flashed. "You have no idea how hard it is for me to trust. I wouldn't sleep a wink if another man were in the house with me. I trust *you*. I don't even know why I trust you, but I do. The rest of them... No. It's either you or nobody."

He considered his options. It was good that Lake had developed a rapport with Ella and her parents, but Ella wasn't the one in danger. And she had Reid and Jacqui in the house to take care of her, whereas Denise was alone. Outside guards would suffice at the Cotes house. "All right. I'll get Lake—"

"Ella needs Lake. I want her to stay there. I'll be fine."

He forced a deep breath and told himself to be patient. "Lake can stay—"

"I will not compromise my daughter's safety. Lake stays with Ella."

"You're serious."

"As a death threat."

He really wished she'd chosen a different simile.

He dropped his head and rubbed the back of his neck. What was he supposed to do now? "I'll talk to Lake."

"I'm not kidding, Jon. Lake stays with Ella, or—"

"No, I mean... She's my partner. I'll ask her what she wants me to do."

"Fine." Denise snatched the remote and started the movie playing again.

This conversation had not gone how he'd imagined, not at all.

He was frustrated and irritated and had no idea what to do. Because he didn't want to leave her alone in the house. Never mind that they did it with clients all the time. It felt dangerous. Too dangerous.

But the thought that kept creeping back in as he let himself out and walked to the guest house was...

She liked him too.

CHAPTER EIGHTEEN

D enise wasn't going to think about what a terrible night's sleep she'd gotten. She'd sounded so confident telling Jon she didn't need a babysitter, that she could stay in the house by herself.

And she could. Of course she could. Only she'd gotten used to Jon's presence. Knowing he was sleeping in the office and would be by her side in seconds if there were any danger... It had helped her rest.

But he and Lake had decided the guards could keep her safe from outside. That wasn't what she'd wanted, what she'd hoped. She'd wanted them to decide Jon needed to stay in the house with her, propriety be hanged.

In the light of day, she knew he'd made the right choice, little though she liked it.

She wasn't supposed to just avoid impropriety. She was supposed to avoid *the appearance of* impropriety. By refusing to stay in the house with her, Jon had protected her.

She should be grateful. She *would* be grateful.

She finished her first cup of coffee and her morning Bible reading and prayer and then showered and dressed. That was one benefit of being alone in the house—she didn't have to get dressed before leaving her bedroom.

A soft knock on her front door had her hurrying to get her shoes on. Jon still had an investigation to run, and all his materials were in her office.

She couldn't help the way her heart raced at the thought of seeing him, even after their argument the night before. He was probably still irritated with her, but even so...

He *liked* her.

He'd said so. He wasn't just attracted to her but developing feelings for her.

Many men had shown interest in her over the years. Since she'd returned to the Lord, she'd dated, even gotten involved with a few guys, but they'd never felt like more than placeholders, men to attend events with, to share a meal with. She hadn't gotten the impression any of them cared that much for her, and she certainly hadn't cared for them. Those relationships had petered out.

But Jon...

She raced down the stairs.

And pulled the door open to a different bodyguard on the stoop. Grant didn't bother smiling and seemed devoid of personality. But then so had Jon at first. "FedEx came."

She took the large envelope, forcing a smile past her disappointment. "Thanks." It was just her daily mail delivery from Monroe. Agent Frank had let them know the day before that Monroe had been cleared of any suspicion and was not a suspect. She was glad to know it. She'd hated to think she'd allowed a serial killer to stay in her house.

The guard bent and grabbed a box on her stoop. "And Amazon." She'd ordered something nearly every day since she'd arrived, mostly stuff for her kitchen. She had a bad habit of online shopping when she got bored or frustrated or lonely. Or scared. By the time the serial killer and the local shooter were in custody, she'd have purchased enough Christmas stuff to decorate the White House and outfitted her kitchen to suit the fussiest chefs.

She carried the mail and package to the kitchen counter and refilled her coffee, trying not to think about Jon.

Jon, who liked her.

Jon, who seemed to believe they weren't suited to each other because he was a bodyguard and she was an actor. He was wrong about that. Denise might live the whole rich-and-famous lifestyle back in LA, but she was still a small-town girl at heart. She didn't need glamour or spotlights to be happy. She liked her work, of course, but all the stuff that went along with it just made her life more difficult. What she needed was a good relationship with her daughter, friends who could be counted on, and a few accountability partners to help her grow in Christ.

And maybe, someday, a man to share her life with.

She hated to admit it, but Jon couldn't be that man. She and Jon weren't suited for each other, but not for the reasons he believed.

She'd spent a good deal of her nearly sleepless night thinking and praying about him, and the Lord reminded her of one very important fact, one she'd wrestled with a lot more than the fear that kept her eyes popping open.

Jon wasn't a believer. And until he was, they couldn't be together.

It was that simple.

And that awful.

Because she was developing feelings for him. And now she knew he returned them.

But God had her best interests at heart. Much as it didn't seem true, she reminded herself that He didn't make rules to ruin people's lives or squelch their joy. He made them because

He knew what was best. So, hard as it was, she would trust Him, which meant, despite her feelings, she had to keep her distance from Jon.

Which was exactly what Jon wanted. That thought didn't make it any easier.

After fixing herself a piece of toast and finishing off her second cup of coffee, she opened the packet Monroe had sent and slid out a couple of bills and a few advertisements. Why did he feel the need to forward those? There was one thick envelope. The return address told her it was from her agent. His office forwarded fan mail occasionally, but those always came in a manila envelope, not a business-sized one like this. Was this a contract?

Had the studio finally agreed to Denise's terms? If so, why hadn't Bruce called?

She sliced open the top with a knife and pulled the papers out.

The top sheet wasn't a letter from Bruce. It was a black-and-white photograph of a beautiful Asian woman.

She looked vaguely familiar, but Denise couldn't come up with her name.

That didn't stop her hands from trembling. Had the killer left another packet at Bruce's office?

If so, why hadn't Bruce called? Why send it along? It was the police who needed this, not her.

It didn't make sense, and flipping to the next page didn't help. It was a newspaper article. The woman's name was Lorelei Cho. She'd starred on a TV show for years but, according to the article, hadn't landed another role after the show's final episode. It was a fluff piece, an article to keep an actor's face fresh in the minds of the viewing audience.

Denise grabbed her phone and dialed. Bruce answered on the second ring. "Are you all right?"

At the worry in his tone, she glanced at the clock. She'd forgotten about the time difference. It was nine fifteen in New Hampshire, which made it six fifteen on the West Coast. "Why did you send me this?"

"Uh..." He cleared his throat. "What are we talking about?"

"Lorelei Cho."

"Lorelei? What about her?"

"Your office sent me an article about her. Is she...?" Denise couldn't say the words, didn't even want to think them. "Did something happen to her?"

"I have no idea."

"Then why did you send me this!" Panic filled her voice and she worked to temper it. "Why would you—?"

"I didn't send you anything, Denise."

"Someone in your office mailed me a letter with an article about this actor."

"Okay, just..." He took a breath. "Why do you think it came from my office?"

"The return address. It's your logo."

"Send me a photo of it, please."

She snapped a picture of the envelope and the article she'd received and sent them.

A moment later, Bruce said, "It's not from us. I have envelopes with our logo and address printed right on the paper. That looks like a sticker."

She felt the edge of it on the envelope. "It is." Which meant she'd been fooled into opening it.

"I'm calling Agent Frank," Bruce said. "Sit tight."

"Wait. Is she...Lorelei... Is she okay?"

"Far as I know. She's one of my clients, but I haven't heard from her in a few weeks. I'll call you back."

The line went dead.

Denise stood in the kitchen, unsure what to do next. Maybe she should call the police? Or call Frank herself. Or...

She hurried to the front door and yanked it open. "Grant!" She hadn't meant to shout, but her heart was pounding.

If this was from the killer, maybe they still had time to save Lorelei. Maybe she could do something besides hide.

The man standing at the bottom of her stoop turned. "Yes, ma'am."

"I need to talk to Jon. Now."

"On it."

She slammed the door and paced until, about two minutes later, she heard a knock.

She yanked open the door, and Jon stepped in. "I'm sorry. I meant to tell you about the fence last night. I know it's ugly, but—"

"I got another package. What fence?"

His eyebrows lowered, and he gave her that intense look she was getting accustomed to. "Never mind. Show me."

In the kitchen, she slid the package across the island to him. He glanced at the photograph first. "Do you know her?"

"No. I talked to Bruce." She explained about the return address, and Jon peered at the envelope.

"He says it's not from his office."

Jon yanked his cell from his pocket and dialed. "Jon Donley and Denise Masters for Agent Frank." He listened, then said, "As soon as possible. Thank you." He ended the call. "Frank's on another call."

"Probably with Bruce. He said he was going to call him."

Jon spread the papers out and read.

Denise rounded the island to stand beside him and skimmed the article again quickly, thinking of the bits of information Jon had on the butcher paper taped to the office wall. Job—out of work; age—thirty-four. Looks—Lorelei was Asian with long black hair and black eyes. Gorgeous, but only one of the other Starlet Slayer victims had been of Asian descent.

Connection to Denise—they were both Bruce's clients. The article didn't say where she lived currently, but she'd grown up in Hawaii.

Hawaii. She was probably the only victim from Hawaii.

But...that thought sparked another. Where were the other victims from?

"Do you mind if I take this back to the office?" Jon asked.

"Go ahead."

He gathered the papers and walked out while Denise tapped the first victim's name into her laptop. Lauren Lahey was from Alabama.

The second victim, Erica Martine, was from Connecticut.

The third victim, Arizona.

Bloomington, Indiana.

Mt. Vernon, Missouri.

Clover, South Carolina.

Thornton, Colorado.

Shannon Butler had grown up in Omaha.

And Lorelei Cho, assuming she was a target, was from Hawaii.

Nine female actors, and not a single one of them from California. Not that it was that unusual. People came to California from all over the country, all over the world, to break into the movies. But California was a very populated state. What were the chances that every single victim would come from elsewhere?

And what did it mean?

Was somebody offended that these women had grown up outside of California? Maybe the killer was from California and wanted to break into the movie business and saw outsiders as a threat?

That didn't ring true.

But what else could they all have in common? How could being from elsewhere...?

Her body reacted before her brain caught up. Her stomach dipped. Her heart thumped.

But it couldn't be. It couldn't be.

With now trembling fingers, she typed in the first victim's name, adding the word *discovered*. It took some digging, lots of perusing of articles. It took patience. An hour, maybe more passed as she stood at her bar and studied her laptop.

But she had the information.

Lauren Lahey had been acting in community theater when she'd gone to a casting call in Birmingham.

Erica Martine had been discovered at a casting call in Hartford, Connecticut.

Jane Sanderson, victim number three, had been discovered at a casting call in Phoenix.

The fourth victim had been discovered at a casting call in Ft. Wayne, Indiana.

The fifth victim, St. Louis, Missouri.

Charlotte, North Carolina.

Denver, Colorado.

Shannon Butler had been discovered at a casting call in Omaha, Nebraska.

Lorelei Cho...Honolulu, Hawaii.

Denise was from Coventry, New Hampshire.

She swallowed, the action painful with the fear building in her throat.

She had been discovered at a casting call in Manchester.

Something slid over her shoulder, and she gasped.

Turned.

Lifted her hand to defend herself and aimed a punch.

He grabbed her arm before her fist connected with his face.

"Whoa, whoa. It's just me." Jon's voice penetrated her fog. "I said your name a couple of times, but..." The surprise leached from his expression, replaced by concern. "What is it?" His voice was low, almost angry.

"I figured it out."

He stared at her as he lifted the phone to his ear. "Frank? I'll call you back." He ended the call. "Tell me."

She would, she had to. She breathed deeply, trying to slow her racing heart. She was safe here. She was safe with Jon.

He wrapped his arm around her waist and urged her to the kitchen table, where she sat and stared toward the slider. The curtain had been pulled closed, but a sliver of glass remained visible, allowing her a tiny glimpse of the world beyond.

Less than an inch of snow had accumulated the day before. It clung to tree branches and rested on grass but left too much green and brown showing for this to be confused with any kind of winter wonderland.

All the snow in the world couldn't cover up the ugliness she wanted more than anything to hide. Maybe it was just a coincidence.

Except it wasn't.

Which meant, she knew who the killer was.

She sat like that a long time.

Jon watched her, but she couldn't bring herself to look his way.

Finally, she worked up the courage to ask, "Lorelei Cho?"

He cleared his throat. "She was at her vacation home at Big Bear Lake. It took a few phone calls and a cop driving up there to knock on her door, but..."

He didn't finish. He didn't have to. "She's dead."

She caught his nod out of the corner of her eye.

"Did you know her?"

"She was one of Bruce's clients. He spoke highly of her."

Jon said nothing, just waited.

"None of the victims were from California."

"Okay. Is that unusual?"

"A lot of actors aren't, but plenty are. Seemed quite the coincidence, nine out of nine." Finally, she faced him. "While you were back in the office, I did some research. All the victims had responded to casting calls near their hometowns. I wrote a list…" She waved toward the counter, and Jon snatched the paper from beside her laptop, where she'd written the nine names, where they were from, and where they'd gone to casting calls.

"What does that mean, casting calls?"

"It's an open audition." Denise toed the curtains open a little more, not caring that they were supposed to remain closed. The scene outside was tranquil, the trees swaying in a breeze, the sky ice-blue behind them. A guard hovered near her back door, but she couldn't see him from where she sat. A black chain link fence had been erected around her property. It was ugly but probably the best they could do, considering how fast it'd gone up.

She didn't care.

It didn't matter.

"So, anybody can go to them?" Jon clarified.

She nodded. "Casting calls are common in LA, of course. Less common in"—she nodded to the paper in his hand—"Ft. Wayne, Indiana."

"Okay."

"There's this one casting director, Hubert Vaughn." The name felt like mud in her mouth. "He used to be a casting director, anyway. Now he's a producer, and a director, and…"

"He wears different hats."

"Depending on the project, yeah. He's known for finding talent all over the country. Used to, whenever he'd cast a movie, he'd do a casting call near where it was supposed to take place, try to find local talent. It ginned up support for the movie, got people interested."

"You think these women all went to his casting calls?"

"I'm sure of it."

"Are you saying you think somebody is targeting women who were discovered at these casting calls?" She didn't miss the skepticism in his voice.

"Not just...somebody. I think..." She swallowed hard. "I think it's Hubert Vaughn himself."

He leaned toward her. "You think the man who discovered these women is killing them? Why?"

She rubbed her lips together.

"Denise?"

Her gaze flicked to his but didn't hold.

"Did you go to one of this guy's casting calls?"

She nodded. Her eyes filled, and a tear escaped. She flicked it away.

"Hey." His voice was calm, gentle. He slid his hand over hers. She fought not to yank it back. "What happened?"

She had to tell him.

There was no other choice. If this was the reason women were dying... Somebody had to tell the truth.

"It was... I was young and depressed and...and there was the casting call. I didn't tell Reid because I knew he'd disapprove. And I mean, of course he would. Ella was just a couple of months old. Why couldn't I just be happy? But since I didn't tell him, I didn't want to ask anybody to watch her because then I'd have to lie, and I didn't want to lie. So I took her with me. It was a long day. A very long day, and she was fussy. But I managed it.

I fed her, I took care of her. I might have been depressed, but I was a good mother. I was."

"Of course you were."

"Brittney auditioned, too, and she watched Ella when it was my turn."

The whole thing had felt bizarre. Before she'd arrived that morning, she'd assumed she'd audition on a stage, though she didn't know why she'd thought that. Instead, she'd read her lines in front of a long table with three people seated on the far side in an otherwise empty office space. She'd recognized Hubert Vaughn, but not the others. She'd been so nervous, so nervous, but she thought she'd done a decent job.

They'd waited in a cramped lobby to hear the results. One by one, the other people had been released, including Brittney.

Eventually, only Denise and Ella remained.

"I thought...I thought he was going to cast me in something. That I'd been good. I was taken back to this office. It was empty except for a table, a couple of chairs, and a sofa.

"It was just me and Vaughn. And of course I had Ella. I left her in her stroller by the door. She was sleeping. He told me how good I was, how I could make it in Hollywood. And then... he just...he was..."

She couldn't say it. But she could remember his words of praise. How amazing she was. How she could be a star. He had just the role for her.

And then he'd joined her on the sofa. Held her there.

Jon squeezed her hand. "Did he hurt you?"

She nodded, then shook her head. "Sort of. I didn't... All I could think was how I couldn't let Ella get hurt. Not that he would have... I wasn't thinking clearly, I guess. I didn't even... I didn't want her to hear me scream. I didn't want her to know. I tried to get away, but..."

Jon touched her shoulder, but she flinched and he dropped his hand.

She said, "I'm sorry. I don't mean—"

"You don't owe me an apology." His voice was gentle, soothing. "And then you left?"

It hadn't been quite that simple, but she didn't need to tell him the whole ugly story. "He gave me a card and told me I had a job if I wanted it. He'd written an appointment time on the back. Said to be there, that I'd be perfect for the role."

"That's why you left your family."

Her gaze snapped to Jon's. "No. Of course not. You think I wanted to go work for that...that...? No."

"Okay." He remained calm, though she saw something in his eyes that belied the rest of his face. "What happened?"

"I just...I couldn't forgive myself. I'd put my daughter in danger. I'd...cheated on Reid."

Jon angled back. "You didn't cheat, Denise. You were raped."

She flinched.

She hated that word.

"Right?" he asked. "Did I misunderstand—?"

"Yes. That's what... But I didn't know how to deal with it." She studied her lap, afraid to meet his eyes. "I felt like I'd betrayed my husband. I went to the casting call without telling him. I took our daughter without telling him. And then that happened. I put Ella in danger. I was with another man."

"You weren't—"

"I know. But at the time, I just...I couldn't process it. I couldn't deal with it. Vaughn made it out like...when it was over...like we'd done this thing together. Like...like I'd had a choice. And it was easier to think that I did. That I'd been in control, allowed it. That if I'd tried harder, I could have escaped. So I must have been in control."

"You couldn't have." The certainty in Jon's voice had her turning to him. "Maybe if you'd screamed, somebody would have come. But probably not. Because if he did that to you, then the people he was with were either gone—"

"Somebody led me to his office."

"—or complicit. Because Vaughn couldn't know if you were going to scream or not. And if you're saying you think all these victims were...assaulted? Then the people working for this piece of garbage had to know." He snapped his jaw shut, and a muscle ticked in his cheek. "I don't care how good of shape you were in, and..." He swore under his breath. "You'd just had a baby. Which means... There's no way you could have fought off a grown man. No way." The intensity in his gaze dared her to disagree with him.

"Okay."

"It wasn't your fault, Denise."

"I know. I mean...sometimes it's easy to let my thoughts...to forget that. He's the one who did something wrong. It's just that what happened that day led to everything else."

"But you didn't go to Hollywood to work for him."

"No. I stayed with Reid and Ella for another couple of months. I tried to get over it. I tried to be happy. But I couldn't make it work. I was so...off. Between the postpartum and then that, I couldn't function. After a while, I convinced myself everybody would be better off without me. So, I left."

CHAPTER NINETEEN

J on had two equally strong desires, and he couldn't act on either of them.

Because even if he knew where Hubert Vaughn was, he couldn't exactly hunt the guy down and kill him.

And Denise didn't seem in the frame of mind for him to take her in his arms and hold her. In fact, she looked as delicate as a soap bubble.

So he paced and tried to think.

Why would Vaughn be killing off his victims? Was he afraid one of the women would come forward? If one did, would the others do the same? That'd happened more than once in the previous few years. Famous men had been brought down by the women they'd abused.

Was that motivating this?

Why hadn't the other victims already outed Vaughn? Jon understood Denise's reasoning. She'd been depressed. Her daughter had been there, which would have added to her confusion and shame. Not that she'd done anything wrong.

The thought of little Ella in her stroller had his hands fisting.

What kind of man...?

No kind of man. A monster, not a real man. Real men protected women and children. They didn't take advantage of them.

In her state, Denise hadn't been strong enough to deal with it.

But why hadn't the others reported it, assuming they'd also been assaulted? Had he threatened them? Or was it something simpler? Something baser?

Denise could have gotten an acting job after that event. She hadn't. She'd stayed, tried to be the wife and mother her family needed. Tried to get over it. But had the other women made the same decision?

Or had they used the event to propel their careers?

He started to head for the office to figure out the answer to that question but caught sight of Denise, still staring out the window. Her mug was empty, so he refilled it with coffee and doctored it like he'd seen her do.

He approached slowly, trying not to startle her. "I thought you might like something warm."

She turned to him, quickly wiping moisture off her cheeks. He slid the mug onto the table in front of her, then snatched a napkin and handed it to her before he sat.

"Thanks."

"Sure."

She wiped her tears and sipped the coffee, her gaze flicking to his when she tasted it. "It's good."

"Are you all right?"

"Just thinking about what happens next."

"Meaning?"

"I'm going to have to tell Agent Frank, right? Once I do that, it'll only be a matter of time before the information is released. Everyone will know."

He hated to think about it, but she was probably right. Regular Janes and Joes got their privacy, but the same courtesy didn't extend to famous people.

"You have nothing to be ashamed of."

Though she didn't argue, the slight, unamused laugh told him she disagreed. "The point is, I need to confess to Reid soon. Immediately. Because once the police know, there's no telling how fast it'll come out. They'll hear. Ella will hear." Denise's voice cracked.

"I'm sorry, sweetheart."

He hadn't meant to add that last bit. Shouldn't have added it.

But she smiled that natural Denise smile he'd come to appreciate.

"In your research," he said, "did you happen to notice if the slayer's victims did what you did—if they rejected Vaughn's offer?"

"Oh." She tilted her head to the side, her dark hair fanning over her shoulder. He resisted the urge to brush it back. "I didn't."

"Would that be hard information to find?"

"Not at all. Easy, in fact. Let's just..." She stood and went to her laptop.

He was glad to see her moving, getting involved. It helped to have a task.

He followed to look over her shoulder while she navigated to a website called IMDb, typed in the first victim's name, then found her first acting job.

"Hmm..." Denise opened another browser and clicked around. "Here it is. Lauren Lahey's first acting job was a supporting role in *Perks of the Pep Squad,* which took place in"— Denise tapped the screen—"Alabama, where she's from. And there he is. Vaughn was the casting director."

She clicked through the other nine names. Though they weren't able to confirm them all, it seemed likely that most of the women's first jobs had been cast by Vaughn.

Denise turned to him, waving toward the screen. "What more evidence do you need? Obviously, he's trying to keep them quiet."

"Someone is," Jon said. "Do you remember the names of the other people who were with him at your casting...thing?"

"Why would one of them—?"

"Why would Vaughn? I'm not saying it's not him. I'm just not convinced. Guy like that, been getting away with it for years. He's probably arrogant."

"No *probably* about it."

"He thinks he got away with it. I mean, if I were Vaughn—"

"You're nothing like him."

"Okay, but if I were him, I'd have targeted you first. You're the one most likely to come forward with the truth because you didn't take him up on his offer. You have nothing to be ashamed of."

"Do you think they do?" The fire in Denise's eyes had Jon scrambling for an explanation.

"No, of course not. But wouldn't you feel a little like...like you'd..." He swallowed hard. "I mean, why didn't you?"

She opened her mouth, then snapped her jaw shut. "I had a family. And...yeah, okay. It's gross, almost like payment after the fact."

Exactly what he *hadn't* wanted to articulate.

"You have no idea how hard it is to break into the business," she said. "The...*thing*...had already been done, so why not take advantage of it? Why not get a job out of it?"

"Why not report it?"

"A nobody wannabe from Podunk, Nowhere, accusing a well-known, well-respected casting director of assault? He'd have claimed consent." Denise gestured toward the laptop as if the man in question stood there. "His word against hers. If he were even charged, he'd hire a great attorney and get off completely or with a slap on the wrist. Meanwhile, the victim would be blacklisted, her dreams of being an actor shattered. Publicly embarrassed. Do you have any idea how often this kind of thing happens? A big-name sports star attacks a woman. She presses charges. He writes a check. She shuts up. Not because she's weak or greedy but because she doesn't believe justice will be done. And will it? I mean..."

She paced away, then turned to face him. "Especially in a situation like that." She pointed at the screen. "Woman goes willingly into a room with a man, eager to please, to get a job. The judge and jury think she was trying to barter for what she wanted. Sleep her way to the top. Isn't that what men think women do?"

"Uh...not—"

"Or they think it's her fault. Even if they believe he forced her, they figure she should have known better. She walked into it. She had it coming. He gets acquitted, and she gets to live with the fact that she was stupid, and now everybody knows the greatest shame of her life."

Jon walked toward Denise slowly. "Okay. I see what you're saying."

"It's just...it's ugly." She looked at her feet, then up but beyond him. At anything but him. "And you feel...powerless. So, yeah, if you can turn it around, make something good come out of it, then you feel like you've taken back some of the power. You're in control. And then you tell yourself you let it happen because it's easier than believing you're that vulnerable. Because if you were that vulnerable once, then you probably still are. And it could happen again."

He understood that, at least to some degree. Lake and her

friends had been incredibly vulnerable—many injured, some assaulted—when he and his team had rescued them. How had Lake responded to that situation?

She'd become a bodyguard. She was the toughest woman he knew. She wasn't about to let evil people hurt her or anybody she cared for. Her reaction might have been different from Denise's, but it stemmed from the same place.

A wave of affection rose in Jon for his cousin, thinking of all she'd endured. And for this woman standing in front of him. He paused a foot from Denise, wanting more than anything to comfort her. But he wouldn't presume. Instead, he opened his arms.

She stepped into them, and he held her against his chest. "I'm sorry that happened to you."

He felt her nod, but she didn't speak, just rested there for a long moment. He breathed her in, this beautiful, frightened, amazingly honest woman.

Too soon, Denise glanced up at him shyly.

"Thank you for explaining that to me," he said. "I understand, I think, to the degree that I can."

"You're not exactly vulnerable, though."

"Yeah. But...I mean, we all are, really. I can be taken down by someone stronger. Or a bullet or an arrow or a car accident or a fall. I'm no superhero."

"Every superhero has his kryptonite."

"Thank you, Ember Flare."

Her smile was slight, but it was there. She stepped out of his arms and returned to the laptop. "Vaughn is the most obvious suspect."

He followed. "Okay, but maybe there's something else at play here. We need to call Frank."

She flinched.

Jon stopped beside her, pulling his cell from his pocket. "Denise?"

When she looked at him, her eyes were wide with fear.

"I can tell him, if you want me to."

She flicked her gaze to his phone as if it might bite. "I don't think I can do it."

"You want to stay and listen?"

She seemed to debate that, then slid onto one of the barstools. "He might need to ask me something. I'll stay."

This was one amazing woman. Not that he had any right to feel proud of her, but he did. He wrapped his hand around her upper arm and squeezed gently.

She aimed that pretty smile his way, and his heart thumped a war beat in his chest.

The woman she used to be—depressed, abused, insecure. Afraid to fight back, afraid of the truth...

That was not the woman who sat beside him now. She was changed. Strong. New.

He thought of something he'd read in the Bible recently—that God made a person new. Or...not God. Jesus. Though, if he wasn't mistaken, they were the same thing, or two different elements of the same being.

He considered himself to be intelligent, but he didn't understand.

In any event, maybe Denise's courage and strength, her *newness*, had something to do with God. And if that was the case, then maybe what she believed, what so many of the people he'd met in Coventry believed, was more than just a worldview with a bunch of rules.

Now wasn't the time to delve into that, but it definitely gave him something to think about later.

He dialed the CBI agent.

CHAPTER TWENTY

"You're sure you want to do this today?" Jon had already voiced the question once, so Denise didn't bother to answer.

It was midafternoon. The skies that morning had been beautiful, but thick clouds had moved in since then.

She was seated in the front passenger seat of the SUV. She'd wondered if Jon would keep his distance today. He'd probably planned to, but after the hours they'd researched together that morning, after everything she'd told him, after eating lunch and planning this excursion—after that hug—he seemed to have forgotten the way they'd left things the night before.

Behind them, the second SUV was filled with four bodyguards. Overkill if she'd ever seen it, but Jon had brought four bodyguards to Portsmouth as well, even though the other times she'd left the house, there'd only been Jon plus three. Whatever the reason, if it meant they could ride alone, the two of them, she'd take it.

Jon was stopped at the light on Main Street, watching her.

She appreciated his concern. The conversation with Agent Frank hadn't been easy. The man seemed utterly devoid of sympathy, battering her with questions until Jon jumped in with, "You treat all your victims like this? Or are you just ticked we figured it out and you didn't?"

At that, the CBI agent had apologized, even managed to feign kindness.

The guy didn't like actors, but that wasn't Denise's problem. At least he was taking their theories seriously.

"We'll bring Vaughn and his assistants in ASAP," Frank had said. "If the killer is any of them, we'll nail him."

Would they really, though? Vaughn wasn't stupid. He'd get a lawyer. He wasn't about to confess to murder.

If only she knew what would happen next. Her hands were clenched together in her lap, and she forced them to relax, closing her eyes. *Lord, You know exactly what's going on. Equip Agent Frank and the CBI to gather the evidence to arrest and hold Vaughn before anybody else gets hurt.*

"Denise?" When she opened her eyes, Jon said, "We can still turn around."

"No, no. I need to do this today, before the information is leaked."

"Frank promised it wouldn't be."

"It will be. Things like this never stay secret for long. Maybe not today, but it's just a matter of time. And if that's the case, then there's no sense putting it off."

She'd been putting it off for years. But one of the things she'd learned in rehab was the importance of doing the hard things instead of avoiding them. She was done avoiding.

The light turned green, but Jon was studying her and didn't notice.

"What?" she asked.

"You don't seem all that worried."

She nodded forward, and he hit the gas and turned.

"I'd already planned to tell them," she said. "I figure the

only way to clear the air between Reid and myself is to be honest about everything. I've known that for a long time."

It wouldn't be easy, but the best things in life were often found on the far side of *difficult* and *terrifying*.

Downtown Coventry was decked out for the holidays. Wreaths with bright red ribbons decorated the old-fashioned wrought iron streetlamps. Storefronts sported Christmas trees, garland, holiday vignettes. Greenery was draped on the benches that were interspersed on the sidewalk. Beside one, a couple of mechanical reindeer looked to be munching on the grass.

She heard a tune and cracked her window. Sure enough, one of the businesses was piping holiday music through hidden speakers, though she wasn't sure *Baby It's Cold Outside* was appropriate for the Christmas season.

The park and lake appeared at the far end of the road. The Christmas tree that had been the focus of Saturday's festival stood tall and proud against the gray sky. With its white lights glittering and its bright star on top, it shone in the low afternoon light.

It was beautiful.

But when Jon reached the end of the road and turned, Denise's stomach tightened.

She'd been thinking about doing this, praying about doing this, for years. But now that she was on her way...

Lord, help me.

He would. He'd get her through it.

It wouldn't hurt that she'd have Jon by her side too. She wouldn't be alone.

He turned down the long driveway and drove through the thick forest that opened up to a big tree-studded yard.

Reid had sold the little split-level he and Denise had bought after college, and he and Jacqui had built this place. Though Denise had offered to pay him alimony a few times over the years, he'd never accepted it, and he'd once told her that every penny she sent in child support went into a fund for Ella's future.

Reid had never wanted anything from Denise. Honestly, she was pretty sure after she left that he would have preferred if she'd never come home.

Though she didn't know how much money he made, she figured Jacqui's income had paid for at least half of his new house. It was two-story, stacked stone and brick, with a porch that looked like it wrapped all the way around. It was larger than most homes in town, she guessed four thousand square feet or more. Gorgeous.

Denise had always wanted to see inside, though she'd never been invited.

Today, she'd invited herself. It only seemed fair to have this conversation in a place where Reid felt comfortable.

Jon parked and, once all the bodyguards were in place, Denise headed for the porch. Before she'd climbed the steps, the bodyguard standing there stepped aside, and the front door swung open.

Jacqui smiled and beckoned her forward. "Come on in."

Denise stepped across the threshold, Jon on her heels, into a foyer that had to be twenty feet tall.

On one side, a curved staircase led to the second floor. On the other side, French doors opened to an office.

She could tell with a single glance it was Reid's office, and not just by the masculine decor. She recognized some of the books on the bookshelves, glimpsed multiple framed photographs of Ella and Reid's family. The mess scattered across his dark wood desk was the biggest giveaway.

Seemed some things never changed.

Jacqui took Denise's hand and gave it a quick squeeze. "I'm glad you're here."

"I'm sorry to pull you away from your work."

When Denise had called, Reid had told her Jacqui was at work and "too busy for your drama." But Denise had wanted Ella's stepmother to hear the story. She'd have to deal with it, just like the rest of them. It only seemed right that she hear it firsthand. So she'd texted Jacqui, who'd promised to be available.

Now, as Jacqui led the way across the hardwood floors and into a great room, she turned back and said, "There are some things more important than work."

Reid was in the kitchen pulling glasses from a cabinet. He turned and lifted his lips in what was probably supposed to be a smile, then frowned at Jon. It looked for a moment like he might question the man's presence, but he didn't. "We have water, tea, soda—"

"I'll take ice water," Denise said.

Jon positioned himself against the wall. "I'm good."

He'd insisted on coming inside with her because he didn't trust Reid enough to let her be alone with him. Silly, but she hadn't argued. She wished Jon would sit beside her, but he was in full-on bodyguard mode.

"Have a seat," Jacqui said.

She chose a pretty French provincial chair upholstered with a sage green-and-white *toile*. From her spot, she could see through the windows that covered the back wall and looked out over Lake Ayasha. Beyond the fenced-in yard, there was a little dock. Ella had told Denise about it, how she'd learned to dive right there, her father in the water, ready to catch her.

Denise let her gaze roam the room. It had personality. Color. The furniture wasn't all sleek and new but comfortably worn. A Christmas tree in the corner was covered in multicolored lights and red ribbon and mountains of ornaments.

Unlike Denise's place, everything about this home was cozy and livable. "Your house is beautiful."

"Thank you. Do you know Tabby McCaffrey? Formerly—"

"Eaton?" Denise asked.

"She decorated it for us."

"Oh, really? I need to call her. The person who did mine seemed more interested in creating a showroom than a home. All gray and white. It's blah."

Jacqui tilted her head to the side. "It's got a lot of potential, though."

That made Denise laugh. "You're very diplomatic."

Her laugh died as Reid set a glass on the table beside Denise, then sat next to his wife on a cream-colored sectional. He rested his arm against the back, the picture of casual. "What did you want to talk to us about?"

Apparently, the small talk portion of their visit was over.

Silently, Jon shifted to stand behind them and met Denise's eyes, giving her a *you've got this* look.

Thank God for him. She wasn't sure she'd be able to get through this by herself.

She took a deep breath and blew it out. "I need to tell you two things, things I should have told you a long time ago."

Reid said, "Go ahead."

Jacqui, kind soul that she was, leaned closer, almost as if to infuse Denise with courage.

"When Ella was kidnapped..."

Reid scowled, all pretense of hospitality gone. His arm came down, and he clasped his hands together.

"I was in rehab."

"You said you were in the hospital." The words were practically barked. "Which I never believed. No wonder... Rehab for what? Why didn't you—?"

"Reid." Jacqui patted his leg. "Let's let her talk."

He clamped his lips shut.

"I'd been drinking a lot." Denise's voice wavered, but she kept going. "And using some drugs. I got hooked. I almost killed myself one night. And maybe..." Maybe, on some level, she'd been trying to kill herself. But she didn't need to tell Reid that. "The point is, I realized I needed to make a change or I wouldn't survive. So, I checked myself into rehab."

"Why didn't you tell us?" Reid's tone was angry, demanding.

Jon glared at the back of his head.

"My contract with the studio has a morality clause. It's not that they care if their actors drink or use drugs, but they don't want that behavior to be public. I only told my agent. When I found out—"

"You should have come home," Reid said. "Do you have any idea—?"

"You need to stop talking." Jon's tone was low and angry.

Reid turned to face him. "I don't remember inviting you in."

"I go where she goes."

Reid turned back to Denise, but under his breath, he said, "I bet you do." The words were laced with innuendo.

Jon stepped closer, a murderous look in his eyes.

She wasn't sure what he was about to say or do, but she figured it wouldn't be good. "It's okay, Jon." To Reid, she said, "I'm trying to do the right thing here. It would really help if you'd behave yourself, maybe pretend to be a grown-up for ten minutes."

He started to speak, but Jacqui rested her hand on his arm. To Denise, she said, "We want to know the story. Go on."

Denise focused on the redhead, trying to ignore the scowling man at her side. "My agent had my phone when my mother called with the news. He came to the rehab center and told me what happened. I'd just gotten through detoxing. I decided to leave, was desperate to get back here. But my counselor said I wasn't strong enough to stay sober. And I...I fought her like crazy, I argued and cried. But she was right. I hadn't stayed sober an entire day for months. She told me that if I came home, I'd have to face all the judgmental looks and words I always dealt with here."

Reid opened his mouth to interrupt.

"Not that I didn't deserve them," she hurried to say. "But all that judgment didn't help. And that would be nothing compared to the fear of Ella being missing. My counselor laid out what would happen. I'd do my very best, but my best wouldn't cut it. Eventually, I'd fall off the wagon. Drink too much, pop a few pills, fall apart. And then you and our parents would have had to deal with me when all the focus needed to be on finding Ella. That would only cause strife and difficulty. Not only that, but the press would have made it all about me. The whole thing would all have become a media madhouse. It was Ella who needed everybody's focus, everybody's attention."

Reid's gaze was hard. "Since we both know you've never minded everything being about you, I'm guessing you were more worried your little addiction secret would have come out. You'd have lost your job."

Tears pricked her eyes. "Believe what you want, Reid. Nothing I say is going to change how you feel about me."

"You're right about that."

"Reid!" Jacqui's reprimand barely earned a glance from him.

Again, Denise focused on Jacqui. "I didn't do anything those days she was missing. I didn't go to the group sessions or see the counselor after she convinced me to stay. I didn't exercise. I didn't eat. I just sat in my room and cried and prayed and begged God...begged God to bring her home." Her voice cracked with emotion, but she didn't give in to the sobs trying to work their way out. She wouldn't. She turned back to her ex. "I know you don't understand. I'm sure you'll never understand, no matter what I tell you. But I love her. I've always loved her."

Again, Reid's mouth opened, but before he spoke, Jacqui said, "Be kind."

Behind him, Jon warned, "Be very careful."

Reid ignored them both. "You say you loved her. Some might argue that people who love *stay*."

"Remember, I told you I had two things to tell you."

"Let's hear it then." He nodded for her to continue.

This was where it got hard. Very hard. She prayed for help. For words. For Reid to stop loathing her long enough to listen.

And then peace brushed across her like a warm breeze, settled in her heart. She was still nervous, but she didn't need Reid's forgiveness or his acceptance. She was forgiven and accepted by the One who mattered.

"When Ella was two months old, I went to a casting call in Manchester. I took Ella with me. I wish... I wish I hadn't." She swallowed the emotion forming a lump in her throat.

Reid's eyes narrowed the slightest bit. "I don't remember that."

"I didn't tell you. I knew you'd be against it. You were so... frustrated with me because I wasn't... I couldn't be happy."

Reid's head dipped and rose, the slightest acknowledgment. "I didn't understand postpartum depression—what a big deal it can be. I've never dealt with depression, so maybe I wasn't as compassionate as I could have been. I just..."

When he didn't finish the sentence, Denise said, "You didn't know. I didn't understand either. We were so young."

Beside him, Jacqui slipped her arm under Reid's and gripped his hand.

Denise wished she had a hand to hold. Her gaze flicked to

Jon's. He didn't speak, but encouragement was clear in the way he looked at her, in the slight nod of his head.

"I did well," Denise said. "At the casting call. I was there with Brittney—you remember her?"

Reid nodded.

"She watched Ella when I auditioned, but then she was dismissed and left. Everybody else was dismissed until I was the only one left. And then..." Her voice shook. Her lower lip trembled until she clamped her mouth shut.

She needed to pull it together.

"I was...I was taken back. I assumed they wanted me to read again. I assumed all three of the people who'd been there before would be there again. I had Ella in a stroller, but she was sleeping. I thought it would be all right. But I was... There was this big Hollywood casting director, and it was just him and me. And he...he..."

She dropped her face into her palms and hid.

"He what?" Reid sounded furious. She was afraid to look at him. "He what!"

"I'm sorry. I never meant... I was... Ella was there, and I was so scared. I'm sorry. I'm sorry. I just..."

She couldn't say the words. She didn't want to say them, not to this man who loathed her so much. She tried to force them out of her mouth, but they were lodged in her throat, holding in the sob that wanted to escape.

Cool fingers slid against her upper arms and squeezed gently. "You don't owe anybody an apology." Jacqui had crouched near, her kindness a whisper in Denise's hair. "He hurt you?"

She nodded, and the sobs escaped.

"That wasn't your fault," Jacqui said.

Denise peeked to find Jacqui looking at her with tears in her eyes.

"I'm so sorry that happened to you."

A couple of tissues appeared in her line of vision, and she looked up to see Jon beside her chair.

She took the tissues and wiped her cheeks.

"Do you want to keep going?" Jacqui asked.

She nodded. "I need to explain it all."

Jacqui settled on the floor beside her and took her hand. The small act of solidarity brought a fresh round of tears.

Jon's palm rested on her shoulder.

Finally, she faced Reid again.

He was still seated on the sofa. He looked stunned. "Why didn't you tell me?" His voice was a whisper.

"I was afraid that you'd..." She took another breath. "That you'd be angry with me for putting Ella in that position. You loved her so much. And that was good, of course. I loved her too. But after she was born, it was like...like I no longer mattered. I mean, I know that's not true. It was just, in the depression, it was how I felt. And things were so hard between us. So...strained."

Reid didn't react, didn't move. Just stared at her with those eyes she'd once loved.

"Maybe you would have reacted well," she said. "I don't know. It wasn't fair that I didn't give you the chance to prove me wrong. I know that. But I was afraid. If I told you what happened, and you got mad at me, or you blamed me—which would have been...I mean, I shouldn't have gone to the casting call in the first place."

He squinted and angled back.

She braced for an attack, but he said nothing.

"I shouldn't have taken Ella with me. Obviously. I should have just... But if you'd reacted with more worry for Ella's well-being than mine... I just... I didn't think I could take that. So it seemed easier not to tell you. But I couldn't get over it. I tried. I really tried. But after a while, between the depression and then that, and our marriage was so...hard. I started to think everybody would be better off without me."

She sniffed, took a deep breath, wiped her eyes.

"I shouldn't have left," she said. "I should have stayed and worked harder, tried harder. I should have seen a counselor. I should have told you the truth. I'm sorry I didn't. I'm sorry it's taken me eight years. I hope you can forgive me."

Reid stood. He didn't move, just looked down at her. There was a look in his eyes she'd never seen before. It wasn't anger or rage or even sadness. He looked...stricken.

And then he walked out.

Just like that.

Jacqui popped to her feet. "Reid!"

"Just one minute." His words trailed him as he marched away.

A door slammed.

Jacqui stared after him.

Jon crouched down beside Denise. "Are you all right?"

She was. She might have wished for a different reaction from her ex, but she hadn't expected one. In fact, she'd sort of expected him to yell at her or call her a liar. Maybe she should be thankful he'd walked away.

"I'm all right. I guess we should just go."

"Give him time," Jacqui said.

Jacqui gave Reid a lot more credit than he deserved, but Denise could wait. She'd done the hard part. It wouldn't hurt to linger a few minutes.

Jon held out the water Reid had set beside her. "Better have a few sips. I'm afraid you're going to get dehydrated—all that crying." His voice held a hint of amusement. He was trying to make her smile.

She liked that. "Thanks." She sipped, more thirsty than she'd realized.

They stayed like that—Jacqui kneeling on one side, Jon standing on the other, all three silent—for minutes that dragged forward like heavy boots through thick mud.

Denise started to count. Sixty more seconds and then she was leaving.

She was halfway there when the sound of a door opening had Jon and Jacqui looking.

Reid was coming back.

Jacqui stood and backed away.

Jon didn't move.

Denise steeled her courage and set the glass on the table. Whatever he had to say to her, she could take it. She felt prepared for his anger or even his cold dismissal.

But he dropped to his knees in front of her. His eyes were filled with tears. He reached toward her but didn't take her hands, just held his there. An invitation.

She slid her palms against his.

He looked toward the ceiling, clearly trying to get his emotions under control.

That gesture had new tears filling her eyes.

And then he looked at her. "I am so sorry."

"You didn't—"

"It's my turn to talk." He attempted a smile, but it didn't hold. "All these years, I've hated you when really, if I'd been half the husband I should have been, none of it would have happened. I mean...maybe the thing with the"—he pressed his lips together, swallowed—"the monster at the casting call. But if I'd been supportive, you could have told me. You could have trusted me to have your back. If I'd tried harder to understand what you were going through, maybe..." He shook his head. "Maybe we could have gotten through it together."

Sobs rose from deep within her.

Reid pulled her close. "I'm sorry. I'm so sorry."

She laid her head on his shoulder, feeling known and understood for the first time in eight years. Because he'd been her husband. Her best friend. He'd promised to love her and honor her, and then he'd loathed her.

And now they were past it.

He leaned back to face her. "Can you forgive me?"

"I forgave you a long time ago, Reid. Can you forgive me?"

He nodded but couldn't seem to speak as he pulled her in again.

They stayed like that a long time, crying. Remembering. Forgiving.

She didn't want Reid back, not as a husband. But now that he understood, now that he'd forgiven her, it felt like they'd come full circle. They'd started out as friends way back in kindergarten. Maybe they could be friends again.

Even better. Maybe they could be family.

CHAPTER TWENTY-ONE

Jon hadn't thought the idiot ex-husband had it in him.

But Reid had surprised him.

Shocked him.

Never had he seen a transformation like that, seen a man go from hate-filled and judgmental to gentle and humble.

Denise and Reid had ended their hug after a few moments, both laughing awkwardly and wiping their eyes.

Now they were discussing when Denise would be able to see Ella again. Wednesdays didn't work because there was some potluck at the church the Cotes attended every week, and Reid didn't want her to miss it.

"I think she'd choose you over it," he said quickly, "but she does really enjoy it."

Denise, Reid, and Jacqui were standing around the wide marble island in the kitchen.

Jon had resumed his spot against the wall. Now that he knew Reid wasn't a threat, he could excuse himself outside. But he'd promised to stay through this with Denise, and he would keep his promise, even if she no longer needed him.

"Maybe you could come to the potluck," Jacqui said. "I bet Ella would love to see you there."

"Oh." Denise looked at Reid, a question in her eyes.

The man nodded, though the gesture came slowly, as if he'd wrestled with his response. "Cassidy and James usually come, and other people you'll remember. You're welcome, of course."

Denise perked up and looked Jon's way.

"We can make it work," he said. "But be warned. We'll stick very close."

She gave him a look he read as *you're such a buzzkill* and turned back to Jacqui. "In other words, I'll have three oversize shadows everywhere I go."

Jon cleared his throat. "Four."

She chuckled, shaking her head. "I think, I hope, that the police are close to figuring out who the Starlet Slayer is. And we might even have an idea who the local shooter is."

Jon had neglected to mention that James had found the name of the kid who'd been obsessed with her. That might lead to something. Might not.

Denise continued. "So maybe it would be best for me to wait until those threats are managed before Ella and I are together in public."

Did Reid's shoulders relax the slightest bit? Jon had to hand it to the guy. He was trying.

"I would prefer that," Reid said.

"Except for Friday night." Jacqui said the words to Reid, then turned to Denise. "You are going to the school play, right?"

"Oh. Is that this Friday? Ella mentioned it but didn't tell me when. I figured she'd have lots of rehearsals leading up to it."

Reid chuckled. "It's not Broadway. I think they rehearse during music class."

"Oh. Right." Denise smiled, shaking her head. "It's been a long time since third grade."

"It's in the high school auditorium," Jacqui said. "Ella is thrilled that you're going to be there." She shifted to face Reid. "We don't want her to be disappointed."

"Of course not." To Denise, Reid said, "You should come."

That elicited one of Denise's true smiles. "Definitely." She glanced at Jon, who nodded. They'd make it work.

"I'd like to see her before then, though. How about tomorrow?"

"You want to pick her up from school?"

They hashed out the details and then headed for the front door. Denise hugged Jacqui and squeezed Reid's hand before walking among the bodyguards to the SUV parked in the circular drive.

Jon was about to follow when Reid said, "Can I talk to you?"

He watched until Denise was safely in the front seat, then tapped his comm. "Stand guard. Be right there."

The guys stood outside the car, facing the quiet forest all around.

"I'll be in the lab." Jacqui kissed Reid's cheek and walked away. She stepped through a door beneath the staircase, which must have led to the basement.

When she was gone, Reid said, "I can't imagine what you think of me."

"Sure you can."

Reid chuckled. "Okay, yeah. You haven't exactly kept your opinions to yourself."

Jon said nothing, unsure where this conversation was going.

"That first day, when Denise was shot at, you accused me of being a hypocrite or a liar. I'm neither, not as a rule, anyway, but I'm not perfect. I have issues I need to work on—big issues. As you well know."

Truth was, Jon had imagined Reid's reaction to Denise's news a few different ways. He'd never imagined what he'd seen today. He wasn't sure if he believed it. Had all of that been for Jacqui's benefit? The guy obviously cared what his wife thought of him.

But he'd kneeled at Denise's feet. He'd shed tears. Actual tears. Which made Jon think he'd been sincere. Which seemed...incredible.

Jon wasn't about to say any of that.

"You said you've been studying Christianity?"

Reid's question surprised him. "A little. I'm curious."

"I just wanted to tell you not to judge Christ by my behavior. He's good and loving and forgiving. He's perfect, and He calls us to be like Him. Sometimes, we're not very good at it. Most of the time, in my case. But that's the thing about God. He loves us anyway." Reid looked at the ceiling for a long moment. When he faced Jon again, his eyes were watery. "The Lord's been telling me to forgive her for eight years, and for eight years, I've disobeyed Him. That's not His fault, it's mine. I just...I don't want to be the reason you reject God. I've been a jerk where Denise is concerned. And an idiot, and stubborn and... Anyway, don't look at *me*." He pointed upward. "Look at *Him*."

Reid had hovered pretty low on Jon's *deserving respect* scale. His behavior for most of the conversation with Denise hadn't urged him higher. Until the very end. He'd walked away, then come back a new person, humbling himself in front of a woman he'd despised for a long time.

That had moved the man up on the scale.

Now, he'd humbled himself in front of Jon. That moved him a little higher.

"Can I ask you a question?"

Reid nodded, obviously wary.

"What did you do, earlier, when you walked away?"

"My first inclination was to accuse her of making the whole

thing up. If Jacqui hadn't been here, I'm ashamed to say I might've."

Good thing Jacqui'd been there, because if Reid had accused Denise of lying, Jon would've throttled him. Then Reid would've ended up in the hospital, and Jon would've ended up in handcuffs.

"Instead, I came back here"—he nodded to his office—"to pray. The second my knees hit the floor, I knew Denise was telling the truth."

"How?"

His shoulders lifted and fell. "God knows the truth. He just filled me with...certainty, I guess. And conviction for all the ways I've disobeyed Him where Denise is concerned. I can't explain it."

Huh. Jon had read enough of the Bible to understand there was a Spirit who was like God, or maybe *was* God. That had something to do with the trinity, a word he'd heard but not found in the Bible. He was still trying to figure that out.

Maybe the Spirit had told Reid?

It all felt very woo-woo and weird.

But the evidence was there.

Jon couldn't imagine what it would be like to hear from God, but he could see the results. Reid had walked away unsure and angry. Five minutes later, he'd walked back completely different. Humble. Contrite. Forgiving.

Jon had never seen such a transformation.

"That gives me something to think about," Jon said.

"If you ever want to talk about anything or...whatever. I doubt you'd want to talk to me, but I have a lot of friends who are better at the Christian walk than I am. I could hook you up."

"Okay."

Reid chuckled. "You don't talk much, do you?"

He did, sometimes. He had the night before with Denise.

But right now, there were too many questions in his head to get much to come out of his mouth.

Reid stuck out his hand. "I hope we can be friends. Or at least civil to each other as long as you're around."

Jon only hesitated a moment before he shook it. "Let's agree to civil."

Reid smiled. "I'll work on the friends thing."

Jon walked out, shaking his head.

Denise and Reid and Jacqui. This summer, Josie and Thomas.

There was something really bizarre about these people. Bizarre and...good.

His guys moved to the second SUV, and Jon slipped into the driver's seat of the first. He figured Denise might want to talk, or process, or cry. She certainly didn't need an audience for any of that.

"What was that about?" she asked as he got settled next to her.

Jon wasn't sure how to explain the conversation, and he wasn't sure he should. "He just wanted to clear the air."

"Is it clear then?"

Her makeup had been wiped away with the tears. Only the mascara remained, framing those dark blue eyes that drew him in. She looked...lighter. Happier. She radiated joy.

Everything in him wanted to take her in his arms and tell her how proud he was of her. How amazing she was. How beautiful.

Instead, he shifted into gear. "We've agreed to be civil."

"Wow, such strides."

He chuckled and drove out the long driveway.

He waited for her to say something, to go over the conversation, to ask him his opinion. But she didn't.

She might not want his take on what'd happened, but he

wanted to share it. "I know I have no right to feel this way, but I'm proud of you. What you did back there, facing him and all his anger... It was impressive."

"Jacqui made it easier."

"She seems really nice. I can't figure out how she ended up with him."

"Reid is a good man, and I abandoned him with an infant and never told him why. He had reason to hate me."

Jon could almost see what she meant.

"I'm glad *you* were there," Denise said.

The road by the lake was winding, but he risked a glance. She was staring at him.

"I did nothing."

"You gave me courage. You were my support."

"Oh, well..." He'd hoped to be helpful. Apparently, he'd succeeded.

He turned at the park and drove through town. It was all fancied up for Christmas. All they needed was snow, and it would be a perfect setting for the holidays.

Denise cracked the window, and the notes of *Hark! The Herald Angels Sing* filled the car.

He felt buoyant enough that he had to restrain himself from singing along.

Denise showed no such restraint, despite her terrible voice. Maybe she couldn't carry a tune, but her joy more than made up for it.

The music faded, and she raised the window as he turned onto Rattlesnake Road.

"Now that Reid doesn't hate me," Denise said, "I can make my home here. I mean, the threats have to be taken care of, but assuming that's managed, assuming Vaughn is caught and stopped, assuming we catch the guy who wants me gone..." Her words faded. She sighed. "That's a lot of assumptions."

"Have faith."

"Faith, huh?" Her voice carried amusement, a bit of a challenge.

Maybe he should have chosen a different word. He meant faith in the police, in himself, not faith in God.

But maybe faith in God wouldn't hurt.

"Anyway," she said, "once the threats are taken care of, I can have a real life here."

"That's what you want?"

"More than anything."

Her words buoyed his spirits even more. If she stayed, and if she wanted to, they could continue to get to know each other, see if there could be something between them besides friendship. Maybe his initial feelings had been right—that they were too different, that their lives were too different. But maybe he'd been wrong.

Maybe, if she stayed in New Hampshire, they could...

What?

Fall in love? Get married?

Was he ridiculous to even let his mind go there?

Probably.

But he liked her. More than liked her. He felt more for Denise than he'd felt for any woman, ever. Which didn't make any sense. He hadn't known her long enough. But he'd seen her at her worst. He'd seen her scared. He'd seen her angry. He'd seen her confident. Brave. He'd seen her as a mother, an ex-wife, a friend. He'd seen enough to know the kind of woman she was.

And he liked what he'd seen.

Not because she was *Denise Masters, movie star.*

Because she was kind, forgiving, courageous, and honest.

This line of thinking had his heart rapid-firing. "What about the movies? Your job?"

"I'll have to travel for filming, of course. A month or two at a time, depending on how big my role is. And then for press junkets. But lots of actors don't live in LA."

"They don't live in New Hampshire, either."

"It's a long flight. But I could—"

A muffled crack came an instant before the SUV lurched.

He gripped the wheel and managed to stay on the pavement, but it was...slippery?

What the—?

Another crack, and the SUV lurched a second time.

Those cracks. Gunshots.

"Get down!" It was bulletproof glass, but better to be cautious. He wouldn't pull over here. It wouldn't be safe.

But the SUV was slipping, sliding. He turned the wheel, but the two remaining tires found no purchase. He hit the brakes, desperate to slow down, to keep the vehicle from careening off the road and crashing into a tree.

They slid off the pavement. The tires gripped the dirt, and he managed to bring the vehicle to a stop.

Beside him, Denise pressed a hand to her chest. "Thank God we're okay."

Voices in his ear. "What happened?"

"Somebody's shooting!"

He tapped his comm. "Quiet. Pull close."

He waited for another gunshot, but none came. The shooter was there, somewhere. Moving into better position?

If Jon could, he'd drive another couple hundred yards on the flat tires, get farther away.

But the road was slick, despite the lack of rain and snow that day. Had the shooter poured water on it? The air was cold enough to freeze it. Between the two blowouts and the ice, Jon hadn't had a chance. With only two tires, they wouldn't get far.

He closed his eyes to think. "Shots came from the left. Agreed?"

Grant said, "Agreed."

Hughes and Marcus echoed him.

This was the reason he and Bartlett preferred to hire former special forces. They knew what they were doing.

"Arm up. Grant, after Ian moves, you, Hughes, and Marcus slip out the right. Stay out of sight. Get into the woods and back-track until you can cross. Get behind him."

"Copy." Grant was in full-on warrior mode.

"Ian, when I say, get out and run to this car. Be seen, and then stay low. Don't get shot." While he talked, he dialed his second team leader.

"Copy." But Ian's voice wasn't nearly as confident. He'd been infantry, so he was trained, but not like the rest of them. And he was young, their newest hire.

"Hold tight. Hughes, call 911."

While Hughes acknowledged the order, team two's leader, Jones, answered Jon's call. "What's—"

"We're under attack. Three miles down Rattlesnake. Careful approach. Road is slick. Come and get Ms. Masters to safety."

"Copy." The man ended the call.

Beside Jon, Denise said, "I'm not leaving you here!"

He ignored her, climbed into the back seat, then into the cargo area. The hidden compartment was meant to be opened from outside the tailgate, but he managed to get the lid lifted.

There were a lot of options in his weapons cache. He chose his favorite, a Browning rifle with a Vortex scope.

He spoke into his comm. "Ready?"

Grant said, "Ready."

Jon climbed into the backseat. "Denise, I need you to move into the driver's seat."

She turned to him. Her face was white. "Why?"

Would she ever follow the rules? Already, two minutes had passed since the second shot. "Do as I say. Now."

She hopped over the console.

"The vehicle is bullet proof. Stay inside. After Ian gets in, keep the doors locked, and you'll be safe."

Fear was etched on her features. "What about you?"

He smiled. "Don't worry about us. This is the fun part." He tapped his comm. "Now."

In the rearview, he saw Ian hop out of the vehicle. He stood tall enough that, from his spot on the hillside to their left, the shooter would be able to see him. He left his door open, then crouched and bolted to Jon's SUV.

While he moved, Grant, Hughes, and Marcus slipped out and into the woods.

Ian climbed in the front passenger seat.

"You good?" Jon asked.

"Yup."

"Team's coming. Stay with her, get her back to the house and inside."

"Copy."

"Wait!" she said. "I'm not leaving you here."

He met her eyes. "You know the drill. Do what you're told. We'll be fine." Before she could argue, he slipped out of the car. He dashed up the street about ten yards, then bolted straight across toward where he guessed the shooter was holed up.

Unlike his men, Jon wanted to be seen.

No gunshots. Strange.

He moved into the woods and started up a steep incline.

Once he was out of earshot of the SUV, he switched his comm so he wouldn't have to tap it to communicate with his guys. "Two things." He kept his voice low. "One, you're all skin and bones—no vests, no helmets. Don't get shot."

They echoed, "Copy."

"Two, this isn't a kill mission. We're in the US of A. You shoot him without being fired on, you go to jail."

"Copy."

Jon's three teammates were hurtling through the woods to get behind the shooter. He'd approach slowly, from the front, try to keep the guy's focus on him.

Considering there'd been no shots after the second one, he guessed the shooter was long gone. This had probably been another scare tactic. But maybe not. Maybe he'd decided to wait for Denise to show herself so he could take her out.

Jon hoped for the second. If the guy was still in the woods, then he and his men would catch him and put an end to this.

He crept forward silently, listening.

Felt like he was being watched, telling him the guy hadn't run.

He kept his gaze, and his rifle, moving as he scanned the forest, the trees overhead, the brush at his knees.

Where are you?

Seconds ticked by. A minute.

Then, Grant said, "Found a four-wheeler."

The shooter was close. Jon could feel it. Rather than risk being overheard, he tapped his ear piece twice to acknowledge.

The guys would disable the vehicle, cutting off the shooter's escape. Their chances of catching this guy had just improved drastically.

So had their chances of getting shot.

He kept moving, kept listening.

Then, someone bolted through the forest just over the next rise.

Jon ran that direction, but by the time he got there, he couldn't see anything.

It was silent again.

"Any sign?" Grant asked.

He whispered, "Moving north parallel to the road."

He hated that he couldn't be more specific.

"Four-wheeler is due west."

Jon tapped the comm again.

Something wasn't right.

The guy should be headed toward his escape. If he knew Jon was following, armed, he should be trying to get out of there. If he'd seen the men, then he should have been running from the start.

Which meant this guy either thought he was too good to get caught, or he didn't care if he was.

In other words, he was either stupid, or he had nothing to lose.

And considering he hadn't been caught yet, he wasn't stupid. Which meant...

Jon cursed.

"What?" Grant asked.

Jon turned back toward where he'd left Denise. He had a bad feeling the target had made himself heard on purpose. And then backtracked silently.

It was what Jon would have done were the situation reversed. Lead the enemy in the wrong direction.

"Back," he commanded. "Now."

"Copy."

He moved quickly, silently, through the woods, taking the shortest distance to where he'd left Denise.

There, just at the top of the hill that edged the road, a man crept behind a tree. He wore camouflage pants and jacket, a black hat, black boots.

The way he moved, the way he'd planned this... No question this guy was military, if not special forces.

Which meant that Jon had to be very careful. Because the

last thing he wanted was to kill the guy. Behind bulletproof glass, Denise would be safe.

Terrified, but safe.

Moving closer, he got the target in his sights. "Today is not a good day to die."

He hoped the shooter would freeze.

Instead, the man ducked and rolled down the hill toward the road.

Jon bolted that direction and scrambled down the hill after him.

Any second, the shooter would lift the rifle and aim at Denise behind the window.

She saw him coming and stared, frozen.

But the guy shifted the gun to one hand and reached into his pocket.

What did he have hidden there?

Jon wasn't about to wait and find out.

He tackled him. Yanked the rifle from his hands and tossed it aside. His forearm pressed into the back of the guy's neck, pushing his face into the slippery asphalt. He yanked his right hand behind his back.

The guy fought, but for all his skills, he wasn't that strong.

"I got him. Little help?" To the shooter, he said, "Stop fighting or you'll wake up in the hospital."

The man went limp.

Just like that.

Ian rounded the car.

"Get the cuffs."

Ian said, "Copy."

The rest of his team arrived. Together, they bound the guy with zip-tie restraints. Jon searched him.

He wouldn't think about the grenades he pulled out of the

pockets of the guy's jacket. He wouldn't think about what could have happened.

Jon handed them to Grant, then stood and brushed himself off.

The car door opened, and Denise stepped out.

"Get back in the car!" He didn't want her anywhere near this guy or the dangerous things he'd brought.

She obviously hadn't seen because she ignored Jon, approaching the man who'd tried to kill her.

Jon gripped her upper arm. "Please, Denise."

The shooter turned her way, and a look of pain flashed in his eyes.

"What did I do to you?" she asked.

"You killed my son."

She backed up a step, another. "I don't... Who is your son?"

"Landon." The man's voice hitched on the name. "He loved you. He *helped* you, and you ignored him. You *ignored him!*" He hurled the words like rocks.

The second team arrived from the house, and Jon could hear sirens coming up Rattlesnake.

Denise looked so shocked, so...lost.

He leaned close. "His name was Landon McLaughlin. He's the kid who changed your tire."

She shot Jon an accusatory look.

"James called last night. The cops were supposed to check him out."

"Can't check him out," the older man said. No wonder he'd been weak. He looked to be in his sixties. "He's dead. Killed himself. Because of *you!*"

All color leached from Denise's face.

Jon wanted to comfort her, but first he needed to get her off the street and to safety. He slid a hand around her waist and walked her carefully over the black ice to the SUV waiting just beyond the slippery area. "Go with Jones and the team. I'll be there soon."

"It's my fault?"

He leaned close, lowered his voice. "No, sweetheart. It's not your fault some random kid killed himself. Just because the guy blames you, that doesn't make it your fault. Go with Jones, and I'll see you when we're done here."

One of his guards stepped out of the back seat, and she slid into the center. Looked like they'd brought reinforcements, probably hoping to get in on the action. But the action had been finished before they'd arrived.

"See you soon."

Jon tried not to notice the concerned looks on his teammates faces just before he returned to the shooter and arriving police.

Because they'd been shot at?

Because of Denise's obvious distress?

Or because he was still on comm...and he'd called her sweetheart.

CHAPTER TWENTY-TWO

Denise paced her living room, glancing out the front window every time she passed it.

The bodyguards had brought her home and escorted her to her door, despite the fact that she'd asked—nicely, she might add —to be taken to the police station.

"Take it up with Donley."

Jon, who wasn't even there.

"Sit tight," one of them said.

Sit tight.

She needed to talk to Jon, to find out what was going on. She'd called Detective Pollard, but he hadn't been available to take her call. Some very nice woman had promised he'd get back to her as soon as possible.

Which wasn't true, obviously. Because it was *possible* for him to call her now. He just wasn't doing it.

She needed to go to town. She needed to talk to that man who'd shot at their car. She needed to know what he was talking about.

Landon McLaughlin. The name wasn't even familiar, though Jon said he was the kid who'd changed her tire.

His father blamed her for his death?

Why?

Because she'd ignored him?

She dialed Bruce.

"How you holding up?"

"Did I ever get a letter from a kid named Landon McLaughlin?"

"Uh... I don't know. Maybe?"

"Can you check?"

He sighed. "It's not like we catalog your fan mail."

"This kid changed my tire for me a few years ago. He's from here, Coventry." Or so she assumed.

"What was his name again?"

"Landon McLaughlin." She spelled the last name for him.

"Actually, that does sound familiar. I can look. You want to hold, or should I call you back?"

"I'll wait."

She set the phone on her bar and put it on speaker. After fixing herself a cup of tea, she started working on building a fire, mostly to give her hands something to do. She wouldn't light it, though. Not yet.

"Denise?"

She snatched the phone. "I'm here. What'd you find?"

"Landon McLaughlin's the guy who was sending you those, er, suggestive letters. The kid who told you how much he loved you and all the ways he wanted to, er, show you, if you know what I mean."

"Oh." She remembered.

His letters hadn't been over-the-top explicit, though they'd been bad enough. Back when she opened all her own fan mail, she'd gotten used to that. But Landon's letters had creeped her out for another reason. He'd been specific about little things on Denise's body, like the strange freckle on the back of her right hand. The way the skin above her nose wrinkled when she was puzzled or upset. The coconut scent of her shampoo.

How had he known those things?

Now she understood. He'd known because they'd met in person. They'd spent a little time together. Just a few minutes, but it had been enough for Landon to become fixated on her.

His letters were the reason she'd started having Bruce and his people screen her fan mail.

"What about him?" Bruce asked.

She didn't want to get into it with Bruce. "I'll explain later." She ended the call and resumed pacing. She knew Jon wanted her to wait for him, but now that Landon's father was in custody, she wouldn't be in danger.

She headed for the front door, snatching her keys on the way. She'd drive herself, if need be. She yanked it open, earning a surprised look from the guard who stood there.

Jones, she remembered. He was probably early thirties, dirty blond hair pulled back in a ponytail, thick brown caterpillar eyebrows that lowered over wide hazel eyes.

"I need to get to the police station."

"Donley will be back soon. You can discuss it with him."

"He can meet me there if he wants to."

"Just sit tight." He turned back around, dismissing her.

"I'll drive myself." She stepped outside, passing him as she descended the steps to her walkway.

"Ma'am, you need to—"

"You can either drive me, or I'll drive myself." She marched down her driveway. "Those are your options."

He kept in step behind her. "Boss, client's on the move... Police station, she said." He paused, then, "I'll tell her."

Denise figured she was about to get reprimanded. That day, she'd relived the worst thing that had ever happened to her, twice. She'd withstood Reid's anger and cruelty, which hadn't been easy even if it had ended well. She'd been shot at, left in a car with a virtual stranger, and accused of being the cause of some kid's death.

She could handle Jon's reprimand.

Her phone rang just as she reached the detached garage behind the house.

She punched in the code to raise the door, then took the phone from her pocket. "Yes?"

"What are you doing?" Jon didn't sound amused.

"I want to talk to that man. I need to know—"

"You don't *need* to do anything. You need to sit—"

"If you tell me to sit tight, I'm hanging up."

That was followed by a beat of silence. His voice lowered, and she guessed he was trying not to be overhead. "Denise, you don't need to be here."

"You're at the police station?"

"Answering questions. Please, just stay where you are."

"I want to talk to McLaughlin. I need to."

"Why?"

"Either tell your guys to bring me, or I'm driving myself. Don't think I won't."

She heard Jon's deep inhale, then long exhale. "You promised to do as I told you. Remember? If I say duck, you duck. If I say—"

"He's in custody. I'm happy to *obey you* when my life's in imminent danger. It's not right now."

After a long pause, Jon said, "Fine. Just do as they say. McLaughlin's in custody, but the Starlet Slayer is not. You're not safe."

She ended the call and faced Jones. Only when she turned did she realize the rest of the team had joined him. She was surrounded by overlarge bodies wearing concerned faces. "Let's go."

~

When she arrived at the police station, Denise was escorted to a private office, where she waited, alone and not-so-patiently, for someone to take her to the man who'd shot at her. Four bodyguards hovered beyond the glass as if every cop in the building had it out for her.

Finally, a sixty-something heavyset man stepped in. "Ms. Masters. I'm Chief Cote." He held out a meaty hand, and she stood and shook it.

"We've met. You're Reid's uncle, right?"

His nod was crisp. "I understand you want to talk to McLaughlin?"

"As soon as possible, please."

He ran his hand over cropped gray hair. "Can I ask why?"

"He holds me responsible for his son's death."

Cote nodded. "Ayuh. But the thing is, the kid killed himself. There's no reason for you to blame yourself."

"I don't blame myself. But there's a reason he blames me. I'd like to know what it is."

He tilted his head to one side. "Why?"

It was a valid question, and she gave it a little thought before replying. "Because his son is dead. He's obviously hurting. Maybe if he tells me why, it'll help him. Maybe he just needs to be heard."

"All due respect, ma'am, I don't see how he's your problem. The guy shot at you three times. If I were you, I'd be demanding his prosecution, not a chat."

"You're not me."

The chief's jaw lowered, then snapped shut. "You got me there. Though I did do a bit of acting back in school. Played Colonel Pickering in *Pygmalion*."

She forced a smile she didn't feel. "I'm sure you missed your calling."

"Not even close." He looked past her, out the window and beyond the bodyguards stationed there, toward the cops buzzing about. "This—police work—this is my calling, and I'm pretty good at it." His gaze found her again. "What do you know about him?"

"Nothing. His son changed a tire for me once."

"Right. Landon McLaughlin. Kid was disturbed. He had four suicide attempts that we know of. Three of them landed him in a mental hospital—two when he was still a juvenile. Meaning, he had issues long before he met you."

She thought back to the young man she'd met. He'd been kind and friendly. He'd seemed perfectly fine. But people weren't always what they seemed.

And she'd been high, so her judgment had been impaired.

"His fourth attempt," Cote said. "Well, you know how that turned out. We learned last night that your bodyguard suspected Landon of the shootings. 'Course we also knew Landon couldn't have done it, but Kenneth McLaughlin's had his share of issues. He was in the service. Honorably discharged after an injury. Coming home... It's not always easy to slide back into a normal life. His wife left him years ago, taking Landon with her. My understanding is that they had a good relationship, saw each other often."

"How do you know so much about them?"

"Told you. We got the call last night suggesting Landon might be behind the shootings. We figured the father was the next best guess, so we tried to find him. No luck, but we tracked down his wife. She tells us that after Landon's death, Kenneth retreated from the world. Started making threats toward people who rubbed him the wrong way. Not sure about all of it, but I'm guessing mental illness runs in the family. This morning, we discovered that he works for Rossi Properties. Not full time, but it looks like he's one of the guys who got your house ready for you. We already figured him for our guy when we got the call about the shooting."

"So he probably has some mental illness." At Denise's remark, Cote nodded. Before he could speak, she continued. "But he's also a hurting father who lost his son. I just want to talk to him, give him the opportunity to say what he needs to say to me. It won't cost me anything."

"Not sure what good would come of it."

"Would any *bad* come of it?"

He stared at her a long moment. "S'pose not."

"Okay, then."

Cote rubbed his lips together, looking like he wanted to say something else. But then he gestured to the open door. She stepped out, and he led the way.

On the far side of the small room, Jon was seated at a desk speaking to Detective Pollard. He caught sight of her and stood. She could tell by the scowl that he wasn't happy to see her.

That wasn't her problem, either. None of these men needed to understand why she felt compelled to speak to McLaughlin. She wasn't even sure herself except that the intensity of it pounded in her chest.

Cote stopped in front of a closed door. "I'll come in with you. You're not going to be alone with him."

"Fair enough."

Before Cote opened the door, another voice said, "I'm coming too."

Jon. Of course.

Cote looked over her head at him. "The guy's cuffed. I might be old, but I can handle him."

"She's my responsibility," Jon said.

Cote looked at her as if waiting for agreement or argument.

"I don't mind."

"It'll be crowded." Cote swung the door open.

Cote hadn't been exaggerating. The room was tiny, barely large enough for the small table where McLaughlin sat awkwardly, his hands cuffed behind his back. He didn't even turn when they stepped in.

But when she rounded the desk, he glared. He started to stand, but Cote said, "Keep your seat."

He lowered back down while Denise sat across from him.

Cote stood in the corner on her side of the room and crossed his arms.

Jon stood behind McLaughlin, who craned his head to see who was there. His eyes widened the slightest bit when he recognized him.

"Mr. McLaughlin," Denise said.

The man turned back to her. His skin was pale, his eyes sunken, his cheeks gaunt, reminding her of pictures she'd seen of people released from POW camps. Starving people. Desperate people.

She closed her eyes, prayed for words, for wisdom. When she opened them, he stared at her with cold loathing.

"I'm so sorry to hear about Landon. When did it happen?"

He blinked, confused.

She waited for him to get his bearings.

"Two years ago. Shot himself with my gun."

"I'm so sorry. I can't imagine. I have a daughter, a little girl. She was kidnapped a few years ago, and I thought...I feared I'd never see her again. The agony of those days... I'm sure it doesn't compare with how you're feeling."

"You don't care about him. You never cared."

"He was a nice kid. He changed my tire, then followed me to make sure I made it back to my parents' house safely. I bet he learned all that from you, am I right? How to change a tire? How to protect women?"

The man licked chapped lips. Nodded.

"He sent me a bunch of letters."

McLaughlin jerked forward, and she leaned back, heart racing.

"And you ignored him!" The words were loud. Spittle flew from his lips.

Jon stepped closer as if to touch him, but Denise shook her head. McLaughlin couldn't hurt her.

"I sent him a thank-you note and a signed photograph for his help."

"All that did was make it worse."

"That wasn't my intention. Make what worse?"

He looked toward the corner, his lips clamping shut and turning down.

The mental illness, obviously. Maybe meeting her had exacerbated his problems, but she doubted it. More likely, meeting her had just given him something to fixate on.

Maybe none of that mattered at this moment.

"Mr. McLaughlin?"

He gave no indication he heard her.

"I just wanted to say how very sorry I am about your son. I'm sure your heart is broken." She pushed back in her chair. "I'll be praying for you and your family."

His gaze snapped up. His eyes, already red-rimmed, blazed with fire. "Don't bother. You and I don't serve the same God."

"There's only One, and I do serve Him, though admittedly, not always very well."

She stood and headed for the door. Jon had it open, and she was about to step through when the man spoke again.

"I published your address."

She froze. Turned back.

Cote, who'd approached behind her, rounded the table again and leaned toward the prisoner. "You did what now?"

The man shifted to face Denise. "I follow news about you. This morning, there was an article at some online site that claimed you'd been threatened by that Hollywood serial killer. Figured the guy didn't know where you were. Thought I'd help him out. There's more than one way to get you to go away."

Her stomach dropped.

Jon scowled.

Cote glared.

But it didn't matter. Vaughn wasn't going to come to New Hampshire. And anyway, they'd probably already arrested him.

McLaughlin smirked, then turned back to face the wall.

Jon gripped her arm and pulled her out of the room. He kept them moving until they were back in the chief's office.

The chief followed them in and closed the door. "What was that about?"

She said, "Probably nothing."

"Nothing?" Jon's voice was too loud. He turned away from her to face the chief, quickly giving him a rundown on the Starlet Slayer.

"You're just telling us this now?" He directed the words to Jon, but Denise answered.

"All the victims were in LA. I'm not in danger here."

As if she hadn't spoken, Jon said to the chief, "It's why she has so much security. Or, one reason, anyway. You just arrested the second reason. We've been working with CBI Special Agent Frank, if you want to call him."

"I'll do that." He leaned over his desk and grabbed a pen. "Number?"

Jon got his phone out and read the numbers aloud.

"Anything else I need to know?" Cote asked.

"I'm not sure you needed to know that." Denise's tone was sharp. She just wanted this to be over. But that wasn't the chief's fault. She took a breath, forced another smile. "Sorry. Thank you for letting me talk to him."

Cote settled in his chair. "Whatever the point was."

"The point was to express my sympathy for his son's death. The point was to tell him I'm praying for him."

He gave her a perplexed look, shaking his head.

Jon opened the door, and she started to follow him out. But then she faced the chief again. "Any chance you could go easy on him?"

Behind her, Jon swore under his breath.

Chief Cote looked up, eyebrows hiked. "The man shot at you, fired an arrow through your window, and set a trap for you on Rattlesnake today. You're lucky you weren't in a serious accident. *He's* lucky nobody else hit that icy spot and wrecked. Somebody coming downhill could've been killed. And you want me to go *easy* on him?"

"He's grieving. He's—"

"Dangerous." The word came from Jon.

Cote huffed his agreement. "Isn't up to me, anyway. The prosecutor will decide. Take it up with her." He lifted his phone, dismissing her.

Jon gripped her upper arm. "Come on."

She walked beside him out of the office, then surrounded by four more bodyguards, out a rear door, where one of the SUVs waited. Jon opened the door to the backseat, and she slid in, another bodyguard at her side.

Jon and a third climbed into the front.

There'd be no privacy on the ride back to the house. Based on the scowl on Jon's face, he wasn't happy with her. Not one bit.

But they had learned one important thing.

Kenneth McLaughlin had broadcast Denise's address to the entire world. Good thing Vaughn would be arrested today. Otherwise, she'd be terrified.

CHAPTER TWENTY-THREE

J on didn't speak during the fifteen-minute ride back to
Denise's house. He needed to get his thoughts in line
before any words came out of his mouth.

In the woods, he'd been focused. Find the enemy and take
him out. He'd learned a long time before how to silence everything but what needed to be done at the moment. He'd trusted
the SUV's bulletproof glass to keep Denise safe until he
returned. He'd trusted Ian. He'd trusted his own ability to catch
and stop the shooter.

When he'd realized the guy was doubling back, he'd stayed
focused.

When he'd tackled the guy, disarmed him, cuffed him, he'd
stayed focused.

He'd answered question after question, rehashing what'd
happened with a uniformed police officer, with Detective
Pollard at the scene, then with Pollard again at the station. All
that time, he'd stayed focused.

But now that it was over, he had to face it.

What could have happened played like a slideshow across
the walls of his mind. If he hadn't realized the shooter's plan, if

the shooter had gotten back to the SUV a few moments earlier...

Denise could very well be dead now.

Ian, too.

The SUV might've been able to withstand one grenade, maybe two. But five?

Thank God. Thank God Jon had gotten to him in time. Stopped him. Saved Denise.

Barely.

He'd been so sure of his and his team's superiority. He'd been cocky.

And he'd almost lost her because of it.

He knew where he'd erred. He'd assumed that the shooter wanted to stay safe, to protect himself.

Jon had also assumed that the guy wasn't trying to kill Denise, just to scare her.

Both of those things had been true at first.

The gunshot at the lake had missed by yards. Someone with McLaughlin's skills...definitely a scare tactic.

The arrow through the window wasn't intended to kill but to warn.

Both attacks had allowed the man to escape, which had convinced Jon that the shooter's freedom was as important as the message he was sending.

Jon had known the shooter was skilled but hadn't believed him a killer.

Jon had also believed the shooter had a sense of self-protection.

Today's events had proved Jon wrong. McLaughlin had been out for blood.

And he'd been willing to die to get it.

And Denise—naive, tenderhearted Denise—felt *sorry* for him.

Almost made Jon want to throttle her.

But not quite. Because...

Aside from his own arrogance, his own monumental inadequacy, he'd discovered something else that day. Something that made no sense at all.

He was in love with her.

And all of that, *all of that*, needed to be dealt with.

He got a text from Lake and knew she was in the guest house, waiting for him. He needed to debrief with her, no question. But there was something else he needed to do first. He texted her telling her he'd need thirty minutes, maybe an hour.

She replied, but he didn't read her message. He could guess it. She wasn't happy with him.

Join the club.

Grant parked, and he, Hughes, and Jon walked Denise to her door. When the other two walked away, Jon stood in the opening. "Mind if I come in?"

She was halfway across the room when she turned. Her smile had dimmed considerably. "Okay."

He closed the door behind him, then checked that all the blinds were closed. No need for an audience.

And then he rushed across the room and took her in his arms.

"Oh," she said. Just that, nothing else. But she wrapped her arms around his back and settled against his chest and held on.

He lowered his head and whispered into her hair. "Thank God you're okay."

"I'm thankful you are."

While he held her, he allowed himself to relax in the knowledge that she was safe and whole. She hadn't gotten hurt. She hadn't even realized how much danger she'd been in.

When his thoughts toward Denise moved in a new direction, unsafe in an entirely different way, he backed up and released her. "Sorry. I needed to..."

"Me too." She gripped his hand and met his eyes. Their gazes held for a long moment.

"There's something else I need to say." Didn't want to end their embrace like this, but it needed to be said.

She tilted her head to the side, all innocent curiosity.

"You have one job, Denise."

"Oh."

"I told you to get back in the car."

"You had it under control."

"You didn't know everything. Neither did I. Please." He gripped her shoulders and bent to meet her eyes. "Please, trust me. Do as I say. It worked out this time. Next time, you might not be so lucky. So when I say duck—"

"I duck. No questions asked." She swallowed, nodded. "I will. I promise."

He released his grip on her arms and stepped back.

"Are you hungry? I could fix you something."

There were things that needed to be dealt with besides food.

"Can we just sit and talk?"

"I'd rather..." She walked into the kitchen and gestured to the barstools on his side of the island. "Have a seat."

Not how he'd hoped the conversation would look, but he wasn't about to argue. Rather than sit, he leaned against the edge and watched her.

She pulled a package of cooked, shredded chicken out of the freezer and stuck it in the microwave. "What did you want to talk about?"

"How are you doing?"

She shrugged, then swiveled and stepped into her pantry.

She emerged carrying a handful of cans and dropped them on the counter.

"Can I help?"

She slid them across the bar to him, along with a can opener. "If you'll do the honors."

"Sure." He started with black beans. "What are we making?"

"Chicken enchilada soup."

"Yum."

She found an onion. "Maybe by the time it's done, I'll be hungry. If not, you can feed it to your team."

"Why make it if you're not hungry?"

"I'm too hyped up to sit."

"Do you want to talk about it?"

"About the fact that a man shot at us today? That you and your team could have been..." Her voice cracked. She shook her head. "Not really."

"The team wasn't in danger." Well, not much, anyway. Ian had been, but Denise didn't need to know all the gory details.

Actually, maybe she did. The police report would be public record. A reporter would learn the facts and publish them, soon.

It wasn't what Jon wanted to talk about, but he should tell her everything.

"*We* weren't in much danger, but *you* were, more than I realized." He told her all the ways he'd screwed up because of his arrogance. He told her about the grenades. He told her how close she'd been to harm.

She stopped chopping the onion, just watched him until he was finished.

"If something had happened to you," he said, "it would have been my fault. I should have left the team with you and gone after the guy myself. I thought I knew what he'd do. I guessed wrong."

Her eyes were watery, though from fear or anxiety—or the pungent onion—he didn't know. She wiped them with a paper towel and pushed the cutting board away. "But you stopped him."

"Even when I realized he was headed back to the SUV, I thought he'd try to shoot you through the bulletproof glass. I thought you'd be safe until I could get there. But with grenades... I was wrong again."

"But you *stopped* him, Jon. You stopped him."

"I might not have. Don't you see? I could have..." He swallowed hard. "I got lucky. *You* got lucky."

"Not lucky. I have a God who protects me. While you were out there, I pulled the ninety-first Psalm up on my phone and prayed it—aloud—over all of us. I'm pretty sure Ian thinks I'm insane."

Jon filed the number of the Psalm away to read later. He wanted to know what she was talking about.

He wanted to know everything that mattered to her.

"God used you to protect me," she said. "He's the One in charge. You did His work today."

"I almost got you killed today."

"You might be my bodyguard, Jon Donley, but you're not my protector. I have one of those, and He's a lot bigger and a lot stronger than you are."

She swiped the paper towel beneath her eyes again and then resumed the chopping.

Just like that.

"You should fire me for incompetence."

She laughed. "That's not going to happen." She nodded to the cans in front of him. "And those aren't going to open themselves." She finished the onion, plopped a pot on the stove, lit the fire, and added some oil. She started chopping a green pepper. When she was finished, she added all the vegetables and sautéed them.

He got the lids off the cans and checked the package in the microwave, which had beeped. It was still frozen.

"Flip that over and set it to defrost for four more minutes."

"Copy."

They worked in silence, but Jon's buzzing phone told him Lake's patience was growing thin. He didn't have much more time.

"So, I've been reading through the New Testament," he said.

She took the package from the microwave, unzipped it, and dumped shredded chicken into the pot on the stove, along with the contents of all the cans. "Find anything interesting?"

He leaned a hip against the countertop beside her. "I remembered something I'd read a couple weeks ago, so I looked it up. It's in Galatians. It says something about how there's no slave or free, no male or female, no Greek or Jew. I think it's about how everybody is equal."

"I think you're right."

"And I was remembering what you said the other night when we were talking about, you know"—he gestured between them—"you and me. How you might be famous, but you're a normal person, just like everybody else."

She'd been stirring but stopped, watching him a long moment. She adjusted the fire on the gas stove, then leaned against the counter to face him. "Okay."

"If that's true, if we're all equal, then maybe you and I could..." He shrugged, embarrassed about his uncertainty. He wasn't the kind of guy to let fear stop him. "When this is all over, maybe we could see where this thing goes, this thing between us."

"Oh."

Not exactly the response he'd been hoping for. She didn't even flash that natural smile he'd come to love.

"The thing is," he said, "and this is going to sound ridiculous, but the thing is... I'm falling for you. I mean, it's more than that." He took a breath and clarified. "I'm falling in love with you."

Her eyebrows hiked, her blue eyes widening. But she said nothing.

"I know we haven't known each other that long." He forced a calm into his words that belied his pounding heart. "But what I feel for you is deeper than anything I've ever felt before."

Did her lips tip up the slightest bit at the corners? Or was that his hope feeding his imagination?

She turned back to the stove and stirred.

Saying nothing.

"Or maybe I've got this all wrong." Was that it? Was he just some...fanboy? Him and Landon McLaughlin and a million others who'd fallen in love with her?

She shook her head. "That's not it."

So he *didn't* have it wrong? He was confused. "I know it seems too soon to be...declaring myself or whatever." Did he just say that like he was the hero from some...romance novel? "It's just...it happens sometimes. That fast."

She looked over her shoulder at him. "Does it?"

"My parents knew each other for nine days before Dad proposed."

"You're kidding." She turned and leaned against the counter again.

"Dad loves to tell the story. He'd been with a group of guys at a concert. In front of them, there was this line of beautiful women. They were all up and dancing and singing along. Behind them, Dad and his friends were paying more attention to the women than to the band on the stage. When Dad caught sight of Mom, he asked his friend sitting behind her if they could switch. But the friend said no, that she was hot"—he couldn't imagine his mother being described that way and didn't want to think about it—"and he was going for it. Dad pulled out his wallet and took out all the cash he had. To hear him tell it, it was a week's worth of food money." Jon chuckled. "He'd decided it would be worth it to go hungry to meet Mom. At this point in the story, Mom always interrupts to say it was twenty bucks of beer money."

Denise laughed, which made his heart do a little flip thing.

"Anyway, he traded places with his friend, and when the concert was over, while all his friends hit on the women in front of them, suggesting bars and drinks and making suggestive *we'll see where it goes* comments, Dad asked Mom if she'd go on a date with him the following evening. She was impressed, said yes. They saw each other the next night—a Thursday—and every day after that. Nine days later, Dad asked her to marry him."

"And she said yes."

"Just like that. I always thought it was crazy, that nobody could fall in love that fast. But then...I met you."

"Oh."

There was that word again. Couldn't she string a few more together?

"It's just that..." She turned, adjusted the heat below the soup, and then paced out of the kitchen. She stopped near the table and leaned back on it.

He followed until he was right in front of her.

She took his hand. "It's just that...that scripture you mentioned? It's talking about people in the church. People in Christ."

"Oh." Apparently, her word was contagious.

"I would love... I have feelings for you, Jon. Strong feelings.

Terrifying feelings. But you're not a believer. And there's this command about not being unequally yoked." Before he could ask what she was talking about, she explained. "It means you shouldn't be joined to someone who's not at the same place as you, spiritually speaking. It means it would be unhealthy for me to get attached to you because we don't believe the same things."

"I see." Heat washed over him, shame and embarrassment morphing quickly into anger, and he had to clamp his lips shut to keep that from spilling out.

She must've seen something, though, because fear flashed across her face.

Fear, as if he might hurt her. As if he ever would.

The expression faded. "It's just..." She took a long breath. "I've spent a lot of my life living outside of God's will for me, so I know what it costs. God only wants my best. If He tells me I shouldn't be with somebody who doesn't share my faith, as much as I care about that person, as much as I might even...love that person, I can't be with him."

He dropped her hand and stepped back. "So because I'm not a *Christian*"—he hadn't meant to say the word with such disdain—"you don't want anything to do with me."

"I didn't say that. I do want..." She sighed. "I just... I can't. If you become a believer—"

"You think I should become a Christian so that you and I can date?"

"No. I think—"

"I don't appreciate being manipulated."

"What? I'm not trying to manipulate you. I'm trying to be honest with you."

"Yeah. Well." He paced into the living area, raked a hand over his hair. "Fine. That's fine." He was halfway to the door when he turned. "I was thinking I'd have to step down as head of your security, but I guess not. Now that we've figured out the connection with the Starlet Slayer, I won't need to stick as close."

"Jon, don't—"

"I'll be around. Doing my job until the guy is in custody." He couldn't get out of there fast enough. "If you need anything, talk to Grant."

"Please, let's just..."

But the rest of her words were lost as he stepped outside and slammed the door.

∼

When Jon stepped into the guest house, his guys looked up from their positions all around the main room.

Grant said, "Lake's upstairs."

Jon took the steps two at a time, desperate to release some of his rage. What he really needed was an hour with his punching bag. And then a long run.

Lake stood at the far side of the upstairs bedroom, gazing out into the dark night. He moved past all the air mattresses and stood a few feet from her, crossing his arms. He focused on the messy room instead of outside or at his cousin.

"'Sweetheart?'" So Lake had heard about his slip at the scene.

"Don't start with me."

She turned to face him, leaning a hip against the wall. At first glance, Lake's eyes looked gray, but when she was scared or angry or frustrated, slight flecks of green flashed. He'd guess frustrated right now. "You're going to have to step down as head—"

"I thought so too."

She pushed off from the wall. "What does that mean?"

"She's not interested. I thought she was. I was wrong."

He turned away from her. He didn't want to see the sympathy, the pity surely displayed on her face.

She slid her hand around his biceps and squeezed. "You want to talk about it?"

"No." He moved out of her reach. Mortified. Embarrassed. He'd told Denise he loved her, and she'd rejected him.

"What did she—?"

"She doesn't date men outside of her little...cult."

"Uh... By cult, do you mean—?"

"The stupid...church." He rounded on his cousin as if it were all her fault. "The whole...Christianity crap. She won't even consider me unless I become a Christian. Can you believe that?"

Lake closed her mouth, but he had a very strong feeling there was something in there trying to get out.

"Just say it."

"Okay." But she didn't, not for a long time. She leaned back against the wall, swallowed.

"What? I don't have time—"

"Give me a second to get my thoughts together."

He should know better than to press her. Lake was thoughtful, careful with her words. He wondered how much of that she'd learned growing up with an abusive father. Jon's uncle Mike had been a bear of a man, quick to anger. Jon never witnessed the guy hurting Aunt Janie, but he'd seen bruises. Maybe, in a household like that, a girl learned to be very, very careful about what came out of her mouth.

Finally, Lake said, "I think Denise is wise to want to be with somebody who believes the same things she does."

Jon spun to face her. "You think it's *wise* to reject me just because I don't believe her stupid woo-woo religion?"

"Putting aside the 'stupid, woo-woo' part, yes. You have no idea what real marriages are like."

"What are you talking about? My parents have been married for over forty years."

Again, she took her time answering. "My parents didn't have a normal marriage. But the thing is, your parents don't either. They"—she shook her head, a small smile appearing for a half second—"adore each other. Always have, as far as I can tell. They're respectful to the point where it's almost funny. They're genuinely grateful when the other does normal household chores. They snuggle together on the couch every night. They laugh at each other's jokes. If they snap at each other, they immediately apologize. Remember we went to that police thing where your dad was honored for heroism? He got onstage and spoke for five minutes about how he wouldn't be who he was if not for Aunt Sally. And she's the same way."

"My parents are happy. What's wrong with that?"

"Nothing, obviously. But your parents are equally matched. They're similar. They have the same ideals, the same values. And then let's take my parents. They came from different backgrounds. Mom grew up in a happy, healthy home."

That was true. She grew up with Jon's father. Their grandparents were pretty amazing people.

"Meanwhile," Lake said, "Dad was abused. Mom was honest and forthright. Dad learned early on how to use his charm to manipulate, to get what he wanted. It's how he got my mother to fall in love with him. She was college educated. He was working class. He believed life is about taking what you need by any means. She believed in love and beauty."

Jon's anger was slipping away as his cousin talked. He squeezed her hand. "She was a good mother. A good woman."

Lake nodded briskly. "The point is, they weren't equally matched. Maybe, if they'd had one or two of those differences, it wouldn't have been so awful. But they had nothing in common. Nothing."

"Your father's a monster. No offense, but—"

"I know that. And you're nothing like him. My point is, you and I grew up with extreme examples of what marriage looks like. The best of the best and the worst of the worst. Most marriages fall somewhere in the middle. Marriage is harder than it looked from where you stood. Why go into it knowing there's this huge, monumental thing you don't agree on? Why start out on shaky ground?"

"Is it really that huge? That monumental? I mean, come on. So she believes in God and I don't. So what?"

"Do you really not believe in God, Jon? Not at all?"

He didn't. Never had. He knew plenty of guys who prayed when bullets started flying, but he'd never seen anybody whose lives were altered because of those prayers.

Well, except for that summer, when Thomas and Josie escaped.

And maybe, *maybe,* Denise had been protected because she'd prayed that afternoon.

Or maybe they'd just gotten lucky.

And then there was Reid, who'd been transformed into a different person after five minutes of prayer.

It was *possible* there was something to what these people believed. "I still don't appreciate being manipulated into following her religion just because I want to get to know her better."

Lake tilted her head to one side. She'd pulled her blond hair from the ponytail she always wore when she worked and shook it out. "Did she really try to manipulate you?"

"I told her I loved her. She told me she couldn't be with me unless I was a Christian. What do you call that?"

Lake's eyes grew round. "You told her you *love* her?"

"Stay on point," he snapped. He didn't want to deal with that.

"You *love* her? Like, for real?"

"She used it against me."

"Or...hang with me here. Maybe she was honest with you about how she felt, and it ticked you off because it wasn't what you wanted to hear."

He was trying to stay angry. If he let the anger slip away, he'd have to deal with what was hiding behind it. All of Lake's... logic wasn't helping.

"Maybe she legitimately doesn't want to fall in love with a man who doesn't believe in something that's vitally important to her. It would be like you marrying a woman who thought weapons were evil and should never be used in any circumstance."

"That's ridiculous. How could weak people protect themselves from stronger people without weapons? It doesn't even make sense."

Lake quirked an eyebrow.

He considered what he'd said. "It's different. What I believe is logical."

"Not everybody believes what you believe."

"Well, those people are...stupid."

Lake laughed. "Don't mince words, cuz." She didn't laugh often, so when she did, it moved him. He'd watched her struggle as a child with her abusive father, struggle because, though she often escaped to his house, often bringing her little sister with her, her older sister and mom usually remained trapped at home. Then he'd watched Lake struggle as an adult after what had to have been the most torturous event of her life.

Lake's laugh made his heart glow.

Not that he'd ever say that out loud. Nobody was intimidated by a man who talked about glowing hearts.

Lake continued. "Is it possible that, to Denise, the fact that you don't believe in God is also stupid? Maybe He's that obvious to her."

He could see what she meant. A little more of his anger chipped away.

Lake's smile slipped. He could tell she had something else on her mind by the way she looked up at the ceiling. So he waited, figuring he wouldn't like it. But he'd always given his cousin space to speak her mind, as she'd always done with him.

Finally, she faced him again. "Reid and Jacqui go to the same church Denise does."

He nodded. He knew that.

"You didn't go on Sunday, but I did. The sermon was...interesting. I always thought Christianity was like every other religion on the planet. You know, do this, do that or you're gonna get it, whatever *it* is."

She'd summed up what he thought of religion in a single line. "Hindus with karma—what goes around comes around. Buddhists and 'enlightenment.' Jews and Muslims and Christians all believe in some form of heaven for good people, hell for bad people. As if there's some cosmic scale out there." He'd studied just enough of all of them to be unimpressed. "If a guy hurts somebody but then gives away all his money to the poor, where does he land? What's the cost of a life? And who gets to decide? And really, is God like some visor-wearing accountant up there, tapping away on an adding machine? It's ridiculous."

"I agree." Lake's head bobbed to emphasize the point. "The thing is, the talk on Sunday made me wonder if I've got it wrong. The pastor said something in passing as if...as if everybody in the room knew it."

"Please tell me you didn't drink the Kool-Aid. They serve it in those little cups. Comes with crackers."

She gave him a look that clearly told him to shut up. "The

pastor said that there was no way anybody in the room was good enough to get to heaven."

"Great. This just gets better and better. Sign me up."

"Do you mind?"

He swept his hand in a *go-ahead* gesture.

"He said that nobody is good enough because God is holy, which I think maybe means perfect? Anyway, He can't, or maybe won't, allow evil in His presence."

"That explains why He never shows up down here."

She'd been about to say something, but her teeth snapped shut. She considered that a moment. "I'm not sure that's true. I mean, if He's real, and if He's the Creator, then maybe everything good is Him showing up. Like...like babies and sunsets and..."

What happened to his tough-as-nails cousin? He must've made a face because she punched his shoulder.

"Ow." It didn't really hurt, but he threw her a bone.

"I'm just saying, there's beauty in the world. And maybe that's from God. And there's also water and food, and we don't all kill each other all the time. Maybe that's God. My mom thought so, you know? Maybe Mom was right. The point is, according to the pastor, God isn't an accountant, weighing good and bad. If He did that, we'd all be lost. Which is the whole point of Jesus. I've heard the story, of course. Mom used to tell us about Jesus. He died on the cross and somehow took our sins with Him, and then He rose on Easter, right? But the rest of it..." She shrugged. "I'm just saying... Maybe it's not real, but it's different from the other religions. It's unique."

He'd read the accounts in the Bible. It was unbelievable. Literally, in that he couldn't believe it'd really happened.

But maybe he was wrong. It wouldn't be the first time. He'd been wrong more than he'd been right that day. One more thing to add to the list.

"According to the pastor, all you have to do to go to heaven is believe," Lake said. "Imagine that? All your sins wiped out"—she swept an arm as if clearing an imaginary board—"just like that. An eternity in heaven instead of hell, just for *believing*? It's bizarre."

"Exactly."

"But what if it's true?"

How could it be true? A man died, then came back to life three days later?

Impossible. But then, they were talking about *God* here. Maybe He could do what He wanted.

Jon wasn't convinced. Wasn't sure he ever would be. "Do you, then? Believe?"

"I asked Jacqui about it. She's pretty amazing. She's like a mad scientist or something. She invented some device that might cure Alzheimer's. The woman's off-the-charts smart, and she believes this stuff." Lake shrugged. "I don't know, but I'm thinking about it. The point is, if Denise believes, it's possible she's not trying to manipulate you. It's possible she'd like you to believe so you can be forgiven and go to heaven. It's possible she told you the truth because she loves you too."

Lake had always had good aim, and those words hit right where she'd intended.

"You were gutsy telling her how you feel," she continued. "But don't discount her bravery. Considering how Reid treats her, I think it took guts for her to be honest with you."

If he were having this conversation with anybody but his cousin, he'd have walked out long before now. But he loved Lake like a sister. More than that, he respected her.

And he had seen *some* evidence that what these people believed might be true.

There was still a problem, though. "It's not like I can just...

conjure up faith. I can't make myself believe something I don't. Wouldn't God, if He's real, know if I was sincere?"

"One assumes, yeah. Jacqui told me to ask God to show Himself to me. She said He likes to answer that prayer. Maybe you could do the same."

He tried to imagine what that would look like. Would he have to get on his knees, like Reid said he'd done that day?

"It's weird, I know," Lake said. "But maybe, if you really love Denise, you can get over the weird and just do it. I mean, how can it hurt?"

Maybe he'd try. Maybe there was still a chance for him and Denise.

But he'd have to figure out this whole God and Jesus thing. And then decide if it made any sense at all. He'd spent a lifetime eschewing religion. He didn't see that changing now.

CHAPTER TWENTY-FOUR

The chain link fence was hidden in the trees behind Denise's property and along the sides, but in front, where no trees separated the house from the street, it stuck out like a scar. From the first moment Denise had seen it, she'd loathed it.

She had a privacy wall around her home in Beverly Hills, complete with a gated entrance. But it was stone, covered with vines and flowers. It added to the beauty of the place. She'd hoped she could skip all that security in New Hampshire. She understood why it was there, of course. With McLaughlin on the loose, it'd been necessary. But that morning, when she'd awakened and looked outside, she'd thought that maybe, soon, they could take it down.

The hours since then had proved her wrong.

Every single time she looked out the window, a car was driving by slowly or stopped completely, many with phone cameras aimed. A bodyguard stood at the end of her driveway, trying to urge the lookie-loos along, but it was a public street.

It was also a dead end, so everyone who continued up the mountain eventually had to turn around at the cul-de-sac and come back down.

She cursed Kenneth McLaughlin for publishing her address.

The allure would wear off. People would forget about her soon enough. And maybe... She didn't even want to consider it, but maybe she'd have to replace that ugly fence with one that would shield her house from the road.

Sometimes she hated being famous.

Fame, intrusive fans, and the threat of killers didn't bring her mood low as much as remembering the way Jon had stormed out the night before.

She'd hurt him—the last thing she'd wanted to do. But she'd needed to be honest, even if the truth was what neither of them wanted to hear. She'd spent a lot of time that morning praying for Jon, for his heart, for his salvation. For their relationship, if there could be one. For both of them to be able to move past this if they couldn't.

She didn't want that, though. She liked Jon, really liked him. More than made sense after such a short acquaintance.

She and Ella had decorated the tree on Sunday but hadn't put up any of the other Christmas decorations. After her prayers, Denise made sugar cookie dough and put it in the refrigerator and then spent the rest of the morning and early afternoon putting out the things she'd purchased to make her home festive. She draped garland from the stair rail and the upstairs hallway that overlooked the living room. She arranged her new nativity scene, which she'd spotted at the store on Sunday and then ordered online. It looked beautiful on the table near the front door. She pulled out the ceramic snowmen she'd been collecting since she'd purchased the house and put them in various locations around the downstairs. And then came her favorite Christmas decorations in the world, which she'd painstakingly wrapped and shipped here a few weeks earlier.

Pictures of Ella sitting on Santa's lap. There were eight of them. In the first, Santa held a sleeping Ella. In the next, one-year-old Ella was gazing at the bearded man with awe. The pictures tracked the changes in Denise's daughter, year after year. All the years she'd missed.

Denise set them on her mantel, along with a few other red-and-green decorations, arranging them among more garland.

By the time she and her security team picked up Ella from school, the empty boxes had been stashed in the garage—the guards had helped with that—and the house looked beautiful.

Ella chattered all the way home, barely leaving Denise time to do much more than nod. But when Denise opened the front door for her, Ella quieted.

She crossed the threshold and gazed around before looking up at her mother. "Mommy, it's beautiful."

Denise felt a wide, silly grin. The room had come together nicely, with all the red-and-green accents. She'd considered doing something more contemporary—maybe blue or even purple—but the traditional colors felt more festive.

"I thought we could decorate cookies." Was that something Ella would like? Was it something Jacqui and Reid usually did with her?

But Ella's eyes sparkled. "Yes!"

They cut out the dough, baked cookies, and decorated them with colored frosting and various sprinkles and candies. Between sugary bites, they talked and laughed and teased.

It was, far and away, the best time she'd ever spent with her daughter.

Exactly what she'd dreamed of for so long.

They were only halfway through the stack of cookies when a knock sounded on the front door. Probably groceries. Denise had put in an order a couple of hours before.

But when she pulled it open, Jon stood on the other side.

She hadn't seen him since he'd left the night before. He

didn't look much happier now. Dark smudges hovered beneath his eyes.

She felt a smile spreading. He might not have wanted to be there, but she was happy to see him. Happier than she would voice. "Come in."

Those eyes narrowed. Maybe he'd expected a different reaction. Maybe he'd expected her to be as guarded as he was. She would have been if he'd come before her prayer time. She'd been horrified at how they'd left things the night before. He'd declared his love, and she'd been honest about her feelings. Honest, but her words had hurt him.

She hated that. She'd also been more than a little annoyed that he'd rushed out as if she'd laughed in his face.

That he'd accused her of trying to manipulate him.

She'd left all of that with God. Jon was lost and hurting. He needed to be loved, not judged. Denise had been judged enough in her life to know the damage it could cause.

So she brightened her smile as she stepped back. "I'm happy to see you."

He moved inside, closed the door, and stayed there. "Can we talk for a few minutes?"

"Ella's here. We're decorating cookies."

He looked beyond Denise, and his lips spread into what she thought was meant to be a smile. "Hey, little bit."

Denise turned to Ella, who had blue frosting on her cheek. And in her hair.

"Wanna help us?" Ella asked.

His gaze flicked back to Denise. "Just need to talk to your mom for a second."

"Why don't you keep working," Denise said. "I'll be right there."

Ella scurried to the table, and Denise turned back to Jon. "It can't wait? I only have her until seven."

"I guess it could wait till then."

"Okay. We can talk after I drop her off. Are you on duty?"

"I was on this morning."

Oh. *That* was different.

"You sure you don't want to join us, then?"

"I'm sure you'd rather I didn't."

By the tortured look on his face, he really believed that—proving he was pretty thick.

She took his hand and tugged. "Come on. I even have an extra apron."

Five minutes later, he was seated at the kitchen table wearing a *Kiss the Cook* apron and a big smile while Ella directed him. "You gotta start with frosting 'cause the candy won't stick straight to the cookies."

It seemed that, according to Ella, the cookies and frosting were just a delivery device for the candy.

Jon attended to her as if she were explaining the origins of life—and there would be a test.

Ella demonstrated with a pastry bag, giving the ornament-shaped cookie a squiggly line. "Now that's not enough frosting for the bigger candies," she said, "but the little ones'll stick. If you want the big pieces"—she plopped a thick blob of frosting on the cookie—"you gotta do something like that."

Jon grabbed a different pastry bag and piped across a Christmas tree cookie. "Like this?"

Ella's little eyes lit up. "Yes! And you can use these"—she grabbed a bowl of red metallic decorations—"for ornaments!"

Jon looked at Denise with a smile.

Realizing she'd been staring, she resumed her work on a star-shaped cookie.

Jon and Ella were so engrossed in the decorating process that they didn't even notice when Denise got up to fix dinner. She sautéed the chicken and vegetables in one pan while rice cooked in another. She put a bag full of breaded chicken in the air fryer. She wouldn't eat it, but Ella preferred it to the "plain" chicken Denise ate. She figured with Jon there, they'd need it all.

She'd bought orange sauce—Ella's favorite—and Thai peanut sauce—hers. She also had Szechuan sauce, which she liked to mix with her peanut sauce to add a little spice.

It wasn't exactly authentic Chinese, but she'd made it for Ella in California, and Ella had loved it.

More than once, she found herself stopping to watch Jon and Ella work. The guarded expression Jon had worn when he'd arrived was long gone, replaced by pure happiness as he decorated—and ate—handfuls of cookies.

"Stop eating them!" Ella was laughing when she said it. "You're gonna spoil your dinner. Mommy only let me have one."

Jon looked up to find Denise watching and smiled. "Am I in trouble?"

"As long as you finish your dinner, young man."

"You know I will."

That she did.

She tossed the chicken in the sauces, leaving some of it plain, just in case, and called the two cookie artists to eat at the island.

"Aw, but Mommy. I'm almost done."

Jon swooped the complaining child out of her chair and tossed her over his shoulder, then carried her to the chair as she squealed. "Delivery for you, ma'am."

"I'm not a delivery!" Ella yelled. "I'm a girl!"

Denise giggled. "Just set it there, kind sir."

He plopped Ella in the seat, and she took in the feast. "Chinese! My favorite!"

Denise had set a spot for Jon. "You know you want to."

He settled in the chair. After she prayed a blessing over the meal, she explained what each bowl contained, and they dug in.

Denise had thought the afternoon with Ella had been perfect already, but Jon's arrival only improved it.

He talked and joked with Ella while Denise ate silently, savoring the moment.

How could this man, this man who treated her little girl with such kindness, who was tough and protective when necessary but also tenderhearted and gentle, who loved her... *Loved* her...

How could he not be the man for Denise?

Oh, God, what are You doing? Because, God help her, she could see herself loving Jon back.

Which meant that, if Denise kept her vow to walk with God, both she and Jon were going to have their hearts ripped to shreds.

Reid and Jacqui had accepted the container of cookies from Ella with praise for the colorful, candy-caked confections. Denise had worried that Reid's kindness from the afternoon before might've worn off, but he'd thanked her for dropping Ella off— with a smile!

And that wasn't even the weirdest thing that happened in the brief exchange at the door.

Jon hadn't joined the team that drove Ella home, so Denise rode in silence back to her house, wondering what he'd wanted to talk to her about.

When she got home, Jon was standing on her front porch. She must've worn a goofy smile because he grinned. "Happy?"

"It was a perfect afternoon. Thank you."

"Me? I didn't do anything but intrude."

"I'm glad you did. Feel free to intrude anytime."

His grin faded, their conversation from the night before suddenly hovering between them.

She wasn't sure what to say. Nothing had changed, but their differing spiritual beliefs didn't keep them from enjoying each other's company. "I'm not ready to go inside yet. Can we walk?"

"In the back, if that's all right. Unless you want a crowd of men around you."

She walked toward the side of the house. The sun had long set, revealing a diamond-studded sky. It couldn't be even thirty degrees, but her coat and gloves were warm enough, and Jon wore his as well.

When the silence became oppressive, she said, "So, the strangest thing just happened at Reid's. I thought maybe you could explain it."

"What's that?"

"Your cousin...Celia?"

He shook his head.

"Celeste? Ssss...Stephanie?"

"You're not even close. What about her?"

"She *smiled* at me."

He chuckled. "She does that from time to time, though usually when she thinks nobody's looking."

"But actually *at me*. Like, on purpose. Any idea why?"

He shrugged one shoulder but said nothing.

Interesting.

Did Denise dare assume that maybe Jon and Lake had talked about her? Maybe, despite Lake's consummate serious-ness, she could approve?

It seemed too much to hope for.

"She talked me down last night," Jon finally said.

Denise wasn't surprised that Jon had brought up their conversation from the night before. He wasn't one to avoid difficult subjects. She was surprised that he admitted he'd needed *talking down.*

What kind of man was this who threw everything out in the open? Who didn't feel the need to dance around the truth or pretend he didn't care when he did?

A very unusual man, no question.

"I'm sorry I accused you of trying to manipulate me."

"It's all right. You said some very"—she searched for the best word—"honest things to me. You weren't expecting my answer."

He dipped his head. "Lake helped me see it from your perspective."

It didn't change anything, but she was glad he understood.

When she reached the backyard, Denise continued to the edge of the forest, gazing between the trees into the darkness. She couldn't make out the fence, but she knew it was there.

"So I'm looking into it," Jon said.

Whoa. What was that?

He stared straight ahead, watching the ground beneath them as if it might shift.

"What do you mean?"

"If it's that important to you, it seems the least I can do is figure out why you believe what you believe. It feels…" He didn't finish that statement. "But maybe you're onto something. Maybe it's not just some bizarre woo-woo belief."

"Woo-woo?"

His lips twitched. "You know. All that spiritual stuff. The idea that there are spirits we can't see and voices nobody can hear. It's weird."

"So how are you 'looking into it'?"

"You ever heard of C.S. Lewis?"

She couldn't help the short laugh. "Uh, yeah. Hadn't you?"

"I didn't know anything about him except that he wrote those kids books, and he's quoted a lot. I guess he was an atheist, and then he did some research and decided he believed in Christianity."

"There are others." She yanked out her phone and started searching. "There're lists of them, but two who've written recently are Lee Strobel and Josh McDowell. I've never read Strobel's books, but McDowell has this...it's like an encyclopedia of reasons to believe the Bible and the Gospel."

"Really?" She didn't miss the skepticism in his voice.

"I bought it for a friend a couple of years ago." Her housekeeper, a proud atheist who'd looked at the thick volume with disdain. When she hadn't taken it home, Denise had perused it, shocked by the pages upon pages of evidence backing up the veracity of the Bible, the history it tells, and the story of Jesus and His apostles. She'd already been a believer, but that book had solidified her faith. "I have a copy back in California. It's amazing."

"I'll look for it."

She tapped her Amazon icon, found the book, and bought it. "It'll be delivered tomorrow."

His look told her he wasn't happy. "I can afford to buy my own books."

She pretended he'd said nothing. She slipped her hand around his arm and squeezed. "The fact that you're willing to consider Christianity... You can't know what that means to me."

"Maybe you didn't understand what I was saying last night."

"I think I did."

"Well, that's what love does, right? It doesn't hold onto its... for lack of a better word, *prejudices* out of stubbornness or pride. It's sacrificial."

Every once in a while, ideas came out of Jon's mouth that could have come straight from the Bible. For a man who claimed not to believe, he sure seemed to understand a lot. Maybe that was his natural disposition, though knowing what she did about mankind in general, she doubted it.

More likely, God had been drawing Jon close since long before he'd met her.

"Doesn't mean I'm going to believe." His voice took on a hard edge. "And I refuse to pretend, just to make you happy or to...to make this work."

"I wouldn't want you to. If you did that, you wouldn't be the man I think you are."

He nodded and said nothing.

They reached the far corner of the property and turned back toward the house. The trees thinned here. She gazed up at the blanket of stars above. There were so many.

She wandered toward the center of the yard, still looking toward the heavens. Jon took her hand and returned it to his arm. "Wouldn't want you to fall."

"Such a gentleman." But she didn't look his way. She couldn't take her eyes off the show overhead. "There are no stars in LA." She laughed at that. "Ironic, right? The only 'stars' there are the pretend ones—the human ones. And the ones cemented into a sidewalk, I guess. But real stars burn bright, not for a season or a couple of decades but for thousands and thousands of years. Those stars were overhead when Jesus walked the earth. When Moses led the Israelites to the Promised Land. When Noah's ark rolled over stormy waters. The vastness of it, the beauty. It's...it's overwhelming."

When he said nothing, she glanced at him for a reaction and found him watching her. He averted his gaze quickly, then pointed. "The North Star. You see it?"

When Denise's mom had pointed out constellations and told her the names of stars, Denise never paid much attention, but she remembered how to find the North Star.

"It's the only thing in the heavens that doesn't move," Jon

said. "To me, it's always represented truth. Foundational ideas. Like, there are some things that simply don't change. The value of a human life. Good versus evil." He shrugged like he was embarrassed.

"I love that. What a great metaphor."

The woods were silent, almost reverent, and it felt for a moment like Denise and Jon were the only two people in the world. Two frail humans and a great big God whispering His love on the breeze.

The sound of a squeaky hinge yanked Denise out of the fantasy. One of the guards jogged toward the front of the house. If he'd seen them, he gave no indication.

"Anyway." Jon stepped away and faced her. "That's not why I came over earlier."

"Oh, right. You wanted to tell me something."

"I hate to ruin the moment."

She didn't like the sound of that. "Those kinds of moments never last anyway."

Jon had been about to speak but didn't. His eyes narrowed the slightest bit. His head tipped to one side.

"You know—silent, reverent moments. Moments when you can feel God. Or...well, I guess maybe *you* didn't but..." She shook her head, forcing herself to shut up.

Jon studied her, then gazed into the forest, up to the heavens. "Huh."

She didn't know what that meant.

Another beat passed before Jon faced her again. "Agent Frank called. About a month ago, Hubert Vaughn told his kids—they're grown and out of the house—and his assistant that he was going to Europe on an extended vacation. He gave them the name of a hotel where he was planning to stay, claiming the need for a 'sabbatical.'" Jon made air-quotes around that word. "The assistant and kids have texted with him a few times. He's told them stories about his vacation, how much fun he's having, all that."

Denise's heart sank. "If he's in Europe, then—"

"He's not. At least, not where he'd claimed to be." Jon went on to explain that Agent Frank had called the hotel, but the clerk had no record of his being there. In the last two weeks, the assistant and the kids had all tried calling him, but the calls had gone straight to voice mail.

"Frank got a warrant to locate his phone, but it's been turned off. Vaughn's off the grid."

"Oh." She should say something more, but Jon's words were rattling around in her mind.

"Looks bad," Jon said. "Frank and his team think he's their guy."

"And you?"

"They're the pros. I'm pretty new at this investigating thing, but I tend to agree with them. I mean, why else would he disappear?"

"But nobody knows where he is." Her words were barely a whisper.

Vaughn could be there now, watching them.

Jon squeezed her hand. "We're not going to let him get within a hundred yards of you. Unlike McLaughlin, Vaughn has no military experience, no experience with weapons that we can find. Which tracks with the killings. They're not exactly precision murders, you know?"

She had no idea what he was talking about and wasn't sure she wanted to.

Jon didn't read her expression. "They're messy. There're much more efficient ways to kill a person, but Vaughn..." He must've seen something in her face because he changed tack. "The point is, if he wants to hurt you, he has to get close. And in order to get close, he's going to have to get through me and my team. He won't. You're safe here."

The last thing, the very last thing she wanted was to come face-to-face with Vaughn. He'd done unspeakable things to her the last time she'd been in his presence. And this time, he'd have a weapon.

But she didn't want Jon or any of his men having to face him either.

"Hey." Jon took her gloved hands. "I promise. We won't let him get anywhere near you."

"Okay." She tried to infuse confidence in her voice, but it didn't work. Because Vaughn had been able to get to all the other women. He'd been patient, bided his time.

Denise wouldn't be safe until Vaughn was behind bars. And at that moment, not a soul in the world knew where he was.

CHAPTER TWENTY-FIVE

"You're not listening to me."

Jon was listening. He just didn't like what he was hearing. "It's a bad idea."

In the backseat, Denise huffed her frustration as Hughes drove in the drizzle along the highway that edged the lake.

"Where are we going?" she asked.

He ignored her. He'd insisted she get in the car with him, that they had someplace to go. When she'd questioned him, he'd played the *you promised to do what I said* card, and she'd complied.

The story had broken that morning. The *LA Times* had been the first to report the connection between the Starlet Slayer's victims and Hubert Vaughn. Thanks to the explosive allegations, other news outlets—papers, radio, and TV—had picked up the story.

Denise's name had been released as one of Vaughn's assault victims—and the person who solved the mystery. Her phone had been ringing all morning. Concerned friends, other actors. Her parents had called and told her they were planning to fly back early to be with her, but she'd talked them out of it, explaining to Jon after she hung up that she had as much drama as she could manage at the moment.

Too much drama, more so because of Kenneth McLaughlin. If Jon could get his hands on that guy…

McLaughlin was behind bars, but thanks to him, everybody knew where Denise lived.

The vultures were already swooping in. Media were buzzing over Coventry like flies, and the trickle of traffic Jon had seen driving by Denise's house the day before had turned into a steady stream. The fans now had to drive single-file past the multiple media vans parked out front.

A couple of them had tried to follow the SUVs when the team drove away a few minutes before, but a wall of bodyguards stepped into the road to block them.

Jon had plenty of experience with famous clients. His agency had hired more bodyguards, who'd already arrived. He'd need all hands on deck until Vaughn was captured.

Frank was now convinced that Vaughn was their man. He'd questioned his two longtime assistants, but they had alibis for the murders. They'd admitted to *wondering* what happened with Vaughn and the actresses he called behind closed doors, but they both claimed to never have believed their boss was a rapist.

Obviously, they both lied, but Frank hadn't charged them with anything.

Meanwhile, the more they looked into Vaughn, the more the evidence pointed to him. According to his calendar, he'd been in town and had no alibis that the police could discover for any of the murders. He'd even been in San Francisco the weekend Jane Sanderson was killed on location.

Vaughn was their guy. Now they just had to find him.

All that, Jon could handle. He and his team could keep her safe as long as it took to find the killer.

It was Denise's ridiculous plan that was pushing him to the breaking point.

"What are we doing?" she asked for about the fifth time since they'd left the house.

Hughes turned down a long driveway and parked.

"I'll explain inside." Jon climbed out of the car and slammed the door.

Denise had summoned him that morning to tell him she was leaving. Her words echoed in his mind. *"I'm not willing to lure a killer to the town where my family lives, where my daughter lives. Now that my address is public, now that we know Vaughn is in hiding, it just seems wise to return to California."*

She'd actually used that word—*wise*.

To return to the place where all the other murders had taken place.

Yeah. Brilliant plan. Right up there with the Edsel and New Coke. Except in those cases, only *products* died.

Why not just paint a big red-and-white target on her back and be done with it?

He took the front steps two at a time and banged on the front door.

James Sullivan pulled it open, his longish hair hanging on either side of his face, bringing to mind the young king from the *Lord of the Rings* movies. The baby resting on his shoulder ruined the image.

"Thanks for doing this, Mr. Sullivan," Jon said.

"It's James. And my wife is Cassidy. We don't do that mister-and-missus stuff here."

He offered a crisp nod. "I just need to clear the house."

James stood back. "Have at it."

It was an older home, not unlike the one where he'd grown up. The downstairs rooms were separated by walls and doors, different from the one-room open concept thing newer houses had. Though the place was old, the grayish-beige walls, the freshly painted trim, and the furnishings made it look fresh and modern.

After checking upstairs—bedrooms and baths, nothing unusual—he entered the kitchen, where Cassidy was arranging an appetizer tray as if this were a social occasion.

She smiled at him. "Glad you reached out."

He hadn't known what else to do after Denise's ludicrous announcement that morning, so he'd called The Patriot and asked James if they could meet.

Jon wasn't above using peer pressure. He wasn't above using any means necessary to talk some sense into his client.

Reid and Jacqui were in the living room and stood when he stepped in.

"Thanks for being here," Jon said.

"Of course." Jacqui gave him that pretty smile.

Cassidy followed him in and set the tray on the coffee table. "Help yourselves."

Reid snatched a cracker and a slice of cheese. "What's going on?"

"I'll let her explain when she's inside." He returned to the front door and spoke to James. "No media hanging around? No unexpected guests?"

"It's been quiet here, unlike at the restaurant. All the press is in town."

"Sorry to pull you away."

"Friends trump business every time."

Jon left James there and jogged back to the SUV. The air was heavy with moisture, and a chilly wind blasted across the lake and through his thin jacket. The forecast called for the rain to turn to snow, but it wasn't supposed to switch over until late that night.

When he opened the SUV's rear door, Denise looked up at

him. "You're making me nervous. Has something terrible happened?"

"This is the Sullivans' house."

"I know where we are." He didn't miss the hint of frustration in her voice. "James has lived here as long as I can remember."

Jon stepped back as the other guards gathered around. "Come on."

She huffed but marched to the door.

Inside, Cassidy pulled her into a hug. "How you holding up?"

"Okay, I guess. It's just media."

"And a serial killer. Why didn't you tell us he was after you?"

"I wasn't sure. And it's not exactly lunch conversation."

Cassidy leaned back and, if Jon weren't mistaken, looked offended. "It is with friends. Everything that matters to you matters to us. Is what they're saying true? Did that man, all those years ago...?"

Denise nodded.

"I'm sorry I wasn't here." Cassidy pulled her into another hug. "I'm so sorry that happened."

When Denise stepped back, she wiped tears. "It's over. We're here now."

Jon hadn't meant the low "Hmm" that issued from his throat.

Denise shot him a look as Cassidy hooked their arms and led her to the living room.

Denise froze at the door. "Oh. Hi."

James, Reid, and Jacqui all stood and greeted her, though nobody smiled.

"I got you water." Cassidy indicated the glass on a side table.

"Thanks."

After Denise sat in the empty chair, Cassidy settled beside her husband, catty-corner to Denise.

Everybody looked at Jon.

"You've all read the articles?"

Reid fielded that. "They think the Starlet Slayer is Hubert Vaughn. He's the man who..." He glanced at Denise but didn't finish the sentence.

Denise just nodded. "But we're not here to talk about that." Then she shot Jon a look. "Right?"

"Right."

"They think he's murdering his victims?" Jacqui's voice held a hint of disbelief. "Why would he do that?"

"To cover his tracks, maybe?" Denise said. "Except this has done the opposite."

"I'll say." Cassidy lifted her phone. "A few women have come forward this morning already, and I'm sure there'll be more. Guys like that... They get away with it once, they think they're invincible. One of the victims said today that she thought if she told the truth, he'd have no reason to kill her. If anything, this is going to bring everything out into the open."

Denise's eyebrows rose. "That's one good thing. I guess we can be thankful—"

"There's nothing to be thankful for," Jon snapped. "And the man's motives are irrelevant. The police are convinced Vaughn's their man. A month ago, he said he was going to Europe, but he isn't where he said he'd be, and his phone is off. He was already a suspect. Now, there's an all-out manhunt for the guy."

"Here's hoping somebody takes him out." Reid looked murderous enough to do the deed himself.

Jon agreed entirely. "Until he's caught, Denise needs to remain guarded. I've asked you all to come here because she has this...idea, and I wanted you all to weigh in."

"What idea?" Jacqui leaned forward, all kindness and curiosity.

He guessed Cassidy knew her friend well because her eyes narrowed. "Let's hear it."

Denise glanced at him, suddenly nervous. "Is that why we're here?"

"You weren't interested in my opinion. I thought theirs might have an impact."

"It's not that I wasn't interested, it's just..." But her words faded as she took in the faces of friends. "I'm going back to Califor—"

"Are you out of your mind?" Cassidy was on her feet so fast, he'd hardly seen her move. "Why would you do that?"

"My location isn't secret," Denise said. "I'm no safer here than I would be there."

James and Reid looked at Jon, perhaps trying to read his thoughts. Maybe inviting him to weigh in. But he'd already done that, and Denise had discounted his opinion.

Jacqui's head tipped to one side. "I thought you came home because you wanted to be near Ella."

"Or was that a lie?" Reid said. "Are you only here because of this killer?"

"Of course not." Denise leaned toward them. "I came here for Ella. For...all of you. I wanted to come home." Her voice hitched, and she shook her head slightly. "This is my home." She straightened. "I'm not luring a killer—"

"You have protection here." Cassidy waved toward Jon. "Not just that, but you have people. I mean, I know you have friends back in LA, but not like us. Not family. You'll be safe here."

"It's not about me." Denise took a deep breath. "I'm not about to put anybody else's life in danger to protect myself. You guys, Ella...that's why I have to leave. Don't you see?"

"No." James shook his head. "I *don't* see how you putting your life in danger protects anybody else. I don't see that at all."

"He could use any of you to get to me."

"That's not his modus operandi," Jon said. "He corners women when they're alone. He doesn't take on husbands or friends or bodyguards. He waits until his victim is vulnerable. Which is exactly what you'll be if you go back to LA."

"There are security agencies there too. I can hire bodyguards."

His frustration boiled over. "We're not all created equal, you know. We're not interchangeable."

"I know that. I know—"

"You're not going to find a single bodyguard in LA who cares more about your security than I do."

"Oh." That silenced her.

He figured the rest of the people in the room were reacting to that little tidbit, but he couldn't take his eyes off her. "And where do you get off deciding your life is less valuable than your daughter's or your friends' lives? You keep telling me you believe what the Bible tells you. But if you really believed that, you'd take your own security as seriously as you take everybody else's."

Denise shot to her feet. "Is that what you think?"

"It's obvious."

"You're wrong, Jon. I know who I am. I know *Whose* I am. And I know where I'm going when I die. I don't have a death wish. I get that I'm no more—or less—valuable than anybody else in this room."

"Doesn't look like it from where I stand."

Denise stepped toward him. "Did you and your team put yourselves in harm's way yesterday to protect me?"

"We would again in a heartbeat."

"Would you take a bullet for me?"

"Without blinking an eye."

"For any of your clients, right?"

He realized he was stepping into a trap but couldn't quite figure out how to yank himself back out. "It's our job."

She turned to Reid. "You once threw yourself over Ella to keep her from getting hurt, right?"

His lips pressed closed. After a moment, he nodded. "But that was—"

"And you." She rounded on James and Cassidy. "You two stalked a kidnapper and murderer to rescue *my daughter*, and nearly got killed in the process. Is that or is that not true?"

James rubbed his jaw, nodded. "We did."

These were stories Jon wanted to hear.

Denise turned back to him. "I'm not planning those kinds of heroics, but I do need to protect Ella and the other people I love. Why is it acceptable for everybody else to risk their lives but not me?" She faced her friends. "Isn't that what love does? Sacrifice?"

Her question was met with silence that hung in the room for a long moment.

And then Reid leaned forward. "Love isn't stupid."

That made Denise chuckle, though the sound was half sob and followed by a sniff. She wiped a few tears and sat back down.

"I'm serious," he said. "The truth is, as long as people know Ella is your daughter, there's a risk to her. But that's life, right? There's no such thing as risk-free living. I've been told"—he glanced at his wife—"that I'm the most overprotective father in existence, but I can only do so much. You and I...we have to trust that God is going to protect her and do our best to keep her safe. But we also have to keep ourselves safe. Because a big part of Ella's well-being is wrapped up in us. Jacqui, me"—he nodded to Denise—"and you. If something happened to you, she would *not* be okay. Denise, you told her you're staying. If you leave…" He shook his head. "You have no idea how much that'll hurt her."

Denise's eyes filled again. "I'm only trying to protect her."

"She won't understand. You need to know the cost." Reid sat back.

Denise seemed too stunned to speak.

"Nobody's going to harm Ella," Jon said. "And if you stay here, if you let us protect you, Vaughn won't get close to either one of you. Chief Cote's already posting his picture all over town. If he shows his face here, somebody will see him."

"If he dares come to Coventry," James said, "this whole town will stand between him and you."

"That's exactly what I *don't* want!"

James smiled at her. "That's the thing about friends, though. We get to love sacrificially too."

Cassidy reached across the space and gripped Denise's hand. "You've always had a really big heart, and I love that. But I'm with Reid on this one. Don't be stupid."

Denise seemed to vacillate, and then she dropped her head. She sat like that a long time before she looked at her friends. "Fine. I'll stay."

"Yes!" Cassidy raised a mug. "To not being stupid!"

The friends echoed the sentiment, smiling.

But Denise stood and approached Jon. She spoke so low that only he could hear. "And you called *me* manipulative."

He tried very hard not to look triumphant. "Some battles are important enough to win—even if you have to play dirty to do it."

CHAPTER TWENTY-SIX

Denise was embarrassed by her tears, but it had been that kind of a day. The online articles. The press watching her house. The "intervention" by her friends. Jon had been personally offended by the idea that she would be just as safe in California. Maybe she wouldn't, but the people she loved would be safer if she left. Her friends. Ella.

And Jon himself, though considering how much he berated her for not prioritizing her own safety, he didn't seem all that worried about his.

Was there any truth to his accusation that she didn't value herself?

Back when she'd still been drinking and using drugs, she'd deluded herself into believing her press. She'd surrounded herself with sycophants who told her whatever she wanted to hear. She used to find her worth in fan mail. Giving up the substances, returning to Christ—those were humbling experiences, and she'd sworn she'd never forget who she really was again.

Maybe she'd gone too far. If, as the Bible said, humility was believing others were better than herself, she'd achieved that.

But maybe she'd come to see herself as so lowly she'd forgotten the part of the Bible that said that, like everybody else, she was valuable. Precious. Jesus hadn't saved her because he'd had to. He'd chosen her.

Jon had seen through Denise and called her on her hypocrisy. He challenged her to see herself neither as lofty and special nor as lowly and unworthy. Jon—and Denise's friends—challenged her to see herself as she was. A child of God, forgiven and cherished by her Creator.

All those thoughts swirled in her head as she gazed at the stage in the Coventry High auditorium. Ella attended a private Christian school nearby, but they'd reserved this room for the evening. Not surprising, as it was the only stage in town.

The conversation with her friends earlier contributed to Denise's tears. Being back in this building that held so many memories didn't help.

She barely followed the story, so intent on watching her daughter delight the audience.

Ella was far and away the best actor in the play. And the most beautiful. And maybe, just maybe, Denise was a little biased.

Jacqui nudged her shoulder and handed her a tissue.

"Thanks," she whispered. Her joy was overflowing in tears. To be home. To be able to watch this.

If not for the killer who no doubt had Denise in his sights, it would be the perfect night.

The kids gathered to sing the final number and took a bow.

Denise was the first to stand, but the rest of the parents followed suit. So it wasn't Broadway. These beautiful little innocents deserved a standing ovation.

After the lights came on, the audience made its way down the hall to the cafeteria, where refreshments would be served. Jon, Grant, and three other guards surrounded Jacqui, Reid, and

Denise as they followed the throng. James and Cassidy were there as well, along with a new couple Denise had met before the show started, Andrew and Grace. She'd learned that Andrew worked with Jacqui, and Grace worked with Cassidy, and they all loved Ella.

Of course they did. Denise's daughter was eminently lovable.

Denise's attendance at the play had posed more than a few problems for the school because of the media presence in town, not to mention the throng of bodyguards. When she'd reached out to the headmaster that afternoon, he'd been nothing but kind and eager to help. The school had stepped up, ensuring that everybody who made it inside was a friend or family member of a student. All that checking off of names when the people entered had slowed the process, but the play had only begun a few minutes late.

The cafeteria looked just like it had when Denise had been a student there. The cinder block walls had been repainted a lighter color, but the fold-up tables with their long benches, the laminated floor...

Reid sidled up beside her as they followed the crowd toward the refreshment table. "It's like stepping back in time, isn't it?"

"It's bizarre."

He smiled down at her, and her tears threatened again.

She and Reid were becoming friends. It was more than she'd dared to hope for.

She turned to smile at Jon, but he wasn't looking her way. His attention was riveted toward the cafeteria entrance. Denise couldn't see over the heads of the people to know what he was looking at. "What is it? Are the kids coming?" They'd gone back to change out of their costumes and would be escorted by their teachers—and a few guards and police—to the cafeteria soon.

"Did you invite Ms. Boatright?" Jon asked.

"Brittney?"

"She's at the entrance, obviously looking for you."

Denise stepped out of the line and tapped Reid's elbow. "There's somebody I need to talk to. I'll be back." She walked toward where Jon indicated, Jon and the crowd of armed men all around.

Sure enough, there was Brittney in the wide entrance to the large room, a police officer at her side. She'd looked so put together when Denise had seen her Tuesday, but tonight her brown hair was pulled back in a severe ponytail. She wore no makeup, and her skin was pale. Her jacket was open, revealing a ratty sweatshirt so old that Denise remembered it from when they'd lived together.

Brittney caught sight of Denise and started her direction but was stalled by the officer.

When Denise was close enough, she spoke to the cop. "She's an old friend. It's fine." The man nodded and moved away, and Denise turned to Brittney. "What is it? What happened?"

Brittney gripped her forearm. "I need to talk to you." Her gaze flicked to the men all around. "Alone."

Before Denise could respond, Jon said, "Not alone."

With barely a glance his direction, Brittney leaned closer and spoke into Denise's ear. "It's about Vaughn. I think I can help. But I can't... What happened to you today, them printing all that stuff... I can't face that. I can't."

Denise struggled to catch up. Had Brittney been one of Vaughn's victims? When had that happened? How...?

"It's imperative. Please."

"Okay." Denise took her hand and started walking, ignoring the frustration wafting from Jon like too much cologne. Most of the school was closed off, but the classrooms nearest the auditorium were accessible. The kids had used them as dressing rooms and staging areas, so they should still be unlocked.

In the hallway, they passed students moving in tidy lines toward the cafeteria. Denise caught sight of Lake, then found Ella beside her.

Her daughter looked confused. As she approached, she said, "Are you leaving?"

Denise pasted on a bright smile. "I'll be right there. Save me a cookie."

Ella moved past, and Denise prayed her words would be true. She loved Brittney, but she didn't want to ruin this magical night with talk of serial killers and sexual assault.

Once upon a time, Brittney had been not only her *best* friend but her *only* friend. Denise owed her a few minutes of her time.

The end of the hallway was deserted, so Denise paused by one of the doors, turning to Jon. "Why don't you guys just wait down the hall?"

He scowled.

Brittney said, "Can't we go inside so nobody will overhear?" She shot Jon and the other men a worried, suspicious glance. "You never know."

"Ma'am," Jon said, "my team is—"

"I know. I'm sure you can be trusted." She was wringing her hands. "I'm sorry. I'm just... This is hard."

Denise stepped into the classroom, pulling Brittney along with her. Through the doorway, she shot Jon what she hoped was a placating look. "We'll be fine. I'll be right here."

He looked like he wanted to push through the door, but she closed it before he could. Hopefully, he'd forgive her for that later. If Brittney was going to say what Denise guessed, she'd need to be away from hovering, hulking men. And if she really had information that might help locate Vaughn, Denise had to get it.

Jon would thank her later.

The window in the door was covered by construction paper to afford the girls privacy when they'd changed into and out of costumes. This room and the one across the hall had been filled with boisterous and nervous children earlier in the night. Long, long before that, Denise had studied English in this room. She could still remember Mr. Halpern waxing philosophical about the use of everyday language to paint vivid word pictures. The students had to memorize a poem and recite it to the class, and Denise had chosen "Stopping by the Woods on a Snowy Evening."

Whose woods these are I think I know. His house is in the village though...

She'd always loved Robert Frost. She flipped on the light. "How did you find...?" She turned, and her voice faded.

Brittney was close. Too close.

She had a knife in her right hand, held high like she'd been an instant from stabbing it into Denise's heart.

A scream caught in Denise's throat. She tried to force it out, backing up until she bumped into the wall.

"Silence," Brittney said.

Denise clamped her lips closed.

They stood like that, saying nothing, while indecision played in Brittney's eyes.

And then she backed up, and Denise saw a gun in her other hand.

A backup plan.

Denise couldn't catch up. Surely Brittney wasn't a serial killer. But what else would explain this?

If she was, then she'd already murdered plenty of women. Why the hesitation?

Brittney's gaze flicked all around the room.

She seemed...confused. But then the indecision slid off her face, replaced by determination.

"Come on." She grabbed Denise's arm and propelled her away from the door, not letting up her firm grip. "If you scream or try to alert the men out there, I'll shoot you. And they'll burst in here, and I'll shoot them, starting with the one in charge."

Jon.

And his men. They were all in danger.

"There's no escaping this for me." Brittney yanked Denise past desks that had been pushed to one side toward the back corner. "By tomorrow, everybody will know the truth, so I have nothing to lose. Absolutely nothing. You understand what I'm saying?"

Denise didn't. She couldn't comprehend what was happening.

Brittney stopped and whirled Denise so they were face to face. Her eyes were bulging, her skin mottled. She barely resembled the put-together woman Denise had met at the park earlier that week. "You understand?"

Terror bubbled up from Denise's middle, tried desperately to claw its way out. But Jon was outside that door. And the other men. And, just down the hall, Ella.

Hadn't Denise just lectured her friends about sacrificial love? Hadn't she just claimed to be willing to put herself in harm's way to protect others? It was time to put her love to the test.

"I understand."

Brittney pushed her toward a door on the side wall. "Open it."

Denise did and was shoved into the next classroom. It was dark, the only light spilling in from the room they'd just vacated and the moon outside.

They headed toward a window. "Leave your phone here."

Denise pulled her phone from her pocket and set it on a nearby desk.

Brittney nodded to the window. "Go on. Lift it."

Denise disengaged the lock and pushed the window up.

"Climb out. If you take off, I'll shoot you. And I won't stop with you. It'll be a bloodbath." She'd sheathed her knife and now patted the pocket of her jacket. "I brought plenty of rounds. Everybody will pay for what you did. I'll make sure of it. Don't think I won't. I've done as bad or worse already."

Images assaulted Denise. People shot, bleeding to death. All those children. Teachers. Reid and Jacqui. James and Cassidy.

Jon.

Ella.

Jon wouldn't let that happen. He'd take Brittney down. Unless she took him down first.

Either way, if Denise didn't do what she was told, she wouldn't be alive to see how the story ended.

She climbed out and dropped to the grass. Everything in her wanted to run, but there were no trees nearby, no bushes. Nowhere to hide. And even if she could, she wouldn't put anybody else's life in danger. The faster she could get Brittney away from the school, the better.

Brittney landed beside her, grabbed her arm, and rushed around the building, not toward the parking lot but straight toward the tree line.

Denise kept up, half running, half being dragged, as they crossed the grassy area behind the school, skirted the field, and entered the woods. They reached the chain link fence that surrounded the grounds. Brittney must have planned to escape this way all along because one section of it had been cut and pulled back. They barely slowed as they made it through.

Brittney and Denise entered a back yard, ran between the

houses, and came out on a quiet street. There were no lights, and the houses were far enough from the road that they afforded little illumination. A van was parked just ahead. Brittney yanked open the back door and shoved Denise inside.

Denise crawled across the metal floor, away from Brittney and the gun pointed at her middle.

With her free hand, Brittney yanked a cell phone from her pocket and lit the flashlight, aiming it into the cargo space. The light landed on a set of zip-tie cuffs that had been threaded through a door handle. "Put them on."

"I don't understand, Brittney. What are you doing?"

"I should have just..." She shook her head. "It's fine. It's better this way."

"Why are you—?"

"Because you were my friend! Or so I thought." She wiggled the gun. "Put them on. Now."

Denise did as she was told, keeping the ties wide enough that she could wiggle out of them when Brittney wasn't looking.

But Brittney hopped into the van, checked the zip ties, and yanked them so tight that the plastic dug into Denise's wrists. Then she closed the rear door and climbed into the driver's seat.

A moment later, they were turning out of the neighborhood, away from Ella. Away from Jon. Away from safety.

CHAPTER TWENTY-SEVEN

J on glanced at his watch. What was keeping Denise? He understood that she wanted to talk to her friend, but Ella was already in the cafeteria, probably eating cookies and looking for her mother. Whatever Brittney had to say, it could have waited a couple of hours. Was Brittney working for some media outlet? Would she sell her story to the highest bidder? Whatever information she had—assuming she had anything at all—ought to be turned over to the CBI, not debated with Denise.

The whole thing felt fishy.

He should have put up more of a fight, but what trouble could the two women get into in a high school classroom? With Jon and his team in the hallway, nobody would be getting inside.

At the four-minute mark, he started to worry that Ella wouldn't be the only one missing Denise. What if the media or somebody else had seen them go down the hall? Could somebody get photos from outside? He spoke into his comm unit. "Ian, head around back by the classrooms on the north side and stand guard. Make sure nobody's looking in the windows."

"Copy," the youngest bodyguard said.

"What you thinking, boss?" Marcus asked.

"Just taking precautions."

The comms went silent. After three minutes, Ian said, "All's quiet back here."

"You see them inside?"

"No, but only a portion of the room is visible."

"Stay and guard," Jon said.

Fourteen more minutes passed.

Jon was pacing outside the doorway. Debated knocking. When he passed the door to the neighboring room, a chill wound around his ankles.

A chill?

He pushed open the door and stepped into the darkness.

A window was open.

Swearing under his breath, he rushed to the back, where a door connected the two classrooms. He stepped into the brightly lit room.

Empty.

Hot rage mixed with cold fury, neither of which would help. He tapped his comm. "They're gone. Out the window. Ian, start a search behind the school. Hughes..." He gave more instructions while he yanked out his phone.

He wouldn't think about the way his hands were shaking. He needed to focus.

Fast.

Before she got too far away.

He tapped the locator app and saw the tiny blue dot already miles from the school. They must have left before Ian got in place. He told his team to gather and bolted toward the parking lot. He was nearly there when he dialed Cote.

"Chief Co—"

"Denise Masters has been taken."

"When?"

Jon appreciated that the police chief didn't ask how it happened or any of the other stupid questions that would need to be answered later. "Twenty minutes ago. She's wearing a locator. She's on a road called"—he glanced at his phone—"Shasta."

"Goes up Mt. Coventry."

"Suspect is Brittney Boatright. My team and I are en route. We're going to retrieve her. I need you to—"

"I appreciate that you guys are trained, but so are we. We'll—"

"I'm taking point, but I'll appreciate your help."

"Now, listen here. This is my town, and I'm in charge of law and order. Your team needs to stand down."

Jon was only half listening as he climbed into the passenger's seat and connected his phone to the navigation system.

Cote was still talking, now the sound coming over the speakers.

Hughes started driving toward the blue dot, which was winding its way along a road that switchbacked up the mountain.

Cote finished with, "You understand me, son?"

"We'll let you know where they stop."

The man was shouting when Jon disconnected.

"Team two's on their way," Hughes said. "What's the plan?"

Two more guards had piled into the backseat, and another SUV followed. They were all connected on comms.

"Get her back," Jon said.

Hughes nodded, lips pressed closed.

These were bodyguards, not special forces. Yes, they were all trained, but they'd never gone on a mission like this before, not together anyway.

That summer, when Jon had lost his client, his partner had been shot and incapacitated. Jon and a friend of his client's—a guy he hadn't liked or trusted prior to that—managed to locate the client and capture the criminals who'd taken her.

He'd wished for a team then. Now, he had one, but would it be enough to rescue Denise?

Or would he lose her like he'd lost that other one so many years before?

Images filled his mind—all those young women. Beautiful, innocent, terrified. Fourteen had been kidnapped.

Thirteen had been rescued.

He'd never forgiven himself the stray bullet that had taken the young model's life. It hadn't been *his* bullet, but he hadn't stood in the way of it either.

He'd replayed that moment a million times, thought of a hundred ways he could have protected that girl.

All the things he should have done differently.

Despite the family's heartfelt thanks when he returned their daughter's body, he'd never let himself forget.

Never.

And now...

He imagined a similar circumstance, only instead of a stranger's body, it was Denise's.

Instead of a family he'd never met before, it was Ella who would grieve forever.

Reid's words from that afternoon rang in his ears. If something happened to Denise, Ella would not be okay. She would never be the same.

No. No. He wasn't going to return with a lifeless body. Not this time.

"You okay, boss?"

Hughes twisted around a corner, then glanced Jon's direction.

Jon didn't know what he'd said or done to elicit the other man's question. "Drive faster."

Hughes nodded forward. "Trying to keep us on the road."

Snow fluttered in the beam of the headlights. It'd still been drizzling at the school, but the higher they climbed, the colder it must be. It already stuck to the narrow country road.

One more obstacle. What else could go wrong?

The little blue dot on the navigation system stopped. When it stayed stationary, Jon dialed the chief again.

"Where are you?" Cote demanded.

"Almost to Shasta." He enlarged the map to see the names of the roads. "Looks like they stopped at the corner of Shasta and Overlook."

"Shasta and... Okay, there's an empty building there. Used to be a video store. I'm assembling a team, and we'll—"

"The last thing we need is for this to turn into a hostage situation. It'll be better if you don't go in with sirens and lights. We don't want to alert Brittney that we know where they are. Let my team go in and take the suspect out and—"

"You mean kill her?"

"I mean *stop* her." Though he wouldn't hesitate to do whatever he had to do to save Denise's life.

"I'm on my way now," the chief said. "There's a farm stand about a half mile before the video store. It'll be deserted. Meet me there, and we'll make a plan when I arrive. Don't do anything until I do."

"Copy." He acknowledged the order, even if he had no intention of following it.

Because the police had to follow a bunch of rules. They had limits to what they could do in order to secure Denise's release.

He wasn't concerned with rules. He was going to get her back or die trying.

CHAPTER TWENTY-EIGHT

The only thing keeping Denise sane was her steady stream of prayers. God knew where she was. He knew exactly what Brittney was planning.

Assuming any of this had been her plan.

Denise didn't think so, certainly not Plan A. That knife... that knife said Plan A would have been a lot quicker.

Brittney had planned to stab Denise like she'd stabbed the other victims—and leave her to die. She hadn't intended for Denise to leave that classroom alive. But...

But.

Maybe it meant something that she hadn't been able to go through with it. Maybe it meant something that she'd brought the gun as backup.

Even though Brittney had been driving, paying Denise little attention, Denise was careful not to look at her watch, at the tiny silver charm dangling from it. The last thing she wanted was to alert Brittney to the tracker.

Surely Jon knew by now that they were gone from the school. Surely he was closing in. She prayed he would do so stealthily. She didn't want to know what Brittney would do if she saw him coming.

"There's no escaping this for me."

Did Brittney think she'd end up in prison? Or did she plan to kill herself?

If the second, would she hesitate to take Denise with her?

The van had slowed, turned, and come to an abrupt stop a few moments ago. Brittney had cut the engine and climbed out.

All was silent for a minute, maybe two. Denise didn't bother to try to get out of the plastic cuffs. She'd wasted enough energy on that, but they were cinched too tightly.

The rear door opened, and Brittney climbed in.

"Where are we?"

But her former friend ignored her as she approached.

If Denise had any self-defense ability at all, when the cuffs came off might be the time to try to get away. But Brittney was taller, stronger. She'd spent hours in the gym back when they were roommates, trying to mold herself into the perfect shape, hoping that being physically fit would open doors for her. It hadn't, but she'd continued with the training anyway, claiming she enjoyed the feeling of power it gave her. CrossFit, boxing, martial arts. She'd competed, earned belts.

Denise had only ever exercised enough to keep her figure. No way she could defeat her—even compete with her—in a fight.

Brittney cut the plastic and stepped back, transferring the gun to her right hand.

Denise shook out her aching wrists. "What now?"

Brittney climbed out of the van, never taking her eyes—or aim—off Denise. "Come on."

Denise did, sliding out onto asphalt covered in a half inch of snow. They were at the back of a small, squat building surrounded on three sides by trees.

Brittney grabbed Denise's arm and propelled her forward. "Move."

Denise stumbled toward a door that was propped open with a rock. She pulled it open—it was metal and heavy—and stepped into a space lit by an electric lantern sitting on a desk a few feet away.

It was a tiny, windowless room, smaller than Denise's closet in Beverly Hills. The desk had been pushed up against one side, a chair beside it. A file cabinet and a few racks of empty shelves lined one wall. A door on the far side of the room was closed.

The rear door slammed with a heavy *whump*, blocking out the sound of life outside, leaving deadly silence.

"Sit," Brittney said.

Denise headed for the only chair, but a strong hand gripped her shoulder and redirected her. "There. On the floor."

She settled with her back against the wall while Brittney moved the chair and sat a few feet away, looking down at her. The floor was concrete, freezing cold. The lantern gave off just enough light for Denise to see Brittney—and the gun aimed at Denise's head.

She was trapped in this tiny room with no escape. With a madwoman bent on her death.

Terror bubbled up, and she swallowed a scream.

What now?

She quelled the question, feeling it would be wiser to let Brittney lead. At least she wasn't bleeding to death on the floor of her high school, but would she die here, miles rather than feet from the people she loved?

Brittney glared at her, the look so murderous that Denise's already racing heart picked up speed.

"This is your fault," Brittney said.

"Okay."

"You should have told me."

"Told you what?"

"About Vaughn! You should have told me what he did. He raped you, and you never said a word."

She wasn't sure why her having been one of Vaughn's victims made her Brittney's enemy, but in Brittney's eyes, it clearly did.

It didn't make sense, though. If Brittney was the serial killer, then she'd been sending Denise information for a week, targeting her days before the stories had been released that day.

She didn't understand.

"Why didn't you tell me?" Brittney's voice was loud in the small space.

"I didn't tell anybody. It was a very difficult—"

"Don't give me that crap. He attacked you, and you got a job out of the deal."

"I didn't *take* it. Vaughn had nothing to do with my success."

Brittney wiggled the gun, and Denise pressed her back against the concrete wall as if another few centimeters could save her.

"Come on, Denise. Tell the truth. It's just you and me here now."

"The truth? Is that what you came for? Fine. Vaughn raped me. I was so... You know how I was back then, so deep in post-partum. When he did that...it wrecked me. I tried to pretend it never happened, to make life with Reid and Ella work. But I couldn't do it. Guilt, shame, depression... My emotions lied to me. They told me I wasn't good enough for my family. So I left, went to LA. With you—my friend." Her voice cracked on the last word, and she had to quell a sob.

Because Brittney had been her friend, for a time her very best friend. How had it come to this?

Brittney's hard expression didn't soften the slightest. She

glanced at her phone. Denise couldn't see the screen, but it glowed on Brittney's face. What could she possibly be looking at?

"I went to California," Denise said. "I went to auditions. I landed an agent. I did all the things—"

"And you're claiming that none of that had anything to do with Vaughn."

"I never spoke to or had any contact with Hubert Vaughn after the casting call in Manchester. I saw him from afar a few times, but I went out of my way to avoid him. I wanted nothing to do with him. He has nothing to do with my career. Nothing."

Brittney's eyes narrowed, seeming to seek the truth in Denise's statement. "He probably put in a good word for you or something."

"If he did, I'm not aware of it. If I had been, I would have spurned his help. I never wanted anything from him."

Brittney stared at her a long moment, then shook her head fast. "Doesn't matter. Doesn't matter. He raped you. You should have told me."

"You think I owed that to you? Why?"

"He's a rapist! Somebody should have stopped him."

Denise nodded slowly, trying to read the truth in her old friend's expression. "Did he...?" But she clamped her lips closed, not ready to ask that question. "How did you find the other victims?"

A smile spread across Brittney's face. "You remember Ricky Rybold?"

Denise didn't think she'd ever heard that name before. She shook her head.

Brittney exhaled frustration. "Rybold. Come on, Denise. Vaughn's assistant. When we auditioned, it was Vaughn, Ricky, and Tennison."

"I never knew the others' names."

"Why doesn't that surprise me? You only ever cared about you."

The words hit their mark. Denise had once been that self-absorbed. But... "I cared about you."

Brittney glanced at her phone again. What was on there that kept capturing her attention? Or was this such a run-of-the-mill situation for Brittney that she was bored? "Right up until you got famous," Brittney said, "and then you forgot all about me."

"Did you think we'd live together forever?" She'd moved out of their shared apartment and moved on with her life. Now didn't seem the time to remind Brittney that she'd also covered most of the rent in that *shared apartment* for years, that Brittney's odd jobs never seemed to earn enough money. Denise didn't bring up the fact that Brittney had been so angry at the time—at Hollywood, at the unfairness, and at Denise—that she'd been nearly impossible to live with. "I didn't forget about you. I just—"

"This isn't about that. It's about what *you knew.* Ricky remained Vaughn's assistant for years. I got to know Ricky. Dated him. Gained access to his accounts. It didn't hurt that the guy liked to party. He has no memory of me taking his phone and digging through his emails while he was passed out on the bed. I found his travel plans, years of confirmation emails from their travel agent. I put that information together with casting calls, and then with actors who were *discovered* at those casting calls. Actors who chose not to take him down but to profit off him." She glared at Denise. "Actors like you."

The accusation made Denise itch to defend herself. She held her tongue. She needed to be careful here. Very careful if she wanted to survive.

CHAPTER TWENTY-NINE

J on moved through the woods, giving the small building a
wide berth. Because of the snow, he couldn't get closer
without risking footprints being seen.

He'd had Hughes drive past the building at normal speed,
then stop about fifty yards beyond it. Jon and Grant had
climbed out.

Like him, Grant had been a Green Beret. He was the only
one on the team Jon had served with. He was experienced, and
Jon trusted his skills more than he did anybody else's.

Marcus and Smitty climbed from the second SUV. As soon
as they were out, both SUVs did a U-turn. Hughes would hang
close while the other headed to the farm stand.

Jon led Marcus silently through the woods toward the rear
of the property.

Grant and Smitty had jogged on the opposite side of the
road and would check out the front and the far edge of the
property.

Everybody was silent in his ear, though the remainder of his
team and the police were assembling at the farm stand down the
road. Cote would be demanding to speak to him, demanding to

know what was going on. Jon's team would put him off as long as they could.

Jon angled toward the back of the structure and caught sight of a van parked near the rear door. The van had no snow on it, but the ground beneath it was covered with fresh powder.

It was the confirmation he needed. He took a photo with his phone and sent it to Hughes, who would share the information with the rest. Jon wouldn't risk speaking. With the snowfall muffling noise, the only sound was the whisper of the breeze through the branches overhead. His voice would resonate. Even the snap of a branch would carry in the stillness.

So he moved slowly, carefully. Behind him, Marcus did the same.

Brittney couldn't know they were onto her. The last thing he wanted was to alert her to their presence. That would only serve to hurry her up.

The back door was closed, the van parked right in front of it. He moved to put the vehicle between himself and the door and jogged in that direction. As long as the woman didn't round the van to the passenger side, she wouldn't see the footprints. If she did come out, he'd be there. He'd take her down.

He peeked into the van, hoping to find Denise, but it was empty.

The women had to be inside the building.

Jon tapped his comm twice to let Grant know he was coming, then returned to the woods. He kept his voice so low it was hardly audible in the silence. "Stay here and keep watch. You see any movement, you let me know."

Marcus nodded, and Jon picked his way toward where Hughes would have left the van.

When he was far enough away that, even if Brittney were listening, she wouldn't hear, he broke into a run, dodging brush and bushes and downed trees. He met up with Grant, who'd left

Smitty to watch the street-facing side of the structure, and together they jogged to the waiting SUV.

Hughes and Ian stepped out.

"Rear door's closed," Jon said. "Probably locked. No windows on that side."

"It's an old store," Grant added, "with lots of windows in front. All quiet. No lights."

Jon asked, "Can we get in?"

Grant lifted the tailgate, rifled through their supplies, lifted a tool. "No problem."

"Silently?"

Grant gave him a *don't ask stupid questions* look.

"Good." Jon dug through the supplies himself, grabbing what he'd need. He found the items he'd packed into the SUV, never believing he'd have to use them, and handed them to Hughes. "You got this?" He'd been an explosives expert, back in the day. Jon trusted him with the task.

"The van?"

"It's close to the building and the woods. Let's not start a forest fire."

"I got it."

His confidence boosted Jon's. He turned to Ian. "Stay in the woods and provide cover. Keep one eye on the back door."

"Got it," Ian said.

"A simple distract and grab." Jon met his teammates' gazes. "We'll figure out where they are, set the charge, then enter from the opposite door."

All three men said, "Copy."

Jon took the synchronized response as a good sign as he led them back to the building.

CHAPTER THIRTY

Denise's first inclination was to argue with Brittney's assertion that she'd *profited* off the rape.

It was ludicrous.

But the other women had done just that, in a way. Hadn't she and Jon reached the same conclusion? What had he called it?

Payment after the fact.

Denise understood the women's reasoning. There was no undoing what Vaughn had done. Why not squeeze the lemonade from the lemon, so to speak?

Denise hadn't had the emotional wherewithal to do even that.

Neither of them spoke. Brittney stared at her, daring her to disagree. If Denise stayed quiet, would it stretch out this moment, or only hasten the end?

How do I get through this, Lord? How do I survive?

When Brittney glanced at her gun, Denise decided talking was the better bet. "I didn't profit from it."

"Right. You're just like the rest of them. One of the many who got famous because they kept their mouths shut."

"He offered me a job, Brittney. I didn't take it. You were with me. You know how I got started."

Brittney glared at her. "There were a couple who reported him to the local police. But Vaughn had a team of lawyers. No prosecutor ever wanted to take him on. Add to that the promise of fame and, for some, a huge payoff, and it was enough for all of them to keep silent. Did you go to the police?"

She shook her head. "I wasn't in the frame of mind. I just wanted to pretend—"

"It doesn't matter!" Brittney shot to her feet, glaring down at her. "I don't care, don't you see? If you'd told me, then I'd have been warned." She tapped her chest with her free hand. "Then it wouldn't have happened to me!"

Any compassion Denise felt for her was quickly chased away by fear. And a little bit of frustration. Did Brittney only think of herself? Yes, she'd gone through something horrible, and yes, Denise should have told the truth long before. But...

But some of Vaughn's victims—and Brittney's victims—had been attacked before Denise. She didn't blame them or hate them because they hadn't told. She felt compassion for them. Where was Brittney's compassion?

Gone. Maybe swallowed up by her anger and bitterness. This wasn't the Brittney Denise had shared her dreams and disasters with. This wasn't the woman she'd once called friend.

But there had to be some of that friendship left, didn't there? What else would explain the fact that Denise was still alive? "Can I ask you a question?"

Brittney's anger seemed to wane the slightest as she settled in the chair again. She gave a go-ahead nod.

"Why did you send me the information about the murdered victims?"

"I wanted you to tell the truth."

Obviously that wasn't true, or at least not all of the truth, because Denise had told the truth, and yet, here they were. Had Brittney wanted Denise to figure it out? Maybe she'd hoped Denise would be able to stop her? She wanted to question her about it, but she couldn't figure out how without potentially making this already bad situation worse.

"You should have warned me." Brittney's words were cold, emotionless. "You claim we were friends, but you never told me."

"It was—"

"You let me go to that casting call."

"I didn't know. If I'd known—"

"What? You would have confessed everything?"

"Yes." Denise never would have sent her friend to audition for Vaughn without warning her.

Brittney was right, though. Denise's silence had allowed other women to walk into that situation. Her silence had been damaging. Could she have stopped him?

Maybe. Maybe not at the time—nobody would have listened to her. But later. When she gained fame and fortune, she could have told the truth.

Should have told the truth.

She could admit that now. Admit that her shame had kept her silent. And had put others in danger.

"You didn't tell me you were going to one of his casting calls." Denise kept her voice gentle. "Where was it?"

"Philadelphia. There was a boxing movie."

"Oh. I didn't know—"

"And how could you have? You were all wrapped up in filming, in your own success. Riding your star to the top." Her words dripped with derision. "And now that you've achieved all that, you come home, and everything goes back to normal for you. Wasn't that Reid beside you in line at the school?"

"It was."

"So you get the husband back, get your daughter back, keep your success. No consequences for people like you."

"Wow." Denise probably should have kept the humorless chuckle inside. "And you say I didn't care about *you*. You obviously know nothing about my struggles, what I've dealt with."

"Wah, wah, wah. Hold on while I grab a tissue."

"Up until yesterday, Brittney, Reid *despised* me. The only reason we have this tentative truce is because I told him everything—about Vaughn, about rehab. About why I did what I did. And that truce is brand new. I don't have Reid back. I'll never have him back." Not that she wanted Reid, but it wouldn't help her to say so.

The man she really wanted was probably out there now, planning to put his life in danger to save hers.

The thought of Jon nearly brought a fresh round of tears. If Brittney killed her, would Jon blame himself? She could still see the look on his face when she'd closed the classroom door. Frustration, irritation.

Denise should have listened to him. She should have trusted his instincts over her own.

Even though this was her fault, Jon would blame himself. If Denise died here, would he ever trust in Christ?

Brittney said, "It's just a matter of time before he falls at your feet like everybody else."

"Reid is happily married. They're about to have a baby. And Ella? You think that's a walk in the park? I'm trying to rebuild a relationship with her after abandoning her." Anger leached into her tone. "So don't sit there and act like everything works out for Denise Masters. It hasn't been all rainbows and puppies for me, you know."

Brittney's eyes hardened, and she lifted the gun, staring through the sights. "Are you really trying to make me feel sorry for you?"

A tactical error. She should be appealing to Brittney's sympathy, not challenging her to a whose-life-is-worse duel.

Mostly, she wanted to keep the conversation going. Maybe, when Jon got there, he'd get her out of this. Maybe he could save her. *Please, Lord.*

Protect me. Protect Jon and his team.

"I'm sorry." Denise took a breath, trying to *look* sorry, even if she didn't feel it. "I don't mean to diminish what you've gone through."

Brittney lowered the gun slightly.

"Trying to break in for all those years," Denise hurried to say, "being denied, even though you're every bit as good an actor as I am." Though that was questionable. Brittney was decent, but her arrogance had never helped her. "And then you had to deal with…Vaughn and his evil. Me, on the other hand—I got my agent, some early work. Then Ember Flare. That was luck. I know that. And I know you didn't have the same fortune on your side. I don't know what would have happened to me if I hadn't had that early success. Would I have gone home, made a life with Reid and Ella? Probably not. More likely, I'd have found solace in a bottle, in drugs. I probably would've overdosed." The truth of her words hit her anew.

She owed so much to God. She could give her success and fame credit for the turnaround her life had taken, but those hadn't saved her. If anything, they'd made everything worse. Only God had the power to pull Denise out of that trap.

Only God could save her now.

"The point is…" Denise continued. What was the point again? Oh, right.

Keep Brittney talking.

"The point is, you and I shouldn't be enemies. We were both hurt. We both dealt with it in our own ways. I wish I'd done everything differently. Told Reid. Reported the attack to the police. Sought counseling and overcome my depression and anxiety and...all the things resulting from Vaughn's attack—and the postpartum. I wish I'd done that instead of running away. I live with regret every single day of my life."

"Sure you do." By Brittney's tone, she didn't believe a word Denise said.

How was Brittney any different? She'd been attacked, and for that, Denise was sorrier than her ex-friend would ever believe. But her reaction was to murder the women who'd been attacked before her?

That was insanity.

Pure insanity.

"Explain something to me," Denise said. "You're angry with me for not having told you what Vaughn did. You're angry with all those women you murdered because they didn't tell. And yet, as far as I can figure, *you* didn't tell either. Maybe if you'd come forward—"

"I made it stop."

"By killing the victims? How did that stop Vaughn?"

A slow smile spread across Brittney's face. "Trust me."

"Weirdly"—Denise nodded toward the gun—"I don't."

Brittney's expression morphed to irritation. "I was going to report him, but I did enough research to know that reporting him wouldn't do any good. The police wouldn't believe me. Vaughn would offer me money to keep me quiet. So instead, I got close to Rybold and figured out who else Vaughn had done this to. Then I presented the evidence to Vaughn—what I knew, my plan to get each of his victims to admit what happened. I figured if we all agreed to come forward together—publicly—no prosecutor could refuse to look into it. He agreed that would be... 'unfortunate' was the word he used. So he started paying me."

Denise leaned back, shocked. "You're angry with those

women for profiting off their rapes when you blackmailed him?" You did the exact same thing." That answered one question that had dogged Denise for days—where Brittney had gotten the money to start an art gallery. And traveling to find new artists was the perfect cover for her visits to the West Coast.

"It wasn't the same." Brittney jiggled the gun as if to emphasize her point. "It wasn't. I told him if it ever happened again, I'd tell the whole story. *I* stopped him."

But how would Brittney know if Vaughn ever did it again? How was Brittney to know if there were new victims who kept silent like all the others had?

Denise wasn't stupid enough to point out the obvious, and she couldn't quite figure out how Brittney went from stopping Vaughn to murdering his victims. A check in her spirit stopped her from asking. Maybe she didn't need Brittney rehearsing the reasons why Vaughn's victims had needed to die, not while Denise sat on the wrong end of a gun.

Where was Jon?

Even if he made it to this little building in the middle of nowhere, how could he possibly rescue her? There were no windows. All the doors were closed. Jon wouldn't be able to see inside, to see where Brittney and Denise were situated.

If Brittney wanted to murder Denise, she would.

Simple as that.

Lord, You see me. You know. Give Jon wisdom. Guide him and his team. Protect them.

Save me, Lord. I don't want to die here.

CHAPTER THIRTY-ONE

J on moved silently through the woods, Grant at his side. They both carried flashlights, but neither lit them now. There was enough light from the moon shining through the clouds and the reflection on the snow, and they didn't want to alert anybody to their presence.

This would have been better with more men, but enlisting the help of the rest of the team would have meant involving Cote and the police.

He didn't know the older chief very well, but he figured there was no way the guy would have authorized this plan.

Jones had related what was going on at the farm stand. Cote was waiting for Jon to let him know what he'd learned. Placating him. He could imagine Jones now. *Be patient. Jon's never in any hurry, but he knows what he's doing. When he has a handle on the situation, he'll let us know.*

Cote was probably fit to be tied, pacing, knowing Jon and his guys were at the abandoned store. But Cote wasn't stupid. He wasn't going to let his pride jeopardize the opportunity to rescue Denise.

For that, Jon respected the local police chief. He'd worked

with plenty of arrogant cops in his life, the kinds who'd rather lose than take outside help.

At the signal—nobody would miss the signal—Cote and his guys would rush up, swarm the building, Jones and the rest of the team offering their assistance. God willing, by the time they arrived, Denise would be safe.

God willing.

Jon had faced his share of danger. He'd tracked down terrorists and gone head-to-head with drug lords. He'd rescued a dignitary once, not to mention thirteen kidnapped models. He'd done all that with his team, relying on his own skills and the training he'd received from Uncle Sam.

He'd never once expected God's help.

Honestly, he'd never thought he needed it. He was capable of doing what had to be done all by himself, thank you very much.

Talk about arrogant.

Even when it had been Lake and her sister who'd required rescue, he'd relied on himself and his team. Even then, he hadn't lifted a single prayer for help.

Was it because of the conversations he'd had this week about God? Was it because he'd seen Josie and Thomas's faith that summer—and seen them survive when they probably should have been killed?

Or was it because this wasn't a stranger or a client or even his cousin? This was Denise.

The woman he loved.

He didn't know for sure what had him whispering prayers now, but they slipped out of his mouth—soundlessly, but no less there.

Save her.

Help us save her.

Protect her.

Guide us.

Did God answer those kinds of prayers? Did He listen to people who weren't even sure He existed? Jon had no idea. He only knew—hoped, anyway—that the prayers wouldn't hurt.

She loves You, God. She trusts You. Save her.

Please.

He and Grant reached the woods at the side of the building, out of sight of the windows, and paused to wait for Hughes's signal.

The night before, Jon had done what Lake suggested. He'd asked God to reveal Himself. If He was real, then Jon needed to know. He wasn't about to lose Denise because he was too stubborn to at least try to understand what she believed. So he'd asked, and God had been silent.

What had he expected? An angel choir?

Would God reveal Himself now?

If You're really there...

The words that wanted so badly to follow felt like an ultimatum. Would that offend God?

Did he have anything to lose?

If You're really there, and if You really love Denise... If You really love me...

Then do Your thing.

Save her.

Protect my team. Please save Denise.

There. He'd said it. And he hadn't been consumed by fire raining from the sky. Not yet, anyway. So maybe nobody heard his prayers. Maybe there was nobody listening, or if God was there, maybe He didn't care.

Or maybe, just maybe, He was going to help.

Hughes's voice sounded loud in his ear. "Charges set."

"Moving in." Jon and Grant bolted from the tree line beside the building to the front door, crossing in front of the windows as quickly as possible. If anybody was watching, they'd be sitting ducks. But the lack of light in that big room—and the fact that it was exposed to the outside—had him betting that Brittney and Denise were elsewhere.

When no shots were fired, he figured he'd bet correctly. While he stood guard, Grant picked the lock.

Considering that the building was deserted, they assumed there was no alarm system. They assumed, in fact, that there was no power at all. They should be safe to walk right in the front door.

Another risk, but there was no time to contact the electric company to confirm. Anyway, it would only be a matter of seconds, and Hughes and Ian covered the back door.

As long as Brittney's first instinct was to save herself and not kill her hostage, this should work.

Assuming Denise wasn't already dead.

Please, God. Please.

Grant got the door open.

Flashlights shining, they stepped into a large, open room. A counter ran the length of one side. Old racks of very narrow shelves had been pushed to one wall. The floor was covered in thin, cheap industrial carpet, which muffled their footsteps.

They moved to the back of the room, where an opening revealed a short hallway. Jon angled into the space, light shining ahead, prepared to duck and fire. But the hall was empty. There were two closed doors.

A sign on one indicated a bathroom.

The other door would open to a space that led to the rear exit. A dark *Exit* sign overhead confirmed his guess.

A dim light glowed beneath it. Denise and Brittney had to be in there.

He listened. No sound but silence.

Were they both dead? Murder-suicide?

An image filled his mind—Denise splayed out on the floor, blood seeping from a fatal wound. He shook it off. Contemplating the worst wouldn't help. He held his gun at the ready and checked Grant, who nodded.

Jon tapped his comm unit three times. Tap. Tap. Tap.

An explosion shook the building's foundation.

Grant kicked in the door, and Jon stepped through and aimed, searching for a target.

The room was empty.

CHAPTER THIRTY-TWO

It had all happened so fast. One minute, Brittney had been telling Denise about Vaughn and blackmail and victims. Once Denise had gotten her talking, Brittney couldn't seem to stop. Denise guessed she'd been dying to tell her everything she'd done from the first gruesome murder to the last. The woman seemed proud of herself—actually proud—for having gotten away with it, and for the way she'd framed Vaughn. She'd been in the middle of explaining her grand getaway scheme when she'd glanced at her phone, as she'd done multiple times since they'd arrived.

Only this time, she'd popped to her feet, shock evident in her wide eyes and dropped jaw.

And then, she'd pulled Denise up from the floor, yanked open the door, and shoved her into the short hallway. Denise had no idea what was going on, but her questions were met with, "Shut up and do what you're told."

Denise didn't fight as Brittney propelled her down the hall to a restroom. It was a tiny, mold-scented space built for one person, but Brittney pushed them both inside. She closed the door and, by the light of her cell phone, whipped Denise around, putting her between the doorway and Brittney.

It seemed Denise would be playing the part of a human shield.

They stood between the toilet and the wall. The metal edge of a toilet paper dispenser dug into Denise's thigh, but that was easily ignored as Brittney shut off the cell's flashlight and snaked her arm around Denise's neck.

With her other hand, she held the gun against Denise's head.

"What are we—?"

"Shut up," Brittney hissed.

They stood like that, Brittney uttering a stream of curse words under her breath while Denise prayed a stream of prayers. Had Jon found them?

Was he out there?

Before she could allow hope to fill her being, an explosion rocked the building, sending vibrations beneath her feet.

Another sound—a bang—came almost simultaneously.

Denise gasped, but her air was cut off when Brittney pulled her back and squeezed her hold against Denise's airway. Only a second passed before she seemed to get her bearings again and let up a little.

Denise sucked in a breath, grateful for the filth-scented oxygen.

Brittney whispered so low it was more breeze than sound. "Not. A. Word."

With the cold steel of the pistol pressed against her temple, she wasn't about to argue.

As fast as all the chaos had erupted, it died.

The silence was charged, buzzing with tension.

It was only a matter of time before they were discovered. Brittney had to know that. What was her plan? She'd so meticulously strategized the blackmail scheme and all her other murders, working it out so that Vaughn would be the perfect scapegoat. But she hadn't intended any of this.

Suddenly, the door in front of them slammed open.

Brittney aimed toward it and fired, but nothing was silhouetted in the opening. All Brittney had accomplished was to confirm where they were.

Silence reigned again, heavy with pressure.

But now Denise could make out sounds of a third person breathing.

"There's no way out of this for you, Brittney." Jon's voice sounded calm and clear from the other side of the doorway, and Denise's heart expanded.

Of course he was there. Of course he'd come to rescue her. *Please, Lord, don't let anything happen to him.*

"You're trapped," Jon said. "The building is surrounded. Even if you could manage to get away, we know who you are. Why don't you put your gun down?"

"If you come in here, I'll kill her."

The quiet lasted a few beats before Jon asked, "Ms. Masters, are you all right?"

Ms. Masters.

Denise was glad she hadn't told Brittney anything about her feelings for Jon. She started to answer, but Brittney squeezed against her windpipe again, silencing her.

"She's fine."

"If I don't hear her say it, I'm not going to believe it. The only reason I'm out here and you're in there is because I assume my client is still alive. I suggest you let her speak for herself."

The pressure against Denise's neck eased just a little. "I'm..." She cleared her throat, which felt bruised and scratchy. "I'm here."

"Are you injured?" Jon asked.

WREATHED IN DISGRACE   351

"Brittney hasn't hurt me." Not much anyway.

"Good, good." Jon's tone was all business. "Brittney, your best shot is to surrender."

"That's not going to happen," Brittney said. "I'm not going to prison."

"Prison's better than dead."

"I doubt that."

"Oh, I don't know." His tone was matter-of-fact. "The way the justice system works nowadays, you'll probably get off on a technicality or released on parole in a couple of years."

"I'm not stupid," Brittney snapped. "Don't treat me like I am."

"I know you're not stupid. You've gotten away with way too much for anybody to believe that." When Jon spoke again, his voice was low and serious. "What do you want?"

Brittney didn't seem to know how to answer, and Jon's question hovered in the silence, the heaviness weighing them all down.

Because, the truth was, Brittney only had two options here. Death or surrender. And she'd already said she wouldn't surrender.

If she chose death, the only question remaining was one Denise was afraid to consider. Did Brittney plan to take her with her to the grave?

"If you surrender to me," Jon said, "I'll tell the police how you cooperated, how you laid down your weapon because you weren't willing to hurt anybody else. But the hostage negotiators are on the way. Once they get here, I won't be able to help you."

"You don't want to help me!" Brittney's words were too loud, echoing off the hard walls. "You'll say anything to get me to lay down this gun. Well forget it! I knew when I started that this would be the end for me. Denise was my last target. Once she's dead, my crusade will be over. Everybody will remember me—me!—as the woman who brought Vaughn down. Not Denise, not Shannon Butler"—her words dripped with contempt—"or any of those other so-called *starlets*. The world will remember me!"

Denise closed her eyes, but tears leaked between her lids.

She didn't want to die in this filthy bathroom. Not like this. Not now, when things were finally, finally starting to go her way.

She didn't want to die at the hands of her former best friend.

She didn't want Ella to have to bury her mother. She didn't want Reid to stand at her graveside. She didn't want Jon to live with the what-ifs.

Please, God. Please, show us a way out of this.

But if this is the end for me, lead Jon to You. Save him. And protect my baby. Draw her to You. Don't let this or anything else separate her from You.

"You don't really want to kill Denise, do you, Brittney?" Jon asked. "I know she can be...self-absorbed, but do you really want to live with murdering your friend? Maybe she wasn't that great at it, the whole friendship thing, but you two had your moments, didn't you?"

Denise's first instinct was to be offended, but she brushed those feelings aside. Jon was trying to connect with Brittney.

"Denise, Brittney, and Ben and Jerry's, if I'm remembering right," Jon said. "Denise's favorite was Cherry Garcia, but you liked...was it Chunky Monkey?"

Brittney went very still behind her. Maybe...maybe Jon's words were having an impact.

"You were friends then. I'm not saying Denise is perfect— God knows she's far from it. But if you shoot her, then I have to shoot you. And I really don't want to have to shoot you. If you put down the gun, we can all walk away from this. Your old friend will still be breathing, and maybe she'll even have a chance to make it up to you, all the mistakes she made. You'll survive, be able to tell your story." He chuckled. "Heck, you'll probably get a book deal out of the whole thing. Maybe one of those A&E specials."

He'd missed his calling. Jon was nudging all of Brittney's wants front and center. Maybe this would work.

Maybe Jon would be able to get them out of this.

But after a protracted silence, Brittney barked a laugh. "They don't give book deals to serial killers."

"They interview them, though, with cameras and lights. And that's assuming you're convicted. As far as I know, the authorities haven't found anything that links you to the murders. Your name never came up in my conversation with the California investigator. With a good attorney, you may get off scotfree. But in order to do that, you have to put the gun down."

Please, God. Please let her—

"You must think I'm an idiot," Brittney snapped. "There's no way out of this for me. And if that's the case..."

Again, her arm tightened around Denise's neck. She shifted the gun so the end of the barrel pressed against Denise's head, just over her ear. The cold steel pressed through her hair and sent a shiver of terror down her body and a gasp through her lips.

Protect the ones I love, Lord. Hold them close.

Jon sighed, long and loud. "Hey, Denise?"

He addressed her by her first name. Maybe he realized what she had—that Brittney wasn't going to surrender. That this was the end for Denise.

What would he say, knowing these might be the last words he would ever speak to her? Would he tell her again that he loved her?

She wished she could tell him exactly how she felt. Because somehow, after all of this, she knew she loved him. It was new and tender, like a spring flower just peeking out of the ground after a long cold winter. But there was something there, something that could have been...amazing.

"Yes?" She heard the breathless, desperate hope in her single word.

"This is your fault."

She sucked in her shock. "What? What do you—?"

"I had one rule. Do you remember the *one rule*?"

Hurt and heartbreak filled her voice. "Do as you say."

"If I say stop, you stop. If I say jump, you say..."

"How high." The words were automatic, but that was exactly the opposite of what he'd told her. *You don't say anything. You just jump.*

"And you couldn't do it," Jon said, his voice hard. "You couldn't just do as you were told."

But she hadn't defied him, had she? Sure, he'd been uncomfortable with her going into that classroom with Brittney alone, but he hadn't told her not to. He hadn't tried to stop her.

And anyway, that wasn't his favorite example. He'd always said...

Oh.

Brittney laughed. "Still the arrogant little know-it-all, aren't you?" She let up the pressure on Denise's neck. "You always did think you were better than everybody else. There might be three of us here, Denise, but you're going to die alone. Just like—"

"Duck!"

Denise let her legs go out from under her and yanked her head down.

Jon spun into the room and fired.

Denise had barely gotten to her knees when Brittney collapsed on top of her.

The woman's weight was immediately yanked off and

pulled away. Jon dropped her on the floor between the vanity and the wall.

He stood over her, gun aimed at her head.

Grant stepped into the tiny room, gun raised, flashlight scanning the space.

Jon flipped Brittney over. She stared up at the ceiling, eyes open and vacant, a tiny hole on her forehead.

Denise couldn't inhale, couldn't breathe. Before she could force out the scream that desperately wanted escape, Jon scooped her into his arms. "Move!"

Grant stepped out of the way, and Jon carried Denise from the room, through a larger space, and outside.

"Breathe," he said.

She blew out a breath and sucked in another.

"That's good. Again."

She did as she was told.

"You're safe now." He tucked her close to his chest and marched through a parking lot.

The temperature wasn't much colder than it'd been inside, but it was fresh and clean, not tainted with the scents of mold and dust and death.

Blue and red lights spun, illuminating Jon's face. She couldn't seem to pry her eyes away from him.

She still wasn't sure exactly what had happened.

She was alive.

And Brittney was...

She buried her head against Jon's shoulder.

"It's okay," he said. "You're safe now."

Voices rose all around. Men running. Vehicles moving.

Denise couldn't make sense of any of it. She didn't want to.

Jon set her down on something soft and tried to back away, but she wouldn't release her grip on his jacket. She couldn't seem to make her fists unclench.

He spoke over her head. "I don't think she's injured. Just in shock."

"Okay. Ma'am, can you lie back?"

She gripped tighter, leaning toward Jon as if he were her only link to life.

A blanket was laid over her shoulders, but she ignored it. She was freezing, but she didn't need a blanket, she needed Jon's warmth. He would be enough.

Gently, he pried her fingers off. When he had her hands in his, he crouched down to meet her eyes. "Sweetheart, you need to let the paramedics check you out."

"D-don't leave. Please."

He leaned forward and kissed her cheek. "I just need to talk to the chief." He nodded to his right, and she glanced to where the chief of police waited. "And then I'll be right back. Okay?"

She was safe, wasn't she?

Jon met her eyes again. "You did good."

"Very obedient, just like you t-trained me."

"I knew you'd figure it out." He kissed her forehead and backed away. "I'll be right back."

Gentle hands tucked a blanket around her. While the paramedic asked her questions, she kept her gaze on the man who'd saved her life.

The man she didn't want to live without.

CHAPTER THIRTY-THREE

Jon kept one eye on Denise as he answered the chief's questions. He expected Cote to be furious with him for entering the building without clearing it with him first. By the time the chief had figured out what was going on and joined him at the bathroom door—keeping very quiet—Jon had already gotten Brittney talking.

The chief had kept silent at his side, but he'd heard the entire exchange. He'd agreed with Jon's assessment that Brittney had no plan to surrender.

When Jon told him—via scribbled words in the chief's notebook—what he planned, the chief had studied the idea a long time. And then he'd nodded.

Maybe the chief would have to face repercussions down the road, but Jon doubted it. Brittney Boatright was a serial killer. If she'd been a man, nobody would question Jon's judgment.

Funny how it felt different because of her gender.

He'd never shot a woman before. He searched his heart for some feeling of remorse or regret, but all he could conjure was an immense sense of relief.

The fact that Brittney was dead wasn't nearly as powerful to him as the fact that Denise was alive.

He glanced her way but could barely see her seated on the gurney beyond the crowd. Reid hovered at her right, his wife at his side. James and Cassidy were there. Behind them was the other couple who'd joined them for the play, Andrew and Grace. Ella was sitting on her mother's lap. He'd been shocked to see the child there, but maybe, like the rest of them, she'd needed to know her mother was all right.

"Do you have anything else to add?" Chief Cote asked.

He thought back to all he'd covered already—how they'd breached the building, set explosives to take out the van, and burst into the room where the dim light was shining beneath the door. How that room had been empty. How he'd confirmed his guess that they were in the bathroom. "I can't think of anything else right now." The chief had heard most of what Brittney had to say. He'd heard her call herself a serial killer.

"Okay, go ahead then." He nodded toward Denise. "We'll have to interview her next, so you might give her a heads-up."

"Will do. Thanks, chief."

The older man gripped Jon's upper arm. "That's twice now you've done our job for us. Some of my guys are a little miffed that you keep having all the fun."

"You?"

Cote shook his head slowly. "Truth to tell, I'm old enough not to care who gets the credit. I'm just grateful."

That word resonated as Jon walked toward Denise and her circle of friends. Grateful. That was exactly how he felt. He'd done it. He'd saved her, and he could admit it had been against all odds. He hadn't had any idea how he was going to get Brittney to put down her gun or get a clean shot. The idea to warn Denise that she'd need to duck...

Could he take credit for that? For any of it?

No. It'd been an inspired idea. Inspired by the One he'd pleaded with for help.

God had shown up. He'd done amazing things, and He'd used Jon to do them.

Thank You.

Again, the Lord didn't answer, but he felt a sense of peace and well-being like he hadn't known since he was a child. It was weird, especially in that setting, surrounded by ambulances and police cars and fire trucks. It didn't make any sense. But Jon felt God's pleasure.

He reached the group surrounding Denise, and her friends shifted to make room for him. "How you doing?"

She flashed that amazing smile his way. Tears streamed down her cheeks, but he guessed they were joyful, maybe a little overwhelmed. "I'm...alive, thanks to you." She giggled and squeezed her daughter closer. "I was starting to think..." She shook her head, perhaps unwilling to voice her fears in front of Ella.

Ella was a smart girl, though. She slid out of her mother's arms and onto the asphalt, facing him. "Did you save Mommy's life?"

He shrugged. "I think God did it. Your mother and I helped."

Ella launched herself across the circle and collided with him. Wrapping her arms around his waist, she buried her head in his stomach. Her muffled "thank you" vibrated against his jacket.

He crouched down and lifted Ella to give her a proper hug. "You are very welcome." He looked beyond Ella to Denise. "It was a life worth saving."

Reid shifted to face him. "So, is it over?"

"Mostly," Jon said. "We just need to locate Vaughn and confirm Brittney's story."

"I know where he is," Denise said.

Jon wasn't the only one who focused on her.

But Denise's gaze flicked to Ella, and she shook her head. "Suffice it to say, he won't be hurting anybody anymore."

Vaughn was dead?

Brittney must have confessed to that before Jon showed up.

"Cote's going to need to talk to you," he said. "You can give him the details then."

"Now?" she asked.

"Whenever you're ready."

"Maybe you should get some rest," Reid suggested. "Talk to him tomorrow."

Jon was about to protest, but Denise beat him to it. "I'm not as fragile as I look. I can handle it."

Fragile? Despite his initial assessment, Denise Masters was anything but fragile. And she was no more a prima donna than Lake was. Denise was tough, yet tender. Vulnerable, yet strong. Beautiful, yet...

There was no contrast to that one. She was just beautiful, inside and out.

She hopped off the gurney, keeping the blanket around her shoulders. "Let's get it over with." She turned to Reid. "Why don't you take Ella home, and—"

"No, Mommy! I want to stay with you."

Denise crouched in front of her. "How about I stop by your house later and tuck you in?" She looked up at Reid. "Would that be all right?"

Reid nodded. The man seemed too overwhelmed to speak.

Ella said, "You promise you'll come?"

"I promise I'll come. If you're asleep before I get there, I'll wake you up, okay?"

Ella agreed. After Jacqui, James, and Cassidy all hugged Denise, Jacqui took Ella's hand and led her toward the cars parked in the far corner of the lot, James and Cassidy with her. The other couple, Andrew and Grace, were waiting there.

But Reid lingered. He seemed conflicted about something, and then he pulled Denise into a tight hug. "I'm so glad..." Again, he shook his head, unable to speak.

Denise didn't say anything, either, just hugged him back.

Jon squelched the rise of jealousy. Their love wasn't romantic. That Reid adored his wife was as plain as the woman's red hair. What Reid and Denise felt for each other was another kind of love—the kind that held families together no matter what.

Reid stepped back. Turning to Jon, he stuck out his hand, which Jon shook. "Thank you. For saving her life."

He only managed a mumbled "of course" before Reid swiveled and jogged to catch up with his wife and daughter.

Denise watched them walk away. "Wow."

Jon slid his arm around her waist. "You have quite a family here."

She looked up at him, tears shimmering in her eyes. "I'm very blessed."

Blessed indeed. He felt exactly the same.

CHAPTER THIRTY-FOUR

Denise waited outside the front door of Ella's school, watching for Jon. She hadn't seen him since the early hours of Saturday morning, two weeks before. He'd stayed beside her that night as she'd answered all the chief's questions, telling him everything that had happened between the time Brittney had forced her out that schoolroom window to when Jon showed up.

Just before Brittney had seen men on the battery-operated video camera she'd installed near the back door, she'd confessed to murdering Vaughn. Apparently, he'd figured out that she was the one killing his victims—and that she was setting him up for the murders. She always ensured he was close by, planning to meet him to get her blackmail money near where she planned her next kill.

She'd threatened him, telling him that if he went forward with the information, she'd tell the police he was the murderer. He'd let it go on for a while, more worried about saving his own reputation than the women he'd violated. But as the murders became more frequent, Vaughn suffered an attack of conscience and threatened to go to the police.

So Brittney had lured him to a boat dock, murdered him, and dragged his body onto a rented boat. She'd motored out into the deep water and dropped him in the ocean. Then she'd used his phone to text his assistant and his kids, telling them he was going on an extended vacation.

They found Vaughn's phone at Brittney's condo in Portsmouth.

Denise had no idea if Vaughn's body would ever be found. She hoped so, for his family's sake, but she wasn't going to lose any sleep over it. The man had been a monster, obviously. Attacking women was one thing, but then to let them be murdered, one by one, while keeping quiet to protect his reputation?

He'd gotten what he deserved.

The thought brought her up short. The last thing, the very *last thing* Denise wanted was to get what she deserved. *Thank You, Lord, for Your mercies.* She'd sinned enough in her past to pray that prayer every day of her life.

After Denise had answered all of Cote's questions that night, Jon had driven her to Reid's house, where she woke her daughter to kiss her good night. Then, Jon had taken her home.

Though the rest of his team was gone, he'd stayed in her guest house one more time. But the next day, after they'd enjoyed breakfast together, he'd left.

She'd spent the day fearing that their brief non-romance romance was over.

But he'd called her that night, and every night since. In two weeks, they'd talked on the phone for probably two hundred hours. They'd talked about everything from their childhoods to their hopes for the future. And they talked about God—a lot. She'd passed along the thick book about the evidence for the Bible and Christ, and Jon had read it—the entire eight-hundred-plus page book. By the time he finished, he was telling Denise things she'd either forgotten or never known.

The man was brilliant.

She smiled just thinking of their long conversations and brief silences that felt not strained but comfortable. Jon was so much more than a bodyguard. He was...he was a Renaissance man. He knew something about everything. She wasn't sure she'd ever met anyone so intelligent, and the fact that he'd spent his life protecting people even though he could have done so many other things only made him more attractive.

The night before, he'd prayed on the phone with her, trusting Jesus and turning from his sins. His humility, his already swelling faith...

She was in love.

It was ridiculous. She'd known him for exactly three weeks, and they'd never even kissed. But she was head-over-heels in love.

Now she stood outside the school, all alone. No bodyguards flanked her or ushered her inside. She was safe, finally. The media had been frenzied for a few days, but then another story had presented itself, and they'd left Coventry. Even the steady stream of fans driving by her house had waned to a trickle.

Denise was safe in Coventry.

Reid and Jacqui showed up, greeted her, and went inside to Ella's classroom. Denise glanced at her watch. Jon had about four more minutes before she'd have to go in without him.

But seconds later, he pulled to a stop in front of her and rolled down his passenger window. "I'm going to park, and I'll be right there."

"Okey-doke." Her voice was high and excited, but there was nothing she could do about that. He'd come. He'd really driven the hours north from his Massachusetts home to see her.

He had said he would, but the way her heart pounded told her she'd doubted him.

Stupid. If anybody would be true to his word, Jon would.

And she knew why, too. He'd told her a little over two weeks before how he felt about her, and he wasn't a fickle man or one given to whims of fancy.

If he said he loved her, then he loved her. Simple as that.

Simple and...profound and amazing and...

Thank You, Lord.

She bounced on her toes until, two minutes later, Jon jogged toward her. He opened his arms, and she stepped into them for a brief hug before taking his hand. "Come on, we have to hurry."

"I'm sorry I'm late. I ran into traffic coming through town. There seems to be some sort of festival or something."

She laughed. "There's always some kind of festival in Coventry. They really need to fix the traffic problem."

Denise waved to the secretary inside the little office—she'd already checked herself and Jon in—and hurried to Ella's classroom, which was crowded with parents and students. There weren't chairs for the adults, so she and Jon stood beside Reid and Jacqui and watched the kids' presentations.

While the teacher held up each gratitude wreath, each child stood at the front of the room and explained what theirs stood for. As expected, Ella's friend Clara talked all about horses. Jansen the bully talked about being grateful for his little sister. His mother, holding a squirming two-year-old, smiled fondly at him.

Finally, it was Ella's turn.

She grabbed her wreath, which Denise had wrapped in a sheet that morning before driving Ella to school, and handed it to her teacher. Then she removed the sheet with a flourish.

Sometimes, Denise saw herself in her amazing daughter.

When Ella turned to the audience, all smiles and confidence, Denise beamed with pride. Ella didn't look a bit nervous as she pointed to the ornaments, explaining each one. She started with her grandparents then moved on to Jacqui.

Denise caught Reid swiping a tear from beneath his eye when she pointed to him and called him the "world's greatest daddy."

She moved on to the bright red heart. "This one is for my mommy, because she said that I never left her heart. And she never left mine."

Denise had to swipe at her own tears.

And then Ella pointed to something Denise hadn't seen before. It was a red foam cut-out shaped like a flowing cape. There was a yellow S on it. Ella pointed to it and said, "This is a Superman cape for Mr. Jon."

Jon startled beside Denise, and she slipped her hand in his and squeezed.

Ella continued. "That's because he's even more of a super-hero than Mommy. She only *plays* a superhero in movies, but Mr. Jon is like a real one. He saved Mommy's life."

Jon's face flushed as people turned to look.

Reid clapped him on the shoulder.

Denise leaned closer, squeezing his hand again.

Ella waved at him, and he waved back, eliciting chuckles from some of the parents.

It was a sweet moment, maybe a funny moment, but also an incredibly important moment. Because Ella already understood something important—that Jon belonged. Somehow, in the course of the week he'd spent with them, he'd carved out a place for himself in their family.

His two-week absence had done nothing to change that.

The presentation ended with cookies and refreshments.

After that, most of the families took their children and walked downtown to the festival. Denise and her family joined the throng. It was chilly, barely thirty degrees, and a few snowflakes drifted around them, but they were dressed for the weather.

It seemed like there was always some reason for the folks of Coventry to celebrate. Unlike the Christmas tree lighting in the park a few weeks before, this one took place downtown. All the shops had moved some of their wares onto the sidewalks. The scent of pizza wafted from the place on the corner, but they walked right past.

In front of The Patriot, James had set up a little fire pit where, for only a dollar, passersby could roast marshmallows and make their own s'mores. Of course, Ella had to have one. Denise joined her, loving the familiar flavors that brought back memories of her own childhood. She barely noticed the sticky mess left on her fingers.

Cassidy was there, jiggling her baby and handing out wet-wipes. She gave Denise a quick side hug. "I love having you back. How long are you staying?"

Both Ella and Jon turned to watch her answer. Neither had asked her that question recently, but she realized now that they'd both wondered. She'd said from the time she arrived in Coventry that she'd be staying through the holidays, but January was looming.

"I signed a new contract with the studio, but I don't start filming until next summer. I might have a few things I need to attend between now and then, but for the most part, I'll be here."

Before Cassidy could respond, Ella yelled, "Until summer?"

"And then I'll only be gone a few weeks before I come back."

Ella gripped her around the waist and squeezed, probably

leaving a sticky mess on Denise's jacket. Not that she cared. When Ella released her, the pure joy in her daughter's face made the sticky mess—and all she'd had to deal with in order to get here—worth it.

"Did you hear that, Daddy?"

"I did." Reid didn't seem a bit upset.

Ella spun until she found a friend and told her Denise's news. The two girls chatted and giggled as if all was right in the world.

Jon didn't say a word, but he wrapped his arm around Denise's waist and pulled her close, kissing the top of her head.

Suddenly, she wished they weren't surrounded by people.

Together, the group walked to the corner, where Cuppa Josie's had parked its truck. Jon introduced Denise to the brunette in the window—the owner, she guessed, since the woman's name was Josie—and the man beside her.

Denise shook both their hands. To Thomas, she said, "We went to school together."

"Long time ago."

"You might want to get on his good side," Jon said. "He's going to be the mayor in about a month."

"Is that right? Congratulations."

Thomas shrugged. "Thanks. I'm getting excited." Though he looked nervous as he said it.

Josie nudged his shoulder. "You're going to be great."

He grinned at her. "With you by my side."

Jon bought them all hot chocolates, and they continued along the sidewalk. Overhead, *Sleigh Ride* played on hidden speakers, and Jon sang along, low enough that only Denise could hear.

Ella and her friends chatted while the parents visited. Some of them even talked to Denise, making her feel comfortable.

As if she belonged.

And she realized...she did. She was exactly where she belonged.

It was nearly dark by the time Reid announced it was time to head home. Ella whined that she wanted to stay with Denise, but he was firm. "You slept over at Mommy's last night." He stuck out his lower lip in a pout. "Don't you miss me?"

She seemed to vacillate before she slid her hand into her father's. "I'll see you tomorrow, Mommy, right?"

"Christmas shopping, just you and me."

Ella skipped away, Reid and Jacqui on her heels. Poor Jacqui was more waddling than walking now, even though she still had six weeks before the baby would be born.

As soon as they were out of sight, Jon gripped Denise's hand. "Shall we?"

"Where are we going?"

"Dinner, eventually."

Eventually? What did that mean?

He took her hand and led her down the block, away from the crowds and toward the park. He didn't pause as they crossed the street and stepped onto the sidewalk, continuing more slowly toward the towering Christmas tree that glittered against the night sky.

He looked down at her. "I just thought you'd like to see it up close, since you didn't get to the other day."

"I'd love to."

The music faded as they moved. Though a couple of people skated on the rink, most of the crowd remained downtown. Jon led her to the foot of the tree and around to the side, where it was darker.

And then he stopped and turned to her. "I thought they'd never leave."

She giggled. "Were you eager?"

"You have no idea." He set his hands on her hips and stepped close, and she understood why he'd lured her here.

Because, as much as they'd grown to care for each other, they'd never kissed. It was time to remedy that.

Jon leaned close, his deep voice rumbling in her ear and sending shivers that had nothing to do with the cold skimming over her body. "I can't wait any longer." He shifted until they were face to face, pausing a hair's breadth away, giving her plenty of opportunity to refuse.

No chance of that.

She pressed her lips against his, and he kissed her softly. Tenderly.

But like him, she'd been patient. She didn't want to be patient anymore.

She wrapped her arms around his neck and pulled him closer, probing his mouth, tasting hot chocolate and happiness. His hands against the small of her back, he pressed her against his chest. He deepened the kiss, sending warmth to the tips of her toes.

She'd shared kisses with Hollywood heartthrobs, with casual dates, and even with her ex-husband, whom she'd adored. But never, never had she felt what she did in Jon's arms. As if he was the home she'd been longing for.

When they came up for air, he pulled her against his chest, where she felt his heart pounding through his thin jacket.

"Oh, my," she said.

He chuckled. "That was worth waiting for."

"Perfect."

"I'm not sure. I think we'll need to practice, see if we can improve."

She liked the sound of that. They stayed wrapped in each other's arms a long time.

And then, he pressed a kiss to the top of her head. "I don't know what this is going to look like."

She leaned up to face him, not wanting to face reality but knowing it was time. "I live here. That's not going to change."

"I live in Massachusetts, but that *is* going to change—as soon as I can figure out how to make it work. I can't just abandon my partners. Bartlett and Summer deserve—"

"Summer?"

Jon smiled. "Yeah. Lake. She said it was fine if I told you her real name. I mean, if this turns into...well, anyway. She said it was fine."

But Denise was only half listening, turning the name over in her head. "Summer? Your cousin's name is Summer Lake?"

He chuckled. "Her sisters are Misty and Krystal."

Denise cracked up. "That's..." She wanted to say hilarious, but she didn't want to offend.

But he laughed too. "My aunt wanted to give her girls happy names." His smile faded. "Maybe because they didn't live such happy lives. But you can see why Summer doesn't like people to know. Who's afraid of a bodyguard named Summer Lake?"

"Oh, I don't know. She's pretty terrifying, if you ask me."

He shook his head. "Beneath the tough facade, she's got a heart of gold. You're going to love her. I promise."

As if they'd be getting to know each other. As if this wasn't just a passing fancy.

Which it wasn't. Jon had told her he wasn't a casual-fling sort of guy. What he felt for Denise wasn't going to fade away. And her feelings for him grew stronger every single day.

"I can't just leave Summer and Bartlett in the lurch," Jon said. "It's going to take some time, probably a few months, before I can move. After that, I have no idea what I'm going to do." His lips closed, and he looked beyond her for a moment. But then he smiled and met her gaze. "I've been praying about it

—weird as that sounds—and this feels like the right thing." He suddenly sounded unsure. "Unless... What do you think?"

"I think you're amazing, and God must have something even better for you."

He gave her a knowing look. "No doubt about that. Anyway, it's going to take me some time to figure out how to make life in central New Hampshire work, especially if you'll be traveling. I mean, if we're together, I want to be...together."

He wasn't talking about the next few months now. He wasn't talking about the following summer.

He was talking about forever.

He watched her, maybe gauging her reaction. "Does that scare you? Am I coming on too strong?"

She popped up to her tiptoes and pressed her lips against his.

Their second kiss was—impossibly—better than their first. He was right—practice was a very good idea. She wondered as their lips moved against each other's if the kisses would just keep getting better and better.

She pulled away, eliciting a groan from him that sent tingles down her spine. "I'm feeling a whole lot of things right now, but not one of them is fear."

He leaned back and stared at her. "What *are* you feeling?"

She knew what he was asking and contemplated making him sweat for a minute. But no. He'd been honest with her from the very start. Fearless in his honesty.

She could do the same.

Placing her hands on either side of his beautiful face, she gazed into his eyes. "I love you, Jon Donley. It's impossible and ridiculous to say such a thing to a man I've known for three weeks, but I love you. You're—"

But the rest of her words were silenced when his lips pressed against hers.

As snow fluttered all around, they settled into their third kiss, this one even sweeter than the second.

Each one that followed held more promise than the last.

~

THE END.

Courage in the Shadows

When she crosses paths with a killer from her past, can she survive long enough to step into her future?

Ever since she and thirteen other models were kidnapped years before, Summer Lake has fought to ensure that she can protect herself. But when her job as a bodyguard brings her into contact with the man she believes masterminded her kidnapping, her first urge is to run, terrified of being taken again. Instead, she follows the stranger, determined to bring him to justice.

Bodyguard Grant Travino fell in love with Summer the instant he saw her, a fierce protector standing guard over the other endangered young women he'd come to rescue. Years later, Summer still sees him as barely more than a coworker. Grant bides his time, sticking close in an effort to keep her safe and hoping she'll eventually open her heart to him. When her life is threatened, he's not about to allow her to fight her enemies alone. He'll stay by her side whether she wants him or not.

But Summer and Grant have an enemy whose global smuggling organization is so powerful, so pervasive, that it'll be a miracle if either of them emerges from this battle alive.

ALSO BY ROBIN PATCHEN

Legacy Redeemed

Amanda Series

Chasing Amanda

Finding Amanda

Standalone Novellas

A Package Deal

One Christmas Eve

Faith House

ABOUT THE AUTHOR

Robin Patchen is a *USA Today* bestselling and award-winning author of Christian romantic suspense. She grew up in a small town in New Hampshire, the setting of her Nutfield Saga books, and then headed to Boston to earn a journalism degree. After college, working in marketing and public relations, she discovered how much she loathed the nine-to-five ball and chain. After relocating to the Southwest, she started writing her first novel while she homeschooled her three children. The novel was dreadful, but her passion for storytelling didn't wane. Thankfully, as her children grew, so did her writing ability. Now that her kids are adults, she has more time to play with the lives of fictional heroes and heroines, wreaking havoc and working magic to give her characters happy endings. When she's not writing, she's editing or reading, proving that most of her life revolves around the twenty-six letters of the alphabet. Visit robinpatchen.com/subscribe to receive a free book and stay informed about Robin's latest projects.

Made in the USA
Middletown, DE
21 May 2023

31096226R00214